1/22

SHIELDING SIERRA

Delta Team Two, Book 8

SUSAN STOKER

Edited by Kelli Collins

Cover Design by AURA Design Group

Manufactured in the United States

CHAPTER ONE

Fred "Grover" Groves lay on the dirt in the makeshift cell where Shahzada and his buddies had thrown him after taking great pleasure in beating him. His nose and mouth were bleeding, and he knew he probably looked pretty horrible, but he'd had worse beatings in his life. As a Delta Force Operative, he'd taken his fair share of fists to the face. Honestly, what Shahzada had doled out was pretty mild in comparison.

When Grover had come to Afghanistan, he didn't really have a plan. He just knew he needed to do something more than sit around the base back in Texas and wait for someone else to find the information he needed.

Ever since receiving the letter from Sierra Clarkson, he'd been anxious, restless.

Upon meeting her over a year ago, here in Afghanistan, he'd been taken with the diminutive redhead. She was a contractor working in the mess hall and there had been something about her that intrigued him. She was bubbly and happy, like a ray of sunshine in the otherwise morose atmosphere. Most of the

1

soldiers hadn't wanted to be deployed, and the heat, sand, and time away from loved ones was taxing on even the most professional soldier.

Sierra had gifted everyone going through the chow line with a smile. She didn't seem to mind that, because of her size, she had to stand on a box in order to do her job. She greeted everyone—soldier, contractor, translator—with the same enthusiasm. Despite worrying a bit about her naïveté, Grover was immediately attracted to the outgoing redhead, and wanted to know her better. He'd managed to convince her to keep in touch after his mission ended. She'd agreed.

Then he never heard from her.

Not one email.

Not one letter.

He'd assumed she'd blown him off. Which sucked, but Grover wasn't the kind of man who'd force someone to be his friend if they didn't want to. However, as the months passed and his Delta team had gotten more and more reports of missing contractors in the region, Grover had become increasingly uneasy. Especially since Sierra had up and disappeared herself. Just like the other contractors, all her belongings had vanished with her. It had been that very fact that made the authorities slow to react, assuming some contractors had simply had enough of the tough working conditions and left.

That explanation had never sat well with Grover and his team. It was highly unlikely *all* of the missing contractors would have just taken off without saying anything to their bosses or their friends on the military base. Though without proof that the men, and Sierra, had been kidnapped, the authorities' hands were tied.

Then, a month ago, Grover received a letter—from Sierra. It had been dated a week or so after he'd left Afghanistan the last time. She *had* written him. *Had* wanted to get to know him. The damn letter had gotten lost in the mail for nearly a year.

Grover knew without a doubt that something bad had happened.

Regardless, his gut feeling didn't go a long way toward convincing the officers in charge that a full-blown rescue mission should be mounted. There was already a SEAL team in the area tasked with looking into the disappearances, but they'd been reassigned shortly after arrival, deployed for another mission their superiors deemed more important.

As far as Grover was concerned, there was nothing more important than half a dozen missing American citizens.

The sporadic information trickling from Afghanistan was slow and days old by the time it got back to the base in Texas, and the Deltas had been preparing to fly over to investigate themselves. Until Doc's woman, Ember, was almost killed by a stalker, further delaying the mission. Grover had convinced their commander to let him go to Afghanistan ahead of the team, to see what he could learn.

He hadn't planned on doing anything rash.

Hadn't planned on breaking every standard operating procedure that had been hammered into his head since the day he'd joined the Army.

But here he was. Captured.

Grover knew Trigger was going to be pissed. As were the rest of the guys on the team. But he didn't care. He'd done exactly what he'd hoped.

He'd found Sierra.

Most people had assumed the woman was long since dead. Shahzada had a reputation for being ruthless. He didn't keep a prisoner of war for months, let alone a year. He got any information he could out of his prisoners, then killed them.

3

But here she was. Grover couldn't see her from his cell deep in the mountainside, but there was no mistaking the voice of the woman in the enclosure next to his.

His face throbbed, but Grover barely felt it. Adrenaline coursed through his veins and he smiled in relief.

"How are you even here?" Sierra asked in shock.

Grover wished he could see her. But the crude holes dug inside the mountain cave didn't afford him that luxury. He also wished he could touch her, reassure her that he'd get her out of here if it was the last thing he did in his life. Since he doubted he could reach her, he'd give as much comfort as he could with his words.

"It's a long story," he said.

She kind of snorted, and Grover couldn't help but smile again. It seemed she hadn't completely lost her spunk.

"You got anything else to do right now?" she asked sarcastically.

"Well, I was supposed to be playing poker with a bunch of locals, but I guess that's out," he sassed back.

"And my manicure appointment was canceled, so that means I can hang out and chat with you a bit," Sierra replied.

Grover closed his eyes as emotion threatened to overwhelm him. He hadn't been sure he'd be able to find this woman. If he did, he'd expected her to be a mere shell of the person he'd once met. But by some miracle, she sounded...okay. Her voice was raspy from disuse, but she wasn't crying hysterically, didn't seem scared out of her mind. He had no idea what she'd been through in the last year, but it was obvious whatever it was, it hadn't broken her.

He'd known seasoned soldiers who wouldn't've held up as well as Sierra.

The words of the base general rang through his mind. He'd

met with the man when he'd first arrived in the country. *We have to face the fact that she's probably no longer alive. And if she is alive, she's almost certainly working with Shahzada by now.*

Grover refused to believe it. He didn't know Sierra, but practically everything about her personality screamed "goodness." She wouldn't willingly join a terrorist group, even to stay alive. He'd bet his own life on it.

Had *actually* done just that.

"I came to find you," Grover told her bluntly.

Silence met his declaration, so he waited her out.

"How did you know where I was?" she asked. "Hell, *I* don't even know where I am."

"I didn't," Grover admitted. "The disappearance of contractors from the base wasn't coincidental, but no one could find any concrete evidence on where the men, and you, had gone. Everyone's belongings were taken, making some people think you'd all left voluntarily. After all, what kind of kidnapper makes sure to pack up their victim's stuff?"

"Shahzada," Sierra muttered.

"Exactly. When my team and I weren't getting the answers we needed, I was done waiting."

"So you just came over by yourself!? Can you *do* that?"

Grover chuckled. The movement hurt his chest where he'd been hit, but he ignored the twinge. "Sort of. My commander approved it and my team should be here in less than a week. Probably sooner, once the video those assholes took hits the airwaves."

"You sound almost...happy to be here."

"I am," Grover agreed without hesitation.

"You're insane," Sierra told him.

"Actually, my plan worked better than I could've hoped."

"Your plan?"

"Yes. To get myself taken so I could hopefully talk to other hostages, find out if anyone had seen you. Knew anything about you," Grover said.

"Wait, you *purposely* got yourself kidnapped?"

"Yes."

"That's...*crazy!*"

"But it worked. I found you."

"Okay, but now what? You found me, but we're both prisoners now."

"We wait."

"For what?" Sierra asked.

"For my team to do what they do best...kick ass and take names," Grover said without hesitation and with complete confidence.

"Right..."

Grover heard the disbelief and incredulity in her tone, but it didn't faze him. He didn't blame her for being less than hopeful after so long, and he also agreed what he'd done was reckless and over-the-top...but it worked. He was actually talking to the very woman he hadn't been able to push out of his mind. "They'll be here," he told her. "We just have to be smart and stay under the radar until that happens."

Sierra snorted once again.

"What?" Grover asked.

"You want to know how the next few days are gonna go?" she asked.

Grover tensed, but she didn't give him time to answer.

"They're gonna take turns beating on you—gotta give the newest members of the group a chance to practice their torture techniques. You'll be tough and resist answering any of their questions at first, then they'll stop fucking around and get to the more extreme torture. Waterboarding. Beating the soles of your feet so you can't walk for days. Flogging. Dousing you with gas and threatening to set you on fire."

Grover's fists clenched. He wasn't afraid of torture. He'd been through it before and had a high pain threshold. He also knew Trigger and the rest of his team would find him, get him out of there sooner rather than later.

But he couldn't stop thinking of the most likely reason why *she* was so intimately familiar with Shahzada's torture techniques...

"That happen to you?" he asked in a low, growling voice.

"Yeah."

That was all she said, her voice quiet, resigned.

That one word made rage bloom inside Grover so fast, it was almost scary. He was going to kill every one of the men who'd touched her. They'd die slow, painful deaths.

He wasn't sure what to say to comfort her before she went on.

"But not for a while. I think I was their first prisoner. They practiced on me. I learned pretty quickly that the sooner I broke, the faster they stopped. I never thought that psychology degree I earned would do me any good out here, but I was wrong."

She chuckled lightly, but Grover couldn't hear any humor in it.

"Tears have worked surprisingly well on them. At least for me. They love to see their prisoners helpless and crying. So I've learned how to cry on demand pretty quickly. But the most useful thing to remember—never let them know something's important to you. They'll focus on that, do their best to use it against you. For instance, if nudity bothers you, don't complain when they take your clothes. They'll never give them back. It amuses them to make their prisoners suffer."

Grover wasn't surprised by any of her intel. It was something the team had been taught early on in their training. "What'd they use against you?" he asked softly.

"When I was first taken, and didn't know better, I begged them to let me keep a ring given to me by my grandmother. She died when I was fifteen and I inherited her wedding ring. I cherished that ring. But when they learned how badly I wanted to keep it, they taunted me with it for months. Promising to give it back if I gave them information about the base. At first, I believed them, told them whatever I could—which wasn't much. I worked in the damn mess tent. But they had no intention of ever giving me that ring back, of course. They were just using it as a way to further torture me."

"I'm sorry," Grover told her.

"It's fine. They can't take the memories of my mam away, so fuck them."

Grover contemplated her words in silence. He'd been at least partially incorrect. While Sierra wasn't broken...the soft, sweet woman he'd once met was gone, possibly for good.

Replaced by a harder, stronger woman who would do anything in order to survive.

Despite abhorring how it had come about, he didn't hate the change itself. Ironically, it made the two of them more alike. He'd seen and experienced things that had made him harder, stronger...and it's ultimately what you *did* with those changes that mattered. Her captivity had obviously turned her into a survivor; that's why she wasn't broken.

She'd taken the worst thing a human could go through and turned it to her advantage in the only way she could...by letting it make *her* stronger, as well.

The connection he felt with this woman was already strong.

Now it seemed to get more intense with every minute that passed.

It was whacked. They were in a precarious situation. He couldn't even see her, for God's sake, but he couldn't deny he was impressed. Though, his heart bled for her at the same time. He couldn't even begin to fathom the hell she'd been in for the last year. She'd had to become hard to keep herself from going insane.

"My advice is to give in to what they want. I'm not saying to give them any information that will help them hurt, kidnap, or kill anyone else, but the faster you seem to break, the quicker the torture will end."

"Okay," Grover agreed. Nothing she said was a surprise. Putting her mind at ease was his only goal.

"And if they use *me* to get you to react, you have to remain unaffected," she said.

Her words seemed to echo off the rocky walls of their prison.

"What?" he asked, not sure he'd heard her correctly.

"They'll haul me out in front of your cell and beat on me to try to get a rise out of you. If you show any kind of reaction, they'll only do it longer. The best thing you can do is ignore it."

"Motherfucker!" Grover swore. It was a common enough tactic by captors, using one prisoner against another. But the thought of her being tortured right in front of him, and Grover not being able to do a damn thing about it, brought out his rage all over again.

"I mean it," Sierra said. "The more you protest, the more they'll hurt me. And if I don't react when they're hurting *you*, please don't take it personally. It's for the best. They'll get bored and quit as long as I don't say or do anything to try to make them stop."

"Listen to me, Sierra. Are you listening?"

Grover waited for her response before continuing. It took a while, but she finally said, "Yes," very softly.

"I can take whatever they dish out. What I *can't* handle is you getting hurt because of something I did. I promise not to do anything to make your situation here worse."

"Don't promise something you can't deliver," she said without emotion.

"I never go back on my promises," he told her firmly.

He heard her sigh. "That's what the others said, too, but in the end, they couldn't understand why I wasn't trying to help. Why I was 'letting' those assholes beat on them."

"I'm not them," Grover said simply. He got it. He really did. The other contractors who'd been taken were men who didn't have Grover's background and training. And since Sierra had majored in psychology, she also understood their captors better than the average person. She'd obviously learned how to act in order to keep herself alive for the last year. She was smart, resilient, determined...and his admiration rose another notch.

Grover moved so he was lying by the side of his cell nearest her own. It made him feel closer to the woman. He had so many questions, but now wasn't the time or place. He hoped he'd have the chance to get to know her, once they were out of here. For now, he needed to rest. He had no doubt his jailors would be back soon to continue their beatings.

"You okay?" Sierra asked.

The fact that she was asking about him, when *she'd* been the one held captive for so damn long, told him everything he needed to know about Sierra Clarkson.

And he was going to do whatever it took to get her out of here.

CHAPTER TWO

Sierra held her breath as she waited for Grover to answer. She'd heard him moving around and wondered what he was doing. It had been a few months since she'd had anyone else to talk to. And while one part of her hated that her captors had taken someone else...selfishly, she was damn relieved to have company.

Sierra had made the decision a long time ago to not let her captors break her spirit. And so far, they hadn't. But throughout the long nights, in the darkness of the cave, loneliness ate at her. She was occasionally still scared...but thankfully, anger had overridden most of her fear months ago.

She knew Grover being there would make her life a living hell for a while. They'd use her to try to get information out of him. And if he ignored her warning, her pain would last much longer than it needed to.

The last contractor, a man named Guy, had begged them to stop beating her, which only made them continue gleefully. They liked seeing Guy suffer. To be completely honest, Sierra knew her captors weren't even hitting her as hard as they could. When she'd first been taken, they'd *really* worked her over. But now, she put on the best show she could, and it worked most of the time. Their blows eased off and they only half-heartedly smacked her around. They got off more on making the men they captured suffer.

"I'm fine," Grover said. His voice was low and rumbly, and Sierra conjured the image of what he'd looked like the last time she'd seen him. Dirty-blond hair—more on the darker side than actual blond—and warm brown eyes. He was at least a foot taller than her...and when she'd glanced up at him, she'd had the odd feeling that he could slay all her demons.

Sierra still remembered how she'd felt as she'd written him the one and only letter she'd been able to send. Giddy, excited about getting to know him better. Which of course hadn't happened.

And now he was here. Had actually gone and gotten himself *captured on purpose* in order to find her. Who *did* that?

Apparently badass special forces operatives, that's who.

Sierra knew he was Delta. She hadn't really understood what that meant until she'd done a bit of research after he'd left Afghanistan. They were one of the most secretive branches of special forces. There was a lot of speculation on what missions they'd participated in, but very little was concrete. It struck her as funny at the time, because she never would've pegged Grover and his friends as being part of some kind of super-secret, elite military group—members of which she'd kind of assumed might be arrogant, macho jerks. But they weren't. The teammates she'd met were funny, friendly, obviously protective, but very down-to-earth.

"Talk to me, Sierra," Grover said after the silence between them had stretched too long.

"About what?" she asked.

She thought she heard him huff out a breath. "Everything. Are you hurt? When my team shows up, can you run? It's okay if you can't, I can carry you. If I remember correctly, you're no bigger than a bug."

"A bug? Jeez, Grover. Kill a woman's self-esteem, why don't you?"

"Sorry. All I'm saying is that I remember you being slight."

Slight. Sierra kind of liked that. She'd been called short, stubby, little...even midget. Slight sounded so much better than any of those. "I can run," she told him confidently.

Grover didn't respond for a moment. Then she heard him sigh.

"I can," she insisted. "I don't have any shoes though."

"No worries on that. My guys'll have a pair of boots for you."

"They will? How do they even know I'm here?"

"Trust me, they know," he told her.

"For that matter, I still can't get over how *you* knew I'd be here," she said.

"I didn't really. But I had a feeling," Grover said.

"A feeling? You know how crazy that sounds, right?" she asked wearily.

"Yeah, I do. But regardless, I couldn't shake the feeling that you were still alive. And I was right."

The last four words were said somewhat smugly, and Sierra could only shake her head. "Yeah, you were."

"Right, so my team will find us, and they'll have a change of clothes for you, and boots. Don't sugarcoat it, though—can you really walk? And run?"

"Yes," Sierra told him confidently.

"Damn...I wish I could see you."

Sierra's confidence took a nosedive. She ran a hand over her head self-consciously. She knew she looked rough, even without access to a mirror. She'd lost a lot of weight over the long months and hadn't had a proper shower since she'd been taken from her tent on the base. Being hosed down didn't count, even though the water always felt so damn good. "It's probably better you can't," she replied.

"Sierra?" Grover asked.

"Yeah?" she whispered.

"The fact that you're not dead is a miracle. A fucking *miracle*. I don't expect you to look like you walked out of a damn salon. You've been through hell, yet you've come out the other side. I couldn't give one single fuck what you look like. You're here, alive, and from what I'm hearing, it sounds as if you've done a damn fine job of staying sane. I'm gonna get you out of here. So help me God, I am."

Sierra felt a tickle in the back of her throat. She wanted to cry, but the tears wouldn't come. She could only cry on demand when trying to manipulate her captors. They'd already taken all her real tears from her. Possibly forever. "Maybe I'll be the one to get *you* out of here," she quipped after a moment.

"Deal," he said without hesitation. "I'll let you rescue me then."

"I'm sure your badass Delta team would love that. They'd never let you live it down."

"Actually, they *would* love that," Grover told her. "They're probably all super pissed at me right about now, for letting myself get taken."

"I still don't understand that," Sierra said. "How did you manage it, anyway?"

"It was surprisingly easy," Grover answered.

Sitting in the dark, listening to his deep, quiet voice, was literally the best thing that had happened to her in the last year. Sierra had talked with the other prisoners who'd been brought in, of course, but it was often one-sided. They were desperate to ask *her* questions. Where were they? What did their captors want? What were they going to do to them? No one had been as seemingly relaxed as Grover, that was for sure. And no one had sounded as confident, either. Granted, he was a special forces soldier, and the other men had been civilians, but still.

"When I got to the base, I spread word pretty quickly that I thought the stories about people being kidnapped was all bullshit. I pretended to get drunk the first two nights, said a lot of ridiculous shit about how dumb the locals were, how they'd never be able to just take someone from base without others knowing. I generally acted like an asshole, making sure to offend pretty much everyone on the base, from the lowest-ranking privates to the general himself. Then I went outside the gates the next two nights, doing the same thing. Finding men who spoke English and insulting everyone and everything—from the country to the US military to the terrorists, *every-fucking-body*.

"On the third night in town, I pretended to be drunk off my ass and I accepted a ride from a local. He was supposed to take me back to base, but just as I'd hoped, that wasn't his destination."

Sierra listened with equal parts awe and horror. "Won't all of that hurt your reputation? Will you get in trouble with the Army?"

"I don't fucking care," Grover said heatedly. "No one else was doing shit to look into the disappearances. As if they didn't care, or weren't concerned about a bunch of contractors."

Sierra swallowed hard. "I was sleeping," she told him. "I didn't hear the men come into my tent, and they had a hand over my mouth before I even woke up. They forced a backpack onto my back and told me it was a bomb. Said they'd blow up the entire base if I didn't come with them quietly. So I did."

"Fuckers."

The word was quiet, but Sierra still heard it. "They brought me to a house in town and told me I was taken because Shahzada's men needed to practice their torture techniques. The first couple of months were...bad," Sierra said, drastically downplaying the pain she'd experienced those first few months. "They packed all my stuff from the base to make it look like I was a deserter. They knew what they were doing. Apparently, you were right. No one cared too much about a few civilians disappearing. If it had been soldiers, I'm sure the US would've made a huge deal out of it."

"*I* cared," Grover said softly.

Sierra swallowed hard. "I lost track of the days, and eventually...I think it just got old messing with me, and they kept me around. It wasn't that anyone had a problem killing a female, but more like they thought the opportunity might arise when they could use me for leverage or something. And they have, more than once. Still...I've been lucky."

Instead of snorting in disbelief, as she might've expected him to, Grover agreed. "Yes, you have."

Sierra knew a lot of people would think she was insane for believing she was lucky after everything she'd been through. But she was alive, and the other contractors who'd been taken weren't. As long as she had breath in her body, she would fight to live.

She had to change the subject or risk getting depressed. "How will your team know where to look for you?"

"They're the best at what they do. They'll find us."

Grover sounded so confident, Sierra wanted to believe him,

but she'd also had her hopes dashed way too many times. Once, she'd heard soldiers speaking in English right outside the house where she'd been stashed in the small town. She couldn't scream and risk alerting the guard right outside her room, but still... she'd *sworn* she was about to be rescued.

Instead, they'd walked right on by, of course; hadn't even knocked on the door. It had taken weeks to get over that disappointment, the despair of listening to those voices grow distant, then disappear.

Now, she was much less likely to be optimistic about being rescued.

"We're gonna find out who Shahzada is and kill him too," Grover said. "That asshole needs to be stopped. We're gonna make sure he isn't around to kidnap anyone else."

Sierra blinked in surprise. "What do you mean?"

"What do *you* mean, what do I mean?" Grover asked.

Sierra would've laughed at that, but she was too shocked he wasn't aware of Shahzada's identity. "Shahzada was here earlier. He was one of the men beating you up."

Silence met her statement.

"Grover?"

"Which one?" he growled.

"Well, I mean...I didn't see them beating you, but I heard him."

"Would you recognize him if you saw his face?" Grover asked.

"Of course. And you would too. You've met him, Grover."

"When?"

"A year ago. On the base. He goes by Muhammad Qahhar there. He's one of the translators the Army hired."

"Fuck! I knew it!" Grover swore.

Sierra heard loud thumping sounds coming from the niche

next to hers, and she winced. When it was quiet once more, she said, "I thought you knew."

"No," Grover said. "I actually didn't recognize any of the guys beating on me, at least at the time, and no one's ever been able to describe the man. He's been like a ghost. I had a gut feeling that whoever was kidnapping the contractors had to have a connection to the base. It just made sense. I'm guessing some of the other translators are also a part of his faction."

Sierra didn't say anything. She'd suspected that, but hadn't recognized anyone else she'd come in contact with while in captivity.

"I'm going to kill him."

Grover's words were all the more powerful because of the lack of emotion behind them.

"Okay."

"I am," he promised. "Now, talk to me about the schedule around here. Are we going to be interrupted in the middle of the night so they can beat on us?"

Surprisingly, his change of topic seemed to relax Sierra a little. She told him everything she'd learned over the last several months. Described which of the men seemed to be less enthusiastic about torturing the prisoners, and who hit the hardest, relished it the most. Explained that when it was just her in the cave, there could be days when she didn't see or talk to anyone. She described the meals they brought—when they bothered to feed her—and did her best to share everything she saw as their faults when it came to security.

In return, Grover told her exactly where the caves were located. How far the mountain was from the Army base, and how many men he'd seen guarding the opening as he was brought inside.

They exchanged information for the next hour or so, and

Sierra had never felt as valued as she had while they talked. Grover wasn't treating her like she was weak or someone to pity. He praised every scrap of information she offered...and before long, she felt the tiniest trickle of hope welling deep within her belly. It was dangerous to her psyche to hope, but she couldn't help it.

Grover was so sure his team was coming. That they'd both be free soon.

Free.

She'd dreamed of walking out of this cave more times than she could count. Of sitting on the porch at her parents' house in Colorado. Of seeing snow again. Of actually being cold rather than hot all the time. Though that's all they ever were—dreams. She was too afraid to believe freedom was just around the corner.

"I swear to you," Grover said as if he could read her mind. "We're gonna get out of here. Also, I should probably warn you... I'm gonna want to continue to get to know you when we get back to the States."

Sierra blinked. Did he just...? "Are you asking me out?" she blurted.

Grover chuckled. It was a bit rusty sounding, but it still sent goose bumps racing down her filthy arms. "Yes."

"Um...no offense...but...I'm not sure that's a good idea."

"Here's the thing," Grover replied quietly. "You intrigued me when I met you the first time, Sierra. And now that I've found you, and realize exactly how damn strong you are—you have to be, in order to survive what you have—I'm even *more* interested. I have no idea what will happen when we're back home. Hell, I don't even know where you live. But I'm just saying...I want to continue where we left off a year ago. We were robbed of the chance to get to know each other, and that pisses me off."

Sierra's heart was pounding in her chest. Grover sounded too good to be real. Then she thought back to her reaction to him when they'd first met...and realized she wasn't all that surprised by his confidence and assertiveness.

"Fine," she said, trying to sound as strong as he thought she was. "If we get out of here, I'll let you take me out on the usual three dates I give any guy before I decide if we're compatible. But if they suck, all bets are off."

"Deal," Grover said immediately.

For a second, Sierra wondered what she'd just agreed to, but he spoke again before she could reconsider.

"And it's *when*, not *if* we get out of here. Where you from, Bean?"

Sierra frowned. "What did you just call me?"

"Shit...um...nothing. Sorry."

Hearing Grover sound so embarrassed was kind of adorable. "Seriously. What did you say?"

"Bean," he mumbled. "I just...I considered Flame, because of your spark and your red hair, but Bean just popped out. It's because...God. It's because you're small and cute. Shit! Ignore me."

Amused, Sierra shook her head. She'd never had a nickname before, and even though Bean sounded a little juvenile, she couldn't deny she preferred that over Flame. "It's okay," she said. "I know you military guys can't resist giving out nicknames, *Grover.*"

"At least I got mine because of my last name, not because I resemble the puppet."

"Are you sure?" Sierra teased.

"Shit, I walked right into that, didn't I?"

Sierra chuckled—and realized it had been a very long time since she'd laughed about *anything*. Even if the worst happened

20

in the next few days, she'd always be grateful to Grover for bringing a bit of levity to her life in this moment. "My parents live in Colorado. Up in the mountains. They have a big house with an amazing view. I swear I can see for miles and miles. It always felt too remote though. I didn't like being so far from the hustle and bustle of the city, and the winters...lord, they're long and cold. But now that sounds like absolute heaven."

"You're gonna see it again," Grover promised.

"I always wonder how my parents have been holding up," Sierra said quietly. "Sometimes I think they have it worse than me. I can't imagine not knowing what happened to your child. It has to be gut-wrenching."

"Only you would think your parents have it harder than being an actual prisoner of war," Grover said. "But you just need to hold out a bit longer, then you can see them for yourself. And...just sayin'...you're gonna hate being cold."

"I am?" she asked.

"Yeah. After being here in the desert for so long, even mild temperatures are gonna make you seem as if you're freezing. Texas has those same wide-open spaces, and it's warmer," he said, almost nonchalantly. "Not as many mountains, unless you live in the extreme western part of the state, but it's pretty in its own way."

Sierra blinked. Of course, the darkness around her didn't change, but she had to have misunderstood what Grover was implying...hadn't she?

"It's hard to take you on dates when I'm in Killeen and you're on top of a mountain in Colorado," he went on.

Sierra had no idea what to say to that.

"Remember Aspen? She was the combat medic attached to the Ranger team when we were here last. She ate with me and my team?"

It took Sierra a moment to get her brain to switch gears. "Oh, yeah, I remember her. Why? Is she okay?"

"Yes, she's fine. She married Brain. They had a baby boy a couple months ago."

"Holy shit, really?"

"Yup. She got out of the Army and is working as an EMT for a local ambulance company in Killeen. The other guys all are settled down too. Lucky married my sister, in fact."

Sierra wasn't sure what to say to that. "Um...congrats?"

Grover chuckled. "Thanks. All the women are tight. They're there for each other no matter what's going on with the team. You should've seen them when Oz's nephew and niece went missing. They banded together like nothing I've ever seen... outside of my own team, of course. And when I left to come over here, they were organizing meals for another teammate's woman, Ember, after she was shot. They're pretty amazing."

Sierra understood what Grover was doing. It was...sweet. Though rather unrealistic. "I'm sure I have nothing in common with them," she said.

"I wouldn't say that. You already know Aspen. And I think you'd be surprised. Hell, Ember Maxwell is one of the most famous women in the country...if she can fit in, I *know* you can."

"Wait, Ember Maxwell? *The* Ember Maxwell?"

Grover chuckled. "Yup. She and Doc are a couple now. She moved to Killeen and started up a gym for kids to teach them the modern pentathlon sports."

"Oh shit. I forgot the Olympics happened while I've been here. Did she make the team?" Sierra asked.

"Yes. But there was a terrorist incident the evening before she competed, and her shoulder was dislocated."

"Oh no!"

"Yeah. She still managed to come in fifteenth though."

"That's amazing," Sierra said.

"She reminds me of you."

"*Right.*"

"She does. She's sweet and friendly. She's tough. She also knows about you, and is worried enough that she posted your picture on her social media account, asked that if anyone had seen you to report it."

Sierra gasped. "That was *her?*"

"What do you mean?"

"Not too long ago, my captors were in a tizzy because my picture was suddenly all over the internet. They were afraid someone might say something."

"Damn! It worked," Grover said, laughing lightly under his breath.

"I can't believe Ember Maxwell posted my picture. That she knows who I am."

"Everyone knows who you are, Bean," Grover said. "At least in my circle. They've been just as worried about you as I've been. Okay, that's probably not quite true...but they know. And care. And they'd do whatever it took to make you feel more comfortable in Texas...if you decided you might want to make it your home for a while."

"Anyone ever tell you that you're not very subtle?" Sierra asked.

"Not trying to be."

A noise from somewhere in the cave system caught their attention, and when Grover spoke again, his tone was no-nonsense and serious once more. "I can take whatever they dish out," he told her. "Our only job is to hold on until my team arrives."

"Okay."

"Try to get some sleep," Grover ordered.

Sierra nodded, though of course he couldn't see her. Just knowing he was on the other side of the rock wall made her feel so much better. She had no idea if his team would find them or be able to get them out, but for the first time in ages...she thought maybe, just maybe, this time would be different.

CHAPTER THREE

Grover swallowed the moan before it could leave his lips. Every muscle in his body hurt, but he blocked it out. He'd been through Survival Evasion Resistance and Escape training several times. The entire team had. It wasn't something he enjoyed, not at all, but it was necessary. The section on torture was especially brutal, but compared to what real-life terrorists did to him, the training seemed like a walk in the park.

Grover had known what he was in for when he'd purposely gotten himself captured, but he'd do it again a hundred more times if it meant finding Sierra. He was still a little surprised that he *had*. And that he'd actually managed to get captured by the Taliban.

Finding out that Shahzada was working on the military base as a translator? That was a surprise—and unacceptable. The man was ruthless, with a very tight hold on the locals. Grover vowed to kill the man before he left the area.

As for Sierra...it was beyond premature to ask her out, let alone try to convince her to move to Texas, but he hadn't been able to stop himself. Everything he'd learned since landing in that cave only made him admire her more. The fact that she was still alive was remarkable all by itself, but that she seemed to be well-adjusted, all things considered, just proved how incredibly resilient she was.

Grover couldn't help but be drawn to her. He'd thought she was pretty over a year ago. He'd already liked her spunk, her bright smile, and her short stature wasn't a turn-off. Knowing she'd been able to outsmart her captors and use her psychology degree against them only drew him in more, and Sierra seemed receptive to getting to know him.

It was too early to assume either of them would escape this hellhole without serious consequences, though. And while Sierra seemed to have a decent handle on everything that had happened to her, Grover still made a mental note to get in touch with a group of men he knew who ran a retreat in New Mexico, specifically for men and women suffering from post-traumatic stress disorder. Veterans, women, and children who'd escaped from domestic abuse situations, pretty much anyone who needed a quiet space to decompress and find themselves again.

He didn't know if Sierra would require their services, but if she did, he'd make sure she got the help she needed.

Despite his desire to help, though...Grover still shook his head at his own arrogance.

What was he doing? Sierra might not want *any* reminders of what had happened to her—and Grover was going to be one big-ass reminder for sure.

He was likely the first person she'd communicated with in a while. She was probably desperate for human contact of any kind; of *course* she'd be receptive.

He'd get her out of here, or die trying, but that didn't mean she owed him a damn thing. He hadn't been kidding about wanting to take her out, but if she showed even the slightest hesitancy, he reluctantly decided he'd back off.

He wasn't wearing his watch anymore, as his captors had stripped him of that and everything else he had on, except for his pants. But his internal clock told him it was most likely morning by now. He forced himself to pace the small niche he'd been thrown into and stretch out the kinks in his bruised body.

No light pierced the darkness this far back in the cave system—so when someone started in their direction carrying a light, every muscle in Grover's body tensed.

He'd much prefer the terrorists to leave them alone, but that didn't seem to be in the cards today. Damn.

He wanted to reassure Sierra, tell her that it would be okay, but he didn't get the chance.

"It's been a while," one of the men said as he went straight to Sierra's cell. Grover wanted to rage at them, tell them to leave her alone, but remembering what he'd promised, he kept all emotion off his face and his mouth shut. He'd be damned if he did or said *anything* that would make them hurt her more.

A man set up a chair outside his cell, so Grover would have a clear view of whatever they decided to do to Sierra. Two more men hauled her out of her cell, forcing her to sit.

"What are you gonna do?" Sierra asked in a voice Grover didn't recognize from the previous night. It was shaky and high-pitched, and she sounded nothing like the strong, capable woman he'd conversed with.

Grover didn't think too long on her voice, however; he was too busy taking in her physical appearance.

Her gorgeous red hair had been shaved, the small remainder left in uneven patches all over her skull. She was gaunt, about thirty pounds lighter than he remembered her being, at his best guess—and she'd been petite already. It looked as if a strong wind would blow her right over. She wore only panties and a threadbare T-shirt, the latter with rips in the fabric. She was absolutely filthy, as well, her skin and underwear covered in the dirt that coated every inch of the cave where they were being held captive.

Grover felt physically sick. He wanted to throw up. He hated seeing her this way. Her shoulders slumped forward and she continued to whine and plead for her captors to leave her alone. To not touch her.

Just when Grover thought she might've had a mental break in the night, that she couldn't possibly be acting, her gaze met his for a split second.

What he saw in her eyes made every muscle in Grover's body tighten.

Anger. Determination. Hatred for her captors. And a potent strength the likes of which even *he* had underestimated.

This woman looked subjugated and beaten, though she was anything but. Every word out of her mouth was for the benefit of her captors. She *was* acting—and she was absolutely glorious.

He hated the very slight shame he saw in her eyes. If she thought he was disgusted by her condition, she was dead wrong. No one had ever impressed him more than Sierra did right at that moment. When they'd first met, he'd thought she was too trusting and innocent. She'd only been in Afghanistan a short time, and she'd been so excited to serve her country, even if it was just as a food contractor for the military.

The woman in front of him had lost her cloak of naiveté and in its place was a mantle of steel.

Grover knew it was ten kinds of fucked up, but he was so much more attracted to *this* woman than the almost gullible one he'd initially met. Which was saying something, because he'd been plenty interested in *that* Sierra as well, all those months ago.

Her eyes filled with tears as she continued begging the men to leave her alone. To let her return to her cell. To please not hurt her.

Before the men started in on their torture, a fourth person approached, walking down the narrow and uneven cave path.

Shahzada.

Grover's lip curled involuntarily.

He *did* recognize the man, now that Sierra had told him who he was. He'd been arrogant and annoying when Grover saw him in the chow hall over a year ago, and nothing had seemed to change.

The leader of the Taliban's organization in this part of the country stopped in front of his cell, completely ignoring Sierra as she carried on behind him.

"Welcome back to my country," Shahzada said.

"Not much of a welcome," Grover commented.

The man smirked.

"And...it's good to see *you* again," Grover said.

"So, you figured it out," Shahzada said.

"That you're Muhammad, one of the translators the Army trusted and hired? That you have almost free rein on the military post and you've been kidnapping contractors for a year now? Yeah, I figured it out." Grover didn't give him a chance to speak. "I also figured out that you're a fucking coward. You didn't kidnap soldiers, because you knew you were no match for us. You could only handle untrained men and women. You're *pathetic*," he sneered, wanting to turn the man's ire on him and away from Sierra, if possible.

As he'd hoped, Shahzada's face turned red. "You will regret those words," he said in a deadly tone.

Grover opened his mouth in a huge fake yawn. "Whatever," he said after a moment, doing his best to look bored.

Shahzada growled and turned his back on Grover. Without hesitation, he grabbed a long, thick stick from the man nearest Sierra and slammed it down onto her thighs.

Grover wanted to leap up from his spot on the dusty ground, where he'd sat in a show of indifference when Shahzada had joined them. He kept himself still. Barely.

Sierra howled so loudly, it hurt his ears, but Grover kept his face impassive and stoic.

With every blow to her body, Sierra cried harder for mercy. If she hadn't warned him last night, Grover might've added his own pleas for them to stop. It took everything in him to remain where he was.

Objectively, he could see that Shahzada wasn't doing much more than causing superficial bruises. He wasn't breaking her skin, which told him a little of the level of pain she was enduring, and none of the blows were designed to kill. She'd been right —this was a show for Grover's benefit. But that certainly didn't mean he wanted to watch her being abused.

After only a few minutes, Shahzada threw down the stick and scowled at her. She had tears streaming down her face and she hadn't stopped begging.

"So pathetic," Shahzada sneered. "I am tired of this." He turned to look at Grover. "I want *him*."

Grover knew what that look in the man's eyes meant. He was in for another long, painful session at his hands. But if it meant he stopped beating Sierra, he'd willingly take it.

Two of the men hauled Sierra to her feet—she still hadn't stopped wailing—and threw her back into her cell. Grover breathed a quiet sigh of relief when he heard the lock clicking into place once more.

Her beating was over. His pain was just about to start.

Shahzada grinned as his men began working on the lock keeping his cell closed. "I've been practicing on all those 'untrained men and women.' I've learned much about what the human body can endure before it breaks. I'm looking forward to this."

Grover took a deep breath. He could handle anything this asshole and his cronies dished out. Trigger and the rest of his team would be here soon. He just had to keep Shahzada's attention on himself and off Sierra, and stay alive in the meantime.

Instead of putting him on the chair where Sierra had just been sitting, Grover was dragged down the dark path, away from the cells. He knew that wasn't a good sign. He could take a beating, but if they had electric torture set up somewhere in the caves, or any other extreme measures in mind, things could be significantly more difficult.

Before blanking his mind, he had the brief and grateful thought that he was glad Sierra wouldn't have to watch him be tortured. She'd been through enough. The last thing he wanted was to add to her trauma.

Come on, Trigger. Get your ass over here and find us.

* * *

Sierra's tears stopped the second her captors' backs were turned. She'd gotten very good at crying on cue. Her thighs hurt, but it wasn't nothing she hadn't dealt with before. Just as she'd told Grover, the more she cried and begged, the sooner her beatings were over. Shahzada and his followers were predictable as hell. She'd perversely enjoyed manipulating them in the past, taking her victories where she could and feeling like she'd gotten something over on them. But today, all she felt was dread.

Grover hadn't said a word when Shahzada was hitting her, which she was grateful for. She had a feeling for a man like him, standing by and doing nothing while a woman was being abused was a form of torture all in itself. But he'd taken her words last night to heart, which she appreciated.

She hadn't wanted him to see her though. Sierra knew she looked rough.

Right...that was an understatement. She wasn't able to wear her pants anymore because they wouldn't stay up, and she had no belt or anything to keep them around her waist. She'd lost so much weight, she was a mere shadow of her former self. Her period had stopped a long time ago, and as much as she tried to keep up the strength in her muscles by stretching and walking around her cell, she knew she had little stamina.

Then there was her hair.

She used to be so proud of her long auburn locks, her best feature for sure. After weeks in captivity, it became more a liability than anything. Sierra felt bugs crawling in her hair in the middle of the night, and it was so filthy and dirty, it made her cringe every time a strand touched her face. Not to mention, her captors frequently used it as a means to haul her around.

In the end, she'd come up with a simple plan. Every time her captors tortured her, she'd begged them not to touch her hair. She'd get frantic when they did, crying and carrying on. It took a few weeks, but finally they'd used her hair itself as a means of torture, shaving it off. They'd held her down, and she'd fought like a wildcat as they'd used first a knife to hack off the strands, then an old, dull electric razor to give her a buzz cut.

She'd cried hysterically and put on a show they'd likely never forget. Her captors laughed and jeered throughout, finally leaving her cell as Sierra wailed, slowly climbing to her knees to sob over a pile of chopped-off locks.

They'd done exactly what she'd wanted. Sierra felt so much better without her grimy hair, which had begun to form heavy dreads that pulled on her scalp. She felt lighter, cleaner. The latter was a joke, really, since she hadn't been clean since she'd taken her last shower on the base the night she was kidnapped. But still, the relief was immense—and the incident confirmed how easily her captors could be influenced.

Twice since, they'd held her down to shave her head, and each time she'd repeated her performance...kicking and fighting and begging them to leave her alone. And God help her, it felt *good* to manipulate her captors, even in small ways. Though, she knew they hadn't been trying to cut her hair evenly. What remained was patches of varying lengths, and she could only imagine how horrible it looked. While it felt so much better shaved, Sierra knew she had to look like a freak.

And as vain and silly as it was, she *hated* that Grover had seen her that way.

She knew it would be inevitable. That if he was right, and his team would eventually show up, he'd see her sooner or later, but it still depressed her.

The minutes ticked by, though Sierra actually had no clue how long she'd sat in her cell, waiting impatiently for Grover's return. Praying that he *would* return, Shahzada usually kept captors alive for a while, working them over frequently before they disappeared. He could only hope he'd do the same with Grover.

The second she heard voices coming toward her, she tensed. She knew better than to leap up and grab onto the bars of her cell, but oh how she wanted to. The lights their captors carried weren't the brightest, but they put off enough of a glow for her to see Grover.

He was barely able to walk, even with men on either side of

him, holding onto his arms. He stumbled over his feet as they dragged in the dirt. Shahzada was nowhere to be seen, but the other men were grinning as if they'd just had the time of their lives.

Grover now wore nothing but a pair of boxer briefs, and she could see dark areas on his legs and torso. Blood. His face was a bloody mess as well. He'd obviously been hit repeatedly, and it made Sierra's anger bubble under her skin, though she kept quiet and didn't say a word as their captors opened the cell and threw Grover inside.

They turned around and left without a sound, and it wasn't until she and Grover were once again alone, in the pitch darkness, that she left her spot against the far wall of her cell. Sierra crawled over to the other side and lay down. She reached her hand and arm between the bars, bending her elbow. The position was uncomfortable, but if Grover moved closer, she knew she'd be able to touch him. And she needed that more than she'd ever needed anything, ever.

"Grover?"

He grunted.

"Scoot over here. Toward my voice. My hand is through the bars, I should be able to touch you if you get close enough."

She heard slow movement in the cell next to hers and held her breath as he came closer. She jerked at the first touch of his fingers against hers, then grabbed hold when his hand brushed hers a second time. She could feel the dirt from the floor on her own skin, and wetness on Grover's, which she knew was probably blood. But none of that mattered. He was alive, and warm, and she could feel his pulse hammering in his wrist.

She wasn't sure what to say. She didn't want to ask what happened; she already knew it was bad. Sierra thought back to everything *she'd* been through in the last year, and knew he'd probably suffered through as much—or more—as she had in the past.

"I'm okay," Grover said softly.

His words were slightly garbled, and Sierra squeezed his hand. "You kinda sound a little like your namesake right now."

He chuckled lightly, and the sound ran up her spine and curled around her heart. She wracked her brain to think of something to talk about, anything that might take his mind off the pain. "Did my hair look as bad as it feels?"

"No."

She assumed he was bullshitting her. Regardless, for the next fifteen minutes, she quietly told him the story of how she'd manipulated her captors until they actually thought it had been *their* idea to cut it. "I know it looks awful, that I have to look terrible, but it feels so much better this way."

"Smart," Grover said.

"If it makes *you* feel better, they'll probably leave you alone for a few days now. They like us to be relatively healthy and strong before they try to break us again."

Grover grunted.

"So that will give your team more time to get here."

She heard him mumble something under his breath.

"What can I do to help?" She felt useless just lying there. Holding his hand didn't feel like nearly enough.

"You're doing it," he replied. Then he asked, "Did they do this to you?"

"No," Sierra said guiltily. "When they took me, some of Shahzada's followers hadn't ever tortured anyone before. I was practice. At least, that's what I was told. They did really awful stuff, especially the waterboarding. But they didn't usually draw blood. Maybe it's because I'm a woman. Or maybe because I'm not a soldier and had no real useful information. I don't know.

But I feel guilty that they seem to have gone so light on me, comparatively."

"Don't," Grover said. "They took your freedom. That's bad enough."

"I guess. Did you do what I told you?" she couldn't help but ask. "Did you tell them what they wanted to know?"

"Didn't ask anything," Grover said. "Just beat on me. Shahzada especially."

"Assholes," she muttered, the hate easy to hear in her voice. "He's jealous of you. Probably remembers how much your team was respected. From the little I've overheard in the last year...he seems pissed he hasn't been able to get a better foothold in the Taliban network and is taking it out on his captives. I think he wants to move up faster, but he's kidnapping the wrong people to make that happen."

Grover grunted.

"I'm not saying his followers are good men, but they aren't as bloodthirsty as Shahzada. They have families. Wives and children. I get the impression they like the idea of climbing the ranks, but aren't willing to be as violent as Shahzada to get there."

"Still gonna die."

Sierra nodded. "I know. And I don't feel bad about it. Not at all. Their fate was sealed when they sided with Shahzada."

Grover didn't reply, and after several long seconds, she felt his hand go lax in hers.

Sierra didn't let go. She knew her arm would eventually fall asleep from the awkward position, but she didn't care. She needed to keep this connection with Grover. She felt guilty that he'd been hurt so badly. Not once in the last year had she been tortured as heavily as Grover obviously was today.

She ran her thumb over the back of his hand. She'd have to

let go eventually. Go back to the other side of her cell so when their captors hopefully returned with food in the morning, they wouldn't know she and Grover had connected. If they did, Shahzada would certainly use that against them.

But for now, she stayed huddled against the edge of the dirt wall in her cell and held Grover's hand as he slept. At least she hoped he was sleeping and hadn't passed out. There was always the possibility that Shahzada had hit Grover hard enough to rupture something inside his body.

Moving a finger down so she could feel the pulse in his wrist, Sierra sighed in relief at the steady beat.

She'd been afraid to believe Grover earlier, when he'd told her his team would find them, but now she prayed harder than she'd prayed in the last year.

Find us. Grover needs you.

CHAPTER FOUR

Trigger, Lefty, Brain, Oz, Lucky, and Doc sat impatiently around the conference table on the military base in Afghanistan. The general in charge of the post was going over what steps had been taken to try to find the contractors in the past, as well as what the other special forces teams had found out when they were there.

Outwardly, Trigger was listening, but inside he was going over the information he and the rest of the team had found with Grover's belongings. He'd encrypted a file on his laptop and had explained, in detail, how he'd planned on stirring up shit in the village near the post.

But it was the short note he'd left right before getting captured that caught their attention the most.

I have no proof, but I'm thinking this has to be an inside job. Someone on this base is either working with Shahzada, or he's here himself.

The team had talked about it and agreed with their missing teammate. The lack of progress in finding Shahzada, or the missing contractors, had to mean the Taliban leader was getting information ahead of raids and missions to search him out.

"Right, Trigger?" the general asked.

Trigger blinked and glanced over at Lefty. He saw his friend dip his head slightly. "Right," he told the officer, having no idea what he was agreeing to.

"I'm very sorry about your teammate, but reports say that he was out of control when he was here. Acting very out of character, drinking too much and being belligerent."

Trigger wanted to rail at the other man. Ask him if he thought Grover's actions made it okay that he'd been taken.

Of course they didn't. Just as a woman wearing provocative clothing didn't deserve to be assaulted. And it was insulting that the general hadn't even considered the possibility that Grover had been acting out of character for a reason.

But no one knew Grover like his team. And they all knew how desperate their friend was to find information on Sierra Clarkson.

They hadn't expected him to go to such extreme measures, however.

"We understand there are rules that need to be followed," Trigger told the older man. "But we're going to do what needs to be done to not only find our teammate, but put an end to the disappearance of contractors on this post. Shahzada and his band of terrorists need to be stopped. I would like to request that you lock the post down until we find our man. No one comes in or out. That means no translators, no one from the Afghani Army, no local spouses or children."

The general looked surprised. "That's easier said than done."

Trigger leaned forward. "It's our belief, and it was Grover's too, that there's a traitor on base. We don't know if he or she is a local or if it's one of ours. But if no information can get in or out, it'll give us a leg up. It'll make Shahzada uncomfortable. Put some pressure on the organization. We *are* going to find our teammate. And hopefully any of the missing contractors who are still alive as well."

Trigger could see the general was skeptical, but he nodded. "How long?"

"As long as it takes," Oz said.

Everyone on the team knew that wasn't going to happen. They might have a week at best; any longer and the general would have to return to business as usual. But they wouldn't need a week. Nothing would keep them from finding Grover.

After twenty more minutes, the meeting ended and Trigger and his team headed for the tent they'd been assigned. As they checked their gear, Trigger outlined the plan. "I think our best bet is to do what Grover did...head out to the local watering holes. Brain, we'll need you to eavesdrop to see if anyone talks about Grover. If you hear anything, we'll follow that person in pairs. No one goes anywhere by themselves, got it?"

Everyone agreed.

"And we all have our trackers, right?"

Again, everyone nodded. Trigger had learned from Ghost, the leader of another Delta team on post, that a mutual friend, Tex, had supplied his team with the handy devices. Trigger had never been a fan of trackers, but he wasn't willing to lose another of his friends while they were looking for Grover. He regretted not forcing Grover to take one before leaving the States.

Trigger was also kicking his own ass for letting Grover come to Afghanistan alone. He'd known how desperate he'd become over the last year to find out why Sierra just disappeared. Since receiving the letter she'd sent that had gotten lost in the mail, he'd only become more concerned. He should've known Grover would do something drastic. But getting himself taken captive on purpose was even crazier than anything Trigger could've imagined. He had no idea if Sierra was still alive, but had no doubt if she was, Grover would do whatever it took to keep her that way until help arrived.

"We're gonna find him," Lucky said, interrupting Trigger's thoughts.

"I know."

"Do we have a list of all the locals who work on base?" Oz asked.

"The general is supposed to send it over."

"Good. Pictures too?"

"Yup."

"We can show them to locals in town, see if they recognize anyone and what they can tell us."

"You really think Shahzada is working on base?" Lefty asked.

"Yes," Trigger said. "It makes the most sense. It would make it easy for him to pack up the contractors' shit and make it disappear, along with the contractors themselves."

"And he was probably working with others too," Doc added.

"Fuck. No wonder the SEALs didn't have any luck in tracking them down. Shahzada probably knew they were here, even what their plans were," Brain said in disgust.

"If Grover got snatched because he was acting drunk, someone knows something. He's a big fucker, they wouldn't be able to fade into the night without being seen," Lucky said.

"Exactly," Trigger agreed. "Take the next couple of hours to talk to your wives and kids...then be ready to head out at seven tonight. We'll see if we can't find someone who will admit to seeing him and who he was with. We won't be back here until we've got Grover...and hopefully Sierra too."

Trigger needed to talk to his wife. Needed to hear Gillian's voice. He didn't like to think about not making it back to her...

but he made a mental vow that he wasn't leaving the country until Grover was back with *them*.

* * *

Grover had lost track of time. Sierra had been right, after the first beating, he'd been left alone for a couple days—but the third session with Shahzada had been even worse than the second. The man was a sadist and took delight in hurting him just for the sake of pain. Again, he hadn't asked him anything. Wasn't trying to get information. He just enjoyed making him bleed.

Shahzada had let him know he wasn't pleased the military base had been locked down. No one was able to get in or out, which pissed him off. He routinely passed information to someone higher up in the Taliban, which, now that he wasn't allowed on base, wasn't possible.

Grover quickly realized that Shahzada had snowed *everyone*. The US military thought he was this huge player in the Taliban. That he had way more power than he did. As it turned out, Sierra was right again—he was simply one of hundreds of men who wanted to move up in the organization. He'd perpetuated rumors about his power to cause fear in both the town, and in the Westerners who were stationed on the base.

As he was beating Grover, Shahzada bragged about all the times he passed on the wrong information during his duties as translator. Instead of telling the villagers that the military would be helping to repair sewage systems and purifying water, he told them the Americans had no intention of lifting one finger to help. That they were on their own. He'd done everything he could to sow dissent between the soldiers and the locals. Used his position to threaten those weaker than him, warning that if they worked with the soldiers, their families would pay.

All in all, Shahzada was, for all intents and purposes, a schoolyard bully. He was a big fish in a small pond, with dreams of moving up in the hierarchy of the Taliban. He was attempting to do it with smoke and mirrors.

Yes, he had kidnapped half a dozen contractors from the base, but hadn't had the balls to take an actual soldier. Until him.

And Grover was going to be his downfall. He just had to hold on.

He sucked in a harsh breath when he moved too quickly and his ribs screamed in pain. At least a few were cracked, he guessed. His kidneys were certainly bruised. And today's torture session had included his arms being restrained behind his back, his body hung from the ceiling by his bound hands. His shoulders were in agony, and Grover knew they'd been dislocated during the torture session. Shahzada's men had actually done him a favor by stomping on his shoulders when they'd finally let him down. It had hurt like a son of a bitch to have them forced back into their sockets, but it was for the best in the long run.

Now he was lying on his back in his cell, in the dark. One arm was over his head through the bars, with Sierra once more holding his hand. Amazingly, feeling her palm against his went a long way toward easing his pain.

"I *hate* them," she said after several silent minutes had passed. "I mean, I already hated them keeping me here with no obvious plan in place on what to do with me. But now? I want to kill them all. Slowly. Make them hurt like they're making you hurt."

"It's mainly Shahzada," Grover felt obligated to point out.

"I. Don't. Care. They're all in this just as deeply. They've kept me here against my will. They've beaten me when Shahzada tells them to. I don't care if they don't hit me as hard as they could; they still do it. They laugh when I fake cry about my hair. They *enjoy* seeing me beg. They're all culpable—and I hope they die slow, horrible, painful deaths!"

Grover couldn't hold back the smile that crossed his face. It was inappropriate as hell, but he was so relieved Shahzada and his followers hadn't completely doused her fire, he didn't care. "They will," he told her.

He heard her huff out a breath in agitation.

"What's the first meal you want when you get home?" he asked, trying to get her mind off the assholes holding them captive.

"Seriously?"

"Sure, why not?"

"Because I've had nothing but tasteless oatmeal-type shit for months," she complained.

Grover realized that his question had been pretty tactless. "Sorry. Forget I asked."

"I never used to think much about food. I mean, I tried to watch what I ate because with my height, even five pounds would make me look much larger. But I didn't really have a favorite food or anything. Now that I haven't had anything good in months...I realize how much I miss tasting *anything* other than the crap they've given me."

"There's a pizza place north of Austin that has my favorite pizza ever," Grover said. "DeSano Pizzeria Napoletana. The name is super fancy, and I swear I've never tasted anything better. You'd think everything was made in the heart of Italy instead of Texas."

"McDonald's French fries," Sierra said. "The salt on my fingers used to annoy me, but even the thought of salt right now makes my mouth water."

"You could have anything in the world and you choose fast food French fries?" Grover teased.

"Hey, don't judge," Sierra complained.

"Sorry," Grover told her. "What else?"

"Fresh vegetables. A tomato straight from the vine. A huge salad with chopped veggies and cheese. And slathered in ranch dressing."

"Sounds good. What else?"

"A cream-filled doughnut."

Grover chuckled and ignored the flash of pain from his ribs. "You have a sweet tooth, huh?" he asked.

"Yup," Sierra said unapologetically. "Pretty much just about anything would sound amazing right now though. I...I've lost a lot of weight."

He hated the shame he heard in her voice. "You'll gain it back. I'll help you."

Her hand tightened on his for a moment before she relaxed again.

He kept talking. "On our first date, I'll get us a pizza from DeSano Pizzeria Napoletana. I'll make you a huge salad with fresh veggies I'll pick up from a farmers market. Cucumbers, tomatoes, peppers, cheese...you name it, I'll put it in there. We'll go up to the top of the barn that was recently completed on my property. You can see for miles up there. We'll eat until we're stuffed, then we'll let it settle while we talk, and then eat some more. We'll be so full, we won't be able to climb down to leave so we'll have to sleep up there."

Sierra chuckled. "So now our first date has turned into a sleepover?"

"Sure. Why not? We've already slept together here, so why not when we get home too?"

There was a moment of silence before Grover heard the most beautiful sound *ever*. Sierra giggling.

"You're assuming I want to come to Texas to visit you," Sierra said when she had herself under control.

"I am," Grover agreed.

Another minute or so of silence before she spoke again. "You're not like any man I've ever met. You're bossy and too sure of yourself. You think you'll get your way just because you want something."

When she didn't say anything else, Grover asked, "And?"

"And what?"

"I heard a but in there somewhere."

"Yeah. But...for some reason I can't get mad at you for it."

"I'm an upfront kind of guy," Grover told her seriously, hating that he couldn't look into her eyes as he spoke. He squeezed her hand tighter. "When I saw you a year ago, I was instantly attracted. You were like this ray of sunshine in an otherwise pretty dark world. When I didn't hear from you, I admit...I was both pissed and disappointed. But even as month after month passed, and I still didn't hear from you, I couldn't get you out of my mind. When I found out that you *had* written? That was it. I wasn't going to let some asshole terrorist steal my chance to get to know you."

"So you came all the way over here and got yourself taken captive so you could get a date?" Sierra asked.

Grover snorted. "Hey, I'm the last of my team to find a woman, and I'm not getting any younger."

"Please. I'm sure women trip over themselves to get you to look at them. In case it's escaped your notice, you're fairly good-looking, Grover."

"I'm thirty-three, not twenty, Bean. I'd like to think I'm not so shallow as to go home with every woman who decides she wants to sleep with a soldier. I'm not denying I went through that phase when I first joined the Army, but that's not what I want anymore. Not for a long time. And not as many women as you think want to get involved with a career soldier like me. Someone who has to leave at the drop of a hat and can't talk about where he's going or when he'll be back."

"Then they're stupid," Sierra said softly. "I'm not saying it's easy to be married to someone in the military, but I think, for me, I'd be proud of what my boyfriend or husband was doing. I've learned firsthand how important it is to keep the tyrants from taking over the world."

Grover was silent for a while. He didn't know any of the basics about Sierra. Things like whether she was a morning person. If she spread her stuff all over the bathroom counter or kept it all neatly lined up on her side. Her favorite movies or books. The things he *did* know were far more important, and he liked all of it. A lot. She was practical. Smart. Down-to-earth. Compassionate. Loyal. A little bloodthirsty.

He knew that last one wasn't something most people thought was a good trait, but he wanted a partner who understood that killing was part of his job. The Deltas didn't kill on every mission, of course, but when they did, it was *absolutely* necessary.

Grover shifted on the ground and winced again. Damn, he hurt. Shahzada was a vicious son-of-a-bitch, and he wouldn't be sorry to see him dead.

As if she could read his mind, Sierra asked, "Do you honestly think your team will find us? I mean, how will they be any different than anyone else who's looked in the past?"

"They'll find us," Grover reassured her. "And I know because if one of them was missing, I wouldn't stop until I'd figured out where they were being held and rained hellfire down on anyone who dared keep me from them. Besides, I left them notes on everything I did when I was on post, and what I had planned to do the night I was taken. They'll follow up and get us out."

"I don't understand why Shahzada has been so...hard on you," Sierra said.

"He probably has a small penis," Grover said.

There was a beat of silence, then Sierra burst out laughing. Once again, Grover couldn't help but grin at the beautiful sound.

"Well, all right then," she said when she had herself under control.

"In all honesty, I'm not one hundred percent sure myself," Grover said more seriously. "I know he's pissed the base is locked down. And like you said, he's frustrated that he hasn't been asked to move up in the ranks. He's still stuck here in this town. He wants more. And because he's spent so much time on the post, he's probably jealous or resentful of men like me."

"Special forces?" Sierra asked.

Grover shrugged, forgetting the damage being strung up had done to his shoulders. He bit back a pained groan and took a deep breath before continuing. "Of men stronger, bigger, and who don't need to rely on fear and intimidation to be powerful."

"Tell me about your friends?" she asked.

Some people might've thought her question was an abrupt change of topic, but Grover followed her logic. He liked that she thought of him and the rest of his team as the opposite of Shahzada. Honorable.

So Grover told her all about his team. He talked about some of their missions—without including details about where they were or what they were doing. He mentioned a few of their close calls and explained how much they relied on each other.

He told her the story of how Trigger and Gillian met when her plane was hijacked. He described how devastated Lefty had been when Kinley entered the witness protection program, but how he'd never lost faith that he'd see her again. He explained about Brain's amazing ability to speak and read so many languages, and how much it had come in handy over the years. Shared the story about Sergeant Spence, who'd tried to kill Brain and Aspen, and how relieved the other woman was to be out of the Army.

He talked a long time about Logan and Bria, Oz's nephew and niece, and explained his own not-so-great relationship with his brother, after Spencer's actions had almost gotten their sister Devyn killed. He told Sierra about their duties at the Olympics and meeting Ember, and how he wasn't so sure about her at first, but now loved her like a sister.

After talking for what seemed like hours about his friends, Grover's throat was dry, but he couldn't stop. He found himself talking about his home. About how he'd torn down the dilapidated barn on the property and his team had helped frame out a new one. He told her about the beautiful barn doors he'd repurposed and put into his home. About how much he loved waking up, going out onto his back deck, and sitting in silence as he took in the morning. He joked about the media room Devyn had convinced him to put in. There was an odd room at one end of his house that had no windows, so she'd decided it would be perfect for a home theater. He'd put a huge-ass screen with a projector in there so he could watch TV on a move-size screen with rows of super-comfortable chairs.

Grover eventually realized he'd been talking nonstop without letting Sierra get a word in edgewise. He frowned. "Sorry. I didn't mean to blab on and on," he said a little sheepishly.

"Don't be sorry. I...I think I love your friends, and I don't even know them," Sierra said softly.

"They're all good people. Not perfect by any stretch, but

together, we all just seem to work. We love that the women all get along so well. It makes us feel better when we get deployed. We know they'll be there for each other no matter what," Grover said.

"It sounds like it. And you said Aspen had a little boy, right?"

"Yeah. Chance. And Riley had a girl not too long ago. Amalia."

"Wow. From what you said, she and Oz haven't been together that long, right?"

Grover chuckled. "Right. But once Oz experienced the joys of fatherhood with his nephew and niece, he decided he wanted more kids. Immediately."

"Good that Riley agreed," Sierra said dryly.

"You want kids?" Grover asked, then mentally kicked himself for the intimate question. "Sorry...that was rude."

"No, it's okay. It's not like this is a normal situation. If we were on a first date back in the States and you asked, I'd probably send a friend an SOS text and ask her to initiate 'get me the hell out of here.'"

"Do I want to know what that is?" Grover asked. "I mean, I can guess from the name, but still..."

"I can't believe you don't already know. And yeah, it's exactly what it sounds like. A woman and a friend set up an emergency 'out' for a date. The friend will call or text with a fake emergency, allowing the woman to leave early if things aren't going well."

"Really?"

Sierra huffed out an amused breath. "I can't imagine that's ever happened to you."

"Actually, it *did*. But I didn't realize what was happening at the time," Grover said.

"Oh my God, seriously? What happened? Why would someone want to ditch you?" she asked.

"Well, first, thanks for the vote of confidence, but your vision of me being mobbed by women anytime I go somewhere is seriously whacked. I'm awkward, and I put my foot in my mouth all the time...as evidenced by my inelegant question a moment ago. We were at dinner—I'd brought her to a steak house—and while we were looking at the menu, I found out she was vegan."

"Ouch," Sierra said with a chuckle.

"Yeah. We were set up by a friend of a friend of a friend. Apparently, she didn't know I was in the military either. And she was vehemently opposed to any kind of violence. She was a pacifist."

"Strike two," Sierra quipped.

"Yup. I thought I could still salvage the date though. She was pretty and nice. I thought we were getting along pretty well, even with the other stuff. The third strike was my sister."

"Devyn? That's her name, right?"

"I actually have three sisters, but that night it was Devyn who did me in. She was out at a bar with her friends, still living in Missouri at the time. There was some guy who was pretending to be a military veteran. She knew enough about the Army to know he was full of shit. So she kept texting me with the stuff he was saying to one of her friends, as he was trying to pick her up. It was ridiculous and over-the-top, but every time my phone vibrated with a text, my date frowned. I think maybe she thought I had a woman, or women, on the side and was a player. Anyway, not too long after that, she used the restroom. Right when she got back to the table, her phone rang. It was her neighbor saying that when she'd let my date's dog out, he ran away. I offered to go with her to help look for the pup, but she declined and left."

Sierra choked on a laugh, and Grover would've given anything to be able to see her right about now. "I take it you never went on a second date."

"Nope," Grover said.

"Wow, okay, so yeah, you were pretty clueless. Anything you'd do differently if that situation happened again?" she asked.

"Yeah, when I found out she was vegan, I'd have taken her somewhere else."

"That probably would've been smart."

"I couldn't've done anything about my job, but I should've kept my damn phone in my pocket instead of having it on the table."

"A man who learns from his mistakes. Amazing," Sierra joked.

"I still put my foot in my mouth all the time though," Grover told her.

"I think our situation transcends society's rules for what's okay to talk about and what's not when you first meet someone. Besides, technically, we've known each other for a year," Sierra said.

Grover ran his thumb back and forth over her hand. His shoulder hurt from his arm being over his head, but he refused to move. He needed this connection with someone else, as much as he thought she did too. "I want to know everything about you," Grover admitted.

"The answer to your earlier question about children is…I don't know. I haven't thought too much about kids. I mean, I know I'm almost thirty and my parents keep reminding me that I'm getting older, but honestly, I like being on my own. I was able to take the job over here in Afghanistan without having to worry about any children. And now that I've said it out loud, that sounds selfish as hell," she said softly.

"Not at all. Just because you're a woman doesn't mean you have to have kids," Grover reassured her.

"I guess. I suppose I might think differently once I fall in love."

"Maybe, maybe not. But I don't think not wanting kids makes you selfish."

"What about you?" Sierra asked, turning the tables on him.

"I'm like you, I'm not sure. I love being around Logan and Bria, but they're not babies. Logan is eleven going on twenty-five, and Bria is almost seven. They aren't infants, which for me, makes it more enjoyable to be around them."

"Most people wouldn't admit that," Sierra told him.

"Maybe not. You ready to call in that phone-a-friend to end this date yet?" Grover joked.

As he hoped, she laughed.

"You think it would work? If so, I'd do it in a heartbeat. This date kinda sucks, Grover. The food's terrible, the restaurant's dirty as hell, and the lighting is shit."

Without thought, Grover burst out laughing, then moaned as the movement made his aches and pains known.

"You all right?" Sierra asked gently.

"Yeah. Forgot about the love taps Shahzada gave me for a second."

Her hand gripped his tightly. "When he comes again, I'm gonna see if I can turn his attention to me, give you a break," Sierra said.

"No!" Grover barked more harshly than he'd intended. He took a breath and said a little calmer, "No. I'm okay. I know what my body can take. If he follows his pattern, he'll leave us alone tomorrow. That gives my team another day to get to us. But if they don't get here before Shahzada decides he wants to play some more, you need to do just what you've done before. Pretend I don't exist. Hear me?"

"I feel as if you being hurt is my fault," she admitted quietly.

"It's not. I'm being hurt because Shahzada is a bully. A power-hungry asshole. A man who desperately wants to make people believe he's a badass when in reality, he's just another coward who's only brave when he's the one holding the stick," Grover told her, making a mental note to never let another moan or groan pass his lips while Sierra could hear him. The last thing he wanted was to add to her anguish. She'd been through enough in the last year, he wouldn't add to the burden on her psyche.

"You're right," she said after a few moments.

"I know."

"Right, there's that confidence thing again," she teased.

"You'd rather I be indecisive?" Grover asked.

"No!" she exclaimed immediately. "I'm just making an observation."

They lay in silence for a minute or two before Grover said, "It's late. We need to get some sleep."

"I know."

When neither of them moved, Grover chuckled. "Someone has to make the first move and let go first."

Sierra's hand tightened on his once more. "Not it."

"They're comin'," Grover said. "And that's me being confident again. They are. I know my friends, they're gonna want to ream my ass that I went and got myself kidnapped. They won't be able to let that go. So they'll be here."

He heard Sierra give a little laugh under her breath. "I believe you. If you want, I'll even stand between you and them and protect you from their wrath."

"Oh, now *that* I want to see," Grover said, envisioning it in his mind.

"Thanks for not forgetting about me. Sitting here in the dark day after day, for so long, I kinda thought I wasn't worth anyone trying to get me out."

"I never forgot about you, Sierra Clarkson. *Never*."

"I didn't forget about you either," she said in a voice so low, Grover almost didn't hear it. Then she squeezed his hand once more and let go.

It was scary how bereft he felt when her skin wasn't against his own.

Moving slowly, bringing his arm back through the bars, Grover clenched his teeth at the pain the movement caused. But instead of rolling over and sleeping, he slowly got to his feet.

He needed to stretch. To test his body. Because when his team came for them, he needed to be ready. Mobile.

Grover couldn't hear Sierra moving around in the cell next to him, but just knowing she was there gave him the motivation he needed to push his bruised and battered body to the limit. He wouldn't be happy until they were both free of this place, Shahzada was dead, and they were on their way out of the country.

CHAPTER FIVE

Sierra sat up in her cell three days later and blinked, trying to see through the darkness that was all around her twenty-four hours a day...except when her captors brought her food, or wanted to beat on her and brought a light with them. She wasn't sure what had woken her up—but then she heard it again.

Gunfire.

It echoed in the cave around her and she scrambled to her feet. As she and Grover had discussed—well, as he'd ordered her to do—she pressed herself against the back wall of her cell, then crouched down and made herself as small as possible.

"Sierra?" Grover's voice was strained as he called out her name.

"I'm down!" she called out.

"No matter what, don't move!" he ordered.

Sierra wanted to tell him to get down too, but she knew that would be useless.

Shahzada had come to beat on him again yesterday, but this time hadn't removed him from his cell. Sierra had heard every blow landing on his skin, the grunts and moans he couldn't hold back. It took everything she had to sit in her cell and not scream at them to stop, but she'd already vowed not to do anything to make Grover's situation worse.

Shahzada had ordered his men to beat her as well. As soon as they'd reached for her, she'd turned on the tears and started to beg. Her pathetic play-acting did mostly what she hoped. Whether disgusted with her supposed weakness or possibly just bored, they gave up on torturing her even quicker than they had in the past.

She and Grover had talked after they'd left, and he'd gone through different scenarios for how their rescue might go. He never wavered in his belief that his friends would come. And soon. He'd told her to stay in the back of her cell, making herself as small as possible, in case Shahzada's men tried to kill them before they could be rescued.

That thought scared the shit out of Sierra. When she'd first been taken captive, she'd been terrified every day that they'd kill her. But as the months passed, she guessed she was a form of backup plan for the group. In addition to using her against others, they were keeping her as a bargaining chip, if things came to that. At first she was their practice dummy for torture techniques, but eventually she became a second, and third, thought.

But she couldn't fathom surviving what she had for so long, only to die seconds before she was freed. So she'd agreed to do exactly what Grover asked.

Now it sounded like their rescue could be eminent.

Sierra knew she was breathing too hard and fast, but she couldn't help it. Her heart was beating a million miles an hour and she thought she was going to pass out. She ducked her chin to her knees and squeezed her eyes shut as she heard raised voices coming toward the cells.

It took her a moment to realize she was hearing English, and not her captors speaking in their native language.

She raised her head—and looked right into a powerful beam of light.

"Shit!" she exclaimed, throwing up an arm to block the glow.

"Damn, sorry!" a male voice said. "Just making sure you were out of range. Hang tight, Sierra, we'll have you out of there in a bit. Stay where you are."

Sierra nodded and kept her eyes closed. All she could see were bright floaty spots anyway. She heard some loud bangs, then a tremendous crash.

She couldn't keep her eyes closed anymore. She lifted her head.

This time, she blinked in surprise. The bars of her cell had been completely knocked out of the rock they'd been attached to and a large section was now lying in the dirt. She looked up and saw three men standing outside her cell. One held out his hand.

"Unless you'd like to extend your stay, it's time to go."

Sierra stood up so fast, she lost her balance. Throwing out a hand to keep herself from pitching to the dirt, she staggered toward the men. One was holding a very powerful flashlight upward, so its beam bounced off the rocks above them, lighting the entire area. The third man dropped a pack from his back and began to rummage through it as she moved forward.

"I'm Trigger. This is Oz and Doc," the man with the light said. "We don't have a lot of time, but you can't go tromping around the desert like that."

For the first time in a while, Sierra remembered what she looked like. Wearing nothing but a torn T-shirt and underwear, and absolutely filthy, she couldn't imagine what these men were thinking.

"Sierra?" Grover said. Then he was there.

Grover was looking pretty rough himself. He'd obviously gotten a pair of pants from one of his teammates and had already pulled them on. But his chest was still bare, and covered in cuts and bruises. He had a week's worth of facial hair and his poor face was in worse shape than the rest of his body. Sierra had a chance to see his wide, worried brown eyes fixated on her, before her face was pressed up against the very chest she'd been eyeing with concern.

"Grover, we've got to move, man. No time for this," Trigger warned from behind them.

For a split second, Grover's arms tightened, as if he didn't want to let her go, then he nodded and took a step back. His hands didn't leave her biceps.

"Here," Doc said as he shoved some material toward them. Grover turned and grabbed it, then went down to one knee in front of her. He tapped her foot. "Lift."

Confused, she did as he requested and soon found herself in the first pair of pants she'd worn in months. Not surprisingly, they were too big, but Grover quickly threaded a rope through the belt loops and tied it in front. A pair of boots thumped to the ground next to him and without looking up, Grover said, "Hold on to me and lift your right foot."

Sierra wanted to tell him that she could dress herself, but she was so surprised at how fast everything was happening, she did as he asked, bracing a hand on his warm shoulder. She concentrated on his quick, efficient movements as he put a sock on her foot and eased it into the boot. Amazingly, it fit almost perfectly. He helped her get the second sock and boot on before grabbing a T-shirt Trigger was holding out to him, throwing it over his head, then putting his own socks and boots on.

Sierra's relief and excitement almost overwhelmed her—until she took a step forward. Her feet felt like they were being suffocated in the boots and it was actually uncomfortable to walk. It wasn't that they were the wrong size or rubbing against her in any way; it was just that she hadn't had anything on her feet in over a year. It was hard to get used to it again.

"It'll get better," Oz said from nearby. He hadn't missed her discomfort.

She nodded. "I know." She *didn't* know, but decided faking it was better than admitting a weakness right about now. The last thing she wanted was to be a liability.

Grover stood, and Sierra looked up at him—way up. Over the last week, she hadn't thought about their differences in height. Lying on the floor, holding his hand through the bars, was a great equalizer. But now, staring up into his eyes, she couldn't help but feel tiny.

"Here," said a man she hadn't met yet, holding something out to her. Reaching for it automatically, Sierra saw that it was a tan baseball cap.

She looked at it, then at the guy, confused.

"I'm Brain. Figure it will keep your scalp from burning."

"Thanks," she said, her voice only wavering a little bit. She thought maybe the real reason they'd brought a hat was to hide the long red hair they'd remembered her having. But since her captors had recently shaved it off again, she was grateful to have the cap to cover the mess they'd most likely made.

"It's good to see you, Sierra. You *are* Sierra Clarkson, aren't you?" another man asked.

"I am," she admitted.

"Can we cut the chitchat?" another man grumbled. "I'm not

really happy being this far back in this mountain. We need to jet."

"That's Lefty and Lucky," Grover told her, pointing first to the man who'd said her name, then the other. He put his arm around her back, his large hand resting on her hip, and Sierra couldn't help but lean into him.

The second they began walking, she could feel Grover limping. She belatedly remembered the possible rib fractures he'd admitted to, as well, after Shahzada's second beating. He might be acting as if he wasn't in pain, but in reality, it had to be excruciating.

She eased her arm around him and held on to his waistband. She did her best to take some of his weight, but knew she probably wasn't doing a damn thing to help.

Amazingly, he looked down at her and smiled. "Toughest bean in the jar," he said.

Sierra rolled her eyes. "That name is ridiculous."

"I know," he said without apology.

She was glad to see Trigger take up position on Grover's other side. If he needed support, she wasn't going to be much use, but his friend would.

They made their way carefully down the long dug-out tunnel in the cave, toward the entrance. They passed a few bodies along the way, but Sierra noticed that none were Shahzada.

Just when she thought they were going to get out of the hellhole she'd been stashed in for months, shots rang out again.

Grover grabbed her, lifting her off her feet and pressing her back against the tunnel wall, protecting her with his own body. The men around her fired back, and Sierra's ears rang with the sound of gunfire echoing throughout the cave.

"Looks like they aren't happy we're trying to take their guests away from the party!" Oz called out.

Sierra peeked around Grover and saw the other man was actually grinning.

"Take 'em out! Take 'em all out!" Trigger yelled back.

The next ten minutes were the longest of Sierra's life.

Grover pulled her farther back in the cave and made her sit on the ground. Then he went back to where his teammates were firing out of the entrance and joined in. Sierra knew better than to do anything to disrupt their focus. As much as she hated it, she was a liability right now and if she distracted even one of them, they could get hurt. So she sat exactly where Grover put her, wrapped her arms around her knees, and prayed no one got injured.

There was a lull in the shooting, and Brain yelled, "That's it. Time to go!"

Grover was there in a heartbeat, pulling her to her feet and keeping a tight grip on her arm as he tugged her toward the cave's entrance.

Sierra was terrified. Wanted to ask if he was sure it was safe. But she didn't get a chance before she was suddenly outside.

She'd dreamed about this moment. About walking out of the cave a free woman. This wasn't exactly how she'd ever thought it would happen, but she wasn't going to look a gift horse in the mouth.

All around them, men were bleeding and unmoving. She would've felt bad for their deaths except for the fact they were working with Shahzada, and had taken great pleasure in hurting her and Grover over the last week.

"Anyone see Shahzada?" Grover asked.

Trigger barked out a laugh as they made their way to the right, keeping the mountain to their backs. "As if that coward would actually fight alongside his men."

Sierra didn't recognize their location, as she'd been blindfolded when she'd been brought to the cave. But it didn't matter. She was outside. Free. Well...almost.

"This next part isn't going to be easy, Bean."

Sierra looked at Grover. "You mean the last year *has* been?" she said somewhat sarcastically.

Even in the serious situation they'd found themselves in, she saw Grover's lips twitch. "Right. Okay then, this next part is gonna suck monkey balls. We're going down."

"Down?" Sierra asked with a frown. "Down where?"

"There," Trigger said, pointing over the edge of the plateau they'd been walking on.

Sierra looked down in confusion.

"We're going over the edge," Lucky confirmed. "Shahzada's men can't follow us that way. Well, they can, but I doubt they will."

"Right, because they'd be insane! That drop-off is practically straight down!" Sierra exclaimed.

"Yup." Doc sounded almost excited.

"You guys are crazy," Sierra muttered.

Just then, shouts sounded from their left.

Brain translated as the words reached where they were standing next to the rocky mountain wall. "'There they are. Kill the men and bring me the woman.'"

"Fuck that," Grover muttered.

Sierra looked toward where the voices were coming from and saw Shahzada standing with another group of men. Of course he was standing *behind* them all, giving orders instead of leading the charge.

"That's Shahzada!" Sierra said, before yelping in surprise when Grover yanked her down into a squat. Looking around, she realized they were sitting ducks. There wasn't much cover where they crouched against the mountain—and literally the only way out of their predicament was to go over the edge, as Trigger had indicated.

Shahzada had the upper hand. He could keep bringing in reinforcements from the narrow road behind him, and eventually one or more of Grover's team would be injured or killed.

They'd come for *her*; she had to do something to help. She wasn't a badass special forces soldier, but she wasn't a coward either.

She grabbed Grover's biceps. "I'll go toward them and pretend to give up. You guys can shoot them."

It was a crazy suggestion. Even Sierra knew that, but she had to do *something*.

"No."

One word. That was all Grover offered. And it irritated Sierra. "I can be a distraction," she insisted.

"I said *no*," Grover repeated.

"We can't just sit here!"

"Have some faith," he said calmly, as gunfire raged yet again.

Sierra couldn't understand how in the world Grover could be so composed. They were about to be overrun by Shahzada and his followers. If he thought what they'd done to him before was bad, he was wrong. Shahzada wouldn't take their escape attempt lightly. And he'd take it out on Grover and his friends. And her.

"Breathe, Bean," Grover ordered. "This'll be over in a minute."

She opened her mouth to tell him that was nuts—then she realized, amazingly, that the number of shots coming from the Taliban fighters was lessening.

She peeked around Grover—and blinked in surprise. There were almost a dozen bodies lying in the dirt. Even as she watched, another man fell to his knees, then to his face.

"They're not well-trained. They're shooting blindly and

without precision. We're making every shot count," Grover told her.

He wasn't shooting, but his team was. Even handicapped as they were, trying to stay behind the dubious cover of the mountainside, it seemed as if every shot fired by Trigger, or Doc, or any of the others, hit its mark.

"Don't kill Shahzada," Grover said. "He's mine."

For a second, Sierra thought he was talking to *her*.

"Moving in ten," Trigger said.

Sierra felt Grover tense against her.

"Moving? Moving where?" she asked.

"To take care of Shahzada once and for all," Grover said simply.

Her adrenaline was already out of control, but hearing that made her entire body begin to shake.

"Easy, Bean. It's okay."

She wasn't shaking out of fear, but couldn't unclench her teeth long enough to tell Grover. She was mad. *Furious*. So fucking pissed off that she couldn't control her muscles.

"I'm going with them. I'll be back in a minute. Stay here with Doc," Grover told her.

"No." It was her turn to be succinct with her response. "I need to know he's dead."

Sierra was ready to fight Grover if he refused, but he met her gaze and whatever he saw there made him acquiesce. "Okay, but you stay behind Doc at all times. Understand?"

She nodded, more grateful than she could express that he wasn't going to force her to stay behind. She needed this. Needed to know the man who'd kidnapped her was truly gone. Needed to see he could never come after her again. Or anyone else.

She wasn't an idiot. Knew there would be others like him.

More people who had hate in their hearts, who would take it out on others. But knowing Shahzada was dead would go a long way toward making her able to put this entire nightmare behind her when she went home.

And for just a second, the thought of going back to the US was suddenly overwhelming.

Could she go back to her regular life? What *was* her regular life? She'd accepted the job with the contractor because she'd wanted a change. Well, she'd certainly gotten that. She was twenty-eight years old. She didn't want to move back in with her parents, but had no idea where to go, what to do now.

"We're moving," Trigger said in a low tone.

Sierra had no more time to think about her future. She was behind Doc, holding on to the pack on his back and heading toward where they'd last seen Shahzada.

As they passed dead and dying terrorists, Doc picked up weapons and threw them over the side of the mountain road. Someone would definitely retrieve them at some point, but at least no one would shoot them in the back after they passed.

"There he is," Sierra heard Grover say.

She peeked around Doc and saw Shahzada attempting to crab-crawl away from the advancing Delta Force team. Trigger walked up to the man and put his boot on the bullet wound in his leg. Shahzada howled in pain.

Lefty reached down and ripped the AK-47 out of his grasp.

Brain, Oz, and Lucky surrounded them, making sure none of the men lying in the dirt regained consciousness and tried to interfere.

"We don't have much time. Finish this, Grover. Fast," Trigger ordered.

Doc kept Sierra from getting any closer than twenty or so

feet from what was about to happen, but she couldn't tear her eyes away.

Grover pulled a knife out of a small holster she hadn't noticed on his thigh. She supposed his team must've given it to him when they'd freed him from his cell. Without a word, he leaned down and slit Shahzada's shirt open. He said something that Sierra couldn't hear, but it made the man in the dirt thrash violently. He threw an arm out, trying to punch Grover.

Grover just laughed humorlessly and batted Shahzada's hand away.

Then he slashed his chest with a movement so quick, if Sierra hadn't been watching so intently, she would've missed it.

"Maybe you shouldn't be watching this," Doc muttered, moving as if he was going to turn her away from the scene.

"Touch me and die," Sierra hissed.

Doc froze, and she was grateful he heeded her warning. She knew she couldn't overpower the other man, and she'd never attempt to hurt him, but she *needed* to see this. Needed to see Shahzada die. If that made her bloodthirsty, so be it.

She watched as Grover slashed the man's chest a few more times. He was fucking with him. Giving him a little back for what he'd dished out for so long. Grover spoke again, more low words that Sierra couldn't hear.

Time seemed to stand still. Sierra couldn't take her eyes off Grover. She should be disgusted. Horrified. Scared to death.

But she wasn't. It was morbidly cathartic to see the man who'd caused her so much pain, terror, and heartache feeling some of the same emotions she had.

Killing him wouldn't make what he'd done go away. It wouldn't bring back the other contractors who'd died while in captivity. Wouldn't make her hair grow back any faster or give her back the year he'd stolen from her. But it would still make her feel better.

A hell of a lot better.

"Company's coming," Sierra heard Brain say.

Grover didn't need the warning. He'd obviously heard the commotion of reinforcements coming up the mountain road. He reached down, putting his hand behind Shahzada's neck, forcing him to look him in the eye, then plunged the knife into his chest, right over his heart.

The infamous terrorist—or rather, the bully who longed to become famous for his evil deeds—jerked once, then went limp in Grover's grasp.

Without fanfare, Grover pulled his blade from Shahzada's chest, wiped it clean on the man's pants, then sheathed it. He nodded at Trigger and, as one, all six men turned and headed back in her and Doc's direction.

Sierra kept her eyes on Grover. When he got to her side, he gave her what she didn't even realize she was waiting for. "He's dead and can't hurt you, or anyone else, again."

"Thank you." The words seemed inadequate for all that this man had done for her. He'd come for her. Literally gotten himself kidnapped in the hopes he'd be brought to where she was being held captive. He didn't even know she was alive. Didn't know anything about her, really, and yet he'd still moved heaven and earth to find her. From what she understood, he'd done so within a month of receiving the letter she'd sent him that had been lost in the mail. Once he'd had confirmation that she hadn't gone AWOL, and really had been kidnapped, he'd acted.

And while she knew Grover had his own bone to pick with Shahzada—after all, he'd been tortured viciously over the last week—that wasn't what this was about. She knew it instinctively.

No. He'd made sure the man would never be a threat to *her* again.

Grover nodded, then gave Doc a chin lift, and the group headed back the way they'd come. Back toward the edge of the mountain they were apparently going over.

"The plan hasn't changed, huh?" Sierra asked nervously.

"Piece of cake," Lucky said, sounding almost excited about the prospect of their upcoming adventure.

"No ropes?" Sierra asked.

"Don't need 'em," Lefty told her. "Just hang on to Grover."

"Who's gonna hold on to *him*?" she muttered.

They walked along the edge of the mountain road for a beat, and Sierra wasn't sure what Trigger and the others were looking for. But they obviously found it when Oz said, "Here."

Before she knew it, Sierra was sitting in the dirt, her legs hanging over the edge of the drop-off. It wasn't as bad as it looked, closer to the entrance of the cave, but it still didn't look like it would be easy to go down this way. The terrain had an extreme slope and there were scraggly bushes dotted along the landscape. She had no idea how far down the slope went, but she could see trees what looked like miles below them.

"There's a small river down there," Trigger informed her. "And the trees will give us cover. Your job is to slide on your butt slowly and steadily. Let us worry about everything else."

Sierra nodded. She wasn't sure she wanted to do this, but she wanted to be recaptured even less.

"They aren't going to follow us," Grover said in a soothing tone next to her. "With Shahzada dead, they don't have anyone telling them what to do anymore. Some might make a half-hearted attempt to stop us, but more likely they'll scatter and try to hide their association with him and the Taliban."

"Until someone else steps into his empty shoes," Brain muttered.

"Time to go," Trigger said as shouts echoed along the road.

"Slow and steady," Grover said. "I'll be right here."

Sierra nodded and took a deep breath. Without waiting for anyone else to go first or for more reassurance, she scooted her butt off the edge of the road and began to slide downhill.

Surprisingly, it wasn't like being on a slide. She didn't fall out of control and her visions of rolling down the mountain like the Dread Pirate Roberts in *The Princess Bride* never happened. Her ass hurt from all the rocks and sticks she was sliding over, but the scraggly bushes gave her plenty of handholds to control her descent.

Time had no meaning as Sierra concentrated on getting down the mountain. She was keenly aware of Grover beside her in some places, behind her in others. In one particularly steep section, he moved so he was in front of her, protecting her from sliding out of control. His teammates were also nearby, encouraging her quietly and making sure no one was following.

"You did amazing, Bean. Think you can walk now?"

Sierra looked up and saw Grover standing next to her, holding out a hand. Blinking, she realized that she'd been concentrating so hard on scooting, she hadn't noticed the ground beneath her had lost its severe angle. The trees she'd occasionally glanced at to gauge distance were closer than ever, and the ground she was sitting on wasn't so precarious.

Reaching up and taking Grover's hand, she let him pull her to her feet. She swayed, but he was there to make sure she didn't fall. He started to pull her into his arms, then stopped himself. She looked up at him in question.

"I'm sorry."

She frowned. "For what?"

"For you having to see me lose control up there."

Sierra literally had no idea what he was talking about. "Lose control?"

"After everything you've been through, you didn't need to see me play with Shahzada like I did. I should've just let Trigger shoot him in the head and been done with it."

Sierra shook her head. "No. That would've been too fast for him. I'm sorry you didn't have *more* time to give him exactly what he deserved."

It was Grover's turn to look surprised. "You aren't disgusted?"

Sierra reached up and touched a cut on his forehead. It was still slowly oozing blood and it was obvious it would scar. Shahzada had done that. Or one of the men he'd commanded to beat him. "I'm not disgusted," she verified.

Grover reached up for her hand and held it tightly in his own, against his chest. His gaze was intense as he studied her. "You're not like anyone I've ever met, Sierra Clarkson."

Sierra didn't know what he meant by that, exactly. She chuckled nervously. "Yeah, I haven't showered in a year, I'm bald, helpless, and I probably smell like a dead body that's been rotting in the woods for months."

He didn't even crack a smile. "I expected that if I *did* manage to find you, I'd probably find a shell of the woman I'd met back in that mess hall on base. That you'd be broken and maybe even a little crazy after being held against your will for so long. Instead, I found a woman who did her best to comfort *me*. You'd been there for months, yet you still reached out to try to make me feel better. You held my hand and talked to me. When the bullets started flying, you didn't panic. Didn't get in the way. But you aren't meek and mild. You're smart. You're brave. You know when you're out of your league...but you aren't helpless. No fucking way.

"Being dirty and smelly can be fixed, Sierra. Your hair will grow back. But it's harder to change who we are on the inside. What others *make* us become. And you are one hundred percent, completely and absolutely amazing. Don't let anyone tell you any differently...even yourself."

Sierra stared at Grover and swallowed hard. She wasn't close to crying, didn't even know if she *could* cry normally anymore. But this man's words meant more to her than she could ever articulate. She'd felt so lost and alone, for so long. Didn't know if she'd ever see the light of day again. And here she was, standing in the open air, sore, tired, and still so very unsure about what her future held, but free. With Grover's words going a long way toward giving her the confidence she needed to keep moving forward.

She nodded, then slowly leaned closer.

His arms wrapped around her, holding her against him gently. He didn't make her feel trapped. Sierra could step back at any moment and she knew he'd let her go. "Mashed potatoes, medium-rare steak, and hot garlic bread straight from the oven," she muttered.

Proving they'd connected on a deep level, she felt his chuckle rumble through his chest under her cheek, then he said, "Grilled salmon, with green beans slathered with butter, and corn bread." He didn't ask what the hell she was talking about. He remembered and went with it. And she was grateful.

Sierra's mouth watered. She picked her head up and smiled at him. "With a huge piece of chocolate cake for dessert."

"Warm peach pie with ice cream," he said

"Hey, get a move on!" Lucky called out from in front of them.

Sierra started, not having seen the man pass them. Grover steadied her and grabbed her hand, squeezing lightly. "He and Brain went ahead to scout things out."

Sierra realized that Grover had probably purposely distracted her as his teammates made sure things ahead of them were safe, and was grateful all over again. "How far are we from the military post?" she asked.

"I'm not sure, but I know Trigger will have been in contact with them by now. Once we get to the bottom of this hill, we'll figure out our next steps."

"Hill. Yeah, right," Sierra said with an eye roll.

Grover smiled. "You'll do, Bean. You'll do."

It was funny how much so few words could mean. Sierra was hungry, thirsty, scared, and completely out of her league. But somehow, with Grover at her side, she felt as if she could get through anything.

CHAPTER SIX

Grover wasn't happy. He'd hoped they'd be able to go straight to the base and get Sierra some medical attention after getting off the mountain. He figured they were within ten miles of the town and the base, but couldn't be sure of the exact distance. Walking ten miles after being sedentary for so long would be a challenge for Sierra, but his teammates would help carry her if need be.

He'd gladly carry her himself, but he knew he wasn't one hundred percent, which pissed him off. His ribs hurt, but he'd had his ribs cracked and broken so many times, it wasn't difficult to ignore the pain and do what needed to be done.

Sierra couldn't weigh more than a hundred pounds, but Grover wouldn't want to risk hurting her if his body failed him. He'd felt her backbone when he hugged her, and he hated how frail she'd become. But while her physical body might be weak, her determination was as strong as ever.

Her appearance was shocking, even more so than it had been in the cave. She'd somehow lost the hat during the trek down the mountain, and tufts of auburn hair stuck up all over her scalp. She was covered in dirt and grime, and she was right...she didn't smell all that great. But neither did Grover. They were both alive. That was all he cared about.

It turned out, getting to the military post tonight was out of the question. Trigger had contacted the post commander and learned the townspeople were on edge after hearing what had happened up in the mountains. Many had family members who'd been killed in the raid on the caves, and even though the dead men had been working with Shahzada and the Taliban, they were still someone's brothers, sons, and husbands. Shahzada's few remaining supporters had gotten everyone worked up, and there were protests and riots happening outside the post's gates. The general had kept the post locked down for everyone's safety. He recommended Trigger and his team, and Sierra, lie low for the night and come in when things had calmed down.

Grover had hoped a helicopter could come and pick them up, but with the Taliban having access to rocket-propelled grenades, the last thing any of them wanted was to be shot down before they could get Sierra to safety.

So for tonight, they'd be hunkering down and waiting for the dust to settle. They'd report in tomorrow morning and find out what the situation was before making a decision as to their next move.

"It's okay," Sierra said softly, putting her hand on Grover's forearm.

He jerked, mentally kicking himself for being distracted for even a second. She shouldn't have been able to get that close without him noticing.

"Heck, spending the night out here in the fresh air is a hundred times better than being in that cave."

The fact that she was trying to reassure *him* was just another way she proved with each and every minute how damn unique she was.

Even though they were pretty sure they hadn't been followed, no one wanted to risk building a fire. When the sun had finally gone down, it was pitch dark, although Sierra didn't complain. Not one grumble or protest left her lips. She ate what she could of the MRE Oz offered her, drank the chemically treated water, and even allowed Doc to take a look at her feet without saying a word.

If Grover didn't know better, he'd think they were out on a camping trip with friends. But Lefty and Brain sitting a bit away from the rest of the group with their weapons at the ready were a healthy reminder that shit could hit the fan at any second.

Sierra was sitting next to him. She had her legs crossed and one of her knees was touching his thigh. When Grover felt her shiver, he looked at her. They'd broken three glow sticks and were using them to see as nighttime pulled around them.

"Cold?" Grover asked her.

"A little."

Grover turned and rummaged in Doc's pack for a moment. It felt weird not to have his own, but he was grateful his teammates were as well prepared as they were. He pulled out an extra desert camouflage uniform top. It would be huge on Sierra, but should keep her a little warmer.

"Here. It won't fit, but it's better than nothing."

Sierra's eyes widened, and she eagerly reached for the top. Kicking himself for not thinking about it earlier, he couldn't help but grin as she wrapped the top around her and sighed in contentment.

"It's not even that cold out here. My parents will be so disgusted at how wimpy I've gotten when it comes to the cold," she said.

Lucky grunted from across the way. "I'm guessing your parents, and indeed anyone who hears your story, won't think you're wimpy."

"You don't know my parents," Sierra quipped.

Grover could hear a note of...happiness...he hadn't heard before now. He supposed being free would do that. While she'd wanted to believe him when he said his team would come to their rescue, he knew it was nearly impossible until it actually happened.

Once again, he struggled to comprehend the woman had been in captivity for a year. A few months would break almost anyone. Sierra was smiling slightly, acting relatively normal. Grover was relieved she wasn't hysterical, though he had a feeling it would be a long time before she truly got over her ordeal, if ever.

"Tell us about them?" Trigger asked.

Grover was glad his friends were there. He wasn't the best at idle chitchat. He wanted to know everything he could about Sierra but was thankful he didn't have to do all the asking.

"They both grew up in Leadville, Colorado...do you know anything about the town?" Sierra asked.

"It's got a high elevation, right?" Lucky asked.

"Yeah. Ten thousand, one hundred and fifty-one feet, to be exact—or three thousand and ninety-four meters. The average highs in the summer are around the upper sixties and lower seventies. The average lows in the winter are negative fifteen or so. There are only about three thousand people who live there year-round."

Trigger whistled low. "Damn, that's cold."

"Yup."

"And you grew up there too?" Grover asked.

"I did. And I loved it. Skiing was my jam. You can see several fourteen-thousand-peak mountains from town. The view from my parents' back deck is ridiculously beautiful. It's like a post-card," Sierra said.

"But you left," Oz noted.

"I did. I love my parents, and they love me, but I needed… more. I wanted to do something with my life. I went to college in Denver and got a job there when I graduated, but it wasn't fulfilling. I listened to a podcast by the contractor company that eventually hired me, and was intrigued. I decided, after much back and forth, to take the job here in Afghanistan. The money was great, I won't lie…but more than that, I felt as if I'd be doing something good for my country."

Sierra fell silent, and Grover couldn't help but reach for her hand. The second his fingers closed around hers, he relaxed. He met her gaze when she looked at him and couldn't help but love the fact that his touch seemed to help her as well.

"Anyway, so yeah, I was used to the cold. When I first came over here, I thought I was going to die. It was just so darn hot. Don't get me wrong, Denver, despite being known as the Mile High City, gets hot in the summers too, but not like here. Now I can't imagine going skiing in negative temperatures. I've accli-mated to the hot weather, and I have a feeling I'll always be cold in anything less than eighty degrees."

"You'll adjust," Trigger told her. "Remember arctic training?" he asked his friends. "Lord, we were so unprepared for that. Doc got frostbite on his toes and Lucky almost lost the tips of his ears. We learned a lot about how to deal with the cold, but damn, that sucked. Give me heat any day."

"I don't know, that mission we had in Africa wasn't exactly pleasant," Oz said. "It was summer, we were right on the equator, and the humidity was so thick it was hard to even breathe. Our clothes were soaked the entire mission. It was a miracle Lucky was the only one who got trench foot because our socks were constantly wet from the sweat and humidity."

Everyone groaned, remembering that particular mission.

"What are your plans when you get home?" Doc asked gently after a moment. "You going back to Leadville to stay with your parents?"

Grover stiffened, anxious to hear what Sierra would say.

"No. I mean, yeah, I want to see them. I'm sure they want to see for themselves that I'm all right, but I'm almost thirty. I don't want to live at home again. And Leadville isn't exactly where I see myself spending the rest of my life."

Sierra glanced over at him, and Grover couldn't help but tell his friends, "I've invited her to come to Killeen."

"Awesome."

"It's definitely not cold there."

"Gillian would love to meet you."

"Ember too. She'll be so relieved you're all right."

His teammates all immediately added their support to the idea, which Grover appreciated more than he could say. "I thought I might take her to The Refuge," he added.

"That's a great idea," Trigger agreed. "She's probably going to have to deal with a lot of interview requests. Brick and his team can help her with that."

"Ember can too," Doc said. "She's had more than her fair share of dealing with reporters and paparazzi and interviews."

"I know Riley will help with autobiography requests," Oz said.

"The Refuge? Brick?" Sierra asked when she could get a word in edgewise.

Grover worried for a moment that they were overwhelming her with their enthusiasm, but she didn't sound stressed, so he explained. "I think I told you about this when we were in the caves, or at least I meant to. The Refuge is a retreat run by a team of former special forces guys, led by Brick. They all suffered with their own forms of PTSD when they either retired or were medically discharged from active duty. They were SEALs, Delta, Night Stalkers, DSF—which is Coast Guard Deployable Special Forces—Green Beret, and SAS, the British equivalent of what we do. They bought a few hundred acres of land near Los Alamos in New Mexico. From everything I've heard, it's an amazing place for men and women from all over the world, trying to regain balance in their lives after a traumatic experience. And not just while in the military. There are plenty of events that can cause mental distress, and Brick and his team wanted to offer a safe haven for anyone who needs it."

"It sounds amazing," Sierra said softly. "I feel kind of lost, honestly. Don't get me wrong, I'm very happy to be sitting here with you guys and not in that damn cave. But I don't know what I want to do with my life now."

"What did you do before you came over here?" Trigger asked.

"I worked for an Amazon fulfillment center. Not exactly changing-the-world kind of stuff."

"Hey, don't be ashamed of having a job. I'm assuming you had a place of your own, bought your own food, paid your own bills... that's all a part of being an adult," Lucky told her.

"Yeah, but that's why I took the job with the contractor, because I wanted to make a difference. And working in a ware-house wasn't what I had in mind."

"Why didn't you find anything in the psychology field?" Grover asked.

Sierra shrugged. "I realized that while I liked psychology itself, I didn't really want to get into the medical field...and most jobs, at least the ones that pay well, require more schooling. And yes, I probably should've researched it a bit more before deciding to major in psychology," she said a little sheepishly.

"You don't have to decide right this second what you want to do with the rest of your life," Trigger told her. "First you need to take care of yourself. You've handled everything remarkably, but we all know firsthand that sometimes trauma strikes out of nowhere. You can be going about your life, then a memory hits and it does its best to suck you down. Gillian still has the occasional nightmare over two years later. They wake her up in the middle of the night and she can't go back to sleep."

"Riley and I both randomly wake and have to go check on the kids. Make sure they're in their beds asleep," Oz added.

"For Devyn, it's birds. She's gotten a lot better, but sometimes hearing a bird chirp puts her right back in the middle of that forest where she was left to die," Lucky said.

"Executive assistant, part-time vet tech, proofreader, event planner, EMT, and former Olympic athlete turned small-business owner," Grover said quietly. "That's what the other women do. You can be whoever you want, do whatever strikes your fancy. But you don't have to decide right this second. Take a moment to breathe, Sierra. Get your bearings. Eat some good food, celebrate not letting Shahzada win."

He heard her sigh. "You're right."

"I know," he said immediately.

The guys chuckled, and Grover was pleased to see a smile cross Sierra's lips. "None of you guys suffer from a lack of confidence, do you?"

"Why should we? We're the best at what we do, and we have women who love us for some insane reason," Doc answered with a grin.

"And for the record, Grover told me all about your wives. They all sound..." Her voice faded.

"Amazing?"

"Beautiful?"

"Strong as hell?"

Sierra smiled. "Intimidating," she said after a beat.

Doc laughed. "They aren't, promise."

Sierra shook her head. "So says the guy who's with the most famous woman on the internet."

"Seriously," Doc insisted. "I admit that I didn't want to like Ember when I first met her. I'm very private, and she was anything but—or so I thought. I also figured she'd be spoiled rotten and a diva. But she isn't like that at all."

"By the way, Shahzada wasn't happy when she posted my picture on her account," Sierra told him.

Grover didn't mind being left out of the conversation. He was content to sit back, hold Sierra's hand and let her get to know the best friends he'd ever had in his life. It wasn't even a question if the guys would like her, it was just a matter of how long it would take for her to have them wrapped around her little finger.

"Ember's gonna freaking love hearing that it worked. I mean, she was hoping someone would contact the authorities somewhere and say that they knew where you were, but if seeing your picture made your captors uncomfortable, at least that's something," Doc said with satisfaction.

"I still can't believe Ember Maxwell knows who I am," Sierra said with a small shake of her head. "I mean, I'm nobody."

"You aren't nobody," Grover insisted.

Sierra shrugged. "It's okay. I don't mind. But I had a lot of time to think over the last year. If I had been more...I'm not sure what the word is...Important? Charismatic? Loud? I don't know. But I can't help but think if I'd been more...*noticeable*, maybe someone would've tried harder to find me before now."

Shame and regret almost overwhelmed Grover. "*I* should've tried harder to find out what happened to you. I shouldn't have waited until that damn letter was delivered."

"Oh, I wasn't talking about you," Sierra said immediately.

But Grover shook his head. "It's true. One month," he said. "That's all it took from the time I got that letter until I found you. I could've spared you eleven months of hell, and I didn't."

"You can't blame yourself," Sierra told him.

"But I do," he said softly.

"That's totally crazy. Stupid. Ridiculous!" she exclaimed. "Grover, you didn't even *know* me. You can't take responsibility for every person you pass on the street. If you meet someone, and the next week they trip and fall on their face, are you gonna try to take responsibility for that too?"

He stared at her. Her face was in shadows, only the slight green of the glow sticks lightening the area around them. Her patches of hair were sticking up and she was frowning at him fiercely.

He'd never seen a woman more beautiful in his life.

Sierra glanced at the men around them. "Tell him that he's being ridiculous."

Trigger shrugged. "He *did* find you when others failed."

"And I *did* notice you," Grover told her. "Hair net and all."

Sierra shifted so she was on her knees next to him. The long-sleeve uniform top she'd put on swam on her small frame, and even on her knees, she was only eye-to-eye with him. She shook a finger at him. "No! You aren't allowed to feel guilty. If you do, then that'll make *me* feel guilty for not being more careful like you said I should, all those months ago. And if I feel guilty, then I won't be able to get over this as easily as I'd like. I'll have night-mares for years and will probably have to take drugs that turn me into a zombie. I won't be able to hold down a job and will have to go live in my parents' basement and I'll freeze to death because there's no way I can handle negative-fifteen-degree temperatures anymore!"

She was breathing fast and her voice had risen by the time she finished her rant—and all Grover could do was laugh. Not at her, never *at* her, but at the situation.

"Okay, Bean," he said, reaching up and grabbing the finger she'd been wagging in his face.

"Okay *what?*" she asked.

Damn, she was smarter than even *he'd* given her credit for. Grover grimaced. "I'll try not to feel guilty."

"Nope. Not good enough." She turned to the guys. "Tell him," she ordered.

Lucky, Oz, Doc, and Trigger looked lost.

"Tell him what?" Oz finally asked.

"Tell him that he doesn't get to feel guilty about me being taken captive."

"You don't get to feel guilty about her being taken captive," Oz repeated dutifully.

That Grover could agree to. He regretted not taking her disappearance more seriously. He regretted not doing what he could to try to find her earlier. And he regretted not having the time to torture Shahzada as much as he wanted. "I won't feel guilty about you being taken captive," he told her honestly.

Sierra eyed him suspiciously. "Why do I have a feeling you gave in too easily?" she asked.

Grover wasn't about to tell her how right she was. "I may not have had a girlfriend in a while, but even I know better than to argue with a woman when she brings out the finger," he told her.

"He's right," Lucky said. "The one time Devyn did that to me, I was scared shitless."

"Sit," Grover cajoled, gently tugging at Sierra's hand. "And you should eat something again. Small snacks often will get your energy back faster than eating three large meals a day."

"I know you're changing the subject," Sierra grumbled, but she nodded.

Doc and Lucky got up to relieve Lefty and Brain on watch duty.

"What'd I miss?" Brain asked as he sat nearby.

"You guys are conceited—rightfully so—you have amazing wives, and children, and Grover's not allowed to feel guilty about my capture," Sierra said with her mouth full of the bite of banana bread from the MRE they'd opened earlier.

Lefty chuckled. "All righty then. Guess you covered all the bases."

"You think you can sleep, Sierra?" Trigger asked. "We don't know what tomorrow will bring. We might have to walk ten miles, or we could be picked up by chopper, or something in between, but we need to be ready for anything."

"I think so," she said with a nod.

They all fell silent for several minutes, and Sierra stared at the ground, looking deep in thought as she ate the bread. When she finished, Grover felt her shiver. He opened his mouth to tell her he'd get one of the emergency blankets they always carried, when she turned to him.

"Do you think..." Her gaze dropped again.

Grover reached out and used a finger to tilt her face up to his. "What, Bean? Don't be afraid to ask me anything."

"I was wondering...You're big, and I'm not...and you're warm. I can feel your body heat even sitting here next to you. It's not a huge deal and you can say no if it's too weird—hell, never mind. It *is* weird."

"What, Sierra? Don't make me go back on my word on feeling guilty," he threatened.

Her eyes narrowed. "You're gonna bring that up anytime you want to get your way, aren't you?"

"Probably," he admitted. "Now spit it out."

Looking around, Sierra seemed surprised that the other guys had all moved a bit farther away. They were getting ready to bed down themselves, using their packs as pillows and stashing the green glow sticks. The only illumination now was from the lone stick sitting in front of Grover and Sierra. He was relieved his teammates were giving them the illusion of privacy. From experience, he knew they could still hear everything going on around them, but Sierra didn't necessarily realize that.

"I just wondered if I could maybe sit in your lap," she asked, not looking at him, clearly embarrassed by the request. "You know, to share your body heat?"

Grover stilled. He'd struggled to keep his hands off her all evening. The first time she'd shivered, he'd wanted to pull her close to warm her up, but he thought that might be a bit much for her. They hadn't talked about all of her experiences at the hands of Shahzada and his followers. He had no idea if she'd been sexually abused, as well as physically. So he hadn't wanted to do anything that might bring back bad memories.

"Yeah. I told you it was stupid," she said, moving away from him.

Shit. Grover had been lost in his head too long and she'd mistaken his silence for rejection. Moving quickly, he reached out and pulled her closer, then easily picked up Sierra and settled her on his lap.

She squirmed, attempting to climb off. "It's okay, Grover. I'll be okay over there." She pointed to her right, toward a relatively clear patch of ground.

"And you'll be even better here," Grover told her. He wrapped his arms around her, surprised by how perfectly she fit against him. He scooted back a bit, holding Sierra on his lap, until he was leaning against a tree trunk. Rocks dug into his ass, his ribs protested, and he had a feeling his legs would be asleep in less than ten minutes, but he didn't care. He wasn't moving. No fucking way.

It took a minute or two, but eventually Sierra relaxed against him. He felt her muscles loosen as she gave him more of her weight. She'd had her back against his chest, but then she turned, resting her cheek on his pec and curling her legs up so she was almost on her side in his embrace.

"I was right. You *are* warm," she said softly.

Grover felt her breath waft over his bare neck and knew he was a goner. This woman had him in the palm of her hand, and she had no idea. It made little sense, but he wasn't about to question it. He'd held other women, yet hadn't felt like *this* before. As if, should she disappear out of his life again, he'd lose something profoundly important.

"If I get too heavy, just move me," she told him.

"You aren't too heavy," he said immediately.

"Tell me that after I gain back all the weight I lost and still buy another dozen Krispy Kreme cake doughnuts."

Grover made a mental note to get his Bean some doughnuts, stat.

God...*his* Bean.

Shit.

"Thank you for finding me," she whispered, and the words settled in his bones like a warm summer evening.

"You're welcome," he whispered back, the words feeling totally inadequate for what he was feeling inside.

Grover refused to burden her. As it had been pointed out tonight, she had her entire life ahead of her, and the last thing he wanted was to pressure her to be with him, if that wasn't what she wanted. She'd just been freed from captivity after a year of abuse. He couldn't take advantage of her vulnerability and her gratitude. He'd have to give her space to figure out what she wanted, in her own time.

It would suck, but Sierra immediately agreeing to come to Texas, only to decide it was a mistake, would be even worse.

He tightened his arms around her as she shifted, and once again he marveled at how well they fit. Resting his head on the tree trunk, Grover closed his eyes. He wouldn't sleep, he was too keyed up and too attuned to the woman in his arms. But he'd rest. His ribs throbbed where Sierra lay against them and the cuts on his face burned, but he'd never been more content than he was right this moment.

He didn't know what the future held, beyond knowing he'd do anything necessary to make Sierra comfortable. To make her feel safe. He'd also keep in touch with her once they got back to the States. Make sure she knew he wasn't kidding about the invitation to come to Killeen.

He'd fallen fast, just as his teammates had. And if they could make things work with their women, so could he. It would just be a bit more of a challenge, wooing her long distance. She was worth the effort. Grover had no doubt about that.

CHAPTER SEVEN

Sierra's mind spun. Intellectually, she'd known Delta Force teams were treated differently than regular Army soldiers, but she hadn't expected to be on her way back to the United States so quickly. She figured there would be red tape, interviews she'd have to give about her experience, hours of briefing, and *then* she'd have to contact her employer and see how complicated it would be to get to an airport and out of Afghanistan. Not to mention her passport was long gone, along with her belongings.

But from the moment she'd woken up that morning, more rested than she'd been in a year, things had moved at warp speed.

She thought she'd felt Grover's lips on her forehead, but by the time she'd opened her eyes, he'd merely been smiling down at her. They'd gotten up, eaten, then started walking along the river. They'd only had to walk about a mile—which was a good thing, since Sierra had started to think she wasn't going to make it any farther than that. She'd lost so much muscle mass and she had zero energy. She would've been embarrassed about it, but Grover, and all of the other guys, had constantly reassured her that she was doing amazingly well. If she spent much more time with them, she'd get a big head for sure.

Then a huge, noisy helicopter had arrived. She was hauled up by a rope ladder, then watched as the seven men who'd rescued her came up. Within minutes, they'd landed in the middle of the military post Sierra had begun to think she'd never see again. She was greeted as if she were a long-lost relative. It was disconcerting how many strangers said they were so happy to see her.

She was shown to a tent and allowed to take a shower. That's where time slowed briefly. Sierra knew she took way too long, used far more than her fair share of hot water, but nothing had ever felt better in her life. She'd wanted to stay in that shower and scrub herself for at least another half hour, but had instead gotten out reluctantly.

Grover had given her a set of Army BDUs to wear, the battle dress uniform that all the soldiers wore. She didn't know where he'd gotten it from, or how he'd known what size might fit, but she accepted the clothes gratefully. For some reason, she still couldn't get rid of the shirt she'd worn every day for the last year. It had been through hell, just like her, and it felt wrong to simply throw it away. So she packed it up, along with the pants Grover's team had brought her and the toiletries someone had offered.

When she'd come out of the shower tent, Grover had been waiting. He'd taken her bag, grabbed hold of her hand, and walked toward what Sierra knew was the post general's tent. She wondered briefly if he felt obligated to hold her hand; she didn't see many people engaging in public displays of affection on the post, but she didn't have time to wonder about it long.

She'd spent the next two hours telling the post general everything she could about Shahzada and his operation. Where she'd been held, how many captors there were, what names she could remember, and everything about the weapons she'd seen.

While he'd expressed sympathy over what had happened, it was obvious he was more concerned about finding out information on the Taliban's influence in the town, so he could capitalize on Shahzada's death. He also wasn't happy with the fact that Shahzada had infiltrated the military base as a translator. The soldiers who worked on the base relied on the men who were hired to communicate with the townspeople. Knowing one of them had been gathering information to use against the post, and actively sowing discontent with the locals, was a bitter pill to swallow. A lot of changes would be coming to the post, and Sierra didn't envy the general the upheaval Shahzada's— aka Muhammad Qahhar's—betrayal would continue to cause.

She'd been emotionally wrung out when she'd finished talking to the general. She was relieved he hadn't treated her like a piece of glass, but she was ready to not think about her captivity for a moment.

Grover seemed to understand, and he brought her to the mess tent. It was weird being back there. And being on the opposite side of the chow line. Sierra wasn't sure she was even supposed to be eating with Grover and his friends, but she was also relieved she didn't have to try to figure out what to do with her time. She had no idea where she'd be sleeping or what came next, but she'd take things one day at a time.

After they'd eaten, with Sierra feeling as if she was literally going to burst—her stomach had obviously shrunk a lot in the last year—Grover took her hand again and led her outside. She didn't even wonder where they were heading until he started toward another helicopter on the edge of the post.

"Where are we going?" she'd asked.

"Home."

Home.

God, that sounded so good. Sierra didn't really even know

where home was for her anymore, but the thought of getting out of Afghanistan, and away from her worse nightmare, was such a relief.

So, she'd let Grover strap her into a seat and watched in bemusement as the rest of the guys climbed in. There wasn't much room left after everyone got settled, but instead of feeling claustrophobic or uneasy sitting between Grover and Trigger, with duffle bags at their feet and rifles slung across everyone's chests, Sierra felt comforted.

Now she was in a military airplane on her way back to the States. It was almost hard to believe. She hadn't said much as they'd gone from the helicopter to the plane, but that was because she was so relieved, she couldn't put into words how she felt.

She'd never really thought about what the military troops went through overseas. Since there wasn't an "active" war going on, she'd just assumed life would be fairly routine on the military bases in Afghanistan. The contractor she'd signed with had made it seem as if it was just like any base back in the States. But the truth of the matter was, the threat was still very high for anyone who was deployed.

Studying Grover's teammates, she saw them in a new light. They regularly put themselves in danger...for what? For the satisfaction of making the world safer? For the thanks? For the pride that came from serving their country? Sierra wasn't sure. But she was grateful regardless.

"You okay?"

The words were quiet and gentle.

Sierra looked at Grover. He was sitting next to her and had been holding her hand since they'd taken off. They hadn't spoken much, but holding his hand reminded her how close she'd felt to him when they were in their cells back in the caves.

She nodded. "A little overwhelmed I think," she told him honestly.

"That's to be expected. Your world has changed pretty dramatically. Hard to believe less than forty-eight hours ago, we were lying in the dirt in the dark, huh?"

Sierra snorted. "That's like the understatement of the century. What happens next, Grover?"

"What do you mean?"

"Just...when we land in DC, you guys are going on to Texas, right?"

"Yeah," Grover said softly. "We'll have a debrief on the plane, so when we get to Texas, the guys can go straight home to their families. We'll do a more in-depth after-action review later. I'll go to the hospital on post and get checked out. Not much anyone can do for cracked ribs, but it'll all be documented for my record."

Sierra squeezed his hand. "I hate that you were hurt."

Grover shrugged. "I knew what I was getting myself into."

She still couldn't believe that this man, someone she didn't know, who didn't know her, had purposely gotten himself taken captive. It was the kind of thing that only happened in the movies, and yet here she was. Her throat closed up, but no tears formed. "What about me?"

Grover didn't ask what she meant. He knew. It was reason number four hundred and three why she was so attracted to him. "You'll be assigned a military escort, probably a female officer. I'm certain you'll go to a hospital in DC for a full workup. You'll probably spend the night there, have to talk to at least one therapist, as well as tell your story to a few more generals before you and your escort will head to Denver. Your parents have been notified of your rescue, and they'll be waiting for you. After that...it's up to you."

Sierra nodded. Nothing Grover said was a surprise. She felt amazingly good, all things considered, but would welcome a full medical panel. She knew she was too thin and had lost a lot of muscle tone. She'd stopped menstruating and figured her blood work would probably be a mess. But she was alive. She couldn't complain.

She'd thought about asking to borrow a phone to call her parents, but honestly, she wasn't sure what she'd tell them. There was so much going round and round in her brain that she figured it would be best to just have someone else inform them she was alive, then tell them everything when she saw them in person.

Despite knowing her immediate future...she still felt kind of lost. Out of her element. And Sierra hated that. She'd always been independent and not afraid of new experiences. But now, it felt overwhelming to have to think about what to do after seeing her parents.

"For the record, I wasn't kidding about the invite for you to come to Texas," Grover said quietly.

Sierra bit her lip and looked at him. "I'm not sure...How would that work?"

"How would what work?"

"Where would I stay? I have some money saved up, but I'm not sure how long it would last if I lived in a hotel and ate out for all of my meals."

Grover shook his head, looking almost amused. "You don't have to worry about money. You have several choices as to where you could stay. I know without a doubt in the world, any one of the women would love to have you stay with them. Gillian would probably talk you into helping with the events she plans. Kinley would likely find you a job within a week of being there. Aspen will be ecstatic to know you're all right, and both she and Riley will welcome another adult to talk to after being with kids all day. Devyn would try to convince you to adopt three dogs and four cats, and Ember would be over the moon if you came to Texas. She feels as if she knows you already. They've all been worried about you."

"But...they don't even know me."

Grover shrugged. "That might be true, but they've still been worried. And they're more than aware of my feelings for you. That'll be enough reason for them to bring you into the fold, so to speak."

Sierra just stared at him. She wanted to ask exactly what those feelings were...but she was too afraid he'd say something like he felt responsible for her, or still guilty because she was taken. He didn't give her a chance to respond.

"Trust me, you wouldn't be in anyone's way. The other guys on the team would love to have you stay with them. Riley and Oz have the biggest house, but they also have three kids, so it would be pretty chaotic there. But if you don't want to stay with any of my friends...you can always stay with me.

"You're safe with me, Bean. I swear it. I've got a big ol' farm-house on several acres of land. It's quiet, and I have a few spare bedrooms. I've even got that media room downstairs with the huge screen that you can lose yourself in. I don't know if you're a TV watcher, but if so, you can catch up on all the shows you've missed in the last year. The latest season of *Stranger Things* was amazing, though I still think the first season was the best. But if staying in my house weirds you out too much, I can rent an RV or something and park it alongside the barn. Although that wouldn't be my first choice, since you'd be much safer in the house..."

Sierra realized that Grover was almost babbling, his words coming out quickly. He'd obviously given this a lot of thought, and the fact that he was going out of his way to lay out all her options, to make her feel safe, soothed something deep down inside her.

She put her free hand on his arm, making him pause for a moment.

"Sorry. I don't mean to pressure you into anything. But if you decide to come to Texas, I promise it wouldn't cost you anything. I'll make sure you have a place to stay and food to eat. It can be hard acclimating to life after being in captivity, and I just want to give you a place you can do that without worrying about a job, or money, or what people think. There's no judgment in our circle, I can assure you of that."

"Thank you," Sierra said. "Your offer means more than I can say. I...I'm not ready to make a decision right this second though."

"I understand. And...just so you know, the offer to go to The Refuge still stands. You know, the place in New Mexico? The last time I looked it up, I saw they allow POWs to stay for free. No questions asked, for as long as you want or need. They have therapists, and daily activities you can participate in or not. The place looks absolutely amazing, and if you need it, it's there for you."

"You were a POW too," Sierra said.

Grover blinked. "Yes. I guess so. Although I'm not sure I'd qualify since I purposely put myself in that situation...and I'd do it again if it meant getting you out of there."

Sierra felt overwhelmed, but knowing she had Grover on her side made everything seem a little less...scary.

As if he knew how hard it was to think about her future, Grover changed the subject. They talked about nothing important, and he made sure she ate several times during the long flight. At one point, Sierra woke up with her head on Grover's shoulder. She'd fallen asleep, and he'd pulled her into his side, letting her use him as a pillow.

He was considerate, kind, protective...and Sierra knew she'd already fallen head over heels for him. She had no idea if it was because of their situation—the fact he'd traveled halfway around the world and put himself in danger to find her. That would probably make *anyone* fall in love. But the last thing she wanted was to latch on to him solely because he'd rescued her. That wouldn't be fair to either of them.

When they finally landed, Sierra was a messed-up jumble of emotions. She was elated to finally be back in the United States, sad that her time with Grover was about to end, nervous about what the doctors might say regarding her health, and completely unsure about what would come next in her life.

They all shuffled out of the plane, and as soon as they stepped into the fresh air in Washington, DC, Sierra shivered. Her brain knew it wasn't that cold out, but her body had acclimated to the extreme heat of the Afghani desert.

Sierra felt a jacket being placed around her shoulders. Looking up, she saw Grover smiling down at her.

"Figured you might be chilly, so I had it ready," he explained.

Sierra had dated plenty before accepting the job in Afghanistan. She'd even had a few long-term relationships, but no one had *ever* been as in tune to her needs as Grover, and she'd only known the man a matter of days. It was almost scary.

He didn't take her hand as they headed for the small building near where they'd landed—obviously not the main terminal, which suited Sierra just fine. She *did* feel the light press of Grover's hand on the small of her back, which was extremely reassuring.

Right before they entered the building, a man came out.

Sierra had never seen him before, but all of the guys around her obviously knew him.

"Tex! What are you doing here?" Trigger asked.

"Good to see you, man!" Lefty said.

"Can't believe it. Tex in the flesh!" Brain teased.

Everyone shook the man's hand, then he turned his attention to her. Sierra studied him. There was something about the man that seemed to command respect. He stepped toward her, and she absently noted his slight limp. He held out his hand, and Sierra automatically reached forward to shake it.

"Welcome home," Tex said quietly.

"Thanks."

"Things from here on out are going to move pretty fast," he told her. "I recommend just going with the flow. Don't overthink things and don't talk to the press until you're ready. They can wait; your mental health is more important than giving them a story. And if you don't want to talk to them at all, that's okay too. I'm happy to deal with them for you, if you want, but you can let me know later. For now, I've got something for you."

Sierra's head was spinning. She didn't want to deal with the press. Not at all. She might just take the man's offer on that. She didn't know him, but if Grover and his team trusted and respected him, she would too. She automatically accepted the object Tex was holding out to her.

Looking down, she realized it was a phone. A brand-new, top-of-the-line model. "Um...I don't think I can accept this."

She heard Lucky snort lightly from next to her. "Look how cute she is, trying to refuse a gift from Tex."

The man himself grinned and went on as if she hadn't spoken. "It's got an unlimited data plan. It's attached to an account I own, but don't let that weird you out. When you're back on your feet and ready to think about such mundane things as cell phone plans, it can be switched over to your own account. There are no strings attached. The phones are paid for by donations to veteran groups, as are the accounts themselves. There's no time limit on using it either, so don't go feeling guilty for having it, all right?"

"But I'm not a veteran."

"Like hell you aren't," Tex retorted without hesitation. "You might not be in the military, but you sure as fuck went through hell as a result of wanting to serve your country. I've already programmed all of these guys' numbers into the phone, along with their women's. Mine is in there too, as is Brick's...the guy from The Refuge. I've taken the liberty of making you a reservation there, as well."

Sierra opened her mouth to explain she didn't think she needed to go to any kind of camp, ranch, or retreat for PTSD, but Tex held up his hand, stopping her.

His voice gentled. "You've been free for two-point-three seconds, Bean. Trust me when I say demons have a nasty habit of sneaking up on you when you least expect them. I also scheduled Grover to join you in Los Alamos."

"Tex," Grover growled.

"Don't you start too," Tex told him. "I know what you did, and why, but that doesn't negate the fact that you were kept against your will and tortured. Visiting The Refuge and talking with Brick, Tonka, Spike, and the others will do you both good."

Sierra looked up at Grover, saw him glaring at Tex, but then, as if he felt her gaze on him, he dipped his chin to meet her eyes, and she saw the irritation bleed away.

"One month," Tex said. "Go home to your family," he told Sierra. "Relax. Heal. Eat some homecooked meals. Then go to New Mexico. I promise it'll be good for you. For you both."

Sierra could only nod. How could she refuse the generous

offer? She couldn't. She had no idea what the next month would hold for her, but then again, she didn't know what *tomorrow* would bring. She had to take things one day at a time, and knowing this man cared enough to try to help her felt good.

"Oh, and one more thing. My wife, Melody, told me I had to tell you this part; that it wasn't fair if I didn't, and it was an invasion of privacy or some such bullcrap. The phone has a tracker. I'll know where you are at all times when you have it on you. I've learned over the years that it's better to be safe than sorry. I'm not a psycho, I won't be following your every move, but if you disappear, and you have that phone with you, I'll be able to find you. Okay?"

Sierra stared into Tex's brown eyes and swallowed hard. She knew she *should* be upset at the invasion of her privacy. But the simple fact was, she couldn't be. She'd disappeared once and it had taken a year for anyone to find her. If it happened again, Tex would know where she was. The thought brought a level of comfort she hadn't even realized she needed. "Okay," she told him softly.

"All right then. I need to get going, and so do all of you. I'm very glad to meet you, Sierra. Take care of yourself. And don't be afraid to open up to Grover and his inner circle. They'll heal you if you let them."

Tex nodded at her, and the guys, then turned and walked toward the end of the building.

"So...that was Tex," Doc said with a little laugh.

"He's..."

"Sneaky? A little scary? All of the above?" Lucky asked. Then he shrugged. "You get used to him."

"If you don't want that phone, I can get you a new one," Grover told her.

Sierra tightened her hold on the phone. "No," she said quickly. "It's okay."

"He means well," Trigger said gently. "He's helped more people than I've got time to talk about. He knows just about everything there is to know about everyone."

"Like the nickname Grover gave me?" Sierra asked wryly. "How'd he know *that*?"

Oz smiled. "We've learned not to ask questions we know we won't get the answers to."

"For the record," Trigger told her, "I think The Refuge is a good idea. For both you and Grover. And even if you don't feel as if you need it, I've heard it's beautiful up there. Brick and his team have done an amazing job setting it up. You can be busy all hours of the day if you need to be—hiking, fishing, riding horses —or you can lie around in a hammock and do nothing at all."

Sierra nodded. The more she heard about the place, the more curious she got. And knowing Grover might join her there? Yeah, she was pretty darn excited about that too...if he showed up. She knew he was busy, and a month seemed like an awfully long time from now. Being apart, both of them dealing with their captivity, could make whatever this connection they felt now fade.

"Give me a second with Sierra, guys?" Grover asked.

Everyone nodded.

Before he left, Trigger stepped up to her. "May I hug you?" he asked.

Sierra was impressed he'd asked. But she supposed she shouldn't have been. He, and all the guys, seemed very in tune to what she might be feeling. "I'd like that," she told him.

Trigger stepped forward and wrapped his arms around her, giving her a short but heartfelt hug. "I'm glad you're all right."

Then Lefty took his place. And Brain. One by one, each of

Grover's friends hugged her and told her how happy they were that Grover had found her. How strong they thought she was. How much they were sure their wives would love to meet her.

It should've been awkward, but instead, Sierra felt as if she'd known these men forever. Finally, they all headed into the building, leaving her and Grover alone outside.

She looked up at him, not sure what he was going to say...and suddenly she was nervous as hell.

But he didn't say a word. Instead, he pulled her into his embrace.

Sierra lay her cheek against his chest and held on tightly, listening to his heartbeat under his uniform.

"I don't know if I can do this," he said, his voice strained.

"Do what?" Sierra asked, tilting her head back but not stepping out of his embrace.

"Let you go."

She blinked at that.

"I know that sounds ridiculous. We barely know each other. Your parents are waiting for you. You have a life to get back to. Still...I can't help but want to keep you by my side."

Sierra swallowed hard. "I know," she whispered.

Grover sighed, then palmed the back of her head and brought it back to his chest. Sierra held him tighter. "I didn't know Tex planned on being here today, or bringing you that phone. I'd planned on giving you my number, of course, along with everyone else's."

"It's okay," Sierra told him.

"If it was anyone but Tex, I'd have thrown the phone at him and told him I can take care of you just fine without his help."

Sierra didn't know how to respond. Take care of her? What was *that* about?

"But it *was* Tex, and that man cares about his teams more

than anyone I've ever met. So I'm gonna let it slide. Now that you have my number, I expect you to use it, Bean."

"I will," she said.

"I don't care if it's the middle of the night and you can't sleep, or if it's one in the afternoon and you think of something you want to tell me. Text or call. I'll answer every time if I'm able to. I might be in a meeting or training, and if I am, I'll always get back to you as soon as I can. Okay?"

Sierra wanted to ask him what they were doing, where this was going, where this intense connection was coming from...the one she'd felt even before getting kidnapped.

Instead, she simply nodded against him.

"I'll see you in a month in New Mexico, but if you need anything before then, you let me know."

Sierra took a breath and stepped away. Neither let go of each other. Grover's hands moved to her upper arms, and hers flattened on his chest.

It was time she started trying to get her bravado back. She was tired of being a victim. She wanted to be the outgoing, carefree woman she'd once been. The one who wasn't afraid to take a job in Afghanistan because it seemed both useful and like the adventure of a lifetime.

"And if *you* need anything, you let *me* know," she told Grover a little bossily.

He smiled. "I will, Bean."

Sierra tried not to smile. "That nickname is ridiculous."

"Yup."

"You aren't going to stop calling me that, are you?" she asked.

"Nope. It fits you."

"Whatever," she said with a roll of her eyes.

Grover's eyes raked over her face, then her hair and down her body. Sierra expected to feel embarrassed or self-conscious, like she had in the cave. She knew she needed to find someone to fix her hair, for sure. Shave it evenly, something. She also knew she still had some bruises on her face and that her body wasn't anything worth gawking at. She'd lost weight all over, including her chest. But somehow, seeing the longing in Grover's eyes made her feel almost normal.

"I'm gonna miss you," he whispered.

"Same," she said.

"That first time you reached out to me in that cave, after I'd been worked over by Shahzada...I knew," Grover said.

When he didn't continue, Sierra asked, "Knew what?"

"That you were it for me."

She could only stare at him in surprise.

"You'd just been beaten yourself. Had no reason to trust me. Had been held captive for a year. And yet there you were, trying to comfort me. No one, Sierra, has affected me as much as you have from the moment we met. From being disappointed that you didn't contact me after I left Afghanistan the first time, to being worried when we heard you had gone AWOL, to being distraught when we learned contractors were disappearing, to being fucking scared out of my mind when I got your letter. I've never felt as much for anyone as I have you."

Sierra knew she should be shocked. Should be wondering what the hell was wrong with this man. But she wasn't. Because she felt the same. "You made me so mad when we first met," she admitted. "You accused me of being naïve. Looking back now, I know I *was* naïve. I was so gung-ho to serve my country in any way possible and to make a difference, even if it was just by serving food to the soldiers who put themselves on the line every day, that I didn't even consider the fact that I could be in danger. It was stupid, really. But I had to think there was a reason I was still alive after a year. Had to believe that someday, someone would stumble across me and help me get out of there. Then... you were there. Admitting that you'd actually gotten taken on purpose. It was crazy. Insane, really. But the second I held your hand...I wasn't as scared anymore."

"It's gonna suck to watch you walk away from me, but I know you'll be fine. You don't need me to hold your hand or smother you with my protectiveness. You need to get back on your feet and find yourself again, without me."

His belief in her was overwhelming.

"I'll see you in a month," he said again, as if trying to confirm she'd go to The Refuge.

"You will," she replied.

The relief in his eyes was instant. He leaned toward her, and Sierra held her breath, waiting for his kiss. But his lips brushed against her forehead, the gesture so gentle, once again her throat closed up. As usual, no tears formed in her eyes.

"I'm proud of you," Grover said against her skin. "I admire you so much. Don't let anyone bring you down. If they try, tell them to fuck off. That they should try living in a cave and getting beat on."

Sierra couldn't help but chuckle. "I will."

Grover's hand came up and ran over her head. She winced as he touched the uneven patches of hair. "This is your badge of honor. Don't be ashamed of any damn thing you did to survive, Bean. Not one thing. Got it?"

She nodded.

"Okay. I could come up with a million more things to say to prolong this, but you have appointments to get to, and I'm sure the guys are anxious to get back to Texas to see their families," Grover said.

Sierra nodded but didn't step away.

"You aren't helping," he said.

She smiled up at him.

"Fuck," he muttered, then leaned down and kissed her lightly on the lips. They still tingled when he lifted his head. "Come on, it'll be warmer for you inside, and it's time for you to eat something."

Sierra nodded because she couldn't speak. He was always taking care of her. Seemed to only have her best interests at heart. It was quite the change from the last year, when her captives had to be reminded to feed her and didn't give a shit about her basic needs.

Grover's hand was at the small of her back as he led them toward the door. Sierra wanted to stop, wanted to snuggle back into Grover's embrace, but he was right. They both had lives to return to. And she so badly wanted to find the Sierra she once was.

A month. That wasn't that long, really. Especially not after she'd survived a year at the hands of Taliban terrorists. She held the phone tighter. And it wasn't as if she wouldn't be able to talk to Grover.

A month? Piece of cake.

CHAPTER EIGHT

Grover paced his living room.

Back and forth.

Back and forth.

He couldn't sit. Couldn't eat. His porch didn't bring him peace. He hadn't noticed the sunset painting the sky a couple hours ago.

Three days.

That's how long it had been since he'd talked to Sierra. He'd sent her a text to ask if she got home all right, and had received a short reply, but that was it.

He was going out of his skin wondering how she was doing. He wanted to know how the reunion with her parents went. If she'd been able to sleep. If the press was hounding her. If she'd set up a time to talk to a therapist. If she was eating all right.

There was so much he wanted to know, but he also didn't want to bother her. Didn't want to risk bringing back bad memories by trying to get in touch if that wasn't what she wanted.

"Shit!" Grover swore, running a hand through his hair in agitation.

He and the rest of his team had arrived back in Texas and debriefed. He'd been read the riot act by Commander Robinson, and while Grover had said all the right things, apologizing and swearing he regretted his actions...he didn't. Not at all.

He'd done exactly what he'd set out to do. Found Sierra. He was also glad they'd discovered Shahzada's deception and killed the man before he could harm others, but that was just icing on the cake as far as he was concerned.

Sierra had been his goal. His finger itched to call her, but again, he knew he was a reminder of the worst time in her life. Who *wouldn't* want to put it all behind them and move on? Even if he knew from experience that it wasn't that easy.

His ribs hurt as he paced, but Grover ignored the pain. He'd been wounded much worse before. Just when he'd decided to go for a night run—he hadn't been medically cleared to exercise yet, but he was going stir crazy and needed to do *something*—his phone rang.

Irritated that one of his team was checking in on him—*again* —Grover was a bit more brusque than he might've been otherwise when he answered without looking at the screen. "What?"

"Um...is Grover there?"

"Sierra?" Grover's heart nearly stopped beating in his chest. He stopped pacing in the middle of the room and held his breath as he waited for her response.

"Yeah, it's me. Am I interrupting something?"

"No! Absolutely not. I'm currently pacing the floor, literally, trying to outrun my boredom."

She chuckled, and the sound made Grover close his eyes as emotion threatened to overwhelm him. It was so good to hear from her. And to hear her *laughing*? Fucking heaven.

"I'm guessing your appointment with the doctor didn't go as you wanted." She sobered. "Are you all right?"

"I'm good, Bean. It's mostly just precaution. Doc doesn't want me running with my cracked ribs."

"Do they hurt much?"

"No. How are *you*?"

"Good."

She didn't sound good. "Don't bullshit me, Sierra. This is the guy who held your hand for hours in the dark, remember?"

She sighed. "I'm very happy to be home, don't get me wrong."

"But?" Grover asked.

"I just...one second I'm happy, the next I'm angry, and the next I'm so depressed, I wonder why the hell I even survived."

Her words didn't surprise Grover in the least. "That's normal," he told her.

She snorted. "Well, normal sucks."

"It does. How are your parents?"

"They're great. Amazing. It was so good to see them in the airport in Denver. They both cried, and I haven't seen my dad cry...ever. We stayed up all night that first night, talking. I told them a little about what I went through—not all of it, just the basics—and they told me about everything I've missed in the last year."

"Everything?" Grover joked.

"Yeah, well, all the big things that happened here in Leadville, at least. The biggest news in our tiny town is about this spinster woman—I know, that's not the nicest thing to call her, but it's true. She's seventy-two and hasn't ever been married. Anyway...Betty got married! I guess she met a man who came to Leadville on vacation with his grown kids and their families. They met at a restaurant downtown near where he was staying.

His wife died a decade ago, and he and Betty hit it off. He's only fifty-nine, but he extended his vacation and then, two weeks later, came back. Three months after that, he asked her to marry him, and now he lives in town with Betty."

Grover smiled. He loved hearing the happiness in Sierra's tone. "That's great."

"It really is." A short silence fell between them before Sierra said, "Grover?"

"Yeah, Bean?"

"I miss you."

His heart skipped a beat. "God, I miss you too," he breathed.

"I feel so off-kilter. One second I'm happy to be here with my parents, and the next I just want to be alone. But then as soon as I'm alone, I freak out. Which is stupid, since I was alone most of the time in the caves."

"It's not stupid," Grover said. "I'm not a therapist, and I'm not sure I have the right words to help you, but like I said, it's pretty normal. On the one hand, your brain knows that you're safe and free of captivity, but you got used to your circumstances over there. You had to compensate for what was happening to you, made being alone your new normal. It'll take time to acclimate, Sierra. Go easy on yourself."

"I'm trying. I honestly didn't think I needed to go to that Refuge place. I thought everyone was just trying to coddle me. Now I'm not so sure."

"I think it might be a good idea to move up the time frame that we go," Grover told her.

"Oh, but...I wasn't hinting at that," Sierra protested. "Honestly. I'm sure it's just because it's only been a few days. I'll be fine."

"I've had nightmares," Grover admitted. He hadn't told

anyone else about his horrible dreams. Not even his teammates, who he shared just about everything with.

"You have?" she asked quietly.

"Yeah."

"Do you...can you talk about them?"

"They're about you," Grover said.

"Me?"

"Uh-huh. We're back in those caves, and Shahzada drags me out of my cell to torture me and after he straps me up, he brings you out. Then he starts beating you, and there's not a damn thing I can do about it. He doesn't stop. You're bleeding and begging him for mercy, but he doesn't. I can't get loose to help you, I can't do anything but watch."

"Shit, Grover. I'm okay. I'm fine."

He went on. "And just when I'm about to break free of the ropes they tied me with, you look up and ask me why I took so long to find you. Then I wake up."

"Oh, Grover..." She sounded so sad.

He regretted telling her. He should've made up something else, but he hadn't been thinking straight. "I just...I wouldn't mind spending some time with you at The Refuge without having to worry about the Taliban or anyone coming to grab us in the middle of the night to beat on us."

"I don't think my mom would understand if I left too soon," she admitted.

"Two weeks?" Grover asked. He'd need to talk to Brick and see if he even had space for them earlier than they'd planned, but somehow, he'd make it work.

"Well...um, I think that would work," Sierra said quietly. "I don't understand how I can be so erratic. I'm safe. I'm home with my parents, who love me. And yet, I feel...unsettled."

"That's all normal," he insisted once more.

"Is it?"

"Yes."

"I feel so horribly guilty," she whispered, "because every now and then, I have the brief thought that I wish I was still back there. Which is insane. I mean, why would I even *think* that?"

Grover hadn't wanted to hold someone as badly as he wanted to hold Sierra at that moment. "Because it was what you knew for so long. You knew what to expect when you were there. There weren't too many surprises. Now, every day is probably something new, despite the familiar surroundings. You're talking to people you haven't seen in years, who are probably asking uncomfortable questions, and you're trying to pretend you're perfectly fine, when inside you aren't sure you are."

"My mom had her hairdresser come to the house yesterday," Sierra said. "I kinda just wanted my dad to shave my head again, and do it evenly, so my hair would grow back at the same rate and I could decide what to do with it later. But Mom insisted her girl could 'fix me.' It hurt to hear her say that. I know she didn't mean it the way it sounded, but it still hurt. Then I could see the horror and pity in the hairdresser's eyes. It was awful. *You* never looked at me like that. I thought you would, but you—and all your friends—just kind of ignored the fact that my hair looked like a three-year-old had gotten hold of it."

"You. Are. Amazing," Grover said slowly, enunciating each word. "You were covered in dirt and had been in captivity for a fucking *year*, but you still reached out to comfort me despite knowing if Shahzada had gotten wind of it, you would've suffered. If you want to know the truth, I thought you looked a hell of a lot better than I thought you would. I expected you to be rocking in a corner."

"That would've made them too damn happy," Sierra muttered.

"Exactly. I wish I could tell you that the stares and looks of pity will stop, but they probably won't. People never know what to say or how to treat someone like us. Someone who's been through hell and come out the other side. With time, the looks will stop bothering you, but for now, the only thing you can do is ignore them. *You* know how strong you are. *You* know that you conned those assholes into shaving your head. It was for the best, and we both know it. One day at a time, Bean. There will be bad days and there will be good ones. You just have to put one foot in front of the other and take things day by day. Okay?"

"Easier said than done," she muttered. Then she took a deep breath. "How is everyone there? How's Ember doing? I know Doc wasn't that thrilled he had to leave her so soon after she got shot."

"She's good. The other women basically sat on her to make her behave and follow the doctor's orders to take it easy."

Sierra chuckled, and Grover's muscles slowly relaxed. He didn't like that she was struggling with getting back to her life, but he wasn't surprised.

"I looked up her Instagram account. She really did post my picture!" Sierra said, the surprise easy to hear in her tone.

"Yup."

"It's pretty amazing that some people actually said they remembered me. The soldiers who'd been stationed at the base, I mean. I wasn't there that long before I was taken."

"You're memorable, Bean."

"I know you aren't making fun of my size, are you?" she threatened.

"Me? Would I do that?"

"Well, since you're a giant, you might."

He loved this. The teasing. "Fee-fi-fo-fum," he joked.

She giggled. "But seriously, her gym sounds amazing. I love

that she wants to give back to the kids in the area. That's why I accepted the job in Afghanistan in the first place. Because I wanted to give back to my country."

An idea formed in Grover's head. He probably should talk to Ember first, but he was fairly certain she wouldn't have any issue with what he was about to propose. "You know, Ember could use some help."

"Help? With what?" Sierra asked.

"The gym. The kids."

Sierra laughed. "Yeah, right. I'm no Olympian. Not even close."

"You don't have to be. The kids aren't either. She really does need help. Obviously, you don't have to make a decision right now but...it's another reason for you to come to Texas."

"I thought maybe you'd regret inviting me by now."

Grover didn't hear any teasing in her voice this time. "No way. If it wouldn't have made me look like a douchecanoe, I'd have insisted you come to Killeen with us, instead of going back to Colorado."

"I needed to see my parents."

"I know." And he did.

"But I have a feeling two weeks will be more than enough time for me to spend here. If you can do it, I'd love to meet you in New Mexico."

"Done," Grover said, his heart lightening.

"But you probably won't recognize me," Sierra said with a little laugh. "I think my dad has taken it upon himself to person- ally see that I gain back all the weight I lost. I swear, there's more doughnuts and cookies in this house than I've ever seen before. And my mom wants to buy me a whole closet full of clothes. But of course, I don't want to buy anything right now because I'll grow out of them if I gain the weight my dad has planned for me."

"I'll recognize you," Grover said without a trace of doubt in his tone. "Just be sure to gain weight the right way. Eating fatty foods *isn't* the right way, in case you were wondering."

"I know. I saw a nutritionist after I went to the doctor. She pretty much told me what you did. Eat lots of smaller meals. Lots of protein, not a ton of fatty foods, and carbs are fine."

"What'd the doc say?"

"All things considered, I'm good. He says that when I gain weight, my period should start again. My blood pressure is a bit low, but he wasn't surprised. I'm a little anemic, I have asthma now from breathing in all that dirt and dust all the time. I've got some funky skin lesions that should clear up with antibiotics, and he recommends that I steer clear of large gatherings until my immune system builds itself back up. But otherwise, I'm fine."

Grover sighed. He didn't like most of what she'd said, but wasn't all that surprised. "That's good, Bean."

"Other than your ribs, are you good? What about that cut on your head?" she asked.

"I'm fine. Promise."

"Did I thank you for coming to find me?" Sierra asked quietly.

"Yes."

She harrumphed. "I don't think I did. No one has ever sacrificed so much for me before."

"I didn't sacrifice anything," Grover protested.

"You did," she insisted. "You could've died."

"But I didn't. Here's the thing, Sierra. I like you. A lot. And the last thing I want is you feeling *gratitude* for me. You needed help, and I was in a position to offer it. That's done. We're moving on."

Grover worried when she didn't immediately comment, thinking he'd gone too far. That he'd pushed her too hard.

"I like you too," she told him. "But I can't just forget what you did. It's not like you held a door open for me or bought me flowers. You got yourself freaking *kidnapped* without even knowing if you'd find me. I could've been in Iraq, or Iran, or buried ten feet under the desert. You had no way of knowing if I was even alive, and yet you still went and did something unbelievable to try to find me."

"I knew you were alive," Grover said. "Don't ask me how, but I did. It was a feeling deep down inside. Most people would say there's no way I could know, but I was confident enough in my feelings to do what I did. You and I will always have a special bond, Sierra. One forged in dark nights in that cave, holding hands and talking. I won't deny that I'd love to see if we could have more...but if friendship is all that grows between us, I'll take it."

Once again, Sierra didn't immediately reply. He was getting used to her way of thinking things over before speaking. He liked it, even as it unnerved him.

"I...I'd like to start with friendship," she said. "I just feel so *off*, I can't imagine even attempting anything more right now."

"And I wouldn't ask you to," Grover reassured her. "You take all the time you need, Bean. I'll be here for you."

"I'm not saying never, just...not right this second. Besides, I'm here and you're there."

"Yup, but the invitation is open for you to come to Texas, remember? You can work with Ember, live wherever you want, and I still want to take you on that date I promised."

"Sitting in your barn, right?" she asked with a laugh.

"Yup."

"Oh, you charmer, you."

Grover chuckled. "Wait until you see the view. I promise you'll be impressed."

"I have no doubt. I do have a question for you."

"Shoot."

"This Tex guy...he's definitely on the up and up?"

"Absolutely. He's a medically retired Navy SEAL who has helped more people than I can count out of dire situations."

"And my phone really does have a tracker in it?"

"I'm sure it does, yes. There's a team of SEALs out in California, friends of his, who kept having issues with their women disappearing. So now he kind of goes overboard with that tracking stuff. I have a feeling his computer screen in his office probably looks like a plane radar. With all sorts of blinking lights indicating where all his people are." Then Grover thought of something. "Why? Is something wrong? Do you not feel safe?"

"It's not that," she said quickly. "But when I finally looked at the contact list, there's *way* more people in there than just your team and their wives."

"Like who?" Grover asked.

"Ghost, Fletch, Truck, Wolf, Abe, Cookie, Rocco, Phantom, Logan, Rex, Bull...to name just a few. Oh, and he sent me an email just yesterday, reminding me that he's added Brick, Tonka, Spike, Pipe, Owl, Stone, and Tiny...the guys who run The Refuge, in case I have any questions for them before I head down to New Mexico."

Grover couldn't help but laugh. "Looks like he covered all his bases," he told her.

"But I don't *know* any of these people. Why would I get in touch with them?"

"Here's the thing about Tex...when I say he knows people, he *knows* people. And not a single one of them would hesitate to drop everything to come to your aid if you let them know you needed it."

"Do you know them all?"

"No. Some, yes, but not all of them. But if Tex thinks enough of them to put their numbers in your phone, I wouldn't hesitate to reach out to any of them if I needed help. And more importantly, if *you* needed help."

"I'm kinda overwhelmed."

"Just go with it," Grover suggested.

"You guys are all pretty protective, aren't you?"

"Yes," Grover said without feeling an ounce of regret. "We spend our lives doing what we can to help others. Whether that's a person who's been taken against their will, or in a more abstract way, by tracking down terrorists who might someday plan an attack that could kill hundreds or thousands."

"Well, I have to say I'm happy to be included in with those you've helped."

"Me too," Grover told her. "What do you have on tap for tomorrow?"

They talked for another hour and a half. And for a man who didn't particularly like talking on the phone, Grover didn't even realize how much time had passed. When he heard Sierra yawn, and he looked at the clock, he saw that it was after midnight in Killeen. She was an hour behind him, but still, she needed to make sure she got plenty of sleep.

"I'm gonna let you go, Bean."

She sighed. "Okay. You gonna be able to sleep?"

"Of course." It was a little lie. He had no idea if he'd wake up covered in sweat and calling Sierra's name, but he wasn't going to tell her that. She had enough on her plate to deal with. "I'll talk with Brick tomorrow, see about moving our visit up," he told her.

"Are you sure it'll be okay?"

"Yes."

"All right. I'll talk to my parents about it then. Grover?"

"Yeah?"

"It was good to talk to you tonight. I feel as if I can tell you anything. Talking on the phone with you, sitting in my dark room...it's kinda like when we were back in that cave."

"Except back then, I could touch you," Grover said.

"I liked that."

"Me too. And you can call whenever you want."

"Okay."

"Let me know how tomorrow's chat with the *Denver Post* reporter goes."

"I will. I wasn't going to do any interviews, but I kinda figured if I got it out of the way, maybe it would calm everyone down."

"Possibly," Grover agreed. "Besides, the day after, someone famous will do something stupid and you'll be day-old news."

"From your lips, to God's ears," Sierra quipped.

"Sleep well, Bean. Thanks for calling. I needed to hear from you, to know you were all right."

"Same. I'll talk to you soon."

"Later."

"Bye."

Grover hung up and stared out at the dark night. He could hear the crickets even through the sliding windows. They were loud out in the middle of nowhere, like he was. He'd worked hard and saved for a long time to be able to afford this house. It was too big for him, but Grover liked his space. The kitchen was top of the line, had an open concept, five bedrooms, an office, and a huge media room. The barn was mostly for show, he hadn't planned on getting any horses or livestock. But he loved how it looked, and the memories of his friends helping him raise it would last a lifetime.

Looking around his house now, though, Grover realized he was lonely. He was thirty-three. Not exactly old, but given how content and happy his friends were, it struck him even harder how alone he really was. Remembering Sierra's story about Betty, how she'd found love at seventy-two, made him smile, but it also hammered home the fact that he didn't want to be like her. He wanted to find a woman to love and cherish. Wanted to laugh with her and *live* life.

Was Sierra that woman? Grover was pretty sure she was. If she gave him half a chance, he'd do his best to show her that he could make her happy. That they could be good together. He respected and admired the fact that she didn't want to jump into a relationship right now. She'd been through something traumatic and needed to concentrate on her own mental health. But that didn't mean he couldn't be her friend. Couldn't show her the kind of life she could have by his side.

Maybe the connection they had was only because of circumstances. Maybe when they spent time together on more even footing, where she wasn't the rescuee and he the rescuer, they'd realize they didn't click like they had back in Afghanistan.

Then again, maybe they'd find they had an even deeper bond than the one he'd already felt growing.

Time would tell, and Grover had to be patient. He wasn't very good at that though. Sighing, he pushed himself to his feet and headed for the stairs. He wasn't cleared to participate in PT, but he was still going to meet with the team while they worked out. Four-thirty would come early, but Grover hoped that because it was so late, he'd fall asleep quickly and not have any nightmares. Now that he'd talked to Sierra, had found out first-hand how she was doing...he should be fine.

And in two weeks, he'd get to see her again. Commander Robinson had already approved his leave, he just needed to get it switched to two weeks earlier. Grover didn't think it would be an issue. Their commander was a good man who cared about the mental health of his soldiers as much as he did their physical health.

Grover would also talk to Doc and Ember about the possibility of Sierra working at The Modern Kid, her gym. Sierra was right in that she didn't have any knowledge of the modern pentathlon sport, but he was confident Ember could still use the help with the children. Attitude and enthusiasm were more important than technical knowledge at this point.

He smiled, thinking about Sierra hanging out with Ember, Kinley, Aspen, and the other women. He had no doubt they'd get along. They'd all been through their own kinds of hell and would welcome Sierra with open arms.

He had *no* idea what would happen after their trip to New Mexico, but for now, all Grover could think about was seeing Sierra again. Talking to her on the phone was great. Amazing. But seeing her in person would be even better. He'd do his best to be the friend she needed, certain this connection they felt wasn't going to fade. In fact, he had a hunch it would only get stronger as they continued to get to know each other.

Two weeks.

It seemed like an eternity, but good things come to those who wait, and Grover was willing to wait as long as it took for Sierra to see him as someone she might want to spend the rest of her life with.

CHAPTER NINE

Grover stood on the porch at the large reception building at The Refuge. He'd arrived two hours earlier and had spoken at length with Brick and Tonka, two of the seven men who owned and operated the mental health retreat. It was a place literally anyone who needed a break from life could go, be accepted, and hopefully relax. Men and women who were or had been in all branches of the armed forces visited frequently. But there were also police officers, firefighters, nurses, doctors, teachers, and other people with high-stress jobs who sought solace at The Refuge.

Sierra was supposed to arrive with her parents any moment now. Mr. and Mrs. Clarkson had volunteered to drive their daughter down from Colorado. Grover was looking forward to meeting them, but was anxious to see Sierra even more.

They'd spoken on the phone every night over the last two weeks. Long conversations about everything from politics to the pros and cons of wearing socks to bed. Sometimes they were serious, discussing terrorism and hate groups, and other times spent the entire call teasing each other.

Grover had learned Sierra had become somewhat of a celebrity in her hometown, and that she hated it. All she wanted to do was blend in and get back to a regular life. He wanted to tell her that the likelihood of that happening was low, especially in a town of less than three thousand, but he hadn't wanted to stress her out more than she already was.

A minivan appeared over the rise, and Grover straightened. It was almost scary how excited he was to see her. He heard someone come out of the building behind him, but didn't turn to see who it was.

After the minivan had parked, Grover drank in the sight of Sierra as she stepped out of the backseat. He couldn't take his eyes from her. He knew he should walk out to greet everyone, but he felt frozen in place.

She looked good. *Really* good. The two weeks at home had done wonders for her outward appearance. Her hair was short, almost buzzed, but was now cut evenly, for which he already knew she was grateful. She wore jeans and a long-sleeve shirt, but even though she was completely covered, Grover could tell she'd put on a bit of weight. She hadn't been lying about her parents trying to fatten her up. Her cheeks were fuller, and she didn't have the hollow look she'd had back in Afghanistan.

"Welcome to The Refuge!" Tiny said as he walked down the steps of the porch to greet their new guest. The man was only six feet tall, but he was hugely muscular. Grover could only assume that's why he'd been given his nickname.

Grover forced himself to move slowly down the stairs. Suddenly, he was nervous. Even though he'd spoken with Sierra every day, seeing her in person was so different. He followed behind Tiny, approaching the older couple who had driven their daughter to New Mexico.

"It's very good to meet you. I'm Fred. Fred Groves. But everyone calls me Grover." He held out his hand, and Mr. Clarkson shook it enthusiastically.

"We've heard so much about you. I'm Ben. And this is Jody. It's so good to meet you!"

Grover shook Sierra's mother's hand, then tuned out Tiny as he welcomed them as well.

He turned to Sierra. She was standing a little off to the side, looking unsure.

And for the first time, Grover second-guessed being here. Maybe seeing him brought back too many bad memories about what she'd been through. He towered over her, and he hated that his size might cause her even a second of fear.

Stuffing his hands in his jeans pockets, Grover said, "Hey," in a quiet, tentative voice.

* * *

Sierra wasn't sure what to say to Grover, which was stupid, because they'd talked for hours and hours on the phone. She hadn't felt tongue-tied with him at all. But suddenly, seeing him in person made her very nervous. Had he noticed that she'd gained some weight? Was he laughing inside that she was wearing jeans and a long-sleeve shirt when it wasn't cold in the least? What did he think of her hair? It was still obnoxiously short, but she was so much happier with it, now that it didn't look like it had been hacked off by a toddler with a pair of dull scissors.

She watched as he greeted her parents politely, and her brows came down when she realized how stiff he seemed. This wasn't the Grover she'd gotten to know in Afghanistan. There, he was confident, even after each brutal beating from Shahzada. But at the moment, his shoulders were hunched forward slightly and his hands were buried in his pockets.

When his gaze met hers, she bit her lip in consternation. There was so much emotion in his eyes, but she couldn't for the life of her read what he was feeling. Was he regretting coming here?

"Hey," he said in a tone she'd never heard from him before.

Then it hit Sierra.

He was nervous too. Unsure of himself.

It was...endearing.

Without thinking twice, she did what she'd been wanting to do since she saw him through the window of her parents' minivan. Sierra stepped forward and wrapped her arms around him. She lay her cheek on his chest and squeezed him hard.

When he returned the embrace, wrapping his arms around her and holding her to him tightly, she sighed in contentment and closed her eyes. This is what she needed. The feeling of being safe. Protected.

It was stupid, it wasn't as if there were bands of Taliban sympathizers roaming the United States looking for her for revenge, but she couldn't quite shake the feeling of being a captive. It was taking longer than she would've liked to realize that she no longer had to do what others told her to. That she could come and go as she pleased. Eat what she wanted. Sleep when she wanted. Use the bathroom anytime she needed to without worrying about who might be watching.

"Hi," she said softly without lifting her head.

His arms tightened for a moment, but he didn't speak.

How long they stood like that, Sierra wasn't sure, but when she finally lifted her head, she noticed that her parents and the man from The Refuge were no longer standing nearby. She hadn't even noticed them leaving.

Grover lifted a hand toward her head, then stopped himself. "May I?" he asked.

"Touch me? Yes."

She felt like purring when his large hand rested on top of her head. She shivered as he ran his palm over the fuzz on her scalp.

"It's so soft," he said, sounding surprised.

Sierra chuckled. "Yeah. I'm considering leaving it short. Not as short as this, but maybe having it styled into a cute pixie cut or something when it gets long enough. I'm not sure I'll ever be comfortable with long hair again. If it gets dirty, I'm afraid it'll just remind me of...well, you know."

"Short hair suits you," he said, finally meeting her eyes. He moved his hand to the back of her neck. He was just resting his palm there, and it made Sierra feel completely surrounded by this man. She liked it.

"Thanks."

"How are you doin'?" he asked.

"I'm good. You? Did you sleep last night?" She knew he was still having trouble sleeping through the night. He admitted to her that he still woke up just about every time from nightmares.

Grover shrugged. "Some. How long are your parents staying?"

"Not long. They're going to detour to Pagosa Springs on the way north and spend the night there. I think they're as anxious to have a little getaway as I am. I know my coming home was a miracle for them, but I also think it's been stressful."

"Understandable," Grover said. "They're worried about you, and that can be exhausting."

Sierra nodded. "Exactly." She loved that this man didn't pull any punches with her. He said things as he thought about them.

He'd once claimed that he frequently put his foot in his mouth with others, but she'd realized that was because he didn't bullshit anyone. He spoke the truth, always. Some might've taken offense to his observation, but she didn't. It was one hundred percent true. Her parents worried so much about her and how she was acclimating back to regular life, and she knew they had to be tired.

"Come on, let's go inside and I'll introduce all the guys. I'm sure your parents will want to see where you'll be staying before they leave too."

And even that was considerate. A lot of people wouldn't think about making sure her parents were comfortable and satisfied with her well-being before they left. Grover didn't even know her parents, yet still he knew what they needed.

"Grover?"

"Yeah?" he asked, not pulling away from her.

"It's so good to see you."

The smile he gave her transformed his face. He went from looking unsure and worried to being relieved. "Same. You have no idea. I've loved talking to you, but seeing your beautiful face as we talk is so much better."

Butterflies swam in her belly as Sierra looked up at the man she couldn't stop thinking about. She'd told him two weeks ago that she wasn't ready for a relationship, and she still didn't think she was. Despite that, Grover made her feel completely relaxed and safe. She supposed it was because he'd rescued her. She didn't want to be *that* kind of woman though. The kind who only fell for a guy because of some sort of savior complex.

"You're thinking too hard," Grover told her.

"How can you tell?" she asked, legitimately curious.

He lifted a finger and brushed it across her forehead. "Because you have a wrinkle right here."

"I guess I'd better not play poker with you, huh?" she quipped, trying to snap herself out of her weird mood.

"Probably not. Come on, let's go check on your parents."

They walked hand in hand toward the large house that served as a reception building. Sierra didn't even think twice about holding Grover's hand. It felt so right, so natural.

When they walked inside the building, Sierra couldn't help but be impressed. This wasn't some fly-by-night ranch. The interior of the reception building had been professionally decorated, and even from her untrained eye, looked as if it cost a pretty penny. The men who owned this place had spared no expense to make everything welcoming and homey at the same time. There were large leather couches and chairs around a huge fireplace. Bright rugs on the hardwood floors, and they'd left the rafters exposed, which gave the room an open feel. It even smelled like warm cookies fresh from the oven. She had no idea if that was because of some sort of air freshener, or if there really were cookies being baked somewhere nearby.

Sierra had briefly glanced at The Refuge's website before leaving to come down here, but since Grover had said he was looking forward to visiting, and had seemed impressed with the men who owned it, she hadn't thought too much about it. She'd been too excited to see Grover.

He pulled her over to where her parents were speaking with a group of men. They were all tall and muscular. It was obvious they hadn't let their physical fitness routines slack since getting out of whichever branches of the military they were in.

Without letting go of her hand, he nodded at the men in front of him.

One of them stepped forward and held out a hand. Sierra shook it as he introduced himself.

"I'm Drake, otherwise known as Brick. These are my partners in crime...Tonka, Spike, Pipe, Owl, Stone, and Tiny. I'd tell you their real names, but you'd forget them quickly and we probably wouldn't respond to them, anyway," he teased. "Welcome to The Refuge. We started this place because we all needed a place to go when we got out of the military, but couldn't find anywhere we felt truly comfortable. Up here, in the mountains, away from judging eyes and from the constraints of civilization, we were able to find ourselves again. We all met through a mutual friend, and came up here to camp, of all things. Two nights turned into three. Then a week. The next thing we knew, we were meeting with a real estate agent to see about buying some land. And here we are."

Sierra smiled at him. "Let me guess, that friend was Tex?"

"You know Tex?" Pipe asked, his British accent barely noticeable.

Grover chuckled. "She met him at the airport in DC. He appeared out of nowhere, gave her a phone that he said he was tracking, told her he'd made arrangements for her to come up here, and left."

"Sounds like Tex," Stone said with a chuckle.

"Anyway, you're standing in the main building. We've got a big kitchen in the back that's open to you at all times. We serve three meals a day, but if you get hungry any other time, or prefer to eat alone, you're more than welcome to raid the fridge. We'll give you the code to get in the back door so you can come and go whenever you want. Each guest gets their own code, and when you check out, the code is never used again," Tiny explained.

"There are a dozen guest houses, which range from one-bedroom studios to three-bedroom suites. Each has a bathroom and shower, as well as a fridge and microwave. We offer housekeeping every three days if you want it, but you can always simply request towels and whatnot when you want them, and if you don't want any housekeeping, that's okay too," Spike said.

Sierra's head was on a swivel as each man spoke. It was obvious they'd given this spiel many times.

"You can literally do whatever you want while you're here. Down the hill around the back of this building is a barn, and we've got horses, a cow, and two goats. They're all very friendly and completely tame. Melba, our cow, will follow you around all day long if you give her scratches and if you let her. There are several barn cats too, and I've got a three-legged mutt," Brick told her.

"We've got a therapist who comes up from Los Alamos three times a week, and sessions with her are included with your stay. She does both group sessions or one on one, if you prefer. But if you don't want to do anything but sit on your porch and enjoy the silence and the beauty of nature, you can do that too. We want this to be a place where everyone can relax and try to center themselves in whatever way works best for them. If you need anything, or want to do anything, just let one of us know and we'll see about making it happen. Okay?" Tonka asked.

Sierra nodded. Everything sounded amazing. She knew she'd had it easy since she'd gotten back—her parents had cooked for her, done her laundry, taken her shopping. She loved them, and was extremely grateful...but she'd still felt a little smothered, which only made her feel guilty.

Being here, smelling the clean, dry air—similar, yet different from the air across the world in the desert—was already making her feel so much better.

"Everything sounds lovely," Sierra's mom said.

"We try, ma'am," Spike said.

"I can go grab your things if you want to go with Tiny for a quick tour of the grounds and to see where you'll be staying," Brick said.

Her dad handed over his keys and soon they were all following behind Tiny as he showed them the property.

Forty-five minutes later, Sierra was giving her parents a hug as they prepared to head back to Colorado.

"We love you," her mom said.

"I know."

"We just want to see you happy. I know you've been struggling, and as much as it pains us, we know that we can't make things better for you," her dad said.

"You have," Sierra insisted. "I love you guys too, and you've been so great."

"I won't say that I want things to go back to the way they were, because that's impossible, but I hope this place can help you heal," her mom said.

"I'm sure it will," Sierra said. Her mom's eyes watered, and Sierra actually regretted she couldn't seem more emotional for her parents' sake, but even after weeks at home, she still hadn't been able to cry one real tear.

Her mom sniffled and wiped away her own tears as Sierra hugged her dad. "Drive safe and please let me know when you get to Pagosa Springs, and when you get home."

"We will," her dad said. Then he turned to Grover, who had stepped back to give them space, but hadn't left. "Take care of her."

Grover nodded.

"She's our world," her mother said tearfully.

Sierra smiled slightly. "Okay, Mom, enough. I'm good. This place is beautiful and perfect. No one needs to take care of me and nothing's gonna happen up here. I'm gonna eat, sleep, and relax. That's it."

She could see her mom wanted to say more, but she merely sniffed and nodded. "I love you. Email me and let me know how things are going."

"Of course," Sierra told her.

"Feel free to call your old man too," her dad said gruffly.

It took another five minutes for her parents to actually get in their minivan and drive off, but after she and Grover were finally alone, she sighed in relief.

"I love them, but man...they're pretty emotional," she said with a small chuckle.

"The last time they said goodbye, things turned out a bit differently than you all had planned," Grover said seriously.

That sobered Sierra. "I know. And I'm very grateful for everything they've done for me since I've been back. I just..." Her voice trailed off.

"You aren't used to it. You need your space," Grover finished for her.

"Exactly."

"What do you want to do first?" he asked.

Sierra didn't hesitate. "I want to track down some of those cookies I smelled cooking and eat a half dozen of them."

Grover's lips quirked up into a huge smile. It made Sierra's breath catch, and she swallowed hard. Damn, her plan to start as friends only with this man was in serious jeopardy if he kept smiling like that. She respected and trusted the Delta Force soldier who'd rescued her from hell...but this man? This easygoing, charming, gorgeous guy? He was going to be damn hard to resist.

He held out his arm. "My lady? I'm happy to provide an escort."

Sierra hooked her arm with his. "Lead on. And don't dally. If those cookies are cold by the time we get there, I'm blaming you."

It felt good to be silly. It had been so long since she'd had the opportunity to tease. Most of the people she'd spent time with back in Leadville were somber and pitying, almost afraid to joke in her presence. As if her sense of humor had been beaten out of her while she'd been held captive.

For the first time since arriving back in the States, Sierra felt herself truly relaxing. She didn't know if it was being here in this amazingly beautiful place, or if it was Grover. She had a feeling it was the latter.

CHAPTER TEN

Grover lay on his bed with his arm under his head and stared up at the ceiling. It was dark out and all he could hear was the wind blowing and cicadas. It should've been relaxing, and he should've been asleep at least an hour ago.

But he couldn't rest. His mind was full of Sierra, how good she looked...how much more relaxed she seemed in just the half day they'd been here. Clearly she'd needed this place. With each hour that passed after her parents' departure, the more it seemed her personality had come out. There were six other people staying at The Refuge at the moment, and watching Sierra interact with them over dinner was extremely enlightening.

The spark that had caught his attention when she'd been serving food back in that chow hall in Afghanistan had returned. She was charming and friendly, and within minutes of being in her presence, the other men and one woman who were eating with them seemed completely comfortable around her.

She was petite, but her personality and presence were larger than life. After dinner, she and Grover had sat on the back deck of her small one-room cabin until eleven o'clock or so. He could tell she was tired, so he'd said good night and headed next door to his own cabin.

Where he couldn't sleep. Because the changes in Sierra, while wonderful, didn't totally ring true. Not to Grover.

On the surface, she acted as if she was completely fine. But he'd spent hours on the phone with her in the preceding weeks, and he had a feeling she wasn't doing as well as she was trying to make them all think. Hell, *he* was still trying to deal with his time as a captive, and he hadn't been there nearly as long as she had.

If she wanted to do the fake-it-till-you-make-it thing, that was her choice. In the meantime, he'd watch and wait and be there if she needed him.

Grover was still trying to force his brain to shut down, to get at least a couple hours of sleep before he inevitably woke up covered in sweat from another nightmare, when he heard something outside. At first he figured it was an animal of some sort; Pipe had told them all at dinner that they frequently had bears, deer, and foxes show up around the cabins.

Then he realized it wasn't an animal making those sounds. He'd been a special forces operative long enough to recognize the sound of sticks cracking under a slow, cautious tread. The careful gait of a person who didn't want to be heard, but was doing a piss-poor job of being sneaky.

Grover was up and moving before he'd given it a thought. It took him seconds to silently cross to the door, though he wished he had his gun. Weapons of any kind were prohibited at The Refuge, which was something Grover actually approved of.

PTSD wasn't something to mess around with and having guns near anyone who was having a hard time coping with their demons wasn't a good idea.

He looked through a side window and couldn't see anyone lurking in the trees between his cabin and Sierra's, but he couldn't see the small front stoop at all, where the sound was coming from. He was ninety-nine percent sure whoever was outside his door was either one of the guys who owned the property doing security checks, or Sierra. It was the remaining one percent that concerned him.

Making sure he had the element of surprise, he soundlessly moved to the door and wrenched it open quickly—and saw Sierra jerk in fright and almost stumble off the top step of his small stoop.

Grover acted fast, reaching out and grabbing hold of her arm, preventing her from falling on her backside into the dirt. "Sierra? Are you all right?"

"Oh my God, you scared me! I'm so sorry, did I wake you up?"

He noticed that she didn't answer his question.

Looking around to make sure they hadn't disturbed anyone else—which was unlikely, since the cabins were spaced reasonably far apart with plenty of trees between—Grover pulled Sierra into his cabin. He dropped his hand once he'd shut the door and clicked on the overhead light. They both winced as their eyes adjusted to the sudden brightness. Then Grover went back to Sierra and put his hands on her shoulders. "Are you all right?" he repeated.

"Yeah."

"What's up?"

"Um, well...I...Shoot."

Grover waited patiently as Sierra did her best to work

through whatever she was trying to say.

"It's stupid," she finished after a minute.

"It's not," Grover insisted.

Her lips twitched upward. "You don't even know what I'm going to say. How do you know it isn't stupid?"

"Because it's the middle of the night and you're at my door. That's how. Talk to me, Bean."

She sighed. "When I lay down to go to sleep, I realized this is the first time I've been by myself since you showed up in the cell next to mine in that cave. I've literally had someone else with me, or at least nearby, every night since. I started hearing sounds outside...and my brain wouldn't stop telling me it was Shahzada. Which is ridiculous, because I saw you kill him. I know he's dead. But I couldn't help but think...maybe he wasn't *really* dead. And maybe he found a way to follow me back here and has been waiting for the right time to snatch me again. *Then* I started imagining him dragging me off into the forest and stashing me in some dark mountain cave here in New Mexico."

When Grover said nothing, she shrugged. "I told you it was stupid," she said softly.

Still without a word, Grover took her hand and slowly led her to his bed. It was a king, and there was plenty of room for them both. He drew back the covers on the side he hadn't been tossing and turning on and gestured for her to get in.

Sierra didn't even hesitate. She kicked off the flip-flops she had on her feet and climbed onto the mattress. Grover noticed that she wore a pair of sweatpants and an oversized T-shirt, despite the heat, before covering her up with the sheet and comforter. He walked over to the wall and clicked off the light, then headed for his side of the bed.

He got himself settled under the covers, and in the dark,

with the sound of the cicadas loud outside, he reached for Sierra's hand.

The second her fingers wrapped around his, Grover felt something deep within him settle. "It's not stupid," he said softly. "It actually makes sense. There's safety in numbers, and your subconscious knows it. But I can reassure you on one point —Shahzada *is* dead. I wouldn't have left that mountain unless I was one hundred percent certain of that. Not only to protect you, but to keep everyone who lives and works in that area safe, including the Afghani people. It's extremists like Shahzada that give the entire country a bad reputation. Most of the citizens I've met are hardworking, peaceful people."

"I didn't have a chance to get to know anyone outside of the people on base," Sierra said sadly.

Grover didn't really know how to comfort her, so he simply squeezed her hand.

They lay there in silence for a beat before she said, "This feels good. Familiar."

"Yeah," he agreed. "Although I have to admit that it's much more comfortable to be lying in a bed holding your hand than in the dirt, with my arm through the bars and bent at an awkward angle so I could reach you."

Sierra laughed quietly. "Right?" Then she said, "I'm really okay, Grover. It wasn't fun to be held captive for as long as I was, but after a while, they didn't really mess with me too much. I don't know why. The hardest thing was dealing with the boredom and loneliness. Day after day, I had nothing to do, no one to talk to. I think the therapist I saw back home was surprised that I wasn't more fucked up in the head."

"Don't compare yourself to anyone," Grover warned. "I encourage you to meet with the therapist here, but you can't start feeling guilty that you weren't constantly assaulted, or beaten, or anything else. Okay?"

"I'll try," she said honestly. "What about you?"

"What about me, what?"

"Will you go talk to the therapist with me?"

"If you want me to."

She huffed out an impatient breath.

"What?" Grover asked. "What'd I say?"

"I want you to go for *you*," she said. "You're having nightmares. You're not okay."

Grover sighed. "I'm not having nightmares about what that asshole did to me. I've been hurt worse in the past, and likely will be again in the future." He didn't want to elaborate further on the nightmares. But he didn't have to. She knew. He'd made the mistake of telling her in their first phone call when she'd been home.

"They're because of me," she said softly. "I thought we agreed that you wouldn't feel guilty," she told him.

"I'm trying," he told her. "But it's not easy."

"That alone is reason to visit the therapist."

Grover felt Sierra moving next to him. She didn't let go of his hand, but she turned on her side and he felt her scoot closer.

"You're so warm," she said.

Grover smiled. "Are you cold?"

"Not really. I mean, I'm always a little chilled, but I'm trying to learn to ignore it. I know it's just my mind playing tricks on me. Is it okay if I stay here tonight? I honestly didn't mean to bother you. I had planned to sit on your stoop for a while, just to be closer to you, until I got the courage to go back to my place."

"It's more than okay," Grover told her. "It feels nice."

"Yeah," Sierra agreed.

They didn't speak again, and Grover felt Sierra's body

completely relax as she fell asleep. He couldn't help but feel a small thrill that she'd come to *him* when she'd been uneasy. That just being next to him made her relax enough to fall asleep.

He was a little nervous about doing the same. The last thing he wanted was for her to witness one of his nightmares. It usually took him a bit to completely wake up, and he didn't want to risk hurting or scaring her.

But he also wasn't about to move from where he was. Sierra was curled into him, her forehead resting against his shoulder and he could feel her knees against his thigh. Her hand was still in his own, and he could admit to himself that her touch seemed to settle him as much as his did for her.

He lay there, enjoying her nearness and listening to the sounds of nature outside. It wasn't long before his own need for rest finally overcame him, and he fell into a deep, healing sleep.

* * *

Sierra woke up feeling better than she had in a long time. She hadn't realized she wasn't sleeping well at her parents' house, but as soon as she opened her eyes this morning, she knew that her brain had finally allowed itself to completely shut down and relax.

She was certain it was because of the man snoring slightly next to her. She hadn't moved much in the night, was still on her side next to Grover, and amazingly, their hands were still clasped together. Moving up on her elbow, she took the time to study him. His hair was completely mussed and the small lines in his face were relaxed, making him look younger than his thirty-three years. He had a heavy five-o'clock shadow, and she realized that he probably had to shave every morning to keep the facial hair at bay. She recalled how bushy he'd gotten in just the week he'd been in the caves.

Knowing something like that about him seemed very intimate. The sort of thing only a lover would know about their significant other.

Grover's nose was slightly crooked, which she figured had happened at Shahzada's hands. Or maybe it had been that way before he'd been taken captive. She couldn't remember his nose from over a year ago, when she'd first met him. The cut on his forehead was mostly healed. Although he'd probably always have a small scar, it would fade with time. Sierra could see a few streaks of gray in his eyebrows, which made her smile. She had a feeling he would definitely be what women liked to call a Silver Fox when he got a little older. And unlike women, he probably wouldn't give a damn if he had gray hair before he turned forty.

As if he could feel her intense gaze on him, Grover stirred.

Sierra could tell the second he remembered he wasn't alone. He turned his head and she almost melted at the sleepy, affectionate look in his eyes. "Mornin'. What time is it?"

"No clue," she whispered back. She had no idea why she was whispering, it wasn't as if she'd wake anyone else, but it seemed the right thing to do.

Grover lifted his free hand to look at his watch. She couldn't help but feel good that he hadn't pulled his hand from hers when he realized they were still connected.

"Holy shit, it's seven-thirty," he said in a slightly awed tone.

"You miss an important appointment this morning?" Sierra teased. "I mean, it's not like we have anything we have to do, is there?"

"No, but I haven't slept this late in...a long time." He turned to look at her once more, and Sierra couldn't read the emotion she saw in his brown eyes. "And I actually *slept*," he told her. "Once I fell asleep, I didn't dream."

She swallowed hard at hearing that. "That's good, right?"

"Good? It's a miracle," he said with a small shake of his head. "I've had a nightmare every night since we got home. I'd sleep about three hours, wake up, and not be able to go back to sleep afterward."

"I'm so glad you got some rest."

"It's you," Grover said without hesitation.

Sierra frowned. "What?"

"You. Here. Holding my hand. It's like my brain finally knows you're safe. There was no need for me to dream of Shahzada hurting you because you're *here*. With me. Touching me. Thank you."

His voice cracked, and Sierra closed her eyes as emotion threatened to overwhelm her.

She felt his fingertips brush against her cheek.

Getting her feelings under control, she brought her free hand up to his, holding his warm palm against her face. "I'm glad," she repeated.

"Me too. You sleep all right?"

"Like a rock."

"Good," he replied simply. "So...what do you want to do today?"

That was another thing Sierra liked about Grover. He accepted they'd clearly needed each other last night but didn't stretch out the moment, didn't make it awkward. She shrugged. "What do you want to do?"

"Shower, eat, check out this cow who likes to be scratched under her chin, then maybe take a hike. Then come back, eat lunch, chat with some of the others here, take a nap in one of the hammocks I saw behind your cabin, have dinner, then sit around and talk to you some more."

"Wow, um...sounds like you've got quite the day planned. I'm not sure that I've thought that far in advance." She was totally teasing him, but she saw the worry bleed into his eyes. She didn't have the heart to make him worry for a second longer. "I'm kidding. That all sounds amazing."

"We don't have to do any of that," Grover backpedaled.

"Seriously, there's no other way I'd rather spend the day," Sierra insisted.

"Okay. I think the therapist is supposed to be here tomorrow. We probably want to save some time in our schedule to talk to her."

Sierra liked that he said "we." She nodded.

"What time did Brick say breakfast was?" Grover asked.

"I think eight. It's buffet though, and goes until nine-thirty."

"All right, so we haven't missed it. I'll meet you in front of your cabin in about fifteen minutes?"

Sierra frowned and shook her head. "Nope. Sorry. I used to be the kind of woman who could shower and be ready to go somewhere in ten, fifteen minutes. But not anymore." She refused to be embarrassed about it. Out of anyone, she knew Grover would understand. "I can't seem to tear myself out from under the hot water in under twenty minutes. Minimum. I can't help but remember how horrible I felt with a year's worth of dirt and grime on my body." She shrugged, just a touch self-consciously.

"No problem. And for the record...I had an extra-large water heater installed in my house, so you can take all the long showers and baths you want. So...forty minutes? In front of your cabin?"

He kept saying things like that, as if it was a foregone conclusion that she'd be going back to Texas with him. And not only going back, but staying in his house. She wanted to tell him that he was making assumptions about things she wasn't sure she could agree to...but another part of her wanted to curl into him every time he said something like that. It was as if her heart was warring with her brain. And the kicker was, she wasn't sure which she wanted to win anymore. "Forty minutes sounds good," she said after a too-long pause.

"Foot in mouth, remember?" Grover muttered. "Just ignore me when I cross the line. I don't want to pressure you into doing anything you don't want to do. I'm a pushy bastard, and I know it. Feel free to push back, Bean. I won't take it personally. Promise."

"Okay. I...I want to see your house. I want to meet your team's women. Hell, they're already messaging me, and I kinda feel like I already know them. But—"

"Wait. They are? What have they said? Are they bothering you? I love them, but they tend to be a little...enthusiastic."

"And you aren't?" Sierra said with a laugh.

"Okay, I definitely am. But they're unpredictable. They'd bend over backward to help you, especially Ember. When she learned that I'd actually found you, and you were free of captivity, it was all Doc and I could do to keep her from jumping on a plane and flying up to Leadville to meet you. And of course, she's been taking credit for your rescue. Telling everyone that it was her post that led to you being found." Grover rolled his eyes and smiled. "She's delusional, but cute, so we don't contradict her. But seriously...what have they said?"

Sierra laughed and reluctantly let go of Grover's hand. It almost felt weird *not* to be touching him, but she forced herself to climb off the mattress on her side. She slipped on her flip-flops and resisted the urge to run a hand over her head. She didn't have any hair to smooth down, but it was a hard habit to break, especially with the way Grover was staring so intensely at her. "Nothing bad. We can talk about it later. If I'm gonna shower and we're gonna make breakfast, I need to go."

Grover stood up from the bed and stretched. He was wearing a pair of shorts and a T-shirt—and Sierra's mouth watered. If he looked that good mostly covered up, she was almost scared to see him without a shirt on...or more.

Then she immediately scolded herself. She shouldn't be thinking about him without clothes. They were friends. *Just* friends. At least for now.

Shit...she was in big trouble here.

Unaware of her lustful thoughts, Grover wandered toward her, then leaned down and kissed the top of her head. "Okay, Bean. Go shower. I'll see you in a bit. Take your time. If we miss breakfast, we miss it. We'll scrounge around in the kitchen. We won't starve. I'll probably do that anyway, to grab some snacks so you've got something to nibble on while we're out and about today."

There he went again, being all sweet and protective. Not that Sierra was complaining. "Okay, thanks. I'll try not to take too long."

"As I said, take as much time as you want. You've earned all the hot water in the world. And, Bean...?"

"Yeah?"

"Thanks for helping me sleep."

And there's that tickle in the back of my throat again. "Ditto."

He grinned. "Okay, enough. Shoo, woman. Go do your thing."

She returned his smile and headed for the door.

"Oh and you've got a sweatshirt, right? Bring it with you. I have no idea what the weather is supposed to be today, but I don't want you to get chilly."

Sierra nodded, not sure she could talk normally. She could get used to his concern, his need to take care of her. She waved lamely at him, then left.

She heard his chuckle follow her as she headed for her own cabin. And for the first time in a very long time, Sierra realized she was happy. Content. It was a heady feeling, for sure.

CHAPTER ELEVEN

Breakfast had been a fun affair. Everyone seemed to be in a good mood, and the delicious food didn't hurt either. They hadn't taken a hike right after breakfast though. Instead, they'd spent all morning at the barn with the animals. Melba the cow was adorable, even Grover had to admit. She loved to rub her head on any human who came near. She was super inquisitive as well. Wanting to know what they were doing at all times.

The goats were a bit more obnoxious, but because Sierra seemed to love them, Grover put up with them trying to chew on his shirt. There were barn cats Sierra wanted to snuggle, and even though the horses intimidated her because of their size, she still spent quite a while with them too.

They also had a long chat with Tonka. He was former Delta, but didn't talk much about his time in the military. Grover got the impression that something had gone terribly wrong when he got out, but he didn't ask. The man now spent his time working with the animals at the ranch, which seemed to visibly calm him.

By the time they left the barn, it was lunchtime.

"How about we grab something and have a picnic?" Grover asked Sierra.

"That sounds wonderful."

They went to the kitchen and made sandwiches. Even that was fun. Sierra teased him about making a sandwich big enough for three people and he made fun of her for putting ranch on hers, instead of the usual condiments, like mayo or mustard. The owners of The Refuge had thought of everything, and in the pantry they found picnic backpacks that could hold silverware and cups, as well as the food.

They set out not too long later, following a trail Spike had told them about. He said it had the best views and wasn't too strenuous. Grover handed Sierra a granola bar to tide her over until they found a good place to stop and eat.

It felt good to have no agenda. To have absolutely no schedule. Grover loved being in the military and wouldn't trade his Delta brothers for anything in the world, but being in the Army meant his life was very regimented. PT, meetings, sticking to a schedule, it was what made the huge bureaucracy work. Being out here in the fresh air, with no timetable, was freeing.

Grover walked behind Sierra and did his best to keep his gaze off her ass. It was difficult, because even after all she'd been through, she still had a butt that was meant to be admired. To try to take his mind off how attractive he found her, Grover asked, "So...the girls have been texting you?"

She laughed. "That was subtle."

"Wasn't meant to be. I'm not asking you to break any confidences, I'm just curious."

"It's funny," Sierra said. "The first time I got a text from one of them, I was expecting it to be you. I was confused for a second because it didn't make sense that anyone else would text.

It was Gillian. She said she was glad I was all right, then said, 'welcome to the crazy.' I was even more confused."

Grover chuckled. "Things can be pretty crazy, that's for sure. Especially when we all get together. It used to be just a bunch of bros hanging out, having a drink and shooting the shit. Now we cook, change diapers, talk about princesses with Bria, fall all over ourselves to let Logan 'win' at kickball, and have discussions about the things the doctors don't tell you about childbirth before you go in to have a baby."

Sierra laughed. "And you love it."

"I do," Grover admitted. "The dynamic of our team has changed, but I honestly think it's for the better. And it's all because of the women. What else did they say?"

"Are you scared?" she joked.

"A little bit, yeah," Grover admitted.

"They've all been really nice. It kind of floors me how open and welcoming they've been."

"That's just who they are," Grover said.

"Yeah. Devyn's been hilarious. And I should probably warn you, she's in full-on 'set up my brother' mode."

"Shit," Grover swore. "I'll talk to her and tell her to knock it off."

"It's fine," Sierra told him. "It's been somewhat enlightening to hear all her stories about you."

"I'm gonna kill her," Grover muttered.

Sierra giggled, and the sound was carefree and happy. And Grover freaking loved it.

"It's all good stuff," she reassured him. "Like the time she was getting harassed on the school bus and you stood up for her. You got suspended, but those bullies never said anything to her again. Or when she was sick in the hospital and you participated in an Easter egg hunt and brought her all of the plastic eggs you found. She said you guys spent an hour opening them all on her hospital bed. And of course, the lengths you went to in order to help your brother after his gambling thing."

"Yeah...his gambling thing," Grover said in disgust. He knew he'd forgive Spencer eventually for all that he'd put their sister through, but he wasn't quite there yet.

Sierra stopped and turned toward him. She put her hand on his arm. "She loves you."

"I know. And I love Devyn too. But I don't need her help when it comes to women," Grover complained.

Sierra raised an eyebrow, then turned and continued down the trail. "What about Sally Jensen?" she called back.

Grover groaned. "Oh Lord, please tell me she didn't tell you about that."

"How would I know her name if she didn't?"

"In my defense, I was eighteen and a senior. Young and dumb."

"I saw the picture," Sierra told him, glancing back with a smile.

Grover stopped in the middle of the trail and bowed his head. "I really *am* gonna kill her."

Sierra giggled again, and Grover couldn't resist drinking in the woman in front of him. She looked so relaxed and happy, and he ached to do what he could to keep her that way for the rest of their lives.

She walked back to where he'd stopped and glanced up at him. "If it makes you feel any better, it wasn't a very nice thing of Sally to do. And...you were pretty damn handsome, even at eighteen."

"Right. So, the backstory is that she told me she was attracted to guys with a sense of humor. I was *trying* to be funny."

"By dying your pubic and chest hair blue?" Sierra asked, doing her best not to burst out laughing.

Grover sighed. "Yeah. And she laughed all right. And, I might point out, my, er...enhancements...didn't seem to make her any less eager to have sex with me. It wasn't until I was asleep that she took those pictures and showed them to all her friends. Luckily, she cropped out my cock when she posted my naked chest all over the school. My nickname took on a whole new meaning for the rest of that school year."

Sierra lost the hold she had on her laugh, and she literally bent over double as she cracked up. Grover didn't give a shit that she was laughing at his humiliation. He was simply soaking in the sound. At that moment, she didn't have a care in the world.

When she had herself under control, he asked, "So...I should've chosen pink?"

That set her off again.

Grover had to reach out and grab hold of her arm to keep her upright.

"Oh my God, my stomach hurts," Sierra complained, still chuckling.

"You're so damn pretty," Grover said quietly, the words tumbling over his lips without thought.

Sierra blushed, shaking her head in disbelief.

"You are," he insisted.

"I'm sure," she said, running a self-conscious hand over the fuzz on her head.

Grover grabbed her hand and kissed the back of it. "Your hair doesn't make you any more or less pretty. Neither do the clothes you're wearing or how much you weigh. You're beautiful to me because of who you are inside. Because when you laugh, you do so freely and without reservation. Because of your smile.

Because you didn't ask my sister why in the hell she was messaging a complete stranger."

"I wouldn't do that," Sierra insisted.

"I know. Which is all a part of why you're so damn pretty."

Sierra rolled her eyes, but Grover noticed that she didn't take her hand out of his. He eyed the trail and realized it was wide enough that they could walk side by side. So he started forward once more, with Sierra next to him this time. "Moving away from embarrassing stories about me...what else did the girls say?" he asked.

"Riley sent me about four thousand pictures of Logan, Bria, and Amalia. She told me how Logan wants to be a professional baseball player, and how Bria wants to be a princess. She somehow got me to agree to babysit when and if I come to Texas. She's kinda sneaky, isn't she?"

Grover chuckled. "Yup. She seems so innocent and quiet, then the next thing you know, she and Oz are sneaking off to have sexy times while you're holding a baby and staring down at their other two adorable kids."

"She did say that Oz wants more kids."

"Oh yeah, he's made no secret of that. Bought a huge-ass house that he's determined to fill," Grover said, smiling.

"Aspen's been giving me nutritional and medical advice," Sierra went on. "Just telling me things I can do to help my body adjust to normal food and regular activity again. Kinley hasn't messaged quite as much, but she'd still been super sweet, telling me how happy she is that you found me, that she can't wait to meet me. She did warn me that Gillian would try to throw some huge party to welcome me to Texas."

Grover sighed. "I haven't made it a secret with my friends that I'd love it if you came to visit, and maybe even made it your home. Or that I want to see where our friendship can go. I know that you said you weren't ready for a relationship, and I'm okay with that...but until you tell me unequivocally that it *won't* happen, I'm going to be patient and hope that maybe someday you'll be ready. Still, I don't ever want you to feel pressured to do anything you don't want to, by me *or* my friends. And that includes coming to Texas or dating me."

"I don't," Sierra reassured him. "It's nice to be wanted, actually."

"Oh, you're wanted," Grover said dryly.

She shot him a small smile. "I'm a little overwhelmed, I admit, but in a good way. I've been talking to Ember the most. Which, as a side note, is weird. I mean, she's *Ember Maxwell*, and I have her phone number. It's so surreal. Anyway, you know how you said that she would probably let me work with her?"

"Yeah?" Grover asked hopefully.

"Well, she already brought it up. And she said the apartment she rented for her friend—the one who tried to freakin' *kill* her—is still available. She paid for the deposit and then added a few months' rent, because she had hopes of finding someone else to help her with the gym."

"That's a great idea," Grover told her.

"You think?"

"Oh yeah. Although, I have to admit, I liked the idea of you staying at my place better."

"I'm seriously considering her offer," Sierra said.

"Good."

She sighed. "Okay, that's a lie...I pretty much already told her I accepted."

Grover stopped in the middle of the trail once more. It was a good thing they weren't hiking for exercise because they'd stopped about a hundred times since they set out. "You did?"

Sierra wouldn't meet his gaze.

Grover gently tilted her chin up so she had no choice but to look at him. "I'm thrilled for you. No matter what happens between us, you can't go wrong with friends like Ember, Gillian, and the others."

"I was afraid you'd think I was...I don't know...encroaching or something."

"No way. I was the one who brought up moving to Texas in the first place, remember? And I haven't stopped since."

She grinned. "I know. That barn-date thing."

Grover smiled back. "That's the one. But seriously, Sierra. Yes, I'm attracted to you, more with every minute we spend together, but if things between us never move beyond this intense friendship we have...it'll be okay."

Sierra stared up at him for a long moment. "You really do seem too good to be true."

"I'm not. I think I already told you that I've got more than my fair share of faults."

"For the record?"

"Yeah?"

"I don't think it'll be hard to convince me to go on that date with you."

Grover beamed. "Good. But for now, while we're here, we're just two buddies hanging out."

"Buddies who hold hands?" she asked with a quirk of an eyebrow.

"Yup."

"Buddies who sleep together?"

Grover nearly groaned at that, but he managed to nod. "I didn't have nightmares last night," he reminded her. "And I know it's because my psyche knew you were there next to me. Safe. And you came to me because you didn't want to be alone. So yeah, in our case...friends who sleep together."

"You aren't like anyone I've ever met before," she told him.

"I can say the same about you."

Just then, Sierra's belly growled, and Grover chuckled. He let go of her hand long enough to put the backpack he'd been carrying on the ground and pull out another granola bar and some peanut butter crackers. Then he slung the pack on again and opened the bar. He handed it to her, gesturing to the trail. "Shall we keep going and find that pretty spot Tonka told us about?"

Sierra nodded. They resumed their walk side by side.

Thirty minutes later, the trail made a ninety-degree turn to the left, and at the turn was a huge flat rock. Sierra and Grover decided it would make a perfect table and climbed up.

Once seated, the rest of the world seemed to disappear. They were surrounded by trees and chirping birds. The weather wasn't too hot, nor too cold. They got out the sandwiches they'd made and the bag of chips they'd pilfered from the pantry, then ate and talked. And Grover couldn't ever remember being so content.

* * *

Sierra's mind was whirling. She'd been fighting with herself for two weeks regarding what she should do, versus what she wanted to do. She *wanted* to move to Texas, date Grover, and accept the friendship all the women offered. But she had a feeling she *should* be more cautious. Not move so fast. Get her bearings before making any huge life decisions.

But sitting here with Grover in the peaceful forest made the decision feel easy. She liked him. And not only because he'd made such a huge sacrifice to find her. He was a good man, she could see that in every interaction he had with other people.

They were drawn to him, just as she was. Maybe because he made them feel important, as if what they were saying was the most interesting thing he'd heard all day. Or maybe simply because he was so damn nice.

Some people actually thought calling a man "nice" was an insult. But not her. Sierra had been around plenty of "not nice" men, and would much rather have someone like Grover, hands down.

The more time she spent with him, the more comfortable she got. Talking with him every night had been enlightening, and she'd gotten to know him pretty well. Being around him in person was...everything.

The way he stood between her and Melba until he was sure the huge beast wouldn't knock her over. How he paid attention to what she liked and didn't...for instance, packing peanut butter crackers instead of the cheese ones. How he made her a cup of coffee exactly the way she preferred it.

It was the feel of his hand in hers. Of knowing she could crawl into bed with him and not be afraid he'd think she was making a pass or allowing him to take advantage.

Sierra knew she would be no match physically for Grover. He could easily overpower and hurt her if he was of the mind. Instead, he'd been extremely gentle, keeping his space, and making sure no one else overwhelmed her either.

The thought of being intimate with him was...exciting. Not scary in the least.

"They didn't rape me," Sierra blurted, then winced at how harsh the words sounded, how completely out of the blue.

True to form, Grover didn't make her feel weird about her outburst. "Thank God."

"I mean, that first month or two, I was terrified every day that they'd do just that, but they were more interested in figuring out how much they could push me before I broke. And once I figured out the faster I cried, the faster they stopped, they seemed to lose interest in even doing that anymore, unless another hostage was around. I was like this toy that got old, that wasn't fun anymore, and they mostly left me alone until someone reminded them I was there."

"That's a good analogy," Grover said softly. "And I'm glad they lost interest, but that doesn't negate the fact that they took away your freedom. That they touched you at all."

"I know."

"Do you want to tell me why you were thinking about them?"

Sierra sighed. "No. But I will. I was just sitting here, amazed at how happy I am. With you. And about how well you seemed to know me after such a short period of time. That since you're so much bigger and stronger than me, you could hurt me, but you haven't. Which got me thinking about why I felt safe going to your cabin last night and actually getting into bed with you. And *that* made me imagine the two of us being...together...if you know what I mean. It doesn't freak me out. I guess...I just wanted you to know that. I figured maybe *you* wondered if I was raped while I was in captivity, and didn't want to do anything that *could* freak me out."

After a beat, Grover chuckled softly. "I'm not laughing at the fact that you might've been sexually assaulted," he reassured her. "But because of your thought process. And I'm glad the thought of us making love doesn't cause you to panic."

Sierra blushed, despite already being used to his blunt way of speaking.

He scooted closer but didn't reach for her. His thigh touched hers, as if he couldn't bear to *not* touch her in some way. She liked that. A lot.

"I admit that I'm relieved they didn't do that to you. The

thought of anyone overpowering you like that makes me absolutely furious. And sick to my stomach. You'll always be safe with me, Bean. I promise."

"Thanks," she whispered. Then she tilted her head and rested it against his upper arm. He didn't move, but she felt him sigh as if relieved she was touching him back. "Can I tell you something?"

"You can tell me anything. Between the two of us, there's a no-judgment zone," he reassured her.

"I can't cry," she said before she chickened out. "I talked to my therapist back in Colorado, and she said that's normal, but it doesn't *feel* normal."

"It does make sense though," Grover said. "You used your tears to manipulate your captors. So emotionally, your brain associates tears with pain. To keep yourself from *feeling* pain, physical or emotional, your body probably shies away from letting yourself cry. As a defense mechanism."

"I decided to keep my apartment when I took the job in Afghanistan. It was in a great area and the rent was extremely reasonable. I wasn't sure how long I would stay overseas and wanted somewhere to come back to when I returned. My parents packed up all my stuff though, after I'd been missing for several months, and stored it in their basement. Mom admitted that she sold my furniture because it wouldn't all fit in their house. When I saw my things had been reduced to a stack of boxes, I *wanted* to cry. It was so sad and depressing. But I couldn't. Not one tear. It's confusing because I felt such deep sorrow."

Sierra felt Grover shift next to her, then his arm closed around her shoulders. "It hasn't been that long since you've been free. Cut yourself some slack. And while I don't like the thought of you crying over *anything*, I'm sure you will at some point. Real tears, not those fake ones you were able to squeeze out on command."

She shrugged. Not sure it would ever happen. But of course, Grover had a good point. While in some ways it felt as if she'd been home for months and Afghanistan was this distant, surreal memory, it had really only been a few weeks. There were a lot of things that she was still coming to terms with. She just had to be patient.

Sitting up straight, she glanced at Grover shyly.

"You good?"

"Yeah. I'm sure you're right."

"I'm always right. Just ask anyone."

Appreciating his attempt to break up the seriousness of the moment, she rolled her eyes at him. "Maybe I'll ask Devyn how 'always right' you are."

"Oh, that was low," he teased. "Siccing my sister on me."

She grinned at him.

Not surprisingly, Sierra realized she felt better. Her issue of not crying hadn't been solved, but admitting that odd fact felt freeing, like she was no longer shouldering that burden alone. Grover hadn't looked at her as if she was broken. She also didn't regret admitting she hadn't been raped. Sometimes, as completely fucked up as it sounded, she actually felt guilty about that. As if people might think she wasn't a "real" POW, hadn't truly suffered, because she hadn't been sexually abused while in captivity.

She hadn't been sure this Refuge thing was a good idea, but clearly she needed it. She'd only been here a full day, but Sierra already felt calmer. More steady. Maybe it was the mountain air. Maybe it was the friendliness of the men who owned it. But she had a feeling it was none of that. It was the man next to her who made all the difference.

They sat on the rock for another half hour or so until deciding to head back to the ranch. The walk was slow and easy, and he held her hand the entire way. She was getting too used to touching him...but since Grover didn't seem to mind, Sierra decided she wouldn't either.

CHAPTER TWELVE

Thirteen days. The best almost-two-weeks of Grover's life. He and Sierra had spent just about every minute of every day together.

And he was head over heels in love with her.

He didn't know how *she* felt, unfortunately, since he'd done his best to keep his "friend" hat firmly in place.

They slept in the same bed every night, holding hands. He hadn't had one nightmare in those two weeks. And she was looking even healthier. She'd gained more of her weight back and she smiled all the time.

They'd fallen into a routine, eating breakfast, visiting Melba and the other animals, then packing a picnic lunch and going for a hike. They'd been all over the mountain trails and had gotten to know each other better with every step. Grover had told Sierra stories that he hadn't told anyone else. And he'd like to think she'd shared some of her innermost thoughts as well.

After returning to The Refuge each day, they either visited with the therapist—separately, together, and in groups—took naps in the hammocks behind their cabins, or just hung out in the reception lodge, talking with other guests and Brick and his friends.

But their two-week stay was coming to an end. Tomorrow, Sierra's parents would return to pick her up and he'd make the long drive back to Killeen.

Grover had also been in semi-regular contact with his friends —getting updates about an increasingly volatile situation back home. Even though he'd worked hard to keep his worry from Sierra, determined not to derail her peace and therapy, he knew he needed to share what was happening. Especially because she was still considering moving to Texas.

At first, Grover and the rest of the team hadn't been too concerned about the Strong Foot Militia. It was a group from a city not too far from Killeen, railing against the rise of what it considered a tyrannical government—which it believed should be confronted with armed force.

There were three types of "official" militia groups recognized by the US government: the organized—including the National Guard; the unorganized—pretty much all other able-bodied persons between the ages of seventeen and sixty, not already in the National Guard; and state defense forces, which were authorized by state laws.

But then there were groups like Strong Foot, whose members took it upon themselves to take up arms against the government. They were basically armed paramilitary extremists with an anti-government and conspiracy theory ideology.

Grover and his Delta team had long been aware of that particular group, since its home base was in San Angelo, only three hours west of Killeen.

They'd expressed their disdain for just about every aspect of the government, but recently had been extremely vocal in their displeasure with the military—specifically, the fact that the US still had troops overseas.

In just the month since Grover and Sierra had returned from Afghanistan, there had been two unfortunate events regarding the military overseas. The first was in South Korea, where a soldier had been convicted of two murders, three rapes, and a handful of assault charges. Because the man's home base had been Killeen, the Strong Foot Militia had used the media attention as a platform for their own protests.

The second incident happened in Afghanistan, but in a different part of the country than where Sierra had been working when she'd been taken. While attempting to take out another Taliban leader, the US had killed several civilians during air strikes. Grover knew the Strong Foot Militia didn't give one little shit about those civilians; their deaths were simply a handy excuse to push an agenda.

According to Trigger, the group had been protesting outside the main gate of Fort Hood for the last week, getting more and more aggressive with each day that passed. There were several dozen men, holding signs and yelling threats against the soldiers and civilians who drove in and out of the gates.

Tensions were rising in the military town, and the militia group showed no signs of ending their protests, only ramping up their antics. They were thriving on all the media attention they were finally getting, quickly turning the entire town into a powder keg just waiting to explode.

Grover knew Sierra could sense his increasing anxiety about the situation, could see it on his face every time he finished talking on the phone with Trigger. He'd done his best to hide his unease, but obviously wasn't doing a very good job.

He wanted Sierra to move to Killeen, and was terrified any talk of the militia group would give her a reason to put it off, possibly indefinitely. But Grover knew staying silent wasn't fair. She'd been through hell and had a right to know everything about the city she was considering moving to. The good, bad, and ugly.

He knew the Strong Foot group wouldn't always be an issue. Hopefully, they'd slink back to where they came from sooner than later, maybe even disband altogether. Beyond that, he also hated keeping anything from Sierra.

Grover made the decision to talk to her about the group before they left tomorrow. He also hoped to discuss what her plans were once she'd returned to Colorado. Provided the militia didn't scare her away, he wanted to know if she was still accepting Ember's offer, and if so, when she might make the move. He couldn't wait to show her his house and barn. To introduce her to the women she'd been texting with. To reunite her with his team. To take her to his favorite restaurants.

Hell, just knowing she was in the same town as him would be amazing.

Having her constantly at his side these last two weeks had solidified his feelings for her, and he was desperate to know if she felt the same.

They woke up on the last morning of their full day at The Refuge around seven-thirty, as normal. Sierra left his cabin to go to hers and shower, then they had a large, satisfying breakfast. Afterward, they headed for the barn so Sierra could give morning snuggles to Melba, the goats, and the cats.

But instead of returning to the kitchen to pack a lunch, Sierra said, "Would you mind if we didn't hike today?"

"Of course not. What do you have in mind?"

"I was thinking we could go back to my cabin, sit on the back deck. And talk."

Usually when a woman said she wanted to talk, it was bad

news. But Grover was more than willing to listen to whatever Sierra had to say. It would also give him a chance to discuss the issues the militia group were causing, and to reiterate how badly he wanted her to come to Texas. She claimed she wanted to, but he had to be sure. "That sounds great."

They still stopped by the kitchen to grab some food for lunch, which Grover carried to her cabin. They set everything up on the small table on her back deck and ate in comfortable silence. That was one of the things Grover liked most about her; he didn't always have to carry on a conversation. They could sit in silence together and be perfectly happy.

After they'd finished their sandwiches and cleaned up from lunch, Sierra sat back in her chair and said, "This has been the best two weeks, Grover."

"I agree."

"I wasn't sure I really wanted to come, as you know. I mean, I was mostly all right, mentally. I kinda felt as if I should leave the space here for someone who needed it more desperately. But after sitting in on all the therapy sessions, I realized that while I might not have been treated as horribly as I could've been, the experience still affected me more than I'd thought."

Grover nodded. "That's good."

Sierra looked over at him. "But I know I wouldn't feel quite as...calm as I do right now, if you hadn't been here with me."

Grover's heart swelled. "I feel the same, Bean."

"I still can't believe you did what you did. I mean, it was pretty outrageous. Who gets themselves taken by a terrorist group in the hopes that *maybe* they'll find someone who disappeared a year ago? I could've long since been dead, Grover."

"I know." And he did. It *was* a long shot, despite what his gut had told him; a decision made out of desperation. "But you weren't. And here you are."

"Here I am," she agreed. She was quiet for a moment, then asked, "Do you think this is healthy?"

"What?"

"Us."

One word. She didn't need to say anything else.

"Yes," Grover told her immediately.

Her lips twitched.

"Look, I'm not saying what we have is conventional. Hell, most people would probably say it's not normal. But I don't care. All I think about is how I feel when I'm around you."

When he didn't continue, Sierra asked, "And how is that?"

Grover had no problem telling her exactly how he felt. This was the perfect time to lay everything on the line.

"Settled. As if I've finally met my best friend. I don't feel as if I need to be anyone except who I am when I'm with you. I don't have to pretend to not be completely freaked out by spiders because I know you'll kill them for me. You know when I'm irritated and when I'm feeling mellow. I've told you all about my fucked-up family dynamics, and you haven't judged me. I've laughed more in the last two weeks than I have in a very long time, and being around you reminds me why I joined the Army —more specifically, Delta Force. I don't care what others think of our relationship. They can fuck off if they don't like it. They aren't us. They haven't been through what we have."

"That first month after I was taken was the worst," Sierra said softly. "I was so scared and confused, in pain. I didn't know what Shahzada wanted from me, and every day I thought would be my last. And out of all the things I could have thought about...I thought about you," Sierra admitted.

Grover could hear the emotion in her voice, but as normal her eyes stayed dry. He knew she'd talked to the therapist about her inability to cry, and the woman had told her basically the same thing he had. That she needed to be patient, that once her mind and body realized she was truly safe, she'd regain the ability.

"I thought back to when we first met. You annoyed me so bad," she told him with a small smile. "I was irritated that you seemed to only see a naïve little kid."

"I never saw you as a kid. Ever," Grover said with feeling.

"You know what I mean," Sierra protested. "But you kinda redeemed yourself when you asked if we could keep in touch. I didn't think a guy would do that if he wasn't interested. Especially since I'd be in Afghanistan for a while and you'd be back here in the States."

"I was definitely interested," Grover said unnecessarily.

"I just don't want what happened to be the basis of any relationship we might have. I don't want you to constantly see me as the poor civilian who needs rescuing. I need you to see me as a mature, capable woman who can make sound decisions."

"I do," Grover told her without hesitation.

"I like you," Sierra said. "But you also scare the hell out of me."

"I'd never hurt you."

"Not on purpose, no. And I absolutely believe that you won't physically touch me in anger or frustration, but I feel as if I'm on a precipice. Do I take the leap...or don't I?"

"Here's the thing," Grover said quietly. "Can I see into the future? No. I have no idea what will happen tomorrow, and I certainly don't know where we'll be in a month, a year, five years from now. But what I do know with one hundred percent certainty, is that you're going to do amazing things. I don't know what, but I know just from observing you for the last two weeks, everyone you come into contact with is somehow changed for the better, just for having known you. The other guests here seem to light up when you talk to them. You're considerate and genuinely concerned for others. That's rare, Bean. Selfishly, I want to have your goodness near me all the time, to help center me as well.

"As for that precipice...take the leap. I'll be there to catch you."

Sierra stood then. And for just a second, Grover thought maybe he'd gone too far. That she was leaving. Instead, she shocked the shit out of him when she stepped over to his chair and climbed right onto his lap.

In the last two weeks, he'd touched her a lot. Her arm, her back. He'd held her hand as much as he could get away with. And even though they'd slept in the same bed every night, this was much more intimate.

Sierra fit against him perfectly. He loved having her weight on him. Even though she'd gained back most of what she'd lost, she'd never be a large person. She would always be petite, and he'd always be huge compared to her. He liked that difference. It satisfied something deep and primitive inside him.

Her head rested on his shoulder and her short hair tickled the side of his jaw. Grover held her to him securely.

"I'm going to go back to Colorado with my parents," she said.

Grover's stomach plummeted, everything else turning to stone at her words.

"Then I'm going to arrange to move to Killeen."

And just like that, his world changed. "What do you need me to do to help?" he asked.

Sierra lifted her head. "Are you sure about this?"

"Absolutely. Are you?" he countered.

She nodded and rested her head back on his shoulder. "I've thought about it a lot. And I even talked about it with the therapist yesterday. She thinks it will be a good thing. A change of scenery. I want what you have," she said quietly.

"And what's that?" Grover asked.

"A tribe. People who are there for you no matter what. Maybe if I had those kinds of friends to begin with, I wouldn't have felt so restless, wouldn't have been so eager to go overseas. Maybe when I disappeared, one of my tribe would've raised hell until someone did something to get me back. I don't want to go back to being the solitary person I was before."

"You won't," Grover vowed.

"I know I'm taking advantage by trying to slip into your group of friends," Sierra started, but Grover interrupted her.

"You aren't. They're good people, and you already fit in with them. They wouldn't accept you if they sensed you weren't genuine."

"Ember's going to lose her mind," Sierra said with a small chuckle. "She's texted me every day, asking when I'm going to get my butt down there and help her out."

"When?" Grover asked impatiently.

"Now you sound like Ember," Sierra said.

"Well, I did promise you a date in my barn," Grover told her.

"And a huge salad," she told him.

"That too. So? When do I need to ask my commander for some time off so I can help you move?"

"I don't know. But soon, I think. I'm ready, Grover. Ready to shake off the sand of Afghanistan and start living again. This place has been amazing, but I need to *do* something. I can't just hang out here with Melba and the other animals and do nothing but hike the forest every day."

"Be careful what you wish for," Grover told her, not able to stop himself from kissing the top of her head. "The girls will have you busy from sunup to sundown if you aren't careful. They're an ambitious bunch for sure."

"They sound amazing. I can't wait to get to know them. And explore Killeen. I've never been to Texas. I've heard a lot of stories about the state."

"And a lot of them are probably true," Grover said, knowing this was as good an opening as he'd get to warn her about the Strong Foot Militia. "One good thing is that it's hot. You shouldn't be cold there. I mean, the winters get chilly, but nothing like Colorado, and certainly not like Leadville."

"Good. Grover?"

"Yeah?"

"Are you going to tell me what's bothering you? I know you got another call from Trigger this morning, and you've been tense ever since. Are you guys going to be deployed again soon? Because if you are, it's okay. I can deal with that part of your job. I mean, I'll miss you and worry about you when you're gone, but I'm not going to fall apart."

"That means the world to me, but no. That's not what's on my mind." Grover took a deep breath. "It might be a good idea for you to wait a bit before you come down to Killeen."

The words were extremely painful, almost refusing to come out, but the last thing he wanted was to put Sierra in the middle of a powder keg.

"Why? What's wrong?" She didn't sound upset. Didn't immediately get emotional and accuse him of not wanting her there, after all. She was levelheaded, which Grover appreciated a hell of a lot.

"There's a Texas militia group that's been causing problems in Killeen. They've been picketing outside the gates of the Army post and doing their best to cause fear, to terrorize anyone who lives and works there."

"Why?"

Grover shrugged. "Because they're young and dumb? Because they think white skin makes them better than everyone else? Because they like the attention? I don't know."

"Is that what your team has been updating you on?"

"Yeah. I don't normally talk to my friends every day when I'm on leave," he told her with a smile. "I mean, I like them, but jeez."

Sierra chuckled, then surprised him again when she adjusted, straddling his lap to face him. It was all Grover could do not to pull her closer, so his cock was nestled between her legs. She wasn't trying to make a move on him; he knew that. So he forced himself to stay completely still. The last thing he wanted to do was freak her out by acting like a horny teen.

She put her hands on either side of his neck and looked into his eyes. "I refuse to let anything scare me away from my new life. I was held captive by the Taliban for a freaking *year*. These idiots complaining about shit they know nothing about aren't going to make me tremble in my boots."

"You aren't wearing boots," Grover said, the joke falling flat even to his own ears.

"You know what I mean," she said.

"I do. Anyway, they're dangerous," Grover told her seriously, putting his hands on her waist and holding her steady. "Brain's been doing some research. He says they've got a shitload of explosives and are armed to the teeth. They like to show off their stash on social media to try to recruit other racist assholes to their cause."

"Okay."

"They're against pretty much anyone who isn't a white American male. Gay, Jewish, Black, Hispanic. Even women."

"All right."

"And they're planning something. No one knows what. There's talk about some big scheme to show the world how tyrannical and out of control the military is."

"Grover, it's okay."

"I just can't, in good conscience, let you move to Killeen without telling you exactly what you're getting into."

"I *know* what I'm getting into. I'm gaining a group of women who I hope will become my best friends. A badass Delta Force team who will have my back no matter what. And I'm getting a protective, honest, amazing boyfriend who hates spiders with a passion, but who I know would face down an armada of the eight-legged creatures if it means keeping me safe and happy."

Grover barely dared to breathe. "Boyfriend?"

"Yes," Sierra said, and he loved how her cheeks turned pink. "I know I said I wasn't ready for that kind of relationship, but clearly I'm an idiot. The last two weeks have been the best in my life. And I'm not exaggerating. The thought of leaving and going to Colorado is killing me, because I'll be leaving *you*. Even if you were stationed in Alaska, I'd follow you in a heartbeat, and you know how I feel about the cold."

Grover tightened his hands on Sierra's waist and pulled her closer. He needed to feel her against him. Was so relieved that she was going to give him a chance to show her how good they could be together, he wasn't even thinking about shocking her with his arousal.

But she came willingly, squirming to get even closer. She buried her face in his neck and they simply held each other.

"I'm going to do everything possible to make you happy," Grover vowed.

"You already do," she said, her voice muffled against his skin.

Moving a hand to her nape, Grover marveled yet again at how small she was compared to him, how large his hand looked against her delicate neck. He was aware of her height and weight, the fact that she was petite, but every time he held her close, the fact was hammered home all the more. She'd had such a big personality when they met, an exuberance that was coming back a little more every day, that it was hard to believe it could be contained in a package so small.

She lifted her head, and he stared into her eyes.

"I'm happy," he told her seriously.

She grinned. "You don't look it."

"I'm scared to death," Grover admitted.

"Of what?"

"You."

Sierra looked surprised. "Me? I'm no scarier than a flea."

"I don't want to screw this up, and I'm terrified I'll do or say something that will make you change your mind."

"Grover, stop it," she scolded. "I don't expect you to be perfect, no more than you expect me to be. We're *both* going to screw up. We'll say things we don't mean and we'll irritate the hell out of each other. But that won't mean I like you any less."

"You're a hell of a woman, Sierra Clarkson. Don't ever forget that."

She smiled shyly. "I'm not all that amazing."

"Are you kidding? Bean, you survived twelve months of captivity. Not only that, you manipulated those assholes into doing exactly what you wanted them to do." Grover ran a hand over her head briefly, physical proof of exactly how smart she was. "You didn't freak out when my team showed up, you did your best to be an asset instead of a liability. Trust me when I say that doesn't always happen. I'd choose you to be by my side anytime the shit hits the fan."

Sierra tilted her head, studying him for a long moment before saying, "You really mean that, don't you?"

"One hundred percent. Your background in psychology means you have the ability to really *see* people, and you possess an innate skill for figuring out how to get what you need out of them."

"You mean I'm manipulative," she said with a smile. "Aren't you afraid I'm going to turn my so-called abilities on you?"

"Nope. Because if you ever have to resort to those tactics, there's something seriously wrong. Besides, I'll bend over backward to give you whatever it is you want, there's no need to manipulate me into it."

"What if I want a Maserati?" she asked.

Grover knew she was kidding, but chose to make his point. "Then we'll talk about what we need to sacrifice in order to be able to afford it."

"Grover," she whispered. "That was a joke."

"I know. But I want you to recognize how serious I am. I won't always be able to afford the things you want, and I might not be able to move at the drop of a hat, at least not until I retire from the Army...but almost everything's negotiable."

"You're too good to be true," Sierra said softly.

"Scared of spiders, remember?" Grover teased.

"I'll protect you from them," she promised.

Grover couldn't stand it anymore. "Since we're now apparently dating...you think I might get a kiss?"

She grinned, but instead of answering, Sierra leaned forward. It didn't take much, as they were already so close, and the second her lips touched his, Grover was putty in her hands.

The kiss was slow and easy. Intimate and loving. Grover knew there would be time for out-of-control passion later, but here, in this relaxed setting, for their first real kiss as a couple, he wanted to take his time.

Despite that, they were both breathing hard when she pulled

back, and when she writhed against him subtly, he realized she was just as turned on as he was. Grover was no longer embarrassed by his erection pressing against her. She didn't seem fazed.

Licking his lips, Grover could taste the tea she'd had with her lunch. It was intimate, and he was almost overwhelmed with emotion. He made a mental vow to never let this woman down. She'd been through hell and deserved the best life had to offer. The best *he* had to offer.

Sierra sighed with a small smile, then leaned forward once more, resting her cheek on his shoulder. Her warm breath caressed the skin of his neck and he relaxed into the chair. Using a foot, he pulled a small footstool closer and lifted his legs.

They both snuggled into each other as he got comfortable. The trees swayed in a slight breeze and in the distance, they could hear Melba mooing, probably for attention or treats.

"Thank you for coming here with me," Sierra said after a moment.

"You're welcome."

"Brick and his friends have an amazing place. I hope it helps everyone else as much as it did me."

"Me too," Grover said.

After a minute or two of companionable silence, Sierra asked, "Do you really think those militia people are going to be trouble?"

"Yeah, Bean. I do. Don't ask me when or how, but something in my gut says that they've gone too far to back down now. They're going to want to do something to show the world they're serious about their anti-government agenda. And what better way to do that than to mess with the largest military post in Texas?"

Sierra hugged him tight. "Are you and your team going to have to go up against them?"

"I don't know. I hope not." Grover didn't like the idea of going up against American citizens. But the bottom line was that if they escalated their harassment, they could become a terrorist threat.

He couldn't help but think about some of the other domestic terrorist attacks. Patrick Crusius, the man who killed twenty-three people at an El Paso Walmart; the many attacks on synagogues and mosques; the Portland, Oregon, stabbing of several people on a train by a man while screaming he was a "taxpayer and had first amendment rights"; the Pulse nightclub shooting in Florida; the Boston Marathon bombing; Joe Stack, who flew his plane into the IRS building in Austin. Even the shooting in two thousand and nine on Grover's own military base, where a major killed thirteen people.

There was so much hate in the world. It grieved him that he might be called to take up arms against his fellow countrymen.

But at this moment, in this place, all was right in Grover's world.

He honestly hadn't thought he'd find a woman to love like his friends had, even after meeting Sierra a year ago, despite his immediate interest. He'd had some good talks with the therapist here at The Refuge, and was making strides toward relinquishing the guilt he felt about not looking for Sierra earlier. He'd always hold *some* guilt in his heart, he guessed, but was doing his best to not let it consume him.

Sierra was doing amazingly well, and by some miracle, that spark they'd initially felt was still there. And she was moving to Texas.

Tuning out the noise in his head about militia groups, protests, and guilt, Grover closed his eyes and enjoyed this moment with the woman who was fast becoming the most important person in his life.

And Grover knew he wouldn't change one damn thing about that life, if it meant he'd end up right here, with Sierra Clarkson in his lap, relaxed and happy—and all his.

CHAPTER THIRTEEN

Sierra was nervous and excited. It had been a full week and a half since she'd seen Grover, and she was anxious to be with him once more. Talking on the phone or FaceTiming wasn't the same as being able to touch him. To hold his hand.

Her parents had been wary of her decision to move, but supportive. They'd liked Grover from the second they'd met him, and it didn't hurt that he'd had a long talk with her dad the other night on the phone. Neither would say what they'd discussed. She was just glad they got along, so she didn't push the issue.

Her dad had bought Sierra a car earlier in the week, ignoring her protests. He said that he couldn't in good conscience send her off to Texas with no transportation. He'd planned on getting a moving company to transport her car with all her belongings, while she flew to Austin, but Sierra had insisted on driving herself.

Her parents also felt bad about selling her furniture, and replaced most of it. Sierra had sworn it wasn't necessary, but when it was obvious it made them feel better, she stopped trying to talk them out of it.

Things were moving at lightning speed, but that was at her insistence. She was ready to start living again. Ever since she'd returned from Afghanistan, it felt as if the world was moving around her, and she hadn't been ready to step back into the fray. But with her parents' and Grover's patience, and after two idyllic weeks in New Mexico, Sierra was ready.

Ember had texted nonstop, telling her about all the ideas she had for her fledgling gym. Gillian had started a group text with Sierra and all the other women, and it was hilarious to read their interactions. The fact that Sierra had been included at all blew her away. The women had been friendly and supportive since her return to the States, but they still didn't know her. Not really. But the fact that she and Grover were officially dating was enough for them to embrace her completely.

Devyn had also been extremely welcoming. There was one text in which she'd kind of warned Sierra not to hurt her big brother, but otherwise, everything she'd sent had been friendly.

As much as Sierra wanted to move into Grover's big farmhouse, she knew she needed to get her own place. She was always independent...at least, she'd been so before being taken captive. She needed to find that part of herself again.

Though she couldn't deny she was looking forward to spending more time with Grover in the real world. Shopping. Cooking. Dating. He'd be busy working when she got to Texas, and that was all right. As much as she'd loved spending nearly twenty-four hours a day with him in New Mexico, she needed some balance. She wanted to go out with the girls, and have Grover hang with his team too.

She wanted to be *normal*, not just the woman who'd been a "guest" of the Taliban for a year.

Before she could be that person, she needed to satisfy the media's desire to hear every grisly detail of her captivity. She'd done a couple of carefully chosen interviews—one before New Mexico and one after—and had set up a few more. The requests were coming in less and less frequently, so Sierra had hopes that before too long, they'd taper off altogether. Something would happen that would put the spotlight on someone else, as Ember and Grover constantly reminded her. And Ember should know. After she'd been shot by someone she thought was a friend, the media went into a crazed frenzy.

Sierra had been in contact with Grover almost the entire drive to Texas. He'd convinced her to put a location-sharing app on her phone. Tex might be able to track her, but he wanted that privilege too. After all she'd been through, Sierra had no issue whatsoever with that. Besides, she got to see where *he* was at all times, as well. She knew when he was working out with his team in the mornings, when he was at work on the Army post, and when he was at home.

They'd made plans to meet at Grover's house when she got into town late this afternoon. She'd seen plenty of pictures of the beautiful property, house, and barn, but she couldn't wait to see it in person. The plan was for her to spend the night at his place tonight, then he and some of the guys would help her move into her apartment tomorrow. Her belongings were scheduled to arrive in the morning.

Sierra followed her GPS directions to Grover's street, then shortly after, turned down a very long dirt driveway to his house. There were trees here and there, but nothing like what she was used to seeing back in Colorado, or even like there'd been in New Mexico.

The second the house came into view, Sierra smiled in awe. It was beautiful, even more so than the pictures, and nothing like what she'd have imagined a rough-and-tough special forces soldier would have. But if she'd learned anything over the last month or so, she'd learned that Grover was unique in so many ways.

She saw him standing on the steps of the gorgeous front porch, and by the time she'd pulled to a stop in front of the house, he was waiting for her at her door. He pulled it open and the second she climbed out, she was in his arms.

Sierra had wondered if things would feel awkward when she saw Grover again in the "real world," but with the way the butterflies in her belly were swirling, she felt anything but.

"Welcome to Texas," Grover said.

Sierra couldn't help but chuckle. "I've been here for like, eight hours already. This is a damn huge state," she observed.

"Yup. One of the only states you can drive literally all day and never cross the border. How do you feel? You hungry? Stiff? What can I do to help?"

Gah. This guy. "I'm good," she told him, looking around his property with interest.

"You want a tour? It's a little early for dinner, but we can go in and eat anyway, if you'd prefer, and I can show you around after. I've got taco soup in the Crockpot. Figured that would be easiest since I didn't know the exact time you'd arrive."

Sierra had no idea what taco soup was, but it sounded amazing. First, she wanted to see Grover's place. The pictures he'd sent were beautiful, but she could tell they hadn't done the property and views justice. "Tour," she told him.

"You got it. Come on." Grover hadn't taken his hands from her since ending their hug. Before he turned toward the barn, he intertwined their fingers. "This all right?"

"Oh yeah," Sierra agreed. Having his hand in hers felt like coming home. She hadn't realized how much she not only loved, but *needed* to hold his hand, until she got home to Colorado and felt kind of adrift. Grover had been her rock. Her anchor. Being here with him now, and having his hand in hers once more, was exactly what had been missing.

As they walked toward the barn, Grover explained how his team had helped him tear down the dilapidated structure that had been on the property. "The one we built in its place isn't nearly as large as the old one, but it's more manageable. And since I have no intentions of housing a ton of animals, this one suits my needs."

"I don't know, Melba was pretty darn cute," Sierra teased.

"She was," Grover agreed. "If you said you wanted some goats, chickens, or any other farm animals, I'd do it in a heartbeat."

Sierra glanced at him. It was hard to wrap her mind around the fact she'd only known this man for a short period of time. It literally felt as if she'd known him forever. Maybe because in Afghanistan, when she was by herself, alone in the dark, she frequently thought of him. What he was doing. What he was thinking. Where he was deployed. And maybe, once or twice, even fantasizing about him showing up to rescue her.

Damn if that wasn't exactly what he'd done. Not in the way she'd dreamed about, with guns blazing and mowing down her captors, but he'd gotten the job done.

"I'm not sure you should make a commitment to having farm animals just because I think they're cute," she told him dryly.

Grover merely shrugged. "You want them, I'll find a way to make it work. I know nothing about taking care of them, so I'd need to hire someone to help me, but that shouldn't be hard around here. I'm sure there are lots of teenagers who could use the extra money."

Sierra stopped in her tracks, and since she was holding Grover's hand, he stopped too.

"What?" he asked. "What's wrong?"

"You can't do that," she told him firmly.

"Do what?"

"Get a cow simply because I think they're cute."

"Why not?"

"Grover! Because! What if we break up? Having a cow would cost a ton of money, especially if you have to hire someone to look after it," Sierra told him, the exasperation easy to hear in her voice.

"You want a cow?" he asked.

Sierra sighed and frowned at him. "No. Maybe."

He smiled. "If you want a cow, I'll get you a cow. You want a closet full of clothes? I'll get those too. Dogs? No problem. Chickens, handbags, expensive shoes? Done. I'm not rich, but if you want something, I'll do my best to save to get it for you. I told you once that I'd bend over backward to give you what you want and need, and I wasn't lying."

"I don't need *any* of that stuff, Grover," Sierra said seriously. "I lived for a year with just a torn shirt and one pair of underwear. I literally had *nothing*. It wasn't fun, but it taught me how little material things mean. What I wanted most in the world was my freedom, but that wasn't a possibility until you came along. So you've already given me my greatest wish. All I want now is your respect and consideration. And maybe a shoulder to lean on every now and then."

"You've got those and more," Grover reassured her.

"I need something else too," Sierra said.

"Anything."

"I need to not feel like a burden. I need to be treated as if I'm a normal woman, not Sierra Clarkson, former POW. I don't want to be treated like a piece of glass. I'm not going to break if you tell me no. Or if you get mad. Or if you've had a hard day at work and just want to be left alone. I want, and *need*, a give-and-take relationship, Grover. Not one where you protect me from the world or put me on some pedestal I'll inevitably fall off one day."

Grover nodded seriously, and Sierra fell for him just a little bit more when he didn't brush off her concerns, or try to convince her they'd never argue or disagree. That was part of being in a relationship.

"I understand. And while I'll always want to keep you safe, even if it's from me and my moods, I'll do my best to not get all Neanderthal on you."

"I'd appreciate that."

"Now, do you need me to carry you so your feet don't get dusty?"

Sierra scowled—then noticed his lips twitching. "Ha. Very funny, caveman," she said with a shake of her head.

"I know you aren't helpless. Or fragile. I'd be an idiot to think that, after all you've been through. But I have to warn you it's in my nature to want to keep you from being hurt. Physically or emotionally. No one gets to make you feel unsafe ever again."

Sierra liked that. A lot. She gave him a small nod.

"Come on. I can't wait to show you the loft in the barn."

She chuckled as they started walking again. "Was that an innuendo?"

Sierra loved the smile Grover threw her way. "Do you want it to be?"

She laughed out loud that time. Then sobered a bit.

"What? What's wrong?"

God, this man was seriously in tune with her. "Nothing. I just realized that I've laughed more around you in the last few weeks than I have in literally the past year. Thank you."

Grover brought their connected hands up to his mouth and kissed the back of hers. "You're welcome, Bean. Come on, you can take a look at this barn of mine and see if you think it'd be suitable for any needy animals. Because I have to admit, Melba kind of grew on me."

Sierra smiled. She freaking loved that her badass special forces boyfriend had been tamed by the huge brown eyes of a gentle cow.

He had to let go of her hand to manhandle the large barn doors, but the second they were open, he grabbed hold of her once more as he walked them inside.

Grover had said this was a small barn, but it looked pretty darn big to Sierra. There were several stalls on the left-hand side, with no doors on them yet. At the moment, there were boxes and other odds and ends stored in each. There was a small office-type room, but otherwise, the space was large and open. Glancing up, Sierra saw the rafters above their heads had been left open, which made the space look even bigger.

She listened as Grover explained what had gone into building the barn and how he'd tried to keep it simple. As he launched into the schematics, and how the contractor he'd hired had reinforced it in case of a tornado, Sierra tuned him out. The stairs in the back corner had already caught her attention. They were a tight spiral leading up to what she assumed was the infamous loft Grover had told her about.

"Sorry," he said. "I was going on and on, wasn't I?"

Sierra shrugged. "It's okay. So what you're telling me is that this place can withstand anything but maybe a direct hit by an F4 or 5 tornado, right?"

"Yup."

"Cool. Can we go upstairs now?"

He laughed at her impatience. "Of course."

Feeling freer than she'd felt in a very long time, Sierra dropped Grover's hand and ran to the stairs. She headed up, being careful not to trip. The last thing she needed was to hurt herself the first day she got there. Sensing Grover at her back, Sierra concentrated on climbing to the loft.

Grover immediately headed for a set of wooden doors at the far end of the space. It was pretty sparse, only a few boxes up there—but it was the leather couch near the doors Grover was opening that intrigued her. She walked slowly toward him, shaking her head as she went.

"A leather couch?" she asked skeptically. "Isn't it going to get ruined out here?"

Grover pushed the large doors apart, and Sierra forgot her question when she caught a glimpse of the view in front of her. This part of Texas wasn't exactly the most picturesque, but in the distance, she could see rolling hills, and because the barn and Grover's house were located on a bit of a rise themselves, they were above the land that stretched out in front of them for miles.

"Holy crap," she said softly.

"It's nothing like the view from your parents' house, I'm sure," Grover said with a small shrug.

"It's not, but it's beautiful in its own way," Sierra reassured him.

"And yeah, I know the leather couch isn't very practical. When Trigger, Oz, and Doc helped me get the damn thing up here, they gave me all sorts of shit about it. But I like to come out here and enjoy the view. Remind myself that there's beauty in the world, if we only take the time to stop and see it."

Sierra walked closer to the opening, but Grover took hold of her hand as she passed. "Careful, I haven't had time to put up any safety barriers yet."

Nodding, she walked with Grover to the edge of the loft. The drop to the ground was about fifteen feet, so nothing terribly extreme, but if she fell out, she'd definitely hurt herself.

Sierra couldn't take her eyes from the countryside in front of her. Texas was very different from Colorado, that was for sure. But she hadn't lied, it was just as pretty as her hometown...but in a different way.

The area immediately around the barn was landscaped, but just beyond there was tall grass as far as she could see. The strands were gently blowing in the breeze, and she could smell earth and a slight hint of honeysuckle on the warm air blowing through the barn.

She closed her eyes, soaking in the moment. Grover had stepped away, and she vaguely heard noises behind her, but didn't pay much attention to what he was doing.

"Sit," he said softly after a moment.

Opening her eyes and turning to look at him, she saw that he'd pulled the couch a little closer to where she was standing near the edge of the loft. Smiling, she sat, and Grover did the same. Without hesitation, Sierra scooted closer and snuggled into him. She lay her head on his chest and stared out at the world.

She could feel his heart beating under her cheek and the feel of his arm around her shoulders made her sigh in contentment. "This is perfect," she whispered.

"It's nothing like the views we had in New Mexico," he said quietly.

"Nope," she agreed. "It's better because it's your home."

She felt him make a sound deep in his throat. It rumbled against her cheek. "You're right. Sometimes I come up here with the hopes of seeing animals in the grass. Every now and then I'll get lucky and spot a deer, but most of the time I get skunks and armadillos wandering around out there."

"I love the tall grass. I don't think I'd like to go walking in it, since it looks like it'd be over my head, but it gives this place a prairie kind of feel," she mused.

"It does," he agreed. "I could've cut the grass, but I like the wild look of it, especially when it sways in the wind."

"Me too."

How long they sat in the loft of his barn, Sierra didn't know. But when she heard his stomach growl, she knew they should get up and head inside. Lifting her head, she took in Grover's face so close to hers...and the expression that she couldn't quite define.

He didn't ask, simply leaned down and kissed her.

Sierra immediately opened to him. He shifted one hand to the back of her neck and held her still as he took what she freely gave. Making out had never felt so...poignant. She and Grover had a deep emotional connection she'd never experienced with anyone else. As corny as it sounded, it was as if their souls knew each other.

They'd kissed in New Mexico, but this time was more intense. Maybe it was being here on Grover's home turf. Maybe it was because she felt as if she was well and truly on her way back to being the independent woman she'd been when she'd made the decision to go to Afghanistan. Whatever it was, she liked it. A lot.

Moving to a more comfortable position astride Grover's lap, Sierra tilted her head and took control of their kiss. His hand dropped from her nape and pulled her hips closer. She could feel his erection, and that only fueled her need. She nipped his lip, then thrust her tongue into his mouth, loving that he let her take the lead.

By the time she pulled back, Sierra felt a little embarrassed at how aggressive she'd been. Realizing that she'd been practically humping his lap, she gave him a small smile.

"Damn, woman," Grover breathed out.

"Um...do I need to apologize?" she asked, wrinkling her nose.

"Fuck no," he said immediately.

"Did you put this couch up here so you could have sex on it?" she blurted.

"No. I haven't dated since I've moved in here."

Sierra was unabashedly fishing for information, and she wasn't disappointed in his response.

"I've kinda buried myself in building this barn and getting my house set up the way I wanted it during the last year, to distract myself."

She swallowed hard. "From what?"

"From wondering what I did to make you not want to talk to me," he said with a shrug. Before she could apologize, he went on. "And of course I now know that you weren't purposely blowing me off, but that's what was going on in my head."

Sierra nodded. "I'm thinking I like the privacy you have out here," she said.

"It is pretty private, isn't it?" he agreed.

"Yup. And I imagine when the sun goes down, the view of the stars from here is pretty amazing."

"It is."

Sierra put her hand on his cheek and gave herself a short pep talk. This was Grover. She could tell him anything. He'd more than proved that in the two weeks they'd spent together at The Refuge. If she was going to become the woman she used to be, she needed to go after what she wanted. And she wanted *him*. "This couch was a great idea. It's comfortable as hell and I can picture myself sitting out here a lot, relaxing and watching the world go by."

"Yeah, I've spent many hours out here myself," Grover said with a nod.

"I can think of some other things we can do out here together," she said suggestively, wiggling her hips against him.

"Damn," Grover breathed, clamping his hands on her hips to hold her still. "You're killing me, Bean."

She smiled.

"And don't think I haven't thought about taking you here in the last week and a half. I have. A lot. But not two-point-three minutes after you arrive."

"So...maybe six-point-seven minutes then?" she asked suggestively.

Grover's gaze heated. "I want you," he said simply. "I haven't been able to sleep, thinking about what it'll be—"

"You haven't slept? Have you had more nightmares?" Sierra interrupted.

"No nightmares, just staying awake because I've missed having you next to me," he reassured her. "But my point is that I'm trying to take care of you. Hell, I haven't even gotten you in the house yet."

"I've never had sex outside before. Wait...does this count as outside?" she asked.

"I think this is as close to you being outside without clothes on as I'm comfortable with," Grover said.

His words were turning her on. Big time.

"Who said anything about being naked?"

"Okay, we're done here," Grover said. "You need to stop saying 'naked.' I can't handle it. How about we get up and I show you my house? Then we can eat. You've got to be tired after driving so long today. You probably should've broken the trip up a bit more."

"I wanted to get here too badly."

Grover stood then, easily taking Sierra with him, placing her feet on the boards under them. He guided her to the side of the couch, then leaned down and kissed her forehead. "Stay here a sec while I close the doors."

Sierra nodded and watched carefully as he closed and latched the doors. She wanted to know how to do it herself. She loved thinking about a future here with Grover. Again, intellectually, she knew they were both rushing things, but at the moment she didn't give a damn. For the first time in over a year, she looked forward to what tomorrow would bring. It felt as if she had her whole life in front of her.

Looking at the couch, Sierra could practically see her and Grover lying on it, naked, after having made love. The vision was so vivid, she knew she'd do whatever she could to make it come true sooner rather than later.

Some people might assume she was too traumatized by what had happened to her in Afghanistan to want to be intimate with someone so quickly, but that definitely wasn't the case. Maybe if she hadn't spent the two weeks with Grover at The Refuge, she'd feel differently. But since they'd spent almost every second of the day and night together, their relationship had been fast-forwarded.

They'd talked about things she never would've considered telling any of her past boyfriends, even the ones she'd dated for a few months. They'd been through something so fundamentally life-altering and intense, and that had changed them. Made them more open to each other, perhaps.

Whatever it was, Sierra wasn't afraid of Grover. He could smush her like a bug since he was so much taller and heavier than she was, but she knew with every fiber of her being that he'd die before doing anything to hurt her.

"Hold on to my shoulder as we go down the stairs," he said.

And that just proved her point.

She trusted him. Respected him. Appreciated him. Loved him.

Loved...

As Sierra grasped his large shoulders, she realized she wasn't freaked out by the thought of loving him. It was scary, because she knew more than most women how dangerous Grover's job was. But she wasn't going to be scared to get involved with him because of something that *could* happen. Look what she'd survived. Dating Grover wouldn't be a cake walk, but it'd be a hell of a lot easier than being locked inside a mountain, being used as a punching bag by a bunch of terrorists.

They reached the bottom of the spiral stairs and Grover looked down at her. "Should I be worried about what put that sly smile on your face?"

"Nope," Sierra told him happily, as she hooked her arm in his.

"I like you like this," he said as they headed for the large doors that led into his yard.

"Like what?"

"Happy. Confident."

"Me too," she told him. "Me too."

* * *

Grover was so thrilled Sierra was here, he could barely contain himself. He hadn't planned on making out with her quite so soon after she'd arrived, but sitting on that couch with her, admiring the view, had been so much better than he'd even dreamed. He was relieved she found beauty in the land like he did. He'd been a little worried it would be underwhelming after growing up in the mountains, then after spending time at The Refuge.

They made a detour on their way to his house to her car, so he could grab her suitcase. The compact Subaru Impreza wasn't something he would've picked, but for Sierra, it was a perfect size. He knew she'd been a little nervous about the drive from Colorado to Texas, as it had been so long since she'd been behind the wheel of a car, but she'd picked it back up quickly. Her parents had bought her the car and refused to let her feel guilty about it. She'd told him that she was going to pay them back once she was on her feet financially.

Grover was as proud of his house as he was the barn, and could only hope that Sierra would find it as comfortable and relaxing as he did. He held open the front door and followed behind her. He left her suitcase by the door, planning to grab it later after he'd given her a tour. She put her purse on a side table and walked inside the large, open great room with her head tilted back.

"Wow, the ceiling is amazing!" she said.

Grover nodded. "Yeah, it was one of the things that sold me on the place. I love that they're so high, makes me feel less hemmed in."

Grover stood back and watched as Sierra explored his home. She stopped in front of the huge windows at the back of the room and stared out onto his property for a long moment. The back of the house had a similar view as the barn loft, with a manageable expanse of lawn meeting the tall grass. He hadn't fenced anything in, loving how open and vast the land seemed.

Eventually, Sierra turned away from the view and continued to take in his house. There were two more leather couches in the living area, with a coffee table and a few other small tables strategically placed so no matter where someone sat, they'd have a place to put a drink. He had lamps to warm the space and his favorite recliner was in one corner. When he sat there, he had a view of both the TV and the large windows.

Sierra walked into the kitchen next and lifted the lid of the Crockpot. She turned and smiled at him. "Smells delicious."

"It is. It's my mom's recipe and she'd kill me if I messed it up."

Grover was pretty pleased with his kitchen. He didn't care about having all the fancy appliances the salesperson tried to convince him he needed. He ended up going with stainless steel, but nothing over-the-top. His six-burner gas stove was more than he needed, but because the people who owned the house last had a six-burner stove, it made sense to get the same size rather than have to redo the cabinets.

Sierra peeked into the pantry, then turned around and raised an eyebrow at him.

"I know, I know," he said. "It's big."

"Big? Jeez, Grover, you've got enough stuff in there to last you at least three years. Are you a prepper or what?"

Grover laughed. "No. But I like to be prepared. Since I live out of the city a ways, I sometimes lose power. So I've got enough water, paper towels, toilet paper, pasta, soup, and other dry goods to last through any prolonged loss of power."

"I guess that makes sense."

Grover decided not to tell her about the emergency generator hooked up to the house in case he *did* lose power. It was more common to see generators in the north, where the cold weather knocked out the power more often than down here in Texas, but he liked the sense of safety the generator gave him. The truth was, he *was* kind of a prepper. He always wanted to make sure he had what he needed to provide for himself, his family—if he ever had one—and even his neighbors, if a disaster struck.

After she toured the kitchen, they were on their way down the hall so he could show her the media room he'd once bragged about. She stopped and fingered a lamp sitting on a table near the hall. "Is this handmade?"

"It is," Grover agreed. He hadn't wanted to get into this right now, but since she noticed, he figured he might as well admit to one of his quirks. "It's not just a lamp," he told her. He walked over and pressed a small button near where the lightbulb was screwed in, and one side of the wide, heavy wooden base fell open, revealing a hidden compartment.

Sierra jumped slightly when the lamp opened, then she smiled up at him. "Cool!" Leaning over, she saw the small pistol he'd stored inside the lamp. "Why am I not surprised you've got a gun hidden in your lamp?"

Grover didn't return her smile. "Because I'm Delta. Because I've seen too much shit in this world to not be prepared to protect myself."

Tilting her head, Sierra asked, "Do you have more hidden around here?"

Grover finally allowed himself to relax. "Maybe."

"Oooh, I'm intrigued. Will you show me?"

"Of course. I want you to be able to access a weapon if you need to. I love living out here, but I also know it could put me at risk." He turned and motioned to a large clock on the wall. "There's one in there too."

"In the clock?" Sierra asked, immediately heading across the room. She poked at the clock a little before turning to him. "How does it work?"

"Push on the face...right there near the three."

She did, and the Velcro holding the face securely in place

lifted on the left side, revealing another hidden compartment. He had a Glock in there, and a wicked-looking knife.

Sierra turned to him and her eyes were sparkling. "It's like hide and seek! Where else?"

Relieved that she wasn't accusing him of being paranoid or insane for having so many weapons hidden around his house, Grover pointed to the coffee table.

Going over to it and falling to her knees, Sierra motioned impatiently. "Come on, don't make me wait. Tell me its secret."

"The entire top simply shifts backward. So you can access the compartment without having to disturb whatever you have on top," Grover said. "There's a button on the underside on the right that will release the inner latch. You have to push it down, then back."

After struggling with the button, she finally got the safety released and she slowly moved the top back, revealing a shotgun he'd stored inside. He also had another knife there, and some throwing stars. They looked almost decorative, but were extremely deadly if thrown right.

"I could've just put them in drawers and things, but I didn't want someone to accidentally find them. A safe seemed too obvious, someone could just steal the whole damn thing and break it open later. Also, the last thing I would want is for someone who broke in to be able to use my own weapons against me, or go out and hurt someone else with a gun they stole from me," Grover explained. "When my friends' kids are here, I definitely didn't want them to get their hands on any of my...toys. And of course, if there's ever a time when someone gets into my house without my permission, I'd want to be able to surprise them and protect myself if needed."

"You don't have to justify anything to me," Sierra said. "I think it's smart. And these are cool. I want to see more."

Grover chuckled.

He showed her the bathroom off the great room and the office. He didn't really use the latter much at all, but it had great built-in bookshelves along one wall. When Riley saw it, he could practically see the drool coming out of her mouth. She had an impressive collection of books, and Oz had actually come over to inspect it closer, see how it was built, as he wanted to surprise her by turning one of the rooms in his gigantic house into an office for his wife...complete with floor-to-ceiling bookshelves just like Grover's.

He swung open the door to the theater room and stepped back as Sierra entered. It was cooler than the rest of the house, since there were no windows inside. He'd put a screen on one wall with a projector in the back. He'd also spared no expense with the sound system. He didn't use the room all the time, but it was pretty kick-ass to watch his military movies in here. There were three rows of some of the most comfortable chairs he'd been able to find. They were large enough to fit his frame, and the cushions were extremely...squishy. That was the word Kinley had used when she'd first sat in one.

"Wow!" Sierra exclaimed. "This is impressive."

"Yup. And that huge-ass wooden flag on the wall isn't there just as decoration."

She grinned and practically skipped over to it.

"The star section opens up if you hit the button on top."

Sierra turned and pouted at him, and Grover laughed. She wasn't nearly tall enough to be able to reach the top of the hand-made wooden flag. He walked over and reached for the button over her head. Then he opened the hatch. Another gun sat inside. "And if you flick the switch on the bottom to the side, the bottom half opens...careful," Grover warned as she almost got smacked in the head by the door.

"What's that? A phone?" Sierra asked.

"Yeah, it's actually an entire communications system. Kind of like a CB radio truckers use. There's also two satellite phones that don't rely on cellphone towers to work."

She stared up at him. "You really *are* a prepper, aren't you?"

Grover merely shrugged.

"I'm not saying it's a bad thing, but don't you think this is all a bit...overkill?" she asked.

"Probably," Grover agreed without hesitation. "But you have to understand that my entire adult life has been spent trying to find bad guys or saving people from them. I've learned how sneaky people can be, and how even good people can do bad things when their back is against the wall. I'd much rather be overprepared than underprepared."

"I can understand that," Sierra said, nodding.

"You might have noticed that I've got hiding spots that are low, waist height—at least waist height for me—and up higher. I never know what situation I might find myself in and have prepared for anything."

"Anything else in here?"

"Some of the chairs have hidden compartments under them. They aren't accessible to kids, I made sure of it. Those actually have biometric locks. They're programmed to only open with my fingerprint. Which reminds me, I'll make sure you have access, as well. We can do that after we eat."

"I'm not sure that's necessary," Sierra protested.

Grover struggled to find the words to explain why this was important to him. "I need to know that no matter what happens, you can protect yourself. As much as I want to say I'll always be there when you need me, we both know that's not possible. Shit happens, and if shit happens to *you*, I want you to be able to do what's necessary to keep yourself safe. And me, if I'm incapacitated."

"Okay," she said quietly. "Now, can we stop talking about you being hurt and me having to go all Rambo on someone?"

"Absolutely," Grover said immediately. He didn't want to think about the hundred and one horrible situations running through his mind where Sierra was on her own and needed a weapon to protect herself.

He saw Sierra look around the room once more, then visibly shiver.

"What? What's wrong?"

"It's just...this room kinda reminds me of that cave. No windows, dark, cooler than the rest of the house." She shrugged a little self-consciously. "It's not a big deal."

Grover immediately took her elbow in his hand and led her toward the door. He hadn't really thought much about it before, but she was right. He made a mental note to get a contractor to the house to knock a hole in the wall to make a window. He could put in blackout curtains and still make it useable as a theater, but it was probably safer to have an egress point anyway.

Sierra huffed out a small laugh. "You're totally overthinking something, I can tell."

Grover loved that she was able to read him so well. "Maybe," he admitted.

"The room is great," she told him.

"But it makes you uncomfortable, which is unacceptable. I want no inch of this house to bring back any bad memories for you," he said as they walked back into the great room.

"It's not a big deal," she protested.

"It is to me," Grover said simply. "How about we eat now and I'll show you the rest of the house after?"

Sierra put her hand on his arm and stopped their forward progress toward the kitchen. "Grover?"

"Yeah?"

She stared up at him for a long moment. He couldn't read the emotion he could see in her eyes.

"I'm happy I'm here," she finally said.

"Me too, Bean. Me too. Come on, let's have some dinner. I'm making a huge salad too, just like I said I would. I'll order that pizza I promised you another day."

"Awesome. What can I do to help?"

Grover couldn't keep the smile off his face as they got the salad underway. He loved this. Working with her, showing her where everything was in the kitchen, felt good. Intimate. It was the first of hopefully many, many meals they'd prepare together.

CHAPTER FOURTEEN

Sierra sighed in contentment, just as relaxed now as she'd been during their time in New Mexico. She and Grover were on his back deck. He'd poured her a glass of soda and he was nursing a beer. He'd shown her the rest of his house after they'd eaten, which consisted of four bedrooms on the second floor, another full bathroom, and a gorgeous laundry room. He'd told her it used to be a small fifth bedroom, but he'd converted it to the laundry room because he didn't want to haul his dirty clothes up and down the stairs all the time.

She'd blushed a little when he'd shown her the master bedroom and the amazing bathroom attached, but did her best to act cool and composed. It was hard when all Sierra could picture was Grover standing in the glass-walled shower, butt-ass naked. Or in the walk-in closet getting dressed. Or in the huge king-size, four-poster bed that took up the majority of the room. The bed was old fashioned and nothing like what she'd assumed Grover would sleep in every night.

He explained that it had belonged to his grandparents, and

when they passed away, no one else had been interested in keeping it, so he'd claimed it for himself. Hearing that was just another layer revealed on the man she loved. Every time she learned something new about him, she admired and respected him all the more. Keeping an old bed wasn't exactly something most men would care about, but Grover did.

His entire house was a revelation. It was well thought out and Grover had done an amazing job with the renovations. From the doors he'd saved from the old barn on the property, to the modern touches like the second-floor laundry room, to the over-the-top mancave he'd put together. It all just fit him. And Sierra liked every little thing she'd learned about him simply by touring his space.

"What are you thinking about so hard over there?" Grover asked.

They were sitting in separate chairs, which she thought was probably a good idea considering how with every second she spent around him, she wanted him more and more.

"I like your house," she said simply.

"Me too," he said. "I used to be all right with living in an apartment. It wasn't really a home, it was just a place where I spent time between work, hanging out with my team, and deployments. But I got to a point where I needed a refuge. Somewhere I could completely relax and wind down. My job is stressful, so I wanted a home. I know the Army could move me to a different post at any point, but I'll end up back here eventually. I built this place with permanency in mind. If I'm lucky enough to get married, this is where I want to live with the woman I love."

He looked over at her. "I want to do this. Sit here in the evenings, talk about my day and hear about hers. I want to watch for deer and armadillos. Hang out and relax."

A pang of desire hit Sierra, and it was almost painful in its intensity. She wanted to be that woman. Wanted to sit here, just like this with Grover, years from now.

Without breaking eye contact, she leaned over and put her cup on the ground next to her chair. Then she stood and walked over to Grover. As if it was second nature, she climbed onto his lap, straddling him. She'd done this a few times before, but this time felt different.

Grover put his own drink down and took hold of her hips. His large hands were so warm, she could feel his heat through her clothes. She kept her gaze locked with his and reached for the buttons on his shirt. She undid the top one. Then the next.

"Sierra?" he asked, with a small tilt of his head.

She stilled her hands. The last thing she wanted was to do something he wasn't ready for. She was breathing hard, from both nerves and excitement. For the first time in many, many months, she felt desire. There had been no time for anything but survival when she'd been a captive, but now, back in the States, safe, with Grover...her body was coming alive.

"I want you," she admitted, not recognizing the sound of her husky voice.

His hands came up and grabbed her own. "Are you sure?" he asked gently.

Sierra nodded. "Yes."

"A few weeks ago, you just wanted to be friends. You weren't ready for more. I just want to make sure you really want this before we go any further. I know things changed between us while we were at The Refuge, but I don't want to rush this if you aren't truly ready."

"I know, and I am," she said. "When I told you that, I was scared. Scared of how important you were to me after such a short period of time. I was trying to protect my heart. But after those two weeks in New Mexico, I realized I was fooling myself. And that life is short. I know that better than anyone. You're one of the most amazing men I've ever met. And I'm not just saying that because you did something incredibly selfless and brave. I have a feeling even if we met somewhere completely normal and safe, like a bar or the grocery store, this crazy chemistry would've still been there. You make me feel as if I'm the most important person on the planet. You make me want to be better, to be more. I know I'm not explaining myself very well, but Grover...I wouldn't be here, in Texas, at your house, *in your lap*, if I didn't want more between us."

For a moment after her impassioned speech, he didn't move. He simply stared at her as if trying to read her mind. Then his fingers tightened on hers and he inhaled deeply. His nostrils flared, and she could see the change in his eyes. She had a split second to brace herself before he pounced.

His hands released hers and he leaned in, kissing her hard and deep.

He tasted like beer, and while she wasn't a huge fan of the stuff, on him, it was practically an aphrodisiac. Just like that, Sierra realized he'd been holding back all the other times they'd kissed. He took her mouth almost desperately. One hand went to the back of her head to keep her in place and the other gripped her hip so hard it nearly hurt...in a good way.

Grover lost his impressive control—and it was one of the sexiest things she'd ever experienced. He wasn't holding back, not one iota, and she hadn't realized she needed that. So many people tiptoed around her now, not wanting to upset her or bring back any bad memories from when she was a captive. But it was obvious the only thing on Grover's mind was passion. Not trying to go gentle or treating her like a piece of glass.

It ramped up her desire for him even more.

Her hands came up and resumed unbuttoning his shirt. When she had it open enough, she flattened her palms on his muscular chest and lightly dug her nails into the skin.

Grover groaned into her mouth, but didn't pull back. Squirming in his lap, Sierra could feel her body preparing to take him. Her underwear was soaked and her inner muscles clenched in readiness.

Finding his nipples, Sierra pinched them lightly, then harder when she felt his hips thrust toward her. He tore his mouth from hers and rested back on the cushion behind him. He was breathing hard, as if he'd just run a few miles, and knowing *she'd* done that to him, that she'd been the one to get him to this point merely with kisses and her hands on his chest, made Sierra feel extremely powerful.

This was a gift. *He* was a gift. If someone would've told her two months ago that this was where she'd be, what she'd be doing, how she'd be feeling, she would've thought they were practicing a new form of torture. But here she was. With the man she'd never forgotten. The one she'd dreamed about.

Leaning forward, Sierra kissed the soft, vulnerable skin of his throat, nipping and licking as she went. He didn't move his head, but one of his hands eased under her shirt, caressing the sensitive skin of her lower back. Then her side. Then, ever so slowly, he moved his hand to her breast.

Sierra had always been self-conscious about how small she was. She was petite all over. Before she'd been captured, she was a small B cup, and while she'd been gaining the weight she'd lost, her old bra size was still a bit too big. But the second Grover's fingers played with the lace of one of the cups, Sierra forgot all about being self-conscious. Her nipples hardened, as if begging for this man's touch. She arched her back, pressing herself into him and begging for more without words. And he didn't disappoint.

Grover reached inside her bra and flicked his thumb over her nipple. It was her turn to moan, and she arched her back even more.

"You like that," he growled.

It wasn't a question, and the arrogance in his tone might've annoyed her if it had been any other man. "Yesssss," she hissed.

His lips quirked up in a satisfied grin as he rolled her nipple between his thumb and forefinger. Sierra's hips jerked, and it was her turn to let her head drop back. She couldn't do anything but sit on Grover's lap and enjoy the feelings coursing through her body. The arousal felt strange, almost alien, but oh so delicious.

"So fucking beautiful. Hold on, Bean."

For a second, Sierra didn't know what he was talking about. She *was* holding on to him. Her hands had moved up to curl over his shoulders and she'd inadvertently dug her fingernails into the rock-hard muscles there.

Then he stood, and she tightened her legs around his hips. But he wasn't going to let her fall. One hand went under her ass and the other stayed under her shirt, teasing her nipple. Sierra looked at him and shivered at the lust she saw in his gaze. He walked them to the door and said, "You're gonna have to open it. My hands are full."

Sierra blushed, but couldn't deny she loved that he didn't want to let go of her for even a second. She leaned over and grabbed the door handle, amazed that even as she moved against him, Grover's fingers didn't cease their heart-stopping caress of her breast.

He walked into the house and turned back to the door. "Close and lock it."

Grover was being his usual bossy self, but because he was

making her feel so amazing, Sierra didn't call him on it. She liked that he was still thinking about their safety.

The second she turned the dead bolt, he straightened and headed for the stairs. As he walked, he shoved his hand beneath the bottom of her bra and engulfed her entire breast in his large, calloused hand. Sierra moaned again.

Grover strode into his room and went straight to the bed. He didn't let go of her, just bent over, holding her against him until he had her right where he wanted. Sierra felt her back hit the mattress a second before Grover's head dipped. His hand plumped her breast and he took her nipple into his mouth through her shirt.

"Oh shit, Grover!"

He didn't respond as he ate at her breast as if he were a man starved. Sierra squirmed under him. She needed more.

Tugging at his hair, she managed to get him to lift his head. She wanted this man. More than she could put into words. But she was also nervous about him seeing her without her clothes on. It was a vain thought, but she couldn't help it. "I'm not very big," she apologized.

His pupils were dilated and it seemed to take a second for her words to sink in. His hand tightened on her aroused flesh under her shirt. "You're perfect."

Sierra snorted.

"You don't believe me?" he asked a little harshly.

"Women don't spend millions of dollars on breast implants to impress other women," she said.

"Men like boobs," Grover said matter-of-factly. "It doesn't matter if they're big, small, jiggly, firm, or anything in between. I don't know why we're so obsessed with them, but we are. What matters is the woman they're attached to. And when we care about that woman, we'll swear that whatever her size is, it's perfect. You, Sierra, have the most perfect tits I've ever seen. Any bigger and you'd be top heavy. Besides...I like how sensitive you are." He pinched her nipple once more, and Sierra couldn't help but gasp at the erotic pain coursing through her body.

"See?" he said with a smirk.

Sierra swallowed hard. It was obvious by the erection pushing against her thigh that Grover was aroused. She needed to stop thinking about what she considered her flaws and just go after what she wanted. And what she wanted was this man. Deep inside her, making her feel complete.

In response, Sierra moved her hands between them and grabbed the hem of her T-shirt. Squirming, she managed to get it up and over her head. Grover wasn't much help, not with the firm hold he had on her breast. When she threw her shirt to the side, she arched her back and reached under her to undo the clasp of her bra. With that done, she lay back and looked up at Grover. She was breathing hard and still a little embarrassed, but determined to be an adult about this.

Grover slowly drew her bra away, then stared at her for a long moment. He licked his lips and lowered his head.

The first touch of his tongue to her nipple made Sierra jerk with sensation overload. He didn't tease her either. There were no sensual licks. No, Grover latched onto her nipple and sucked. Hard.

She made an unintelligible sound in the back of her throat and grabbed his arm with one hand, the blanket beneath her with the other. All she could do was hold on as Grover did his best to drive her out of her mind.

After a minute of sweet torture, he lifted his head, his lips making a popping sound as they let go of her nipple. He ran a finger over the hard flesh, now sticking straight up. Even that felt amazing. Small currents seemed to flash down her body, straight to her pussy. She was soaking wet and so damn aroused.

"I love these," Grover said, his voice a full octave deeper.

"Clothes off," Sierra ordered almost breathlessly. She needed to touch him. Needed to feel him on top of her.

To his credit, Grover didn't stop to ask her if she was sure. He didn't even hesitate. He reached for the fastening of her pants.

Sierra brushed his hands away. "*Your* clothes off," she clarified.

In response, Grover smirked down at her. "Only if yours come off too."

"Race ya," she said with a grin.

After spending two weeks solid with him, she learned that Grover was more competitive than anyone she'd ever met. She wasn't ashamed of using that against him. In two seconds, he'd ripped his shirt off and was reaching for the button of his jeans.

The only reason Sierra won the competition for who could get naked fastest was because Grover had to step off the bed to remove his pants and boxer briefs. She was able to simply shove hers down her legs and kick them off, her shirt and bra already off.

Grover hesitated at the side of the bed. His cock was long and thick, and she could see a bead of precome at the tip. As she stared at him, he stroked himself, twisting his wrist when he got to the head. Sierra couldn't help but lick her lips.

Without a word, Grover turned. With his free hand, he wrenched open a drawer in the nightstand next to the bed. He pulled out a box of condoms and struggled to open it with one hand. Sierra could've offered to help, but she was too busy ogling him.

There was no doubt about it, Grover was a beautiful man.

He might not like that adjective, but there really was no other word to describe him. He had muscles everywhere, and when he moved, they rippled under his skin. His belly was flat and it looked to her as if he trimmed his pubic hair, which made her smile.

"What are you smiling about, woman?" he growled as he finally got the box open and pulled out a condom.

"You," she said simply. One hand moved down her body and she lightly stroked herself.

Grover's eyes locked between her legs as he climbed back onto the bed. He straddled her legs, and Sierra jerked when his cock brushed against her bare skin, leaving a smear of precome behind.

Her fingers moved faster on her clit and she spread her legs as far as she could, which wasn't far at all, since his knees were on either side of her thighs. As she played with herself, Grover rolled the condom down his length. Sierra was glad he was prepared. She knew they'd need to have a talk about birth control and their sexual health, especially since she'd been in captivity for so long, but for now, she just needed him. The talk could wait.

She loved how Grover couldn't take his eyes from between her legs. She'd never felt sexier. Never felt as if a man was going to die if he didn't get inside her. But that's what the look on Grover's face was communicating. He bit his lip and his chest heaved. He took hold of his cock and squeezed the base, as if he was seconds away from coming, even before getting inside her.

Reaching out, Grover ran a finger between her pussy lips. She moved her hand but he shook his head. "No, keep touching yourself," he ordered.

Eagerly, Sierra brought her fingers back to her clit. The worst thing in the world was being turned way the hell on, but having a man who was more concerned about getting himself off than making sure she had an orgasm as well. She was glad to know that wasn't going to be an issue with Grover.

"I'm big," he said unnecessarily. "I don't want to hurt you. Make yourself come, make yourself nice and wet for me, Sierra. Then I'll fuck you."

Damn, his words were bossy as hell, but such a turn-on. Sierra flicked her clit faster. Grover gently pushed a finger inside her body as she touched herself, and she tightened her inner muscles around him.

"Damn," Grover said on an exhale.

Sierra grinned.

Her smile faded as he added a second finger and began to slowly thrust in and out of her soaking-wet body.

Then she couldn't think about anything other than chasing the orgasm that was quickly rising within her. She'd masturbated for the first time after being rescued when she'd returned from New Mexico. She'd lain in her bed at her parents' house and fantasized about Grover. She came with visions of him bracing himself over her, smiling down at her tenderly.

But damn if the reality wasn't so much better than her fantasizes. She felt herself getting closer to the edge and moved her fingers even faster over her sensitive bundle of nerves.

"So damn beautiful," Grover rasped.

Sierra tried to widen her legs once more, but moaned in frustration when she couldn't. She felt Grover moving, and the next thing she knew, she was spread eagle. He'd moved between her legs and widened his stance, shoving her thighs wide. She couldn't stop herself from thrusting up against his fingers, which were still lazily pumping in and out of her.

"More," she begged.

"Come for me," he said.

Sierra reached up and gripped his biceps with her free hand as she frantically strummed her clit. Her stomach tightened and her thighs shook when she finally went over the edge.

The second Grover realized she was coming, he removed his fingers from inside her and she felt his cock replace them. He pushed inside her even as she thrust against him, lost in the throes of the monster orgasm that had taken over her body.

She vaguely felt an uncomfortable pinch as she adjusted to Grover's size and girth as he thrust inside. Then he pushed her hand aside and used his thumb to roughly flick her clit.

Sierra shrieked and bucked against him, her already sensitive clit desperate for relief. But of course she couldn't dislodge him, he was too big. Too heavy. His caress flung her over the edge once more. All she could do was hold on as the erotic torture continued.

As she squirmed and thrashed under him, he began to thrust. Hard.

There was no finesse to his movements, Grover's hips pistoned fast, prolonging her ecstasy as he took his own pleasure.

It didn't take long for him to come. His entire body stiffened as he thrust inside her body once more, going deeper than anyone had ever gone before. He held himself still as a deep flush spread up his chest as he moaned loudly and came.

After a few deep breaths, he looked down at her face...then his gaze moved to where they were joined and he began to manipulate her clit once more.

"Grover," she complained weakly, but he ignored her plea.

"Come again," he ordered. "I want to feel it on my cock a second time. I was concentrating too hard on not exploding myself before."

Helpless to do anything other than obey, Sierra felt her body shaking and working itself back up to another orgasm. She'd never come more than once while making love in the past. The next was less intense but no less earth-shattering.

Grover moaned as she tightened around him once more and the lust in his eyes was enough to make Sierra feel absolutely beautiful. And powerful. *She'd* done that. She'd reduced this larger-than-life man to an out-of-control animal.

When he removed his fingers from her clit, she sighed in contentment and a bit of relief. He eased back, and they both moaned at the feel of his cock sliding out of her slick folds. He got up and headed for the bathroom and was back before Sierra could get her bearings. Grover climbed onto the bed, rolled to his back, and dragged Sierra into his arms. She draped practically on top of him, and he pulled one of her legs up so it was on top of his thigh.

And inexplicably...Sierra was tongue-tied.

That had been the best sex of her life, but she was already having second thoughts about initiating it. Especially so soon after arriving in Texas. Should she have gone slower? Made sure Grover really wanted to be in a long-term relationship? If all he wanted was sex, she'd just made things very easy for him.

Just as her anxiety was ramping up, Grover ran a hand over her ass in a gentle caress and said, "That was amazing."

Sierra nodded against him.

"I have to admit that I wasn't prepared for it."

"Um...you had a new box of condoms in the drawer next to the bed," she replied.

"Yeah, but I hadn't truly expected us to be here tonight."

She stiffened. Yeah, she was an idiot. She'd moved too fast.

Grover obviously felt her discomfort because he rolled until she was under him. He got up on his elbows and held her face in his hands. Sierra felt surrounded by him, but not smothered. He kept the bulk of his weight off her but there was no doubt he wanted her complete attention.

"I didn't *expect* it, but that doesn't mean I'm not over-the-moon satisfied," he told her. "For the record, in case there's any lingering doubt, when I invited you to Texas, this is where I wanted us to end up. And when I talked about sharing my house with a woman for the rest of my days, you're the woman I had in mind. I'm not worried about how fast things have moved between us, because I've been thinking about you for over a year. I couldn't get you out of my mind after I met you in the chow hall in Afghanistan, and my feelings about you didn't change even though you'd disappeared. And..." He paused, chuckling slightly. "Well, when you hear the stories about Doc, Oz, Brain, and the others, you'll understand. Moving fast is kind of what we do."

Sierra nodded. "When I decided to move to Texas, this is where I wanted us to end up too," she clarified, echoing his sentiment. "Although maybe jumping you on your back deck on day one wasn't exactly in my plans."

"It was hot as hell," Grover said with a smile, leaning down to kiss her forehead. Then he rolled them until he was on his back once more and she was on top of him again.

"Thank you for not...I'm not sure how to phrase this without sounding like an idiot."

"You couldn't be an idiot if you tried," Grover told her.

Sierra wrinkled her nose and decided just to spit it out. "I appreciate you not treating me as if I'm a piece of glass. You know, asking me a hundred times if I'm sure, or questioning if I'm really ready. I know I've still got some things to work through in regard to my captivity, but I wasn't raped. So my sexuality isn't really one of them."

"I wish I could say that all I was thinking about was how

much I respected you and trusted you to know your own mind, but," he shrugged, "I'm a guy. A man who's wanted you for quite a while now. I'm afraid my brain kind of short-circuited when I finally got my hands on you."

Nothing could've made Sierra feel better. She loved that he'd been as out of his mind with lust as she was. "Same," she said quietly.

"With that said...I have to ask. I didn't hurt you? You're petite and I'm...not."

Sierra smiled. "No. You didn't hurt me. Not even close. I've never...Grover, I came before you got inside me. I was wetter than I've ever been." She knew she was blushing, but was thankful that she wasn't looking at him right that second. "You didn't hurt me," she finished.

"Good," he said, and Sierra could hear the satisfaction and pride in his voice. "I didn't last as long as I wanted. I'll be better next time. Maybe. We do need to talk about your health though."

"I'm clean," she said immediately. "When I went to the doctor, they did tests. I don't think they believed me that I hadn't been sexually assaulted."

"I didn't mean that," Grover told her. "I was talking more about your overall health. Has your period started again? You've gained a healthy amount of weight. What do we need to be on the lookout for as far as your body getting back to its normal routine?"

Sierra snuggled into Grover and his arm tightened around her. This should've been an embarrassing conversation, but somehow, with Grover, it wasn't.

"No period yet, but the doctor says that's normal. It could take up to six months, even with my weight getting back to where it should be."

She felt Grover nod. "That's kind of what I thought. It's probably not smart to introduce a bunch of chemicals and hormones to your body when you're trying to get back to normal. I have no problem using condoms. They aren't one hundred percent effective though. If I need to, I can take more permanent measures to protect you."

Sierra lifted her head at that. "What do you mean?"

"I mean, if it takes me getting a vasectomy to protect you from getting pregnant when your body is still healing, that's what I'll do."

Sierra blinked. "But...that means you won't be able to have kids."

"Who says?"

"Um...*biology?*"

He gave her a small grin. "It's probably too early to be talking about this kind of thing, and we can discuss it at length later, when and if we decide we want to have children, but vasectomies are reversible. Also, I could have some of my sperm frozen if adopting is out of the question for you. There are a ton of kids out there who need homes, and we could always go that route if we decide we want children."

Sierra felt that tickle in the back of her throat once more, but as usual, no tears formed. She couldn't believe he was willing to go to such extremes for her.

"I'm in this for the long haul," he said seriously. "But I'm not willing to risk your health. Getting pregnant right now wouldn't be safe. As good as you look and feel, your body is still healing from the trauma it went through. I'll do whatever it takes to make sure you heal at your pace and without adding any more stress to your body."

Sierra dropped her head and pressed her nose to the warm skin of Grover's neck.

"Bean?"

"I just...that's...I can't ask you to do that, Grover. That's crazy."

"You aren't asking. I'm willingly offering. Look at me, Sierra."

Taking a deep breath, she lifted her head again, meeting his gaze.

"This isn't a fling for me. You've gotten so far under my skin, I don't think I'd survive if you left."

He hadn't gone so far as to say he loved her, but Sierra could see the truth in his eyes. She nodded. "I don't know what I did to deserve you," she finally whispered.

"You survived," Grover said simply. Then he leaned up and kissed her lips, before urging her to lie back down. "We can talk about it later."

Sierra took a deep breath. He was right. She wasn't ready to talk about having children. And while she appreciated him wanting to look out for her, she wasn't sure she wanted him to get a vasectomy either. She thought back to their conversation about children when they were prisoners. She'd told him she liked being unencumbered, and he'd admitted that he enjoyed being around older kids like Logan and Bria. That got her thinking about the number of older children who were in the foster care system.

Maybe his idea wasn't as crazy as it seemed. If, down the line, she wanted to be a mother, adoption was definitely an option.

"Sleep, Bean, we can figure out the details later."

"What time is it?" she asked.

"No clue."

"We need to set an alarm. My stuff is supposed to be delivered tomorrow morning," she told him.

"I'll be up," Grover said with confidence. "My body's been

trained to wake up early every morning. After so many years of PT, it's rare that I can sleep in past seven."

"Okay," Sierra said, yawning huge. She'd seen firsthand that he was a morning person when they'd been in New Mexico. If he said he'd be up, he'd be up.

"And I know I'll sleep well tonight, so I'll *definitely* be up on time," he said.

"I thought you said you were sleeping okay since coming back from The Refuge," Sierra commented.

"I have been. But with you here by my side, in my arms, I'll sleep even better."

Gah! He might claim that he always put his foot in his mouth, but he kept saying the sweetest things. "Same with me," she said quietly.

She felt his lips against the top of her head and realized in a moment of surprise that she'd forgotten all about her hair. She was used to getting a lot of looks, people staring at her since she was practically bald. The hairdresser had evened it all up, but it was growing back so slowly, and Sierra was still self-conscious about it.

But tonight, she hadn't given her hair a single thought. Grover liked her exactly how she was, hair or no hair.

Sighing in contentment, Sierra allowed herself to completely relax. She had no idea where she and Grover might be in a month, a year, five years, but she hoped and prayed that she'd always feel as safe and comfortable with him as she did right this moment.

With the sound of his heart beating under her cheek, Sierra fell into a deep, dreamless sleep, secure in the knowledge that Grover would keep her safe from any bogeymen lurking in the darkness.

CHAPTER FIFTEEN

Grover placed the last box from the moving truck down on the floor of Sierra's new apartment. With Doc, Lucky, and Trigger helping, along with the men who'd driven the truck, it hadn't taken long to get her belongings unloaded.

"Looks like that's the last of it," Lucky said.

"I can't thank you guys enough," Sierra told them. "What can I do to repay you?"

Grover opened his mouth to tell her that they hadn't helped her with the expectation of payment, but Doc responded first.

"You can come over to my place this weekend. Ember is dying to meet you, as are the rest of the girls."

"I'd love that!" Sierra said excitedly.

"Great. How about Sunday? Any time after two or so. We'll grill burgers and stuff, it'll be totally low-key."

"Low-key, riiiight," Trigger said with a chuckle.

The others all laughed too.

Seeing Sierra looking a little confused, Grover said, "Whenever we all get together, it's complete chaos. It's never low-key. Throw in two babies and Logan and Bria, and it's mayhem."

"It sounds…nice," Sierra said with a smile.

"Sorry the other guys couldn't come over and help today," Trigger said. "With that damn militia group still harassing anyone who comes and goes from the post, we've been tasked with extra security duty."

"It's okay, you guys were really all I needed. I don't have a ton of stuff, as you can tell," Sierra said. "Is the Strong Foot Militia dangerous?"

It was an abrupt change of topic, but Grover could see the worry in Sierra's eyes.

"They're mostly annoying," Trigger told her. "Trying to get soldiers and family members to engage with them when they're in line waiting to enter the post. They aren't breaking any laws, since they stay on public property, but they've scared enough people that the post commander has assigned the extra duty to be safe rather than sorry."

Sierra nodded. "What are they mad at, specifically?"

"What *aren't* they mad at?" Lucky countered. "They're anti-government and think the military is the root of all evil. They think anyone who's working for the government is the enemy."

"So, what do they hope to accomplish by harassing everyone who goes in and out of the base? It's not like you guys can just quit…right?" Sierra asked.

"Right," Grover said. "Many of the men who're harassing people going on and off post are young. They look like they're in their late teens or early twenties. I think they're just bored and have kinda banded together in a sort of mob mentality. There's safety in numbers, and for now, what they're doing is fun for them."

"There's one guy who's older," Trigger noted. "He kind of

stands at the back of the mob and lets the others do most of the harassing. That guy who's five-ten or so, with a beard and longish hair?"

"That's right. I've seen him. Do we know anything about him?" Lucky asked.

"No. But maybe it would be a good idea to see what kind of information we can dig up. If he's the group's leader, and we can take him out of the equation, maybe the men who are with him will slink back to San Angelo or wherever they came from," Trigger mused.

"It's worth a shot," Grover agreed. "Chop off the head and the snake dies." He looked over at Sierra after he'd finished speaking...and grinned at the expression on her face.

"That's gross," she said.

"But appropriate," Lucky said. "You need us to help you with anything else?"

Sierra looked around at the boxes stacked up here and there in the small apartment. "No, I'm good. Thank you again so much for helping."

"It's what we do," Lucky reassured her.

"We'll see you this weekend," Doc reminded her.

Sierra smiled. "I'm looking forward to it."

"Don't be surprised if the party gets brought up in your group chat," Trigger warned. "The girls like to organize what everyone's bringing. You know, like who's got the desserts and alcohol."

Lucky laughed. "Remember that one time when no one coordinated and all we had was meat and chocolate?"

"If I remember correctly, no one was too upset," Grover threw in. "We all ate the meat and the girls stuffed themselves with the desserts."

Sierra giggled.

Trigger gave her a chin lift, and Lucky and Doc did the same before the three of them headed out of the apartment.

"So, where do you want to start?" Grover asked her.

"Don't you have to go back to work?" Sierra asked.

"Nope. My commander gave me the rest of the day off. He's gotten used to us needing the time off to move our girlfriends in. I think we should start with putting your bed together. You'll need someplace to sleep."

Sierra raised an eyebrow at him.

Grover chuckled. "And no, I wasn't trying to proposition you, although...that's not a bad idea."

She laughed. "You're such a guy."

"Yup," he agreed and stalked over to her.

Sierra backed up as he got closer until she hit the wall behind her.

Grover put his hands on either side of her head and leaned in. "And I'd like to point out that I wasn't the one who went there first, *you* did. I simply made an innocent comment about putting your bed together, you were the one who had to make it sexual."

Her hands rested on his sides, and Grover mildly resented the fact that his uniform top was tucked into his waistband so her hands couldn't slide up and under his shirt.

"Do you blame me? After this morning?"

Grover smiled. He'd woken up early, as usual, and hadn't been able to resist going down on her. Waking her up with his mouth between her legs had been sensual and so damn hot, he'd almost forgotten to put on a condom before sliding inside her.

"It's just that you're irresistible," he said. "It's not my fault."

"Right, not your fault," she teased. "Your tongue just *accidentally* landed between my legs and your dick somehow magically got lodged deep inside me."

Grover burst out laughing. Man, he loved this woman. He dipped his head and nuzzled the sensitive skin near her ear. He'd found out this morning how much she liked being touched and licked there.

"You aren't playing fair," she grumbled, still tipping her head to the side, giving him nonverbal approval to continue.

Grover moved his hands to her waist and did his best not to pull her shirt up and over her head. He really did want to get her bed set up. Everything else could probably wait, but she needed a place to sleep. Thinking about her being here without him wasn't a comfortable thought, but he pushed it to the back of his mind. She wanted, and needed, to be independent. He'd survived thirty-three years of his life without her, he could handle a night or two here and there. He hoped.

His teasing quickly turned into a long make-out session. Despite his good intentions, a hand did end up under her shirt, and the other between her legs. He made her come right there against her wall, and it was sexy as hell. He didn't have a lot of room to maneuver his hand down her pants so it was a challenge to stimulate her, but he didn't do so badly, if the way she undulated against him and moaned was any indication.

After she'd come, he pulled his fingers out of her waistband and licked them clean. The blush on Sierra's face was something he'd never get tired of seeing.

"I can't believe you just did that," she said.

"You shouldn't be so damn tempting," he countered.

"So that was also my fault?" she asked.

"Yup," Grover said with no remorse.

The look of determination on her face gave her away, and he managed to catch her hand before she could grab his cock. "Uh-uh," he said. "We need to get your furniture set up." Grover glanced at his watch. "And it's getting late. I need to feed you."

She harrumphed. "But what about...that?" She motioned to his cock with her head.

"It can wait. That was for you." Grover reached for her hand but she shook her head and sidestepped him.

"I'm not a prude, but you're gonna need to wash that hand before we do anything else."

Grover chuckled. "Right. Why don't you go on into the bedroom and figure out where you want to set up your bed, and I'll be there in a second."

"Okay. Grover?"

"Yeah, Bean?"

"I'm happy."

Two words. That was all it took to make Grover feel content and satisfied. "I'm glad. Me too."

They smiled at each other before Sierra turned and headed for the bedroom. Grover went into the kitchen to wash his hands, thinking about how much his life had changed in such a short period of time. When he'd gone to Afghanistan, he had no plan in mind, but once he realized his best bet to find out what happened to Sierra was to get himself taken captive, he didn't think twice. And he'd do it again a thousand times over if it meant hearing Sierra say she was happy.

He was lucky, and he knew it. The outcome of his capture could've been bad. But Sierra had been worth the uncertainty and pain he'd experienced. Seeing her flourish, laugh, blush, and smile was worth any amount of hardship he'd gone through. Sierra was free. And she was his. She still had a ways to go to get back to normal, whatever that looked like for her, but she'd get there. He had no doubt about that.

* * *

Sierra lay in Grover's bed that night and wondered how she'd gotten there. She'd had every intention of staying in her new apartment. The last thing she wanted was to overstay her welcome at Grover's house. But after they'd put her bed together, Grover convinced her to let him help her unpack a few things. They then rearranged some furniture before returning to his house for lunch. That had led to a quiet relaxing day today before Grover fed her again.

He'd made them orange-glazed pork chops, then talked her into watching the sunset from the loft. Somehow, they'd lost track of time as they talked on the leather couch out in the barn, and the next thing she knew, she was yawning and couldn't keep her eyes open.

Grover had convinced her it would be too dangerous for her to drive back to her apartment when she was as tired as she was. Not to mention the fact that she'd forgotten to unpack her sheets, and she had no idea which box they were in anyway. Since her suitcase was still at Grover's house, it seemed a no-brainer for her to stay.

The moment they'd crawled under the covers, they couldn't keep their hands off each other, and before she knew it, she was naked and straddling Grover's lap. She'd ridden him long and hard, loving being on top. He obviously loved it too, if his moans and the way he couldn't take his eyes off her body were any indication.

Sierra thought back to what she'd said to Grover earlier that day, about being happy. She'd forgotten what true contentment and joy felt like. While in captivity, her entire focus was on surviving each day and not going out of her mind from loneliness. The experience had an odd way of making time stop, until the months of joylessness had felt like years.

She still had a lot to figure out, namely what she was going to do for a living. But she had an amazing boyfriend who cared about her well-being, a group of women who'd embraced her wholeheartedly without even having met her, a roof over her head—even if she hadn't slept there yet—and food to eat. She was unbelievably fortunate. Even with everything that had happened to her, she wasn't capable of feeling bitter. How could she be, with Grover at her side?

Snuggling closer, she smiled when his hand tightened in hers. She was on her side next to him, her legs drawn up, and they were holding hands. They'd slept like this every night while at The Refuge, and it was even more intimate now that they'd made love.

"Sleep, Bean," Grover said sleepily.

Sierra kissed his bare shoulder and nodded. "You too."

"I will now that you're here."

Knowing that Grover seemed to need her as much as she needed him was a heady feeling. He'd finally admitted earlier this evening that he *did* have a few nightmares after New Mexico, when she was back with her parents and he was here. She hated that he still felt guilty about her captivity, and suspected she'd never fully be able to make him feel otherwise. It was just the kind of man he was.

Closing her eyes in contentment, Sierra slept.

* * *

Cory Holliday cleaned his gun almost by rote. He'd been able to disassemble and reassemble any kind of weapon in under ten seconds by the time he was eight. His dad had made sure of that.

Many people would say that Cory had a tough childhood, but he didn't really see it that way.

His father had been in the Marines, had given his all to his country...and then he'd been kicked out without a second thought. Dishonorably discharged. For some bullshit charge that the government had never even been able to prove. When he'd come home, he was no longer the proud man Cory remembered. He was bitter, angry, and vengeful.

After his dad was sent home in disgrace, the goal for the remainder of his life was to show the world how corrupt and abusive the military *really* was. He'd passed his hatred on to Cory. Teaching his only son to hate the government as much as he did.

If his father was still alive today, Cory knew he'd be proud of him. Proud to stand by his side, to participate in what he had planned for the brainwashed soldiers stationed at Fort Hood, and everyone who lived and worked in the area.

Cory was more than ready to move on to the next part of his plan. The Strong Foot Militia had been in Killeen for a few weeks. There were several dozen of them who'd made the journey, taking turns picketing outside the main gate of Fort Hood. Cory loved seeing the discomfort and even fear on the faces of soldiers, contractors, and family members as they entered and left the Army post.

While the main group was camped just outside the city, Cory had handpicked ten of his youngest, loyal, ardent followers for a more important mission. The actual reason they were in Killeen in the first place.

The eleven of them were holed up in an abandoned house at the moment, which had gotten very old. They'd scared the closest neighbors bad enough that no one would dare call the cops. But this place wouldn't make the kind of impact they needed. No—they needed a larger house. A fancier one, preferably occupied.

One that would make everyone cringe in horror when it blew up.

And they needed bait.

Cory knew it wasn't as simple as just taking over some random person's house. No, they needed a reason for the reporters to show up. For the *military* to take notice and do their best to take it back. Cory and his group could egg them on, force their hand. Make them use deadly force to end the siege. Just like they'd done in Waco. The country had been horrified at the government's actions during that siege, and Cory wanted a repeat of the event.

He was ready to die for the cause. As would his followers. In return for their sacrifice, he needed to make sure the country was watching. Seeing firsthand how out-of-control their government had gotten. Everyone needed to witness their murder— then, and only then, would the citizens of this great country finally have the blinders ripped from their eyes. They'd rise up against the tyranny they'd been living under without even knowing.

But again...they needed bait. A highly decorated and respected soldier to dangle in front of the military community. Dare them to try to rescue one of their evil own.

Cory had been watching and waiting for the right person as they picketed outside the gates of hell, otherwise known as Fort Hood. It needed to be someone with a high-enough rank that the brass would care about losing. A private or someone else equally expendable wouldn't do. He and the others had been following soldiers home for days now, and they'd yet to find a house that would work for their plan. They were all too small, in crowded neighborhoods. Too crowded for Cory and his men to control the situation effectively.

They just needed to be patient. Eventually they'd find the perfect soldier. Maybe someone with a family. Kids always ramped up everyone's emotions.

"Pass me another joint," Adam called out.

Cory sat in the back of the room, continuing to clean his rifle, simply an observer as Sam, Cameron, Rob, Adam, and Zeke smoked pot.

Brody, Alan, Tony, Luis, and Kevin were on duty at the moment. Standing outside the Army post, mingling with other Strong Foot members, harassing anyone who went in or out. If they could gain more followers with their protests, great. But newcomers wouldn't be involved in the master plan, nor would the rest of their group. The dozens of members who'd come to join the protest...but couldn't be trusted to carry out Cory's will.

The ten chosen men were from their home base of San Angelo. They were all young, several were high school dropouts, and most were easily managed with the promise of free drugs. Even *they* didn't know his ultimate plan, but they didn't have to. They were true followers. They'd do what he said, simply because he said it.

Putting his rifle on the floor, Cory grabbed the small bag of pot beside him and walked over, handing it to Adam.

"Thanks, man."

Cory nodded and walked back to his spot against the wall. He picked up his rifle once more, continuing his methodical work. Once they found their mark, they'd go to the storage unit he'd rented a couple months ago and collect the rest of their arsenal. The RPG and other weaponry would show the US Military that they were serious—and force them to fight back with the same strength.

Smiling, Cory sat back and closed his eyes. Soon. All his hard work would come to fruition, and his father would be avenged. They just needed to step up their game and find the perfect place and bait. Then the fun would begin.

CHAPTER SIXTEEN

"If you get overwhelmed, just let me know and we'll leave," Grover said.

Sierra smiled over at him. It was Sunday, and they were on their way to Lucky's house for a get-together. The original plan was to meet at Doc's, but as the ladies worked out the details on their group chat, the venue had changed to Lucky's place.

"I will." She didn't bother to say that she'd be fine, they both knew that might not be the case. As much as she enjoyed being around others, she'd learned in Colorado that it was more difficult than she'd thought it would be. Her therapist had reassured her being in large groups would get easier, but for now she was taking things one day at a time.

Even though she'd planned on going back to her apartment Saturday night, she'd fallen asleep on Grover's couch instead. They'd gone to her apartment early in the day and unpacked more of her boxes, but she'd eventually wanted some fresh air. She and Grover went back to his property, and she'd helped him with some yard work, using the riding lawnmower—which was a new experience for her—while he used the weed eater.

Grover had made them another amazing dinner and then turned on *Cheer* on Netflix, something he claimed he'd never watch on his own, but he thought she might enjoy it. Sierra didn't know when she'd fallen asleep, but was vaguely aware of being carried up the stairs and cuddling into Grover's side. It wasn't until waking this morning that she realized she'd once again stayed the night at the farmhouse instead of her own place.

And Trigger had been right. Gillian had initiated a long day of texts in their group chat, about what time everyone was planning to arrive, what everyone might want to bring. It felt nice to be included. She hadn't participated in the conversation much, but she'd loved hearing the *ding* each time a new text came through.

Grover parked his Jeep Grand Cherokee along the road, as Lucky's driveway was already full with the cars of his teammates.

"Shoot, are we the last to arrive?" Sierra asked. "I thought the others planned on getting here around four. It's only three-thirty."

Grover shut off the engine and turned to look at her. "They're sneaky," he said simply.

Sierra eyed him warily. "They planned to get here first? Why?"

"Probably because they love any excuse for a party," Grover said. "Come on, let's go see what's up."

Sierra climbed out of the car and grabbed the bag that held the cookies she'd baked that morning, with Grover's help. He took the bag from her and held her hand as they walked up to the sidewalk to the house.

"I love my friends, but I know they can be overwhelming.

Especially when we're all together. When it was just us guys, we could have a laid-back gathering where we all sat around and shot the shit. But now that everyone's married and there are kids in the mix...our small group of seven has become eighteen, including you. And if Brain and Aspen invited their ninety-something-year-old neighbor, and her granddaughter and grandson-in-law, it'll be even more. I'm serious when I tell you if you need to go, we'll go."

Sierra couldn't deny that she was nervous to hang out with that many people, but these weren't just random strangers. They were Grover's best friends. And all the women had been so kind to her over the last month, she was more than ready to meet them in person. "Thanks," she told him. "I'll see how things go. And the same goes for you. If you get overwhelmed, I'm more than happy to go back to your house and chill."

Grover leaned down and Sierra tilted her head up to meet him halfway. He kissed her hard, then pulled back and gazed at her. She couldn't read his expression, but after a moment, he simply nodded and said, "Let's do this."

He didn't knock on the door, just reached for the knob and walked inside the smallish house.

Sierra caught a glimpse of people everywhere before they were noticed.

"They're here!" a blonde woman called out.

Grover and Sierra were immediately surrounded by women, all talking at the same time.

"It's so good to meet you in person!"

"You're so tiny!"

"You look really good, Sierra!"

"Thank God you're here!"

"How's the apartment?"

Everyone was speaking at once, and Sierra couldn't help but

laugh a little. "I'm here," she agreed. "Do you all always talk at once?"

Trigger came over and hooked an arm around the blonde, who Sierra assumed was his wife, Gillian. "They're a little jazzed. They've worked hard to keep this a surprise for you."

He gestured behind him, and Sierra saw a homemade paper sign strung along the wall in the dining area. It said, WELCOME HOME, SIERRA.

"We figured it had a dual meaning," Gillian said. "Welcome back to the United States, and hopefully to your new home here in Killeen with us."

That damn tickle in the back of her throat was back. Sierra smiled at everyone. "Thank you."

"Come on," said a woman only a couple inches taller than Sierra, gesturing toward a sliding glass door. "The kids are playing out back, and we've set up a seating area for us to hang out. The guys put up two canopies so we can all sit in the shade and not have to be jammed under the deck as they grill stuff."

"She might want to chill inside for a second, Kinley," another woman said.

"How about we all introduce ourselves before we do anything else?" Ember added.

Sierra knew it was Ember because...duh...huge celebrity. She was as beautiful as she was in her pictures on the internet. Her skin was smooth and flawless. Her curly black hair barely held under control by a scrunchie at the nape of her neck. She wasn't wearing any makeup, but Sierra decided she liked how she looked better this way, relaxed and casual, rather than all decked out, as she was in her social media pictures.

"I'm Ember," the dark-skinned woman said.

"I know," Sierra responded somewhat shyly. "I can't thank

you enough for the apartment. Seriously. As soon as I figure out what to do with my life, I'll pay you back."

Ember waved her hand in the air and shrugged. "Whatever. It's just been sitting there empty, so I'm glad you can use it. And I'm hoping after you see my gym, you'll decide to help me out."

"Not so fast!" Devyn complained. Sierra knew who she was, too, since Grover had pictures of his family all over his house. "She might decide she wants to come work part-time with me at the vet clinic."

Sierra frowned. "But I don't know anything about animals."

"We always need receptionists," Devyn said, seemingly unconcerned.

"I'm Gillian, and *I'd* love help with my events, if you're interested in that sort of thing."

Grover held up a hand. "Easy, ladies. First off...Sierra, this is Gillian, Ember, Devyn, Kinley, Aspen, and Riley." He pointed to each woman as he introduced them, and Sierra decided it was a good thing she already knew who three of them were, otherwise she had a feeling it would be a long time before she kept them all straight.

"And secondly, I'm sure Sierra is happy to hang out with you guys and see what you do for a living, but she's not just up for grabs, as you all seem to think she is," Grover said wryly.

Sierra smiled up at him. "It's okay."

"No, he's right," Kinley said with a smile. "We're all acting like a pack of jackals ready to pounce on the newest member of the tribe. We're just very glad you're here and all right. And of course, we want to help you get settled in. If you ever need anything, all you have to do is ask."

"Absolutely," Riley said with a wide smile. She was holding a baby on her chest and Sierra couldn't help but notice how content and happy she looked.

Aspen nodded. "You're always welcome to do a ride-along with me in the ambulance, but it's not the most exciting job... until it is."

"What does that even mean?" Devyn asked with a frown.

"Just that it can be super boring, until we get a call for an unconscious person who needs CPR. Then it gets exciting really fast," Aspen explained.

"All right, you ladies need to move this party out of the foyer," Brain grumbled. He was holding his and Aspen's son in a baby carrier on his chest—and the sight of the man with an infant in his arms, after Sierra had seen him killing terrorists, was a bit startling.

He must've noticed her staring, because Brain winked at her and said, "Anytime you want to hold this monster, just let me know."

"He's not a monster!" Aspen protested. She turned to Sierra. "He just wants what he wants as soon as he wants it," she explained. "And can get a bit loud about it."

Everyone chuckled, indicating they were well aware of the baby's quirks.

She loved that. How everyone knew each other so well, and how comfortable they all were together. Even the talking over each other didn't bother her. It was...homey.

Grover leaned down and kissed her temple. "I'll bring a drink out to you. Any preferences?"

"A water?" she asked.

"You got it."

"Come on, we've got a *lot* to talk about," Gillian said with a huge smile.

If she'd been anywhere but here, with the men who'd literally saved her life, Sierra might've been a bit reticent to leave Grover's side. But even though she'd just met these women for the first time, she *knew* them. She'd been talking to them in texts for a month. They were exuberant and friendly and funny, and because she knew each and every one of them had been through their own kind of hell, she felt an instant kinship.

"I'll take the bag out with me," she told Grover, holding out her hand. "I have a feeling we might need sustenance."

"Tell me there's something sweet in there," Kinley begged.

"Mint chocolate chip cookies," Sierra told her.

"Oh yeah, you'll fit in just fine," Riley said with a smile.

"Hey! Is she here?" a boy called out as he ran into the house.

"Yes, Logan, Sierra is here," Oz told his nephew.

Sierra glanced at a boy who had the same brown hair and gray eyes as his uncle. He was also surprisingly tall for an eleven-year-old. "Hi," she said.

Logan studied her for a long moment, then he stepped toward her and lifted his hand. Before Sierra realized what he was going to do, Logan had run his hand lightly over the hair on the side of her head.

Oz moved at the same time Grover did. Sierra felt Grover's arm go around her waist and pull her backward, as Oz took hold of Logan's wrist and gently pulled his hand away.

"What? What'd I do?" Logan asked, looking up at Oz in confusion.

"It's not polite to touch people without their permission. Remember that bully in your class, and that little girl he touched?" Riley asked.

"But...I just wanted to touch her hair. Not her *boobs*." The last word was whispered as if Logan thought it was a naughty word.

"It's okay," Sierra said, feeling awful at how sad Logan looked.

"It's not," Oz said firmly.

"I've never seen a girl with a shaved head before. It's cool!"

Sierra breathed out a relieved sigh. It wasn't that she needed the little boy's approval, but she didn't want to have to try to explain why her hair was so short.

"We'll talk about it later," Riley said. "Go on back outside and check on Bria. Okay?"

"Okay. I'm sorry if I hurt your feelings," Logan said.

Sierra smiled and nodded at him, then he turned and ran back outside.

"I'm so sorry," Oz said.

"It's okay."

"People used to do that to my sisters all the time," Doc said. "They had the coolest braids and afro, and strangers used to come up to them and without a word, touch their hair. I never understood why white people felt it was all right to fondle Black people's hair without permission."

"It happens to me sometimes too," Ember agreed.

"It's a little weird," Sierra admitted. "I'd never go up to anyone and run my hands over their hair without permission. And I'm sure if I did that to a kid, their parents would probably go ape shit. But the difference is, I'm an adult who's fully aware that consent is important. I don't think Logan was considering that, and he didn't mean anything by it."

Ember smiled. "And he was right about one thing...your hair is pretty cool."

Sierra wanted to roll her eyes. She wasn't so sure about that, but it was nice to hear.

"You should leave it short," Riley agreed.

"I'm thinking about it," Sierra said.

"All right. Out, ladies. You can talk about hair and makeup without us men around," Trigger grumbled.

Everyone laughed.

"You sure you're okay?" Grover asked as everyone headed for the backyard.

Looking up at him, Sierra nodded.

"Thanks for not making him feel worse than he already did," Oz said, interrupting them.

"I'd never do that. He's a curious kid."

"Still, I'll make sure he understands why it was rude," Oz reassured her.

"It's really all right," Sierra insisted. "He wasn't the first and he won't be the last."

"He will be if I have anything to say about it," Grover mumbled.

Sierra shook her head at him. "Down, boy," she scolded.

Oz barked out a laugh and winked at her. "Love seeing someone put Grover in his place," he said before heading for the yard himself.

"On second thought," Sierra told Grover, "I'm thinking I might need a glass of wine or something."

"You got it," he answered. "For the record...you fit in perfectly with this motley crew. Just so you know."

"I like them. They're...real."

As soon as the words left her mouth, she realized that was absolutely true. No one seemed to be pretending to be glad to see her. They were affectionate and genuine, saying silly things and joking around with her and everyone else. She didn't feel as if she had to be careful about what she said back.

Ever since she'd gotten home from overseas, she'd felt a need to watch what she said, desperate not to make anyone else uncomfortable. She definitely hadn't trusted anyone enough in her hometown to say what she *really* felt about everything that happened to her, outside of her parents. She'd put on a brave, happy face and largely said only what she thought others wanted to hear. It was exhausting...another thing she'd realized right at that moment.

This group of people would never judge her for anything she might say or do. Sierra felt it down to her bones. She could truly relax and enjoy their company.

"They're real, all right," Grover said with a bit of exasperation. "Pains in the ass sometimes, is what they are," he mock grumbled. "Will you save me a cookie?" he asked.

Sierra smiled up at him. "Yes."

"You say that now, but wait until you see everyone fall on them as if they haven't eaten for months. Especially Bria—you have to watch her. She'll charm you out of half a dozen if you let her."

Sierra giggled. "I'll watch out for her."

As Grover continued to stare, Sierra recognized *that* look. She licked her lips and did her best to keep herself from pushing him back into a closet or bathroom and having her wicked way with him. The desire slammed into her out of nowhere, but she didn't feel bad about it for a second, since she saw the same need in his own expression.

"Girl time," he said almost desperately. "Go on, or they'll think I'm in here making out with you or something. Not that they haven't done the same thing with their men."

Sierra chuckled. She could totally see the others sneaking off to be with their husbands. That was another thing she'd already noted, that no one was afraid to show their significant other how much they were loved. Going up on her tiptoes, Sierra initiated a kiss.

Grover didn't hesitate, meeting her halfway.

"I'm happy," Sierra told him once more. She hadn't missed how his face had gone soft when she'd said those words the other night. If that was all it took to make him look content and satisfied, then she'd say it every day for the rest of their lives.

"Me too. Now scoot. Go forth and bond with our tribe."

Sierra was still smiling as she made her way to the door. The second she opened it and stepped outside, a little girl yelled, "Cookies!" and made a beeline for her.

All Sierra could do was keep on grinning as she was accosted by the cookie monster she'd just been warned about.

* * *

Grover was sitting with Sierra on his lap when Trigger's phone rang. He stiffened, as did the other men around him. Riley, Oz, Aspen, and Brain had all gone home already with their kids, as it was past their bedtimes. There was no reason to think that someone calling Trigger was related to their job, but they'd all been conditioned to think the worst when they got phone calls outside their normal working hours.

"Trigger," his teammate said as he answered.

He was quiet for a long moment as he listened to whoever was on the other end of the line. Then he said, "I understand, Sir. We'll be there first thing in the morning. Yes, Sir. See you then." He hung up.

Grover braced for whatever his team leader was about to say.

"That was Commander Robinson," Trigger said. "We're on permanent front gate duty until the damn Strong Foot Militia decides to move on."

"Can't they kick them out or something?" Gillian asked.

"They aren't breaking any laws. They're on public property," Lefty answered.

"But they're harassing people," Devyn grumbled. "That has to be against the law."

"It's a fine line," Doc said. "And I'm guessing no one wants to rile this particular group. They've got connections to other militia groups in Texas, and the last thing anyone wants is for Fort Hood to become the epicenter of a massive gathering."

"So you guys have to what, guard the gates?" Sierra asked.

"Pretty much, yeah. We've done so occasionally since this started. But the post commander wants to reassure the contractors, civilians, and military personnel that they're safe coming in and out of the gates," Trigger explained.

"It's not a big deal," Grover said, trying to soothe Sierra and the other women.

"Yeah, and think of it this way, with us on permanent gate duty for the foreseeable future, that means we won't be deployed," Doc said with a smile.

"Ooooh, really? That's great," Ember said. "You can help me with the mini fencing match we're having next weekend then."

Doc mock groaned, and Ember smacked him in the arm.

Everyone laughed, and Grover felt Sierra relax against him once more. She'd straightened when Trigger had started speaking into his phone. He ran his hand down her arm and intertwined his fingers with hers. It was amazing how something so small made him feel so much better.

"What'd you think of The Refuge?" Doc asked Sierra.

"It was amazing. So beautiful and peaceful. The guys who run it have literally thought of everything. The food was as good as any five-star restaurant, but nowhere near as fancy. And we could do as much or as little as we wanted while we were there. The therapist who we visited was also really good. She put me at ease immediately, and even in the group sessions, I didn't feel as if anyone was in a competition to see whose experiences were the worst...if that makes sense."

"It does," Doc agreed.

"How were the cabins? Were they rustic or modern?" Gillian asked.

"Ours were modern. But they also had some that were more sparse. Honestly, they have something for everyone. Oh! And Melba the cow was a highlight!" Sierra said excitedly.

"They had a cow?" Kinley asked.

"Yup. And goats. And a dog and cats. We got into a routine of going to see them after breakfast each day. I miss Melba."

"Well, Grover *does* have a barn," Lucky said with a chuckle.

"Yes! Please, Fred! You need a cow or two! And maybe some of those fainting goats. Oh! And some chickens!" his sister said.

"No," Grover said as firmly as he could, despite knowing he could totally be talked into getting farm animals if Sierra asked.

Devyn pouted, and Grover merely rolled his eyes at her.

He felt Sierra chuckling in his lap and was glad she wasn't the one who'd been lobbying for a ton of farm animals. He wouldn't be able to say no to her. But his sister, he could definitely refuse.

After a bit more ribbing, talk turned to other things. Ember enthusiastically spoke about the increase in enrollment at her gym and how happy she was that she and her parents were talking again. They'd had a tough go of it for a while, after Ember had decided to change her lifestyle completely and move to Texas.

Devyn talked about a few of the cases at the vet clinic, and Kinley went into a long tirade about how inconsiderate some people were. As an executive assistant, she was in charge of her boss's schedule, and it seemed a lot of people weren't very nice when they had to go through her to talk to her boss.

As Gillian told them the details of an upcoming party she was planning, Grover leaned down to Sierra. "You good?" he asked. He'd been checking in on her every hour or so, wanting to be sure she wasn't staying to be polite. It was more than obvious to him, and hopefully to Sierra, that the other women genuinely enjoyed her company. If she wanted or needed to leave, no one would think badly of her.

"Yeah," she said. She was sitting sideways on his lap, resting her head on his shoulder. Despite her reply, she sighed heavily.

"You're tired," Grover said.

"A little."

"We're gonna get going," Grover announced when there was a lull in the conversation.

"Yeah, it's getting late," Trigger agreed.

"We still working out in the morning?" Doc asked their team leader. "I'm only asking because I'm not sure what time our shifts at the front gate will be starting."

"Yeah," Trigger said. "At least for tomorrow. I'll get with Commander Robinson and see what our rotations will be. But he didn't say anything about coming in early, so we're business as usual until we find out otherwise."

"Are we running or doing the obstacle course?" Ember asked.

"I know you were cleared by your doctor, but I still don't think it's a good idea for you to be doing the obstacles," Doc told her.

"Running," Trigger said, ending any argument between the lovers before it could start.

"Cool. I've missed it, and I know I'm out of shape," Ember said.

Kinley leaned forward and mock whispered to Sierra, "She's a little crazy. She actually *likes* working out."

Sierra laughed. "Well, I guess there's a reason she's an Olympian and we aren't."

"Very true," Kinley replied with a smile.

"Come on, guys, working out isn't so bad," Ember cajoled.

"Whatever. I'll stick with my doughnuts and sleeping in,"

Gillian said.

"Oooh, doughnuts," Sierra said. "My favorite."

"We can stop on the way home," Grover told her immediately.

Devyn giggled.

"What?" Grover asked.

"She's got you wrapped around her little finger," his sister told him.

"Yup," Grover said without feeling the least bit embarrassed about it.

"We don't need to stop," Sierra insisted.

"You want doughnuts, you'll get doughnuts," he said easily.

"Great, now *I* want some too," Kinley complained.

"If you come to The Modern Kid to help me out tomorrow, I'll make sure to have lots of snacks in the break room," Ember tempted.

"Make sure you get her to specify what *kind* of snacks," Devyn warned. "She's likely to have all healthy stuff."

Grover smiled, listening to the banter between the women. It was as if everyone had been friends for years rather than the relatively short time it actually had been. They'd truly clicked, and he was so grateful Sierra had been included.

"Fine. I promise to have some cinnamon rolls just for you," Ember told Sierra.

"I already said I'd come and help, you don't have to bribe me...but for the record, cinnamon rolls are my favorite," Sierra told her.

"Noted. The first class starts at ten, since school is out. Come by anytime. Nick and I can certainly use your help."

"I'll be there."

"Great."

"On that note," Grover said. "We really do need to get

going."

He stood with Sierra in his arms and placed her feet on the ground. The others decided now was as good a time as any for them to leave too, and everyone headed through the house for the front door.

It took a bit for everyone to say goodbye to each other, and even that made Grover smile. Once they were on their way, he headed toward his house.

It wasn't until he was bumping along his driveway that he realized he probably should've taken Sierra back to her own apartment. He hadn't even thought about where he was going.

After pulling into his garage, he turned to Sierra, ready to apologize and offer to drive her to her place.

He needn't have worried about her being upset—she was sound asleep. Her head was resting at an awkward angle, her body being held up by the seat belt around her chest.

She'd been excited when they'd stopped briefly at the doughnut place, taking her time deciding which of the sweet confections she wanted. But obviously she'd been more tired than she was willing to admit, because sometime between the doughnut shop and now, she'd crashed.

Grover got out and walked around to her side of the car. He undid her seat belt and carefully lifted her.

She stirred. "Are we home?"

"Yeah, Bean, we are."

"Okay." Then she rested her head on his shoulder and tightened her hold around him.

Her trust meant the world to Grover. Not to mention, he freaking loved that she called his house "home." Though, she might not know they were at his house. She could think she was at her apartment, but he suspected otherwise.

Grover carried her upstairs and gingerly placed her on his

bed, smiling as she immediately turned onto her side and curled into a ball. He removed her shoes, then went downstairs to the garage and grabbed the doughnuts and checked all the locks on the doors. He went back up to his room and, after changing for bed, stood next it, just watching Sierra sleep for a long moment. He'd left the bathroom light on in case she woke up in the middle of the night. He thought about getting her up to change clothes, but decided she'd be okay wearing her jeans and blouse for one night.

He carefully climbed into the other side of the bed, doing his best not to jostle her. But she semi-woke anyway.

"Grover?"

"Yeah, it's me."

"I had a good time tonight."

"Me too."

"You were worth waiting for."

Grover stilled at her words. If she meant what he *thought* she meant, he wasn't sure he could take it.

"I wouldn't have minded staying in that cave another year if it meant I'd end up here."

God. She *had* meant what he thought.

He couldn't hold the words back any longer. "I love you," he said in a low, gruff tone.

She sighed and shifted even closer to him.

Grover realized that she was still mostly asleep. That she probably had no idea what she'd said...or how he'd responded. But that was all right. He hadn't wanted to freak her out by saying "I love you" too soon; there was no doubt it *was* pretty early in their relationship for that. Still...Grover knew.

He reached for her hand and curled his fingers around hers, feeling more settled than he ever had before. Closing his eyes, he slept.

CHAPTER SEVENTEEN

Grover was in a good mood. He'd been woken up in the middle of the night by Sierra kneeling between his legs. She'd had his cock out and her mouth around him before he'd truly understood what was happening. Then all he could do was hang on and do his best not to explode too early. When he'd reached his limit, he'd thrown her backward, stripped her naked, and taken her hard and fast.

He'd left her sleeping while he got up to go to the post to do PT with his team, and when he'd returned, they'd had a not-so-nutritious breakfast of doughnuts and coffee. Grover couldn't remember when he'd laughed as much as he had that morning. The more time he spent around Sierra, the more he *wanted* to spend with her.

There were times in the last few days when he could tell she was thinking about what had happened to her, but then she'd shake off her demons and concentrate on the here and now. She was remarkable, and while he loved her resilient spirit, he also suspected he'd need to keep an eye on her to make sure she was dealing with whatever feelings came up about her captivity.

As he pulled up to The Modern Gym around nine that morning, after letting Trigger know he'd be a bit late coming into work, he had to remind himself that he'd see Sierra that evening. She said she'd have Ember drop her off at his house when they were done at the gym.

"Have a good day. And don't be afraid to tell Ember if you need a break," he told her.

"She's like the Energizer Bunny, isn't she?" Sierra asked.

"Pretty much. Doc had the hardest time making her take it easy after she was shot."

Sierra shook her head. "I still can't believe all that happened to her. Or, for that matter, that I'm about to hang out with *the* Ember Maxwell for the day."

Grover smiled. It had taken some getting used to for him too. "Have a good time. And remember, if this isn't fun, you don't have to make any promises to keep coming by."

"I know."

He reached out and put a hand on the back of her neck and gently pulled her toward him. He kissed her long and deep before pulling back a fraction. He stared into her eyes for a moment, struggling not to blurt out how much he cared about her.

Sierra lifted a hand and put it on the side of his face. "Be careful today. Those protestors sound like they're real assholes."

He chuckled and nodded. "They are. But they aren't anything we can't handle. Especially not after being deployed and facing some of the worst terrorists the world has to offer."

She smiled. "That's right. My big bad boyfriend."

"And don't you forget it," he teased.

She leaned forward, kissed him once more, then turned and

climbed out of his Cherokee. Grover waited until she disappeared inside the gym before driving out of the parking lot and
heading for the post.

When he neared the gate, he realized why their commander
had assigned extra security. There were at least two dozen men
from the Strong Foot Militia outside the gate, and for such a
relatively small group, they were being extra loud and antago-
nistic today. They approached every vehicle on the road leading
to the gate, yelling at the occupants as they waited to enter.

They clearly knew that while they were allowed to say whatever they wanted, even if people didn't agree with them, they
weren't able to truly threaten anyone or incite violence. Still,
that didn't mean their shouting wasn't offensive or fear-inducing.

"Stop being sheep!"

"The military is killing innocents overseas!"

"Think for yourself!"

"Big brother is watching!"

"Watch your back!"

Grover clenched his teeth together. Hard. The line to get
onto base was moving slowly this time of morning, and he had
no choice but to sit there and listen to the jackasses harass
everyone as he waited to show his ID.

A man came up to his Jeep, stood right outside his window
and began to heckle him.

"Hey, look! Here's a baby killer!"

Before Grover could blink, two more men had joined him.
One was quite a bit older than the others. The man he and his
group suspected might be the leader of the group. The one who
normally hung back and egged on the others, rather than engage
military staff and contractors. He looked to be in his forties or
fifties, his average height and frame covered from head to toe in
well-worn, dirty camouflage. His beard was scraggly and he

looked unkempt—but it was the cunning in the man's eyes that told Grover he was someone to be wary of, unlike the young men around him.

"Hey, soldier man, if your bosses told you to bend over and kiss their asses, you'd do it, wouldn't you?" one of the boys asked.

"Of course he would," another young man answered. "He has to, otherwise he'll get in trouble."

"That's right, they're like sheep, doing whatever they're told without thinking."

"He can't think, he's dumb as a box of rocks!"

Grover wasn't offended in the least by their petty taunts. He also wasn't surprised to learn they had no clue what they were talking about.

"He's doing what he's been programmed to do," the older man said. "Obey. He kills law-abiding men who are just trying to live their lives, and when our government calls them terrorists, he blindly agrees without trying to see what's right in front of his face."

His window was down only about three inches, but it was enough for him to hear the militia members clearly, and for them to hear him. He wanted to reply. Tell them they were idiots, but he knew better than to engage. It would only encourage them.

"Hey, Cory, look at all the pretty decorations on his uniform. He's probably killed *tons* of innocents."

"How does it feel knowing you're helping a corrupt government oppress not only its own citizens, but other innocents as well?" Cory, the older man, asked.

Any mellowness he'd felt after a great morning with Sierra was quickly disappearing.

The wind blew through the open window, and Grover could smell the stench of pot coming from the men. He shook his head in disgust. "What's your problem?" he asked, breaking his own rule about not engaging. He kept his voice calm though, not letting one iota of the anger he was feeling toward these men and what they stood for sound in his tone. "You're upset because there are thousands of men and women who are proud of the country they live in, and are actively doing their part to keep everyone who lives here safe?"

"Safe?" Cory spat. "Right. The government threatens to send in the National Guard to take us out when all we want is to bring attention to the fact that our constitutional rights are being obliterated."

"You can't have it both ways," Grover reasoned mildly. "You can't talk about constitutional rights in one breath and disparage the government in the next. They go hand in hand."

The man flushed a deep, angry red. "No, they don't!" Cory insisted. "We're being oppressed, and you're too stupid to see it. Open your eyes, man! The military can kill whoever they want, *whenever* they want, with no repercussions. *You're* a murderer. You go to other countries, where people believe differently than we do, and someone points a finger and says 'kill him'—and you do it! No one throws you in jail. No, they give you medals and say 'good job!' It's *disgraceful*. And one of these days, the people of this country are going to sit up and take notice. They're going to put their foot down and say enough is enough!"

Grover realized the man might be unbalanced. The fact he was riled so easily was a clue. On the outside, he looked normal enough, but if he truly believed Grover—or anyone in the military—could kill at will, he was delusional.

"You're wrong," he replied simply.

"I'm *not*! Mark my words, when the government and military don't get their way, they pull out their guns and do their best to destroy anyone who dares go against them!"

The cars in front of him began to move, and Grover had

never been so relieved. He made a mental note to not let Sierra come onto post until these men had decided they'd had enough and left. The very last thing he wanted to do was expose her to this crap. Besides, she'd probably lose her shit and go off on the protesters. And if anyone made even the smallest move to hurt her, he'd have to react, and he'd probably get in trouble as a result.

Yeah, it was best to keep her away from them altogether.

"I feel sorry for you," he said with a shrug.

Cory glared at him and flushed even darker, while the other two men sputtered indignantly, probably trying to come up with a good comeback.

"Big brother is watching!" one of the them called out as Grover pulled forward.

"Save your soul and get away from the oppressors!" the other shouted.

Grover shook his head. The group had no idea what they were even protesting. They sounded like spoiled brats, pissed at anyone telling them what they could and couldn't do.

When he got to the gate, the young military policeman apologized for the wait and for the harassment from the protestors.

"It's not your fault."

"The good news is that we'll have some additional manpower here at the gate, starting this afternoon," the MP said.

Grover nodded. "Yeah, I'll be one of the ones tasked to offer extra security."

"Oh, great. I guess I'll see you later then."

Grover looked in his rearview mirror as he pulled past the gates and saw the men standing around, still heckling anyone who drove by. At first he'd just thought the group was merely a nuisance, but after experiencing their vitriol firsthand...and meeting Cory...he had a feeling they were more dangerous than he'd realized.

* * *

Cory watched as the Jeep Cherokee drove through the military gates and memorized the man's license plate number. "That's him," he said out loud.

"That's who?" Luis asked.

"That's the guy who'll help us make our point," Cory said.

"Him? He seems...big."

He was. Which made him perfect. He was a senior enlisted soldier, and when Luis had pointed out all the medals on his chest, Cory knew he had to be someone important. They needed to find out where he lived. At this point, it didn't even matter if he lived in an apartment. Maybe that would be better, anyway. More people to displace. To disturb.

Cory had wanted an out-of-the-way venue; something hard to sneak up on, with wide spaces they could easily monitor, similar to the compound of the Waco incident. Now he realized that the building didn't matter half as much as choosing the right person.

Most of the soldiers who passed through the gates did their best to ignore them. The women and children were downright afraid. But this man looked *pissed*. As if he wanted to jump out of his fancy car and beat them to death.

This was the kind of soldier the government coveted. The strong ones who were used as muscle. If Cory could incite the military to try to rescue an important man, someone they desperately wanted to protect, his point would be made all the more clear.

He turned away from the young assholes he was having a

harder and harder time stomaching and pulled out his phone. He dialed the number of a friend back in San Angelo who worked for the Department of Motor Vehicles. Strong Foot had plenty of members who'd infiltrated various government agencies. They needed to keep an eye out, find out what their oppressors had up their sleeves, and what better way to do that than to work for them?

Smiling when his friend answered, Cory looked down the road where the man had disappeared. Yeah, he would be perfect...even better if he had a family and children who could be exploited.

* * *

Sierra stood in Grover's kitchen, smiling like a crazy person as she prepared a simple dinner of baked chicken. Doing something so...ordinary...felt like a gift. When she arrived in Colorado at her parents' house, they'd done all the cooking for her. And again at The Refuge, she hadn't had to prepare any food beyond simple sandwiches. She'd eaten fast food on her way down to Texas, and even since arriving, Grover had prepared most of their meals.

This was the first time she'd made a meal from start to finish all by herself since she was freed, and it felt surprisingly liberating. It was silly, it was just baked chicken, not a huge gourmet offering, but it was one more step toward gaining everything that was taken from her. In getting her independence back.

She was well aware of the fact that she hadn't spent even one night in her apartment yet, contradicting her own goal. She'd been so adamant about having her own place, standing on her own two feet. Despite that, she was more than content to be here with Grover. He made her feel normal. As if she wasn't Sierra Clarkson, former POW.

Then there was the sex...

She never thought she could enjoy sex so much. And she had no doubt it was because it was with Grover, and not anyone else. They connected on a cellular level. She didn't feel awkward when she was with him. After that first time, she hadn't felt self-conscious about her body, her hair, or anything else.

When Sierra heard the sound of the door opening, she turned to greet Grover as he entered from the garage. The cheerful welcome died in her throat when she saw the look on her man's face.

He wasn't happy. Not in the least.

She hurried around the counter to meet him. "What's wrong? Are you all right? Is everyone else all right? Shit, where's my phone? I haven't checked it for a while." Sierra was looking around, trying to remember where she'd left the darn thing, when she felt Grover's arms close around her from behind.

"Everyone's fine," he reassured her, resting his chin on her shoulder.

Sierra knew the position couldn't be all that comfortable for him, so she turned in his embrace. "Talk to me," she begged.

"It's that damn militia. They're...annoying."

Sierra blinked. "Annoying? I realize I don't know you all that well, but I think after spending two weeks with you in New Mexico, I learned enough to know that you wouldn't be this upset with someone who was just *annoying*."

"You're right. They're fucking assholes who get off on scaring people and spouting utter bullshit. They're domestic terrorists who are doing their best to spread fear and hate—and it makes my blood boil."

Well...all right then. This reaction fit the man she'd gotten to know much better. Sierra flattened her hands on his chest and rubbed gently. "What happened?"

Grover sighed, and Sierra could tell he was trying to get his ire under control. "Nothing they haven't been doing for the last couple weeks," he said. "But this time I got a front-row seat to five hours straight of them harassing anyone who came in or out of the gates. They're offensive, and they don't even realize they have no idea what the hell they're talking about. They're making stuff up and twisting the truth to fit their own warped agenda—or their *leader's* agenda, most likely. And it's impossible to tell what they're really trying to accomplish. I have no idea what they hope to get out of their protests in the first place. It's not like the Army is going to shut down the base or anything. I don't like not knowing what they might be planning...it makes me nervous."

Sierra wasn't sure what to do to help him. "I'm sorry."

Once more, Grover sighed, then he closed his eyes. When he opened them again, he seemed to have gotten himself under control. At least a little. "No, I'm sorry. I'm being a downer."

"Grover, you don't have to always be upbeat and happy. That's not how relationships work. When you're upset, I'll do what I can to cheer you up, and when I'm not happy, you'll do the same. Now, tell me what I can do to make you feel better."

More of the angst bled out of his eyes as he looked down at her. "You're doing it. You're here. And something smells really good."

Sierra shrugged. "It's only chicken."

"Do you know when the last time I walked in here and had dinner waiting for me was?"

"No."

"Never," he said succinctly. "Thank you for cooking for us. How was your day?"

"Good. Why don't you go up and change. Maybe take a shower. It'll help. I mean, I know that a nice long shower has helped *me* when I've gotten overwhelmed recently. Maybe it's because I went so long without that luxury, but something about standing under hot water seems to clear my head. It might do the same for you."

"Sounds good. Then I want to hear all about your day with Ember at the gym," he said.

"Deal. Do you want green beans or corn with your chicken?"

"Beans. There's garlic bread in the freezer too."

Sierra smiled up at him. "Okay. I'll get everything ready while you change."

Grover lowered his head and rested his forehead against hers. "Thanks for being here, Bean."

"Of course. Are you sure I'm not overstaying my welcome? I mean, I *do* have a perfectly good apartment I can stay at."

"No!" he barked, lifting his head.

Sierra blinked.

"Sorry," he said with a small shake of his head. "I didn't mean to be so...loud. And if you want to go stay at the apartment, I'll pout, but I won't stop you."

"I feel weird because I made such a stink about wanting to be independent, to stand on my own two feet. And now here I am, happily shacking up with you every night. I haven't even unpacked all my stuff."

"You *are* standing on your own two feet," Grover protested. "Cut yourself some slack. You're figuring out what you want to do next, you're making friends, and getting on with your life. Where does it say in the "what to do after escaping captivity" manual that you have to be by yourself while you figure everything out?"

Sierra wrinkled her nose. "I just don't want you to think I'm using you in any way."

"I don't. Maybe I'm using *you*," Grover said. "I mean, you did make dinner tonight. And I hear the washer going. I'm assuming you didn't just put your stuff in there."

"Whatever," Sierra told him, rolling her eyes.

"Damn, I love that."

"What? Me being obnoxious?"

Grover laughed. "If that was you being obnoxious, then I've got an easy sixty years ahead of me."

Sierra blinked again, then smiled, charmed by the fact he thought about them being together so far in the future. Neither of them knew what tomorrow would bring, never mind sixty years from now, but she felt all gooey inside thinking about him wanting to be with her forever.

"Thank you, Bean."

"For what?" she asked.

"When I walked in here, I was in a piss-poor mood. Have been all day. That militia group really got to me. But now I'm laughing and thinking about us being ninety years old and still teasing each other. And it's because of you. So thank you for being here, for just being you."

"You're welcome," she replied softly. "Go shower and change. Dinner'll be ready when you get back down here."

Grover leaned down and kissed her once more. "I'm thinking tonight we need to look at the stars from the couch in the loft out in the barn."

Sierra could see the lust in his eyes, and just like that, her nipples got hard. Make love with Grover in the fresh air of his loft? She was totally up for that. "Sounds good," she said as nonchalantly as she could.

Grover grinned mischievously as he backed toward the stairs. "I'm happy, Bean," he told her as he went.

"That's my line," she complained, but returned his smile.

"Yup." That was all he said before he turned around and headed up the stairs, taking them two at a time.

Sierra stared after him for a beat, then returned to the kitchen to finish their dinner. She thought back to what she'd told Grover last night. That if she knew she'd end up here, happier than she could've ever thought possible, she would've gladly spent twice as much time in that mountain prison cell. She hadn't lied. Being with him was worth any sacrifice. Everything wouldn't always be sunshine and roses, but for now, she was going to hold on to her happiness with both hands. She knew better than anyone how quickly life could change.

She renewed her vow to live for the moment, and hopefully she'd have years and years of "moments" with Grover.

Starting tonight, with a new memory...making love to the man she treasured under the stars.

Knowing she was once again smiling like a crazy person, and not caring, she reached into the pantry for a couple cans of green beans. As she heard the water turn on in the upstairs shower, Sierra couldn't help but close her eyes for a moment in gratitude. And for the first time, she understood a little of what Grover must have felt when he'd received her lost letter.

She'd do *anything* to keep this life. Even if it meant putting herself in danger. She'd do her part to keep this relationship happy and healthy.

CHAPTER EIGHTEEN

Four days later, Grover was struggling to keep his bad mood from affecting his relationship with Sierra. He was well aware she didn't want him to keep things from her, but the assholes in the Strong Foot Militia were pressing on his last nerve. It was as if they'd locked onto him, going out of their way to be especially nasty when he was on duty at the front gate.

Even Doc had noticed, commenting on how maybe he should talk to the commander and see if he could be excused from the extra shift.

But Grover didn't want to do that. Didn't want to leave his teammates to do the dirty work while he stayed back in the office. So he was sucking it up and doing his best to ignore the jibes and jeers they often yelled his way while he was helping at the front gate.

That meant by the time he got home in the afternoons, he wasn't in a good mood. He hated being this way around Sierra. He did his best to be happy for her each day when she recounted the time she spent with the other women, but it was difficult.

And it wasn't as if she'd missed the fact that, just over a week into her move to Texas, Grover wasn't one hundred percent present in their relationship.

They were currently lying in bed, and she'd just gotten done telling him all about her day spent with Riley and the kids. They'd gone to one of Logan's baseball games, and he'd caught a flyball that had turned the tide for his team. They'd won eight to seven, and Logan had been extremely proud of himself, once again telling everyone who would listen that he was going to be a professional baseball player, an outfielder just like his idol, Shin-Soo Choo.

Grover had been nodding and smiling in what he thought were all the right places, but when Sierra lifted a leg and straddled his stomach to stare down at him, he knew he'd probably spaced on whatever it was she'd been saying.

"I hate seeing you like this," she said softly.

"I hate *being* like this," he admitted.

"Can't the cops kick them out or something? It seems ridiculous that they're still here after all this time. Still scaring people and yelling stupid shit."

Grover shouldn't have been surprised she knew exactly what was bothering him. "Technically, they aren't doing anything illegal."

"Harassment isn't illegal?" she huffed.

"They're very careful not to cross a line that would get them in actual trouble," he told her.

Sierra lay down, flattening herself on his chest. She nuzzled the skin on the side of his neck as she mumbled, "Well, I hate them for how they're making you feel. I know that not all soldiers are as honorable as you and your team, but painting everyone with a broad 'all soldiers are killers' brush just pisses me off."

Not surprisingly, her compassion and understanding made Grover feel better. "Thanks, Bean."

She nodded, and Grover sighed. They lay like that for several minutes, before she wiggled a bit and slid off him to lie at his side once again. One leg was still thrown over his, with an arm stretched across his chest.

"Hummm, I like this position," she said drowsily.

Grover huffed out a laugh. "Me too, but in about two-point-three seconds, you'll need some space."

"True," she said with a small chuckle of her own. "As long as you don't let go of my hand, I'm good."

And she was. Grover had no idea how other couples slept, but he didn't really care. They'd forged a bond back in those mountain cells, holding hands through the bars even though they couldn't see each other.

Sierra fell asleep shortly after, and just like he'd predicted, she shifted off him, onto her side with her knees tucked up. But he kept hold of her hand, and she settled quickly.

Staring up at the ceiling in the dark, Grover felt restless. Things with Sierra were good. Better than good. She was settling quickly into life here in Killeen, and he couldn't be more thrilled. His friends were all happy and healthy, as was his sister. He should be content and ecstatic that he'd found someone he wanted to spend the rest of his life with.

But deep down, the situation with the Strong Foot Militia nagged at him. Something just wasn't right. They'd been protesting too long. Not that there was a timeline on how long someone should or could rally, but everything about this seemingly pointless protest seemed...wrong.

There also seemed to be two distinct groups. The men who were older and marching around with signs. They seemed almost bored. Then there was the younger group, usually accompanied by Cory, the man Grover was now almost certain was in charge. They looked like they were barely out of high school and sounded as if they were parroting someone else's words, not what they truly felt.

They also seemed...on edge. Unlike the other protestors. As if the young men were looking forward to something.

Commander Robinson had done some digging and learned that the older man was named Cory Holliday. He had a record, but only for a few minor offenses. Drug possession and trespassing. He was born in Wyoming, and his father had been kicked out of the Marines for insubordination. There were really few details on him other than that.

The team had talked, assuming the father had passed his hatred of the military on to his son, and all these years later, Cory was still mired in that hatred.

Because the Strong Foot Militia consisted of Americans, the Deltas—and the military in general—had to tread carefully. The last thing they wanted was to cause a bigger incident. But Grover didn't like the look in Cory's eyes. He was planning something, he felt it in his gut, but until the group actually acted on whatever it was they had in mind, his hands were tied.

Grover had no doubt the group was armed, they were just smart enough not to openly carry while they were protesting. It was the uncertainty that was eating at him. He and his fellow Deltas relied on information to form a plan of action. Without intel, he felt decidedly at a disadvantage. And since the group had seemed to take an extreme interest in him, Grover was even more uneasy.

Thank God he was only working a half day tomorrow. Trigger had seen how stressed he'd been, with Cory doing his best to antagonize him, and had scheduled Grover for the Saturday morning shift. Since they had no upcoming missions for the foreseeable future, he was then free to leave early.

Sierra was going to be working with Gillian tomorrow, helping her with a fiftieth anniversary party. He wanted to do something special for her to make up for his mood this week. Make a fancy dinner, then maybe they'd sit outside on his deck and watch the sunset. It didn't really matter what they did, as long as he got to spend time with her.

She needed to head over to her apartment and grab some more clothes too. Grover knew he should feel guilty that she still hadn't spent even one night there, but he didn't. He could've volunteered to stay at the apartment with her, but he preferred his house.

Glancing over at his nightstand, he could just see the outline of the tissue holder sitting there. He hadn't shown that hiding place to Sierra. The entire top lifted up, concealing another weapon.

He knew all his guns were overkill, but he'd rather be safe than sorry, especially now that he had something precious to protect.

Grover squeezed Sierra's hand involuntarily, and she stirred next to him.

"Grover?"

"Sorry, everything's fine. Go back to sleep," he said quietly.

"Mmm, kay."

When she'd settled again, Grover took a deep breath. He needed to stop seeing problems where there weren't any. Several therapists he'd seen over the years had told him that he was overly protective. Of his family, his team, his house. It wasn't anything he didn't already know. But he'd rather be overprotective than not prepared.

He leaned over and kissed Sierra on the forehead before lying back. "Love you, Bean," he whispered.

To his surprise, she said, "Love you too."

Smiling, Grover could only shake his head. One day soon, one of them would get the courage to say those words when they were fully awake, in the light of day. But for now, he'd hold her words close to his heart. He was a damn lucky man. He had great friends, family, and now a woman who loved him. Everything would be all right. Life was good.

* * *

Cory stood in front of his chosen members of the Strong Foot Militia, the ones he'd handpicked to help him demonstrate the increasingly alarming control of the government.

"It's time," he told the others. "Tomorrow, we take action. We know where our target lives, and we were led to him for a reason. His house is perfect. It's isolated, and the government won't hesitate to take action, to show the world how far they'll go to protect their secrets."

"Cool!"

"This is gonna be fun!"

"We'll only be in jail for a little bit, right?" Kevin asked. "My little sister turns ten in two weeks and I promised her I'd be home for her party."

Cory kept the sneer off his face...barely. These punks had no idea what they were in for. They thought they were going to follow the soldier home, harass him a bit, get the newspapers to show up, then make a big show out of being arrested. Little did they know the mission they were about to embark on was so much bigger.

They'd all be household names for years to come. They

would be written about in history books. They were going to make the ultimate sacrifice. Just like David Koresh and his followers.

When their fellow Americans saw how out of control the military had become, how they were willing to use deadly force on their own citizens to shut them up, they'd open their eyes. They'd stop blindly supporting a corrupt government. They'd stop paying taxes and funding murderous missions.

"Don't worry," Cory told Kevin and the others. "Tomorrow, Americans are going to understand how badly they've been duped by their leaders. They'll no longer thank military members for their service. They'll see how wrong they've been, how the very people they're thanking are nothing but murderers. The wool will be removed from their eyes once and for all. And they'll have us, the Strong Foot Militia, to thank for it."

"I don't understand how taking over one guy's house is gonna do all that," Tony muttered.

Cory was moving before Tony had finished speaking. He punched the kid square in the face, sending him flying backward. The joint he'd been smoking flew out of his hand and landed on some old newspapers in the corner of the room. Zeke and Cameron quickly snuffed out the fire so it didn't burn the abandoned house down around them.

"You aren't here to *think*," Cory snarled. "I've been a part of Strong Foot since before you were born. You don't question me, understand?"

"Yes, Cory," Tony said quickly.

Cory glared at the others. "Any other cowards want to speak up? Maybe you're too scared to do the right thing tomorrow. Maybe you're just little boys who can't handle standing up for your country. Is that it?"

Everyone shook their heads.

"Either you're with me, and our great nation, or you're against me. So which is it?"

"We're with you," all ten men said at the same time.

"Damn straight you are. And tomorrow we'll show the world that the Strong Foot Militia isn't to be messed with. No more signs. No more words. We'll use the weapons we brought and that we've acquired since we've been here. If the military thinks they're the only ones with firepower, they're gonna find out how wrong they are. Right?"

"Right!"

"Damn straight!"

"Hell yeah!"

"Can't wait to finally get to shoot!"

"We gonna get to use the RPG?" Brody asked.

Cory smiled at the young blond. He was only seventeen, but he showed the most promise out of everyone he'd handpicked for this mission. He had a hatred in his heart that matched Cory's. The military had fucked over *his* dad, as well, and he was willing to do anything necessary to get payback. He almost regretted that the kid would mostly likely die, but his death would fuel his two brothers to follow in his footsteps for sure.

Everything Cory did was for the greater good, and Brody dying at the hands of their own government would surely make others like them around the country rise up in retaliation.

"Oh yeah," Cory told Brody. "We're definitely going to use the rocket-propelled grenade tomorrow."

Brody smiled huge. "Awesome."

"So, here's the plan..." Cory began, explaining everyone's role in the next day's activities. "Any questions?"

Everyone shook their heads, and Cory turned and rummaged in his bag, pulling out a fresh bag of weed he'd bought that morning and holding it up.

Everyone cheered. It had been a while since they'd had some really primo pot. As everyone got to work rolling joints, Cory sat back and watched with a satisfied smile on his face. It was the least he could do for the boys. After all, some were going to die for the cause, even if they didn't know it. He might as well let them have some fun.

Tomorrow would be the start of a brand new world...just not for all of them.

CHAPTER NINETEEN

"You see the younger guys?" Grover asked no one in particular the next morning as they stood at their positions near the front gate.

There were the usual few dozen men standing with their signs and heckling those arriving and leaving the post, but Cory —and the younger men who were always at his side—weren't anywhere to be seen.

"No clue," Doc said.

"Something isn't right," Grover muttered.

"You feel it too?" Brain asked.

Grover nodded. The men who were there that morning were merely going through the motions. They weren't as energetic as the younger group, nowhere near as vocal as they were when Cory was with them.

"I'm gonna enjoy the break from their blabbering," Lucky said with a disgusted snort. "Maybe if we're lucky, they're thinking about moving on."

"We can only hope," Brain agreed.

The morning went by fairly smoothly, and Grover was glad when just before lunchtime, they were relieved by Trigger, Lefty, and Oz.

"Any trouble?" Trigger asked.

"Nope. The protestors who showed up this morning were pretty subdued," Lucky said.

"Thank God," Lefty replied. "I'm sick to death of this shit."

"Same," Doc agreed.

"Grover?" Trigger asked.

"Yeah?"

"Try to relax this afternoon. You've seemed really tense the last few days."

Grover nodded. "I will."

"And tell Sierra hi for us. Gillian was really thankful she could help her out today, especially since one of her assistants is home sick."

"I will," Grover promised, before heading for Doc's Durango. He'd driven them all up to the front gate, and he'd take them back to the office before they went their separate ways.

Within ten minutes, Grover was headed back toward the gate in his own vehicle. He waved at Trigger and the others as he passed, glaring at the men who were still holding their signs and harassing people.

He drove straight to the grocery store and headed inside to get everything he needed to make a decadent steak and lobster dinner for Sierra. He still wanted to get them that pizza he talked about while they were in Afghanistan, but for tonight, he wanted to spoil her with surf and turf. After getting the ingredients for a fresh salad, he headed toward the back of the store. There was a fairly long line at the butcher's section, and Grover waited impatiently for his turn. He went by the ice cream freezers on his way to the check-out and grabbed some of the double dark chocolate caramel ice cream bars Sierra liked so much.

Thinking about the upcoming evening made the tension in Grover ease a bit. He was looking forward to some quiet time with Sierra and trying to put some of the tension of the last week behind him.

He felt his phone vibrate briefly on his hip but ignored it since he was driving. If it was an emergency, whoever was texting him would've actually called instead.

It was a warm day, like usual, but Grover knew storms were in the forecast for later. He'd never been afraid of tornados, but now that Sierra was living with him, he decided he needed to look into getting an emergency shelter put in. He had plenty of room on his property to bury a storm shelter. Better safe than sorry.

He was lost in his thoughts about the possibility of tornados, and where he and Sierra would go in case one blew through, as he drove down his long driveway. The sight of his house and barn went a long way toward making him feel even more relaxed.

Until Sierra had practically moved in, he'd considered the place his refuge, but still just a house. She'd made it something even more special. A home.

Grover pushed the button to open the garage door and pulled inside. Glancing down, he reached for his phone to read the text that he'd received while driving.

Before he could unlock his phone, his door was wrenched open and something hard was pressed against the side of his head.

"Don't move, soldier boy, or I'll put this bullet through your skull."

Grover froze.

Fuck.

He saw several of the young men he recognized from the militia swarm around the front of his car. Each and every one of them was armed to the teeth, holding semiautomatic weapons and with rifles slung over their shoulders.

Grover now understood why they hadn't been protesting outside the gates of the post that morning. They were here, waiting to ambush him.

Carefully, so as not to alarm Cory, whose voice he recognized, Grover raised his arms, showing the militia leader that he was unarmed.

"Step out. Slowly," Cory growled.

Itching to take the asshole out, Grover complied. He had no doubt he could take Cory down, but with the amount of fire-power the others had, they'd kill him before he could deal with them. If his team was here, things would be different—but he was on his own.

Until he found out what the hell the group wanted, his best bet was to keep who he was, and how deadly he could be, on the down low.

Grover had the fleeting thought of how glad he was that Sierra wasn't with him. Knowing she was in danger would've pushed him to do something rash. For now, he'd stay calm and mentally take notes.

They'd mess up, and when they did, they'd regret fucking with him.

* * *

Sierra's face hurt from smiling so much. She had no idea how Gillian did this job day in and day out. She was a bundle of positive energy and simply being around her was exhausting for Sierra.

There was no doubt that Gillian was good at what she did. Everyone, from the happy couple celebrating their fiftieth wedding anniversary to the youngest great-great-grandchild, seemed to have the best time at the party. Gillian kept everything running smoothly and even when there were hiccups, she handled them so easily, no one even knew something had gone wrong.

While Sierra loved hanging out with her and helping, she already knew this wasn't something she wanted to do full-time. Or even part-time. Being around so many people wasn't as easy as it once was for her, though Sierra refused to feel bad or guilty about that.

So as much as she'd enjoyed the day, Sierra was more than ready to get home.

Home.

Damn, when had she begun to think of Grover's house as home?

She really should at least try to pretend she was using the apartment Ember had so graciously let her have, but the thought of going there without Grover wasn't appealing in the least. So she'd basically...what...moved in with Grover?

Yup, that's exactly what she'd done.

But he didn't seem to mind.

Sierra thought back to the night before. She'd been on the verge of sleep when she felt him shift next to her. He'd kissed her on the forehead and told her that he loved her. Without thought, as if it was the most natural thing in the world, she remembered telling him she loved him back.

"What's that smile for?" Gillian asked.

"Nothing. Okay, that's a lie. I was thinking about Grover," Sierra admitted.

"You guys are perfect together. You just fit," Gillian said. "It's hard to explain, but it's almost as if you've known each other for years and years. You're so comfortable together."

"I *feel* like I've known him forever," Sierra agreed.

"Well, I think it's awesome." She opened her mouth to say something else, but her phone rang. Giving Sierra a sheepish grin, Gillian reached for her cell. It had been ringing off the hook all day as she communicated with various people about the party.

"Hello? Oh, hi, Trigger. Yeah, she is...we're done for the day and heading to our cars right— Why? Um...*why?* What's wrong? You know I'm gonna have to tell her more than that."

Sierra tensed. She knew without having to get clarification that Gillian was talking about her. And she didn't like her friend's tone. She was worried...in a way that she hadn't been all day when putting out fires and talking to vendors about the anniversary party.

"Is he talking about me? What's wrong?" Sierra asked, alarmed at the change in Gillian's expression as she listened to whatever Trigger was saying.

Gillian shook her head—and suddenly Sierra was swamped with the feeling of being left out. When she'd been a captive, every decision had been made *for* her. She *hated* never knowing what was going on, what might happen to her from one moment to the next. And right now, it was more than obvious Gillian's husband was saying something Sierra *needed* to hear.

Without thought, she reached out and took Gillian's phone out of her hand.

Never in a million years would she have done something so rude prior to her kidnapping, but she was less concerned with niceties now and more worried about getting as much information as possible about anything that might affect her.

"Hello?"

"Sierra?"

"Yeah. What's going on? What was Gillian supposed to tell me?"

Gillian's husband sighed. "I need you to go with Gillian back to our place."

"Why?"

"There's been an incident."

"What does that mean? Stop beating around the bush, Trigger, and tell me what's going on. *Now*."

"Okay, but we've got this under control."

That didn't calm Sierra, not in the least. She held on to her patience by the skin of her teeth as she waited for Trigger to continue.

"Put it on speaker," Gillian insisted.

Sierra did, and she and Gillian both hovered over the phone as Trigger began to speak.

"You know the Strong Foot Militia has been a pain in our asses lately. Today, they took things to a new level. Some of the more vocal members were missing from the protests this morning, which we thought was odd. Grover, especially, seemed bothered by it."

Sierra wanted to scream at Trigger to hurry up and say what the hell was wrong already, but she bit her tongue.

"They were waiting for Grover when he got home," Trigger said solemnly. "Around a dozen members of the group are now holed up inside his house, with Grover as a hostage. But we're on this, Sierra. We're gonna get him out."

Everything inside Sierra froze as numbing shock and pure terror swept over her.

Yet her mind raced with questions. What would they do to Grover? Why had they taken *him* hostage? Why at his house and not at the place where they were protesting?

"Sierra? Are you all right?" Trigger asked. "I want you to go with Gillian. Go wait at our place. I'll keep you updated as to what's going on and the second we get him out, I'll call."

"Okay," Sierra said flatly.

"Okay?" Trigger asked, obviously surprised at her easy acquiescence...or perhaps disbelieving.

"Yeah." She was barely aware of what she was saying. She needed to think. She wanted to do something—but what? She wasn't a soldier. Didn't have the training Grover's team did. Hell, there was an entire Army post filled with people who had more experience than she did in rescuing hostages.

But could she sit back and do *nothing*?

"Good," Trigger said with a sigh, interrupting her thought process. "Again, we've got this. We're here, and so is another Delta team we work with. And just about every law enforcement agency in a twenty-mile radius. Rumor has it the FBI and ATF are on their way too."

"That's good."

"We're gonna get him out," Trigger repeated.

"I know. Thank you for calling," Sierra told him.

Gillian took the phone off speaker and Sierra vaguely heard her speaking softly to Trigger. "I'm so sorry," she said after hanging up. "I know your car is here, but you can come with me. You shouldn't be driving." She took Sierra's arm, walking them toward her RAV4.

"I'm okay," Sierra told her woodenly.

"You don't *sound* okay," Gillian said doubtfully, unlocking the car.

Once they were both inside, Sierra took a deep breath and

turned to her friend. "I don't know *what* I am right now," she said honestly.

The look of compassion and worry on Gillian's face nearly broke Sierra, but she swallowed hard and pushed away the almost overwhelming emotions threatening to take over. She needed to be clearheaded. Needed to figure out what she was going to do.

Gillian's phone rang again, making both women jump at the sudden loud, jarring noise.

"Hello? No, I'm still here." Gillian sighed. "It's not a good time right now. Can you— Right. No, it's okay, I'll be inside in a second. Just keep her calm until I get there. I know. We'll talk about it later."

Sierra looked at her in question when she hung up.

Gillian frowned. "That was my assistant. One of the older guests came back and said she couldn't find her purse. She swears that someone stole it and she's freaking out. This was the woman who insisted someone had taken her meal and thrown it away before she was done eating...remember? Who'd gotten turned around and forgotten where she was sitting? Her half-eaten meal was still where she left it and no one had stolen anything." Gillian shook her head, exasperated. "I'm sure this is something similar. She probably put her purse down somewhere and just forgot. Of course, she doesn't want to talk to anyone but *me* about it, and she's giving my assistant a hard time. It won't take me long to deal with this. I'm so sorry."

"It's fine," Sierra said. She could use some time alone to think.

"When I get back, we'll go to my place. I'll call the others and we'll all wait to hear what's going on together. Okay?"

Sierra nodded.

Gillian put a hand on her arm. "This is going to be fine," she said firmly. "I know my husband and the rest of the guys on the team are going to get Grover out of this. They're good at what they do."

Sierra knew that. She'd seen it firsthand. "I know they are." She felt a little robotic, with her short, flat responses, but she couldn't muster up the energy to say more than a few words at a time.

Gillian squeezed her arm and nodded. "I'll be right back," she said, then climbed out of the car and hurried back toward the building.

Now that she was alone, Sierra closed her eyes, trying to decide what to do.

What she *should* do was sit right where she was, wait for Gillian to get back and go home with her. She knew the other women would join them. Keep Sierra calm while they waited to hear any news about what was going on at Grover's.

But the longer she sat there, the more that option didn't feel right.

She'd been forced to sit around and let others decide her fate for an entire year. And the *only* reason she'd gotten out of that situation was because Grover had made the decision to go to Afghanistan, on his own, to find her. What would've happened if he hadn't taken such a huge risk? If he hadn't gone against every protocol he knew?

She'd likely still be in that mountain cell. Or even dead by now.

The longer she sat there and thought about Grover being held against his will—in his own house, no less—the more anger churned inside her. She'd been scared and almost numb when Trigger called, but now white-hot rage threatened to consume her.

How *dare* those militia assholes threaten him. Especially

after everything he'd done to try to keep Americans safe. Grover had put his life on the line time and time again, not for fame or glory or fun...but because it was necessary. Because it was *right*.

Could she do any less for him now?

Running a hand over her scalp, Sierra felt the soft hair growing there. It brought her back to those dark caves...made her think about the terrorists...how she'd manipulated them so easily.

Could she do the same again? She wasn't sure—but how could she not *try*?

Looking down at her watch, Sierra saw that mere minutes had passed since Gillian had gone back inside. It felt like hours. And she could only imagine what those same minutes felt like to Grover.

The longer she sat there, the more harm those assholes could do to the man she loved.

Moving without hesitation, Sierra pulled open the door to the car and headed for her Impreza. Gillian would be worried, but Sierra had made her decision.

She had no idea how she was going to get to Grover, and a huge part of whether she could help him or not depended on what she found when she got to his house. But she'd never forgive herself if she didn't at least try.

Sierra took the time to send a quick text to Gillian, telling her she needed to be alone and would call her later. It was likely Gillian wouldn't take her words lightly; she'd probably head to her apartment to check on her. But as much as Sierra hated deceiving her friend, she had to. She couldn't sit around when Grover was in danger.

* * *

Ten minutes later, Sierra scowled at the cars and military trucks parked sideways, blocking the entrance to Grover's driveway. There was no way they were going to let her through.

Thinking hard, she drove another half mile down the road and abruptly turned off into a field of tall grass, like the stuff at the back of Grover's house. It was tall enough to hide her car, but she couldn't do anything about the tire marks leading into the field. Hopefully anyone passing by would be more concerned about all the military vehicles nearby to even think twice about a car driving off the road into the grass.

Her inner voice was screaming at Sierra, asking her what the hell she thought she was doing, but she did her best to shut it out. Grover would have sacrificed his life for hers, and he didn't even know her at the time. She loved the man. She couldn't *not* do this.

She fought to open her car door in the thick grass, then headed in the direction of Grover's house, moving slowly, thankful for the camouflage the grass and trees gave her as she neared. Her heart was beating a million miles an hour but oddly, the closer she got to the house, the calmer she became.

It took much longer than she wanted to get to the house because twice she'd had to change direction, quietly slipping away when she spotted police officers and an FBI agent guarding the perimeter around the property.

She was currently on her belly, peering through the grass at the absolute chaos surrounding Grover's house. There were firetrucks and police cars parked all over the lawn to one side of his long drive. She assumed there were a lot more she *couldn't* see from her position. She also noted a few military Humvees and a large RV with the words "Incident Command" emblazoned on the side.

As she watched, a van sped down the dirt driveway, dust

billowing out behind it as it raced toward the scene. As soon as the vehicle stopped, half a dozen men climbed out, all with large white letters on the back of their vests, declaring them to be FBI.

To her surprise, she saw several shapes bleed out of the landscape around the house, heading for the van. With a start, she realized it was a few of Grover's teammates—and she hadn't spotted a single one until that moment. They'd clearly been surveilling the house, blending perfectly into their surroundings. Now that some sort of bigwig in the FBI had arrived, she guessed, they were moving to talk to him.

Her heart racing, Sierra realized she never would have gotten any closer to the house if whoever was in that FBI car hadn't arrived right then. The Deltas had been watching, waiting...they would've stopped her in a heartbeat.

This was her chance. Probably her *only* chance to get inside.

It was insane. Completely crazy. And there was a chance Grover would never forgive her for what she was about to do. She knew he still felt guilty about not rescuing her sooner, no matter what she or any therapist said. He might consider her actions today a betrayal of the huge sacrifice he'd made for her in Afghanistan. He'd gotten himself taken captive, tortured, only to have Sierra throw herself in the middle of a situation that could ultimately get her and Grover *both* killed.

But she couldn't get over the thought that if Grover died here today, and she did nothing to try to help, her life would essentially be over.

She couldn't live with herself if she sat around twiddling her thumbs while his life was on the line. Maybe the Sierra she'd been before she was taken captive could've left Grover's rescue to the professionals, but she wasn't that person anymore. She'd changed.

If she and Grover got out of this in one piece, and he was so pissed at her that he couldn't forgive her...so be it. At least he'd be alive. It would hurt not being with him, but she could at least go on, knowing he was still living and breathing.

Her mind made up, Sierra studied the area one more time. She could see at least three officers using trees as cover. There was another man standing beside the barn as well, his rifle pointed toward Grover's house. She suspected the front and sides were equally well-covered. There was no way the militia members would be able to get out of the house alive.

At that thought, Sierra frowned. Taking Grover hostage in his house made no sense. The militia *had* to know they'd be trapped. That once word got out about what happened, the house would be fully surrounded.

She didn't know who had alerted the police or military to the situation...but a tight ball of dread formed in her belly.

Even her captors back in Afghanistan had been careful not to trap themselves inside the houses where she'd been kept before moving her to the mountain prison. So why in the hell would the Strong Foot Militia barricade themselves inside a house? It made no sense to—

Sierra's racing thoughts screeched to a halt.

Unless they had no intention of giving up.

Unless they *wanted* to die.

Shit.

She needed to move. Needed to get to Grover.

Once she broke free from the cover of the grass, there would be no way to hide what she was doing. Any number of things could go wrong, but she hoped she'd have a short head start, since the officers' eyes were glued on the house, not on the land surrounding it. The last thing they'd expect was for someone to try to get *in*, instead of out. She had to be fast enough to stay out of reach, to get inside the house before they could tackle her. She was counting on it, in fact.

At any time, Trigger and the others could finish their conversation with the FBI and head back to their positions around the house. She had to move.

Mentally counting down from three—when Sierra got to one, she sprang into action, running as fast as she could toward the back door of Grover's house.

The officers spotted her almost immediately, yelling at her to stop. But she wasn't going to turn around now. No way.

She let out a screech of fright when the first gunshot went off.

She half-expected to feel pain blossom in her chest, but when she didn't, she kept running.

As if that first shot had broken the ice, what sounded like war broke out all around her.

The militia members in the house were shooting out the windows—but surprisingly, it didn't seem they were aiming at *her*. They'd turned their weapons on the men and women stationed around the house. Several had broken cover to yell at her, giving away their positions, and two gave chase, from what she could tell by her peripheral vision as she ran.

They quickly changed course, the militia itself holding them off with their gunfire.

Sierra had no idea why no one was shooting at her. She guessed she was probably a lot less threatening—a lone woman, wearing civilian clothes, not carrying any obvious weapons. She was a lesser target than someone armed to the teeth.

Shockingly, the militia had done her a favor. They'd kept the police from reaching her. From tackling and keeping her from her objective...namely, getting in the house.

More scared than she'd been since her first night in captivity in Afghanistan, Sierra ran straight up onto the deck, making sure to keep her hands up to show she was unarmed. She'd managed to get this far; she wasn't going to mess up now. She had one chance to make this work—and even *she* thought it was a long shot.

CHAPTER TWENTY

"What the fuck?" one of the men standing in his living room exclaimed.

Everyone nearby turned to see what had alarmed the man.

Grover's heart stopped—and he watched in disbelief as Sierra ran onto the back deck.

He had no idea where the hell she'd come from, who the hell had allowed her to get so damn close to the house, but he was pissed as fuck!

He opened his mouth to scream at her to run, but he wasn't fast enough.

"Let me in! I'm with you guys!" she yelled. "I've been watching you for weeks and I want to join!"

Grover blinked in surprise. What the *hell* was she doing?

Cory pushed his way through three men who were standing at the sliding door, staring stupidly through the glass at Sierra. The men upstairs were still firing at whoever was in the back-yard, not allowing anyone to get near enough to Sierra to pull her back.

Cory pointed his automatic rifle at her through the glass. "Get the fuck out of here!" he yelled.

"No, listen!" she insisted. "I hate the military! They ruined my life! I'm not lying. My name is Sierra Clarkson. Google me, you'll see I'm telling the truth! *Please* let me in!"

Fuck!

Grover knew immediately that Cory would do it. Let her in. Bring her into this fucked-up situation.

He wanted to scream in frustration and rage. But he kept silent.

The last place he wanted her to be was inside this house.

He knew it was too late. She'd already piqued Cory's interest. She'd have to continue with whatever insane plan she had.

She was lying about wanting to join the militia. He had no doubt whatsoever about that. He remembered only too well how she'd manipulated her captors back in Afghanistan. She'd gotten them to do exactly as she wanted, with no clue they were puppets on her string. Was she hoping to do the same here?

This wasn't the desert, and Cory wasn't Shahzada. This could go wrong a thousand different ways. He knew she thought she was helping, but she wasn't. She'd just made the situation so much worse—because now it was personal for him. If one hair on her head was hurt, he'd completely lose it.

"It's her!" Alan exclaimed.

Grover had already memorized all the names of the men around him. He'd been learning everything he could about them, in fact, in the hopes he could use that knowledge against them at some point.

"Look," Alan told Luis as he showed him his phone. "She's still got the shaved head and everything."

"What's it say?" Cory asked. His rifle had never wavered from Sierra's chest.

"She was a POW for over a year," Alan said. "In Afghanistan. She was rescued not too long ago."

"Interesting," Cory said. Then he motioned to Tony with his head. "Let her in. Then search her. If she makes one wrong move, shoot her."

Tony moved toward the doors. The men had moved one of his recliners up against the glass and it took him a moment to scoot it out of the way.

It was just one more thing that proved these assholes had no idea what the hell they were doing. A fucking chair in front of a *glass door* wasn't going to keep anyone out for long.

"In," Tony ordered Sierra.

She slid inside the room, keeping her arms up and away from her body.

Grover noted she was moving slowly, not making any jerky movements, and she kept her eyes on Cory, as he was the one giving the orders and obviously in charge.

"Thank you for letting me in!" Sierra said. Then her voice hardened. "The house is surrounded. The only reason I got through was because the stupid cops were looking for people coming out, not going in. Thank you for shooting at them to help me get in here. They've got some serious firepower out there. I'm assuming you've got enough to hold them off?"

No one answered as Tony searched her for weapons.

Grover didn't like how the man's hands lingered a bit too long on Sierra's chest and between her legs, but he didn't let any of his thoughts show on his face. He needed to play this smart until he figured out what Sierra intended. She hadn't acknowledged him in any way, and he needed to do the same. If Cory knew how much Sierra meant to him, he'd use her against him.

For a brief second, his mind flashed back to Afghanistan, when Sierra had warned him about that very thing.

He *hated* that they were right back in the same situation.

"She's clean," Tony said.

"The second I heard what was happening, I jumped in my car and came over. I didn't have a chance to stop for my stash. My weapons," Sierra told the group. Then, looking around, she said, "I thought there were more of you."

"There are," Tony said. "We've got lots more people upstairs."

"Shut up," Cory hissed angrily.

"It's not like a little thing like her is gonna overpower us or anything," Luis scoffed.

Cory stalked toward Sierra, and it took everything within Grover not to react to the danger coming off the man in waves. Not that he *could* do anything...not with Brody holding a weapon at his head.

Two months ago, before he'd met Sierra, Grover wouldn't have hesitated to act before now. He would've sacrificed himself so his team, and other law enforcement personnel, could storm the house and take these assholes out. But now that he'd found Sierra? No. He needed to stay alive. He had more to live for than he ever had before.

Cory reached into the holster at his side and pulled out a pistol.

Without hesitation, he coldcocked Sierra in the face.

She fell to her hands and knees, her head hanging, and every muscle in Grover's body tightened.

Then she looked up, met Cory's eyes—and smiled.

It was a chilling look. If Grover didn't know her as well as he did, he might've seriously thought she was unbalanced. "Nice hit," she said calmly.

"What are you *really* doing here?" Cory growled.

"I want to join you," Sierra repeated. "I *hate* the military. The

Army especially. I went to Afghanistan to serve my country. I was too short and weak to join the military, so I got a job as a contractor to serve that way. I thought we were doing the right thing over there. That we were trying to help. But I was wrong. So damn wrong..."

She laughed bitterly before continuing. "The Afghani people don't need help. They don't *want* help. They're doing just fine. All the military does is interfere in their way of life. How would *we* like it if someone invaded our country and told us were doing everything wrong? If they told us our religions were wrong and immoral? Americans think we're saving people, but in reality, no one wants or needs us to save them."

"This is true," Cory said matter-of-factly, holstering his pistol.

Grover barely dared to breathe as he listened to Sierra con the evil man standing above her.

"For a long time after I was taken, I thought the government would come to my rescue. Surely they'd help an American citizen, right? But they didn't. They didn't give a *shit* about me. Because who was I to them? No one! A useless contractor. A *female*. I was worth less than the sand on their boots. They left me there to suffer. To be tortured. To let the frustrations of an entire country be taken out on me for an entire year! It wasn't fair. But did they care? Fuck no!"

"But they *did* rescue you," Tony said. "It says in this article that an Army unit saved you."

"They did," Sierra agreed. "But only because one of their *own* was taken hostage. Do you know how long he was held? One week. *One...fucking...week* before his people came for him. They basically *had* to take me when they discovered I was there too. But they didn't come for me. I would still be there if it wasn't for the bad luck of that soldier getting taken."

"Hmm." Cory was clearly listening...and Grover noticed that he'd lowered the barrel of his rifle a bit, his stance slightly relaxed.

He was damn glad his role in Sierra's rescue had been kept out of the media, that it hadn't been released *he* was the soldier who'd been taken captive.

She was doing it.

Damn if Sierra wasn't winning this asshole over.

"I don't know what your plan is...but I want in," Sierra pressed. "Especially if it means taking some of those military bastards *out*."

Cory nodded, making a decision. "Fine—but you won't be left alone."

Sierra shrugged as if she didn't care about that.

"And we aren't giving you a weapon," he continued.

At that, Sierra pouted. "How am I supposed to kill anyone without one?"

"You can be bait," Cory said with a smirk. "When they see you in here, they'll be even more desperate to do something stupid."

"Ah, cool. Okay. I can play the damsel in distress," Sierra said, smirking back. Then she looked over and met Grover's gaze for the first time.

He thought he might see worry in her eyes. Maybe she'd try in some way to communicate with him. But all he saw was hatred.

He actually had to remind himself that she was playing a part. That the anger in her eyes wasn't directed at *him*.

"What about him?"

"What *about* him?" Cory said belligerently.

"He's one of *them*," she spat. "He's dangerous."

"He's a pussy," Brody said with a laugh. "He hasn't moved a muscle, not with this rifle pointed at his forehead."

Sierra glanced at Cory. "I know I'm just a chick, and you're probably way smarter than me, but you have to be careful with these military assholes. They'll try to surprise you and catch you off guard. I saw it happen more than once when I was on base in Afghanistan. You can't trust him, even with a gun pointed at his head."

Cory seemed to ponder her words.

She pressed on. "Is there someplace you can stash him? Like a storm shelter or something? There are lots of tornados in Texas, right? Wouldn't this place have a room for that? Something secure?"

"There's that media room down the hall," Luis said. "It doesn't have windows."

Grover's heart began to beat wildly in his chest. *Fuck*, his woman was smart. He hated *how* she'd learned to manipulate people so well, but he was proud as fuck at that moment. He still wanted to beat her ass for putting herself in this situation in the first place, but he couldn't believe how she'd almost turned this entire fucked-up scene around in just a few minutes.

Of course, nothing had been decided, so he couldn't get his hopes up quite yet.

But he'd do what he could to help the situation.

"Don't," he croaked.

Cory turned to look at him. "Don't what?"

"I'm being compliant. I'm doing what you want. I can just stay here."

Cory eyed him for a long moment, and Grover thought for a second maybe he'd overplayed his hand. Cory looked back at Sierra. "Why?"

"Why stash him? Because I don't trust anyone in the military! Not for one second. And why put someone on him and waste a gun anyway, when you could be using them to watch what's going on outside? Also, look at the size of him. Unless you plan on just shooting him, if he *does* decide to do something, it'll take several of your guys to subdue him." She shook her head, as if her logic should be obvious. "Putting him in a closet, or that room with no windows or whatever, means he can't signal to anyone and he can't escape. It's not like he can dig a hole through the floor." Sierra laughed as if that was the most ridiculous thing ever.

"I swear I won't do anything," Grover argued, almost whining.

"Fuck, man, you're pathetic," Brody said with a roll of his eyes.

"Stay here with her," Cody ordered Tony. "If she moves a muscle, shoot her."

Tony looked unsure for a moment. "Um...okay."

Grover was positive the guy wasn't going to shoot Sierra. He looked extremely uncomfortable with just the thought of it.

Cory stalked over to where Grover was sitting. His arms had been zip-tied to the chair, and he couldn't defend himself as Cory once more pulled out his pistol. He whipped Grover in the face once. Twice. Then a third time.

Grover could feel blood dripping down his cheek. He moaned as if the beating had broken him.

Cory smiled in victory. "Take him into the damn media room. Remove anything that even remotely looks like it could be used as a weapon. Then lock him in there and barricade the door. Oh—and shoot the lights out."

Finally, he turned back to Sierra. "Welcome to the Strong Foot Militia, little girl."

She grinned. "Thanks."

"If you do *anything* that makes me think you're not who you say you are, I'll make you wish we'd shot you the second you walked into this house," he warned.

Sierra slowly stood. She'd wisely stayed on her hands and knees throughout the conversation with Cory, wiping away blood from the split in her lip where he'd hit her. "I'm exactly who I say I am. And I'm ready to see the Army pay for what they've done to me."

"Take her upstairs," Cory ordered Tony. "Tell the others what's going on." He looked at Sierra once more. "You...put on a show in that window in the front room. Cry, carry on, beg for help. It's about time we got this show on the road."

"Sounds fun," Sierra said with a grin. Then Tony grabbed her arm roughly and practically dragged her toward the stairs.

Grover wanted her to look back. Wanted to communicate with her somehow. Tell her how much he loved her. That he was proud of her. But she didn't look back as she disappeared up the stairs.

"Cut the ties," Cory told Brody.

The younger man did as ordered, not caring that he cut Grover's wrist in the process of removing the zip-ties.

When the plastic cuffs fell to the floor, Cory ordered, "You. Stand up." He poked Grover with the barrel of the automatic weapon as he spoke.

Grover stood, purposely stumbling a bit, making it seem as if he was unsteady on his feet.

"Go check out the room, I'll bring him to you in a second," Cory told Brody. "And you, go back to the damn door and make sure no one else decides to join our party."

When the two men were out of earshot, Cory leaned in close to Grover and lifted the pistol he still held. He jammed the barrel against the underside of Grover's chin.

For a second, he thought the man was going to shoot him right then and there.

Instead, he said quietly, "It's too bad you're gonna miss the show. But the bitch was right. It'll be better to not have to worry about you when the shit hits the fan."

"What're you talking about?" Grover asked, sounding as scared as he could. He needed information—and he had a feeling this was his last chance to get it.

"A fireworks show," Cory said with a dark chuckle. "We've got an RPG. Did you know?"

Grover shook his head.

"We've been priming the area for weeks. Everyone knows our name, knows the Strong Foot Militia is here and unhappy. The media's been tripping over themselves to talk to us, to film us. When they hear about *this*, about how easily we overtook one of the big bad soldiers we've been protesting against, they're gonna want in on the action. Once they all arrive, get those cameras set up—and we both know they're gonna show in droves; no one's gonna want to miss the most exciting thing to happen around here in ages—we're gonna use that rocket to get this party started."

Grover pressed his lips together in dismay.

"I'm gonna light up the sky. And no one will be able to stop themselves from returning fire. They'll set your pretty house ablaze like it's the fucking Fourth of July. *Everyone* will hear the screams from the poor men—and one woman—trapped inside. They'll see firsthand how far the government is willing to go to silence dissenters. That they'll kill their own citizens...for what? For holding signs and protesting? It'll open their eyes. The country will finally see that we're right. The government is nothing but a big damn bully—and it's time to revolt. To rise up against them."

"Do the others know what you're planning?" Grover couldn't help but ask. He wanted to remind the asshole that when they died, it wouldn't be because they'd waved a few signs. It was because they took someone hostage and shot a damn RPG at the military.

Cory snorted. "Those pussies? No way. All they care about is smoking pot and not having to work. I need their fear and screams to be authentic. But they'll be heroes in the end. Martyrs for the cause."

"It's ready!" Brody yelled from down the hall in the direction of the media room.

"Walk," Cory ordered, jamming the pistol into the flesh under Grover's chin harder.

With no other choice, and his mind spinning with how the hell to end this insanity without dozens of deaths and his house burning down, Grover did as he was ordered.

CHAPTER TWENTY-ONE

"Fuck," Brain muttered. "This is completely out of hand."

Trigger couldn't agree more. Not only was his team there, and another Delta Force team headed by Ghost, but the Texas Rangers, FBI, and the Bureau of Alcohol, Tobacco, and Firearms. The Killeen local police had also shown up in droves.

There were too many people, not enough action, and all eyes were on Grover's house.

Not only that, but somehow this already FUBAR'd situation had gone from bad to worse when Sierra had gotten herself inserted into the middle of the shit show. She was supposed to be safe at his house with Gillian, but no—she ran up to the back door and walked right in.

No one had any idea what was going on inside that house. They didn't know if Grover was still alive or what the Strong Foot Militia hoped to accomplish.

Trigger heard a commotion behind him. He turned to see that a news van had somehow gotten past the outer perimeter and was barreling down the driveway toward them.

The last thing they needed was for this standoff to be broadcast live on television and the internet for everyone to see.

"They planned this," Lucky muttered in disgust, staring at the house.

"Yeah, they absolutely did," Trigger agreed, turning his attention back toward getting Grover and Sierra out of the house safely. He'd let the FBI deal with the media.

"But for what?" Doc asked.

"And what the hell is going on in there?" Lefty muttered.

That was the ten million dollar question.

If it had been up to the Delta team, they would've stormed the house already. The dozen or so militia members were no match for them, especially with Ghost's team there as well. But minutes before they'd planned to storm the house, the FBI showed up and they'd been forced to meet. Meanwhile, with every minute that passed, Grover could be in big trouble. And the addition of Sierra meant they now needed to act with even more caution.

The phone on Trigger's hip vibrated, and he cursed. He didn't have time to deal with whoever was calling him. But because he knew Gillian and the others would be scared out of their mind—and it wasn't as if they were actively doing anything at the moment, much to his disgust—Trigger pulled out his phone.

Glancing at it, expecting to see Gillian's name on the display, he was somewhat surprised to see that whoever was calling had blocked their number. It could've been just about anyone from the base at that point. Trigger wouldn't be surprised if it was the damn President calling to see what the hell was going on.

"Trigger," he said as he answered.

"Is this as big a shit show as it seems to be?"

For just a second, Trigger thought he was hearing things. He turned and took a step away from the group of ATF agents who were standing nearby. "*Grover?*" he asked incredulously.

"I'd appreciate it if you can keep everyone from burning down my damn house," his friend said in frustration.

"Holy shit, man! Where are you? Are you all right? Do they know you're calling me?"

"In my media room using my satellite phone. Yes. And no."

Trigger motioned to his team, and they all moved even farther away from the chaos unfolding on Grover's front lawn. "Talk to me," Trigger ordered.

"The team there?" Grover asked.

"Of course."

"Right, so here's what I know..."

For the next five minutes, Trigger listened as Grover gave them all the information he had on the men inside the house, and what they'd planned.

"Holy shit!"

"Yeah, and the kicker is, Cory's the only one who knows this is a suicide mission. The other guys just think they're here to get attention and they'll end up in jail by the end of the night," Grover said in disgust.

"And Sierra?"

"I have no idea *what* she thinks, but she's the one who made it possible for me to be talking to you right now. She convinced Cory it would be a good idea to stash me away."

"In your media room. Where you have a communications system and weapons under every damn chair," Brain said, incredulous.

"Yup. When I gave her a tour of the house, I showed her all my hiding places. She's fucking incredible—but I'm gonna beat her ass when you get us out of here. Trigger?"

"Yeah, man. What's up?"

"I'm gonna do as much as I can from here, but I need you to cover Sierra. Cory's gonna be pissed when he realizes his plan isn't working."

"Of course."

"I can't live without her," Grover said gruffly.

"And you won't have to."

"Don't let them blow up my house," he said. "When that fucking RPG goes off, people are gonna lose their minds. Cory's definitely right about that."

"We'll take care of it," Trigger promised. "After we make sure the FBI knows what the plan is, and we're sure they aren't going to interfere, we're gonna come in fast and hot. I'll give you a heads up when it's about to go down."

"Sierra went upstairs."

"Yeah, we saw her," Trigger said. "Your woman's a hell of an actress. She was crying and yelling through an open window."

"It's all fake," Grover said.

"We know," Trigger reassured him.

"But do the *other* four hundred and fifty-two people out there know?" Grover asked.

It was a good question, but a moot one at this point. Whether or not Sierra's tears were real and what she was doing wasn't important right now. What *was* important was taking off the head of the snake. The team had done it before, many times, most recently with Shahzada in Afghanistan. Grover had suggested that once Cory was out of the equation, the rest of the men would quickly back down.

Trigger believed him.

"I hate not knowing what's happening," Grover said.

"This is gonna be over soon," Trigger said. "Give me a bit of time to talk to Ghost, the ATF, and FBI. I've already got a plan."

"Famous last words," Grover joked.

Trigger took a deep breath. If his friend could make a joke at a time like this—when Sierra, his house, and literally his life was at stake—everything was going to work out. He knew it.

"I'll be in touch. In the meantime, lie low."

"I don't have a choice," Grover complained. With a sigh, he added, "They're young and dumb kids, Trigger. Don't forget, they have no idea they were set up on a suicide mission."

"I know," his friend said. "We're gonna do everything possible to *not* make this a lethal takedown."

What Trigger didn't say was that if someone was dumb enough to fire on them, all bets were off. Grover would already know.

"Call me back in fifteen minutes and I'll have an update," Trigger said. "We've got your back, Grover."

"Ten-four."

Trigger hung up the phone and turned to his team, giving orders. They had a lot of people to talk to in a short period of time. The sun was quickly sinking below the horizon, and if Grover was right—and of course he was right—Cory would be itching to use that damn RPG. Everyone needed to be on the same page when that happened, otherwise everything could literally go up in flames right in front of their faces.

Spotting Ghost standing with his team, Trigger felt renewed energy move through him. Between his own team, and Ghost, Fletch, Coach, Hollywood, Beatle, Blade, and Truck...he had every confidence that things would turn out in their favor.

He strode toward Ghost, ready to explain the plan.

* * *

Sierra stood in the back of one of Grover's guest rooms and did her best to seem as excited as the men around her. Cameron and

Rob were standing on either side of the window, taking turns shooting rounds. From what she understood, they weren't actually aiming at anyone; they were just shooting every now and then to make sure no one outside came too close to the house.

Adam and Zeke were doing the same thing from other windows upstairs. Between them, they were keeping the back and front of the house covered.

"More ammo, Sierra!" Zeke called out. She'd been tasked with making sure the guys had ammunition at all times. She went into the hallway and grabbed another box of bullets, then headed for the master bedroom. It was painful for her to see the room where she'd been so happy, and felt the most relaxed, get defiled by the Strong Foot Militia.

She handed the box to Zeke, then turned to head out of the room. The less time she spent in there, the better for her sanity.

She almost ran into Kevin in the hallway. Cory was behind him...and she shivered at the look on his face.

"It's time," he said with a grin. "The media is here. Only one van, since the assholes are keeping the others back at the road, but one camera is all we need. Their footage will go viral around the world."

Kevin whooped and asked, "Can I get the RPG ready?"

Sierra almost wanted to roll her eyes. It was as if he thought he was playing a video game or something, not about to put together a weapon that could kill dozens of people with one shot.

Cory nodded. "Sure. Set it up in that small room over there. It has the best view of the front of the house, where the assholes have parked their fancy vehicles."

Sierra wasn't sure what to do. She was only one person. Cory and his followers outnumbered her eleven to one and they were very well armed. Yes, she knew where Grover had hidden weapons in the house, but even if she could get to them without being seen or stopped, she wasn't sure how to use them. They might have safeties on them, or maybe they weren't even loaded.

She'd worked hard to get these guys to trust her, with the split lip to prove it. The last thing she wanted was to ruin that, not if she could do something else to help the Deltas.

She knew Grover had probably talked to his team. That phone system in his media room was the main reason she'd suggested Cory put him in there. His team needed to know what was going on in the house, and Grover could help coordinate their rescue. She hoped.

Not knowing what else to do, she went back into the room where she'd left Cameron and Rob.

"Shit, man. I need some weed," Rob bitched.

"Same. Think Cory'll let us take a break soon?" Cameron asked.

Sierra knew they had to realize she was there, but they obviously didn't care. Tony had explained who she was when he'd brought her upstairs. The other men accepted the story she'd weaved without question. The longer she was in the house, the more she realized that these men—boys, really—were even more naïve than *she'd* been when she'd accepted the job overseas.

They weren't here to truly hurt anyone. This was almost like a game to them. A bit of excitement for a bunch of bored kids. And if Cory had been supplying them with drugs and food and anything else they might need, why *wouldn't* they simply go with it?

Glancing toward the door, she didn't see Cory. She heard him and Kevin putting together what she assumed was the damn RPG. She didn't have a lot of time.

"How'd you guys hook up with Cory, anyway?" she asked.

Rob fired his rifle and laughed. "Did you see that? I didn't think that old guy could move that fast."

"Watch this," Cameron told his buddy, shooting off a few rounds of his own.

Sierra clenched her teeth, hard. She hated that these jerks were aiming at her friends or other innocent people because they thought it was *amusing*.

Desperate to get them to stop fucking shooting, Sierra blurted, "You know we're all gonna die, right?"

She had no idea what she was saying, but she needed to do *something* to take their attention off the windows.

Cameron turned to stare at her. "What?"

"What the fuck you talkin' about?" Rob asked.

Sierra thought fast. "Remember Waco? Oh, wait...that was before you were born. But surely you heard about it. The ATF and the military, the same people who are outside right now, got frustrated when they couldn't get into the Branch Davidian compound in Waco. So they took a tank and rammed the place and it burned to the ground, killing like seventy people who were inside. Men, women, and children. I don't see how things for us will turn out any differently."

She didn't mention that it was likely the Branch Davidians actually started fires inside the compound before the tank broke through the wall in the first place.

Rob and Cameron were quiet for a moment. Then Rob shook his head. "No. Cory said we're just putting on a show for the media. And they're out there right now, filming. Once the world sees how dangerous and out of control the military is, we'll surrender."

Sierra let out a harsh laugh. "You really believe that?" she asked. "The second we walk outside, we're dead meat. Those military guys are pissed way the hell off that they're being shot at. They'll fire on us, then later claim we were holding weapons. They always spin shit to make themselves look good." She shook her head. "Nope, we're all gonna die today. But that's all right with me. I'm already fucked in the head after everything I've been through. I'd rather die for the cause than live with the night-mares and flashbacks I've got because of the fucking military."

Cameron and Rob shared a nervous look, and Sierra was thrilled that she'd at least planted a seed of doubt in their minds. It was about time they started using their damn brains instead of following Cory blindly.

"Sierra! I need more bullets!" Adam shouted from another room.

"Duty calls," she told Cameron and Rob. Then she turned and headed out of the guest room. She almost tripped over Kevin again, who was moving a large wooden box out of Grover's office.

"Watch it!" she barked.

"*You* watch it," Kevin retorted.

"Wow, you guys got it set up already?" Sierra asked, her stomach dropping.

"Yeah, it wasn't hard. Cory's getting it ready. There's a huge SWAT van parked right in front of the house and behind it is a military Humvee. He thinks he can take both out with one shot," Kevin said excitedly.

"Awesome! What then?"

"What do you mean?"

"What are our plans after that? It'll probably make everyone outside fire back. So what are we gonna do after we blow their shit to smithereens?" She kept her voice down, not wanting Cory to overhear. Her lip still hurt from where he'd hit her. Of course, that blow was nothing compared to what she'd experienced at the hands of Shahzada.

"Not sure, but Cory will tell us," Kevin said, unconcerned about anything other than shooting the large weapon he'd just helped set up.

"Sierra!" Adam yelled once more.

Bending, she picked up another box of ammo and went down the hall to where Adam was pretending he was in a video game. Without a word, she dropped the box at his feet, then turned and left. She heard Adam bitching about the bullets spilling out, but Sierra didn't care. She hadn't lied to Tweedledee and Twee-dledum in the other room. She didn't have a good feeling about what would happen after Cory shot off that RPG.

She could hear someone yelling through a megaphone, trying to get someone to talk to them, to negotiate. But no one seemed inclined to answer. And if Cory didn't want to negotiate, that meant he probably didn't care if he lived or died. Or if those he brought with him did either.

Sierra supposed some people watching this mess might think exactly what Cory wanted them to. They might agree that the government and military had overreacted. They wouldn't care that the men and women outside were goaded into whatever they might do.

Standing uncertainly in the middle of the hallway, Sierra was out of ideas. She'd done what she could to help Grover, then spread uncertainty among some of the idiots blindly following Cory. Now all she wanted to do was run. But she'd gotten herself into this situation, and there was no running from it.

Kevin exited the room Cory was in and called down the hallway for everyone to hear. "Five-minute warning!"

The others upstairs at the windows let out shouts of

acknowledgement, and she heard the men who were still downstairs do the same.

Kevin met her gaze and grinned. "Ready for the fireworks? It's gonna be off the hook."

"Cool," Sierra managed to say. Luckily, Kevin was too excited to notice her lukewarm reaction.

Sierra strongly reconsidered finding one of Grover's hidden guns and stopping Cory from doing what would surely incite the officers and soldiers outside to retaliate. But the same obstacles remained. She didn't know how to use any of the guns, and any hesitation could get her killed.

All she could do was hope that Grover had been able to use his secret phone, and weapons, and was even now on his way out of the prison cell she herself had suggested they put him in.

Sierra moved to the end of the hall and pressed her back into a corner, doing what Grover had ordered in those caves in Afghanistan. She slid down the wall until her ass hit the floor. Wrapping her arms around her knees, she did her best to make herself as small as possible.

While nowhere in the house was safe at the moment, at least she was away from the windows. She had no doubt that bullets would start flying the second Cory aimed that damn rocket-propelled grenade.

For a moment, it *felt* as if she was back in Afghanistan. Trapped. Waiting for her fate to once again be decided by others. Except this time, she'd willingly made herself a hostage.

Closing her eyes, she rested her forehead on her knees and prayed.

* * *

The second he'd been left alone in his media room, Grover had gotten to work. Brody had shot the lights out, as ordered, but Grover didn't need them. He knew where he'd stashed every weapon in this room. His thoughts briefly turned to Sierra, but if he concentrated too hard on what she might be going through, he wouldn't be able to function.

He started with the reclining seats.

It took some maneuvering, but he was able to remove one of the knives he'd hidden in a compartment under one of the chairs and cut the second set of zip-ties Brody had put on him. Grover could feel blood on his skin from where he'd cut himself, and where Brody had sliced him earlier, but he didn't even feel any pain. He was too focused. Within a minute, he'd removed the phone from its hiding place behind the decorative flag on the wall and was talking to Trigger.

His team leader had asked for some time.

Grover's first inclination was to burst out of this fucking room and take out whoever dared stand between him and the woman he loved. But he trusted Trigger, and his team leader needed to make sure everyone was aware that Cory had an RPG and was planning to use it.

He'd designed the damn media room to be practically sound-proof, and Grover regretted that now. He couldn't hear what was going out outside, or even inside his damn house. To keep himself busy, he collected as many weapons as he could comfort-ably hold. He holstered a pistol on his thigh and another at the small of his back, strapped a knife onto his calf and another at his waist, then grabbed a rifle as well.

He didn't want to kill anyone...

Yeah, that was a lie. He wanted to take Cory down, and if any of the other stupid punks had hurt Sierra, he'd take them out too.

After arming himself, Grover paced the room.

What seemed like an hour later, but was in actuality closer to the fifteen minutes Trigger asked for, the phone vibrated in Grover's hand.

"Talk to me."

"Looks like Cory's about to make his move," Trigger said, and Grover could hear him breathing hard, as if he was moving while talking. "I've informed everyone as to what the hell is going on, and they've agreed not to bring the house down. They're going to make a lot of noise though," Trigger warned.

"Sierra could be hit if they fire into my house!" Grover growled.

"Everyone's been instructed to fire high and low, not right at the windows."

Grover wasn't exactly happy with that, but he also knew it was the best he was going to get at the moment.

"They'll keep them occupied as we come in from the west, and Ghost and his crew come in from the east. The garage is a weak spot. From what we can tell, they don't have eyes on it."

"They put shit up against the back door," Grover warned.

"Yeah, we saw. It won't slow any of Ghost's crew down. Be ready, Grover. Two minutes and we're in. We're coming in quiet rather than balls to the wall."

"Ten-four."

"See you soon. This'll be over in five. Over and out."

Grover slid the phone into his back pocket and headed for the door. Cory and Brody had barricaded the door of the media room with several chairs from his living room, but they were no match for Grover. A few hard, quiet shoves and he was entering his hallway.

He paused to listen, hearing nothing but the sound of someone on a megaphone outside, attempting to get Cory to talk. Grover felt his heartbeat slow as he regulated his breathing and crept down the hallway toward his living area, completely focused on the task at hand.

An extremely loud whooshing sound startled him—followed by a massive explosion that literally rocked the house on its foundation.

He heard someone shout with excitement in the front room. Glass shattered somewhere, probably from the blast wave of the RPG exploding, as it hit whatever Cory had aimed at.

Then the air filled with the sound of gunshots.

It sounded like Grover was in the middle of World War Three. There was no need to be quiet anymore, as no one in the house would be able to hear anything but the report of dozens of guns.

More shouts came from upstairs, men yelling that people were coming toward the house from the backyard.

It sounded like the Strong Foot Militia was panicking.

Good. It would make things easier for him and his team.

Moving quickly, Grover crept up behind Alan. He was staring dumbly out the back door toward the yard, his rifle pointed at the floor.

He put a hand over the militia man's mouth and wrenched the weapon away from him. Alan grunted in surprise, his eyes wide, but he didn't put up a fight.

Hearing something behind him, Grover turned—and saw the most beautiful thing he'd ever seen in his life.

Six figures coming down the hallway, from the direction of the garage.

His team, led by Trigger.

Doc grabbed Alan, and Grover motioned toward the small dining room at the front of the house. Within two minutes, there were four men lying on Grover's living room floor, their arms bound behind them, tape over their mouths so they couldn't warn their friends.

Doc stood over them with a rifle, as the rest of the team headed for the stairs. This would be tricky. The sounds of a huge gun battle still raged outside, and Grover prayed that Trigger was right and no one was shooting live rounds into his house. He didn't give a shit about his things; all he cared about was that Sierra didn't get caught in the crossfire.

Trigger let him lead the way up the stairs, and Grover went slow and steady. When he'd climbed a few steps, he held up his hand to stop the others, then peeked over the bottom edge of the hall banister to see what the situation was.

Eyes widening, Grover saw Sierra sitting at the far end of the hallway. She'd stuffed herself into a corner and was huddled into a ball.

He was so damn proud of her at that moment. That was exactly what she should've done. Gotten herself away from the windows and made herself as small a target as possible.

Her eyes widened when she spotted him and without any prompting, she pointed at the master bedroom and held up two fingers. Next, she pointed to one of his guest rooms and held up one finger. Then she did the same with the other rooms, letting him know where everyone was. Grover didn't know who was in which room, but at the moment, that didn't matter. They all needed to be subdued.

Looking back at his team, Grover wasn't surprised to see Ghost, Fletch, and Truck standing at the bottom of the stairs. They'd obviously made their entry into the house as well. They had the numbers now to easily take out the remaining militia members, it was just a matter of if they'd be smart and surrender easily, or if they'd do something stupid.

Moving quickly, because they all knew they could be discovered at any second, the Deltas burst up the stairs and scattered into the various rooms.

Just as Grover was about to get to Sierra, Cory came out of the office.

He didn't hesitate, grabbing Sierra and wrenching her off the floor.

She shrieked and fought him as hard as she could, to no avail.

Cory dropped the rifle he'd been holding and pulled out a pistol. He easily pulled Sierra in front of him and jammed the weapon under her chin, just as he'd done to Grover. Sierra's head was forced back so Grover couldn't see her eyes.

"Stop, or I'll kill her."

Grover immediately stopped in his tracks. Trigger at his side. The sound of men surrendering could be heard all around them, but Grover only had eyes for their leader. He held his own pistol with steady hands. All he needed was for Cory to give him an opening, and he was as good as dead.

The noise of the gunshots from outside faded. One of the Deltas must've communicated that things inside the house were under control. Mostly.

"It's over," Trigger told Cory. "Your plan failed."

"It didn't fail," he crowed. "That explosion was seen by millions! As was the resulting firefight. Americans shooting at Americans. *Everyone* has seen how little the government cares about its people!"

"No one saw anything," Trigger explained. "The one news crew out front stopped filming. See, we knew you had an RPG— and we knew you were going to use it."

Cory's face flushed red beneath his beard. "No!" he screamed.

"Yes," Trigger said calmly. "As far as the American people know, the protestors who've been harassing innocent civilians for weeks went over the deep end and took an innocent woman and a decorated soldier hostage. No one sees you or your group as the victims here. You're done."

Sierra had gone still in Cory's arms when he'd shoved his gun against her vulnerable flesh...but movement out of the corner of Grover's eyes caught his attention. Sierra's hand.

She held up one finger.

She wasn't wasting any time. Wasn't going to give them a chance to talk Cory down. But honestly, Grover wasn't sure the man *could* be talked down. He was trapped and he knew it. His plans shot to hell, literally.

Two fingers...

Grover's field of vision narrowed. He sighted his weapon between Cory's eyes. The man was trying to keep himself hidden behind Sierra's slight body, but the second she made her move, Grover would be ready.

No one threatened his woman. *No one.*

Cory was ranting and raving about the corruption of the government, how he might've failed today but his followers would take up where he left off, proving to the world that the military was immoral, full of nothing but killers.

Ignoring the irony of Cory's statement, Grover saw Sierra lift a third finger.

She whipped one hand behind her and grabbed Cory's dick, even as the other shoved the gun from beneath her chin.

She squeezed as hard as she could, and Cory reacted predictably. He screamed. He reflexively shoved Sierra away from him as he bent over double.

While she was still falling, Grover's weapon discharged.

Two bodies hit the hardwood floor in the hallway only a moment apart, but Grover only cared about one of them. He dropped his weapon on the floor and raced for Sierra.

As Trigger and Lefty went to Cory to make sure he was

disarmed and no longer a threat, Grover grabbed Sierra by the arms and hauled her upright, until she was standing in front of him. His mind was in chaos, otherwise he never would've yanked her up so roughly, but he was desperate to make sure she was uninjured.

She blinked at him as he frantically searched for any signs she'd been hurt.

"Sierra?" he barked.

She frowned and shook her head, wincing.

"Sit rep!" a voice from behind them shouted. It was Lucky.

"Shots fired!" someone else yelled.

"No shit! Who was hit?"

The hallway was cramped and crowded as everyone tried to figure out what was going on. Grover vaguely heard someone yelling cease fire, obviously to whoever was in charge of the men outside, to make sure they didn't start firing again after hearing more shots, but he could only stare at Sierra.

"Are you hit?" he asked her.

She licked her lips and took a deep breath. When she shook her head, Grover's knees almost buckled right then and there. "Are you sure?"

She nodded and tried to look behind her. Grover took her head in his hands, preventing her from looking anywhere but at him. "Talk to me, Bean."

"My ears are ringing from the shots but I...I think I'm okay. Is he..."

"He's dead," Grover said unemotionally.

Cory was right about one thing: the military was full of killers. And the most deadly of the bunch had been standing right in front of him.

He gently ran his thumb over her split lip, where Cory had

hit her. In return, she raised her own hand and ran it over his cheek, where *he'd* been hit.

All around them, people moved, taking the young men down the stairs from the rooms where they'd been holed up and trying to assess the situation. But all Grover could do was stand there and stare at Sierra.

To his shock, tears filled her eyes, quickly spilling down her cheeks.

Fuck. Sierra didn't cry. They'd both discussed it at length, with each other and with therapists.

And here she was, crying.

"Sierra?" he whispered, his own voice breaking.

To his amazement, she smiled. Tears dripped off her chin and she was fucking smiling.

"I'm okay!" she reassured him. "I'm just so relieved it's over!"

Pulling her close, Grover did his best not to smother her as he held her against his chest. He could feel her tears wetting his shirt, and the feeling was one he'd never forget. "I love you," he said. He put his hands on her shoulders and eased her back slightly. "I love you," he repeated, louder.

"I love you too," she said, still smiling and crying at the same time. "Maybe tonight is a good time to break in my apartment. Your house seems a bit...drafty."

A loud laugh sounded from behind him, and Grover turned to see Brain. "That's because most of the windows were blown out from the RPG blast," he told them. "I'm thinking it might be a few days before you're gonna want to return home."

"We're moving," Grover informed his friend.

"What? No, we aren't!" Sierra countered with a frown as she wiped her face.

"You can't want to live here," Grover argued.

"Why not? I'm not going to let some crazy person chase us out of our home!"

Grover pulled her into his arms again and turned to get the hell out of the hallway. He didn't want Sierra to see Cory's body, even though he suspected it wouldn't upset her as much as it might someone else. She'd been through hell and back. He guessed not much would faze her in the future.

"We've got hours of meetings ahead of us," he said as he walked her to the stairs. "We'll have to tell not only the FBI and ATF everything that happened here, but my commander as well. We need to call Gillian and the others, make sure they know we're okay. We also need to call our parents. I have to get in touch with a security company to come out and arm this place with the best shit they've got, then I need to find someone to replace all these windows—"

"I'll take care of the windows," Ghost said, interrupting him.

They were at the bottom of the stairs now, and Grover could hardly believe the number of people who were in his house. He thought space was limited when all his teammates and their wives were over, but that was nothing compared to the bodies crammed inside at the moment.

Grover nodded at Ghost. "I'd appreciate it. Thanks for being here."

"Wouldn't have been anywhere else."

"Hey, at least your house didn't get blown up like mine did," Fletch joked.

Grover remembered that event from a few years ago. All he could do was nod. "True." He turned back to Sierra. "Anyway, as I was saying, we're gonna be busy for a while. But when we're done, I'm taking you to your apartment and we're not coming out for days. I didn't get to make you the dinner I had planned, and that pisses me off."

She smiled up at him. "Not making me dinner pisses you off, but not the fact that your house was just in the middle of a freaking war zone?"

"Oh, I'm pissed about that, for sure. Especially that you put yourself smack dab in the middle of this shit show. And that Cory hit you. And that these stupid kids didn't realize what he had planned for them. And—"

Sierra reached up and put her hand over his mouth. "I get it."

Suddenly, everything that had just happened hit Grover all at once. He couldn't get the sight of Cory holding a gun to Sierra's head out of his mind. He swayed on his feet.

"Get me a chair," Sierra barked loudly. Everyone around them froze, and she snapped her fingers impatiently. "Now!"

Grover couldn't help but smile slightly as several people rushed to do as she demanded. His woman was a tiny dynamo. She was stronger than anyone he'd ever met.

He sat, pulling her down with him. Sierra snuggled into him as if she didn't care who was watching. And he supposed that was the case, because *he* sure as hell didn't.

As men and women scurried around them, going about the business of figuring out what the hell had happened and how an unassuming American had gotten his hand on a freaking rocket-propelled grenade, Grover closed his eyes and held on to the woman he loved more than he could ever put into words. They'd had a close call, and they both knew it. But they were both all right now. And he was going to make sure they stayed that way.

CHAPTER TWENTY-TWO

Sierra glanced up from her spot on the back deck. Grover was standing inside and, as if he could feel her looking, he turned to meet her gaze.

"You okay?" he mouthed.

Sierra nodded and smiled at him. She was chilling on the back deck with Devyn, Gillian, and Aspen.

The week since he'd been taken hostage and his house taken over had been insane. Sierra's parents flew in to check for themselves that she was all right. Grover's parents had also come down from Missouri. Apparently, having a bomb go off in their son's front yard was way scarier than knowing he risked his life regularly on top-secret missions for the Army.

It turned out Trigger had been lying to Cory about the press not filming. There was no way they'd have agreed to that, and no one could legally stop them. Even the cameras at the end of the driveway had caught the huge plume of black smoke that had risen in the air after the RPG was fired. But the one news outlet that had gotten near the house—how they'd managed that,

Grover and the rest of the team still had no idea—had of course caught everything happening live.

Including how the police and military snipers were shooting at nothing, acting as a distraction for the Delta teams to breach the house.

Cory might've wanted the American people to turn against the military, but the opposite had happened. Thanks to the news footage, support for the Armed Forces seemed to be higher than ever.

Grover hadn't left Sierra's side since it happened. He seemed to be taking everything that happened harder than she was. He'd lost it completely one night, yelling at her for being so reckless and foolish. She'd let him rant and rail, knowing he needed to get it out, and when he'd finally wound down, she walked into his arms and held him tight. "I was so scared for *you*," she told him. "I couldn't leave you in there on your own."

"Never again," he'd told her. "I don't care that you being there and doing what you did saved us. My heart can't handle anything like that ever again."

"Okay," she agreed immediately. It wasn't as if she wanted to ever go through something like that again herself.

All the other women had come over to see her in person over the last week. It had been emotional for Sierra to see how much they all cared so deeply. She wasn't someone they'd known for years, but friendships in the military seemed to be stronger, more immediate.

And speaking of friendships, the other Delta Force team who'd come to help out that night had gone above and beyond in getting Grover's house put back together. All the windows had been replaced in a single day, and while the scorch mark from the cars that Cory had blown up remained in the front yard, everything else was basically as it had been.

Tex had even gotten involved, arranging for a security gate to be put up at the end of Grover's driveway. The militia members had simply driven right up to his house and broken in, waiting for him to get home. Grover hated the gate, and it was likely he would have it removed in the not-so-distant future, but for now, it kept the lookie-loos away.

Regardless, *no one* would be able to get onto Grover's property without his knowledge again, not with the amount of security he now owned.

But Sierra didn't mind. She couldn't deny that all the gadgets and bells and whistles were intimidating, but it gave them back a sense of safety that Cory and his followers had almost destroyed.

The men who'd joined Cory in his insane plot were all still in jail, and would be for quite a while. They all claimed they had no idea Cory had planned a suicide mission. They truly thought they'd just shake things up, put on a show for the media, then get a slap on the wrist when everything was said and done.

Personally, Sierra thought they were all stupid as hell, but she supposed she'd made some dumb choices herself when she was their age. Not as dumb as joining an outlaw militia group, but still.

Things were just now getting back to some semblance of normal. As normal as they could be for two former POWs who'd been thrust into the spotlight. Sierra was taking each day as it came and trying not to get overwhelmed with the fact that once again, everyone wanted an interview. Ember was assisting a lot with that, using her knowledge and experience to help her navigate the tricky waters of the media.

Today, everyone had gathered at Grover's place to celebrate life, friendship, and simply being alive. And by everyone, Sierra meant that literally. Grover's team and their women, Ghost's team and their families, her parents, Grover's parents and siblings—minus Spencer, who was still in rehab for his gambling addiction. Even Commander Robinson was there, as was Aspen and Brain's elderly neighbor, Winnie, and her granddaughter and her family.

Gillian had somehow arranged for everything on extremely short notice. She'd called in a lot of favors, but had blown off Sierra's thanks, saying that she might as well use the connections she'd made for their own enjoyment.

There was food on every available surface, and while there weren't enough chairs for everyone, no one seemed to care. Kids were running around everywhere and it was complete chaos... and Sierra couldn't have been happier.

"This is insane," Devyn said with a small laugh. "I mean, seriously, who *are* all these people?"

Even though Sierra had told Grover she was fine, he still came outside to see for himself. As he approached, he heard his sister's question. "They're my friends," he said, putting his hand on Sierra's shoulder.

"You have friends? No, that can't be right. My brother's a hermit," Devyn joked.

Everyone laughed, and Sierra reached up and squeezed her man's hand.

He leaned down to whisper in her ear. "I'm thinking we need to escape back to The Refuge. Get away from all these people."

She chuckled and tilted her head to look up at him. "I'm definitely okay with that. But maybe not right this second. That would be rude."

Out of the corner of her eye, Sierra saw Grover's parents approach. Grover straightened and greeted them. Then she saw him smirk before he said, "So, Devyn...when are you and Lucky gonna get married?"

Sierra smothered a chuckle. Everyone knew she and Lucky

were *already* married—everyone but her parents. They hadn't really meant to keep it a secret from them, but it just kind of happened. Lucky wanted to get married so Devyn would have the benefits the Army could provide her as a military spouse, and Devyn had no problem with that, because she loved him so much. The issue was that her parents wanted a huge traditional ceremony back in Missouri. She hadn't wanted to disappoint her parents by telling them she and Lucky had already done the deed, and they hadn't had time to work out the details of a big wedding and reception.

"Oooh, yes. Let's talk about that, shall we?" their mom said, clapping her hands together eagerly.

Devyn glared at her brother for a beat. "We will, Mom."

"Promise?"

"Promise," Devyn said with a sigh.

As soon as the older couple wandered off, Devyn threw a balled-up napkin at her brother. "That was mean, Fred."

Grover chuckled. "I know, sorry. But I had to say *something* to get her to stop hovering over me and Sierra."

"So you threw me under the wedding bus?" Devyn asked.

Grover shrugged. "It worked. Besides, the sooner you let Mom have her ceremony, the sooner she'll get off your back about it."

"Yeah, then she'll be harping on me to have kids," Devyn said with a sigh.

"Is that a bad thing?" Sierra asked.

Devyn blushed and shrugged. "Not really."

"I'm gonna be the best uncle ever," Grover said. "I'm gonna fill your kids with sugar, then send 'em home for you to deal with."

Devyn sat back in her chair with a smirk. "You will too."

"Yup."

Sierra loved this. It was hard to believe not too long ago, her life was so different. So bleak. And now, here she was, surrounded by people who treated her as if they'd known her forever. Who genuinely cared about her well-being.

"Hey, Aspen!"

Everyone glanced up to see a teenager making her way toward them.

Sierra had met her earlier. Her name was Annie, and she was Emily and Fletch's daughter. She had dirty-blonde hair and blue eyes, and the second she met Sierra, she'd declared her hair to be "rad" and said she was going to ask her mom if she could get hers cut the same way.

"Hi, Annie," Aspen said, keeping her voice down so as not to wake the sleeping infant on her chest.

"Will you go over tourniquet wraps with me later?"

Without missing a beat, Aspen nodded. "Sure."

"Great! Thanks!" Annie said happily, then skipped off.

"What was that about?" Sierra asked when the girl was out of earshot.

"Annie wants to be a combat medic when she grows up. She heard that's what I did when I was in the Army, and now she wants to learn as much as she can about medical stuff. I think she wants to get her EMT license as soon as she's old enough."

"Wow, that's ambitious," Sierra said.

"Yep. And she'll do it," Aspen said with a small smile. "She's one of those people who, once she decides what she wants, she goes after it."

"Yeah," Grover added. "She's got a boyfriend who lives out in California who she met when she was like seven or eight. She says she's gonna marry him one day. And while I'd probably lose it if my daughter told me that when she was so young, I think

Fletch loves it because it means she's not interested in dating anyone else."

Everyone chuckled.

"Somehow, I'm not sure Oz would be quite as supportive if Bria came home and declared that she'd found the boy she wanted to marry," Gillian said with a laugh.

"Right? Oh my God, no way," Aspen agreed.

"Walk with me?" Grover asked Sierra quietly as the others discussed how hilarious Oz's reaction was going to be when his niece decided she wanted to start dating.

She nodded and stood. Grover immediately took her hand. "We'll be back," he told the group. Everyone smiled at them as they headed across the yard.

Sierra didn't have to ask where they were going. She knew.

Grover led her to the barn, and she grinned at the empty stalls—one of which would soon be filled. Grover had surprised her last night by telling her he'd arranged for a cow to be joining their family. Apparently, it had been rescued from a life of neglect and the rescue group needed a place for her to go where she'd have nothing but love and all the grass she could eat. Sierra had cried when he'd told her.

It seemed as if she cried all the time now. The tears welled up in her eyes at the drop of a hat. When she was happy. When she was surprised. When she was sad. When she was scared. She was a virtual crybaby, but surprisingly, Sierra was perfectly all right with that. It meant she was moving on from the horrors she'd experienced in the Middle East.

Grover led her to the stairs and followed behind closely as she headed up to the loft. Sierra was somewhat amazed that they were alone. That no one had followed them into the barn. It seemed as if there was always someone who wanted to talk to

Grover. He was liked and respected by just about everyone he met.

He walked them over to the couch and she sat. Grover took a seat right next to her, and Sierra blinked in surprise. Usually the first thing he did up here was open the large doors in front of them, so they could look out at the land or the sunset.

But today, he took her hands in his and simply stared at her for a long moment.

"Are you all right?" she asked tentatively.

"Yes," he said without hesitation. "I'm great. For a while last week, I wasn't sure if I'd get to do this again. Sit here with you and simply be. I'm good, but even *I* knew I couldn't overpower a dozen men. I had planned to just go with it, wait for an opening if one came, and if it was my time to go, I was comforted by the fact that you were somewhere safe."

"Then I walked in."

"Then you walked in," he confirmed. "I've never been so scared, and so determined to live, as I was in that moment. And then you proved how smart I've always known you are. You manipulated Cory into putting me right where I needed to be. I'll never underestimate you. I'll never take you for granted. I'll never stop loving you, Bean. We were meant to be together, and I can't wait to spend the rest of my life with you."

Sierra's heart nearly stopped beating. Was he saying what she thought he was saying? She felt that tickle in the back of her throat, but instead of her emotions getting stuck, tears immediately welled up.

He chuckled a bit at seeing them. "I never thought I'd be so glad to see a woman cry in my life," he said softly. "For the record, I have no problem with your tears, you go ahead and cry whenever you want."

Sierra chuckled. "I don't even know why I'm crying now. It's ridiculous, really, but I suppose my body's just making up for all the tears I didn't shed after I was rescued."

"Well, why don't I give you something to cry about then?" Grover said gently.

Sierra frowned. She was about to ask him what he was talking about when he stood and headed for the large doors. He pushed one door back, then the other, then held out his hand and wiggled his fingers at her.

She stood and took a step toward him—freezing as her gaze focused on the yard.

All their friends and family were gathered below.

They'd arranged themselves so their bodies spelled out the words MARRY ME.

When Sierra turned back to Grover, she found him kneeling on the dusty loft floor. He was holding a ring box open, but she barely glanced at it. "Grover," she croaked, the tears falling in earnest already.

"I know it's fast. And I know people probably think we're crazy. But I knew you were it for me over a year ago. I don't know how, it was just a feeling deep down inside. And when I lost you, I was devastated. I had to go about my business, pretending it wasn't tearing me apart, but it was. Nothing was going to keep me from you once I got that letter. *Nothing.*

"Marry me, Sierra Clarkson. Let me love you for the rest of our lives. I don't know what's ahead for us, but hopefully it won't include militia members on a suicide mission."

She chuckled through her tears. "Yes. Of course I'll marry you," she told him softly.

Grover stood up and Sierra threw herself into his arms. He almost dropped the ring box as he went to catch her.

"What'd she say?" someone yelled from below.

Sierra turned her head and saw that the words now looked

more like gibberish than the carefully planned message they'd been a moment ago, as people broke formation. She laughed as parents tried to wrangle their kids back into place, without luck. Gillian was trying to get everyone to look at her so she could take a picture, but no one was paying any attention. The scene was unruly, and Sierra knew she'd never forget this day for as long as she lived.

She felt Grover sliding the ring onto her finger. She looked down—and gasped.

"Oh my God, Grover! How did you—"

"It's not your mam's ring," he said quickly. "Unfortunately, when Shahzada took it from you, it disappeared forever. I did embellish it a bit more though, I hope that's okay."

It was more than okay. He'd added an emerald-cut diamond to the simple setting of her grandmother's original ring design. The old and new together created a unique look that fit her perfectly. "You got this done in a week?" she asked.

Shrugging, Grover said, "No. I had the guy start on it before we met up in New Mexico. I spoke to your dad on the phone, told him what I wanted to do. He got with your mom, and they sent me some pictures of what the original ring looked like, and I found someone to replicate it."

Sierra could only stare at him in shock. "Seriously?"

"Yeah. I knew even then that I wanted to be with you forever. How could I not? You're everything I've ever wanted in a woman. From the second you offered to hold my hand in those caves, I was a goner."

"Damn," she breathed. Then, ignoring the heckling the guys were giving Grover from below, she wrapped her arms around his neck and stood on tiptoe.

"I love you, Fred Groves. With all that I am. I know I'm a mess. I have an apartment with my stuff in it that I've only slept in once, I have no job, and I somehow talked you into getting us a cow when neither of us have any idea how to take care of it... but I'll do whatever it takes to be a good partner to you."

"I know you will, just as I will to you," Grover answered. "I don't care about your apartment, and you never have to work a day if you don't want to. We'll figure out the cow thing together. All I want is you. Holding my hand, by my side. We'll deal with whatever life throws at us as we go."

"Deal."

"Deal," he returned, then leaned down to cover her lips with his own.

As their friends and family cheered from below, Sierra kissed the man of her dreams. The man she loved.

EPILOGUE

Five Months Later

"Whose idea was this again?" Grover complained as he tugged at the tie around his throat.

"Yours," Lucky said with a laugh.

"Well, it was stupid," Grover grumbled.

Their entire team laughed.

They were all standing in a back room at the church his parents had been going to since they'd moved to St. Louis. One night in the middle of a mission, when Grover and Lucky were lying in the dirt in Siberia, waiting for a man they were watching to make a move, Lucky commented that Grover's mom was driving Devyn crazy, continually asking when she was going to get married.

Grover knew exactly how pushy his mom could be, and he'd casually made the suggestion that maybe he and Sierra could have a double ceremony with Lucky and Devyn.

He'd also mentioned it to Devyn, and she'd mentioned it to their mom...and now here they were. In St. Louis. Waiting for the signal to go out in front of the minister and watch their brides walk down the aisle.

This wasn't Grover's thing. And he didn't think it was Sierra's either. But they'd both sucked it up because his mom was so excited. And Sierra's parents were too. Before anyone knew it, the two mothers had planned everything. So they'd all flown up to Missouri and now they were getting married.

"Bet you wish you'd just done the courthouse thing like Gillian and I did, huh?" Trigger asked.

Grover growled at his friend. He was cranky. And hot. And he hadn't seen Sierra all day. His mom had insisted it was tradition, but he found himself missing her dreadfully.

"Hey, I *did* do the courthouse thing," Lucky reminded them.

"It'll be worth it when you see her," Lefty said, ignoring Lucky and slapping Grover on the back.

"And when we get to the party...er...reception later," Lucky added.

Grover nodded. He was tired of waiting. He wanted this done. He couldn't wait to make Sierra his, legally. She was already his in every way that mattered.

Finally, the time came for them to go out into the church. The entire team lined up at the front and waited for the music to start.

When it did, Grover was confused at first. Because instead of the wedding march he'd been expecting, "Let's Get It On" by Marvin Gaye blared out of speakers in the walls around the interior of the church.

He heard Trigger snort first. Then Lefty joined in. Grover couldn't hold his chuckle back. Then everyone in the church was laughing so hard, the music could barely be heard.

After Gillian, Kinley, Aspen, Riley, and Ember walked down the aisle, Devyn and Sierra began walking toward them, arm in arm. They were both wearing floor-length white dresses, each carrying a huge bouquet of flowers. Grover had no idea what kind they were; he only had eyes for his woman.

Her pixie hair—at least that's what she called it—had a flower pinned to the side, and she looked absolutely radiant. She'd gained back a healthy amount of weight and her cheeks were rosy, either because it was a bit warm in the church or because she'd had a few mimosas with the girls. But most of all, she looked happy.

So damn happy.

Grover remembered when she'd turned to him and said those two words. *I'm happy.* That was all he wanted for her. He'd do whatever it took for the rest of their lives to keep her that way.

He couldn't wait for her to see the wedding present he had waiting back in Killeen. He'd found two miniature donkeys that needed a home. They'd be added to their growing animal sanctuary of a cow, two goats, and countless chickens.

"Damn, I've never felt luckier than right this second," Lucky murmured.

Grover couldn't agree more.

Instead of waiting for Sierra to make it all the way down the aisle, Grover jogged toward her. He heard more laughter around him, but didn't take his eyes from Sierra.

"Hi," she said when he was standing in front of her.

"Hi," he returned.

Then she reached out a hand for him, and the second Grover's fingers closed around hers, he breathed out a sigh of relief. This was what he needed. His love by his side, her hand in his. She made everything right in the world.

Lucky had followed behind him, and the four of them walked

back up to the front of the church to stand in front of the minister.

"We are gathered here today..."

He tuned out the words as he looked down at Sierra. She squeezed his hand, and he smiled. Then he looked over at his sister and Lucky. And past them to Trigger, Lefty, Brain, Oz, and Doc. Glancing to his left, he saw Gillian, Kinley, Aspen, Riley, and Ember. He was surrounded by the most important people in his life...

Grover was happy.

* * *

Lucky headed back to his wife with the mango margarita she'd asked for. His *wife*. Even though they'd been married for a while, it hit him suddenly that she was well and truly his, not just in secret. He was a lucky son-of-a-bitch.

The smile on his face faded quickly when he couldn't find Devyn. She wasn't sitting at the table where he'd left her.

Looking around, Lucky frowned when he didn't immediately spot her.

After putting her drink down, Lucky wandered the room, searching for her, wanting her right by his side. She looked gorgeous in her wedding dress, and as much as this fancy shindig was a pain in his ass, he wouldn't have denied Devyn anything. Seeing how happy her parents and siblings were made it all worthwhile.

The only blight on the day was her missing brother. Lucky hadn't wanted to invite Spencer, not after everything he'd done to Devyn, but his woman, being the compassionate and forgiving person she was, had insisted.

But, to Lucky's relief, Spencer hadn't responded to the invitation. He was out of rehab and, from everything Devyn's parents said, doing better...but Lucky wasn't quite ready to forgive the man yet.

"Lose your wife already?" an older gentleman joked as he passed Lucky.

"Misplaced, not lost," Lucky told him with a smile.

"Well, I saw her heading for the door about five minutes ago," the man informed him.

"Thanks," Lucky said, then headed for the entrance to the ballroom. He had no idea why she might leave the reception. At this point, he was just mildly curious, but if something was wrong, he wanted to be there for his wife.

Lucky nodded at some of the guests as he passed and headed for the front of the hotel. He was relieved to see Devyn standing just outside the revolving doors—but his relief quickly turned to unease when he saw who she was talking to.

His steps sped up as he hurried to get outside. He pushed through the revolving doors, mentally cursing when they didn't move as fast as he wanted them to.

He opened his mouth to ask what the hell *Spencer* was doing there, when Devyn stepped close to her brother and hugged him.

Lucky stopped. He *wanted* to pull Devyn away from the man who'd caused her so much pain, but he checked himself, hovering behind the siblings as they embraced.

Devyn pulled away from Spencer, then, as sensing Lucky standing behind her, turned her head and gave him a small smile.

Spencer took a step back and shoved his hands in his pockets. He nodded once at Lucky, then turned to walk away.

Lucky immediately wrapped an arm around Devyn's waist and pulled her against him. "Are you all right?" he asked.

She nodded. "Yes. He sent me a text and said he was out here. He asked if I would come see him for a minute."

"And?" Lucky asked when she didn't continue.

Devyn turned in his embrace and looped her arms around his neck. "He's doing really well," she told him. "He feels awful about everything that happened...and I believe him when he says that he's changed. He just wanted to congratulate me."

Lucky knew he and Spencer would never be friends, but Devyn loved her brother and wanted to repair their relationship. He would respect her decision.

"That's good, Dev."

"It is," she agreed.

"I got your drink," he told her, ready to change the subject. Thinking about Spencer on today of all days wasn't high on his list of things he wanted to do.

"Yeah?"

"Uh-huh. But you know, I have a better idea."

"What's that?"

"We could go up to our room and order a bottle of champagne from room service."

Devyn laughed and shook her head, but he could see the desire in her eyes.

"We can't," she said. "We still need to cut the cake. And do the first dance. My parents would be so upset if they didn't get pictures of all that."

Lucky sighed dramatically, then grinned. He knew she was going to say that, but she couldn't blame him for trying.

She went up on her tiptoes and kissed him. "I love you, husband."

"And I love you, wife," he returned.

As they entered the lobby of the hotel to head back to the

reception, Lucky turned to look in the direction Spencer had gone.

Devyn's brother was standing outside, his gaze locked on his sister. When their gazes met, Spencer dipped his chin respectfully.

Lucky returned the gesture and watched as Spencer disappeared around the corner.

"Thank you for not freaking out," Devyn said softly.

Lucky leaned down and kissed her temple. "He fucked up. Huge. But he loves you, and I can't blame him for wanting to see you on your wedding day."

"And that's one of the million and one reasons why I love you so much," Devyn said with tears in her eyes.

"Come on. Let's get you back in there before your *parents* freak out," Lucky said.

"I wasn't gone that long," Devyn protested.

The second they stepped inside the ballroom, Devyn's mom rushed up to them and exclaimed, "There you are! The photographer is getting the cake set up for pictures!"

Lucky looked down at his wife and raised an eyebrow.

She burst out laughing. "Okay, you were right."

Lucky kissed her once more. "Go on. I'll be right there."

Devyn nodded and walked toward the table with their wedding cake, accompanied by her mom. There was another table nearby with Grover and Sierra's cake. It felt right sharing this moment with his teammate. Lucky might not have chosen a huge reception, but it was a small price to pay to see the happiness in Devyn's eyes.

Life wasn't all sunshine and roses, but moments like this, spent with loved ones, somehow made the bad stuff fade. Lucky couldn't wait to experience every second of his life with Devyn. This was just the beginning.

. . .

Two Years Later

"Never again!" Riley seethed between clenched teeth.

"Okay," Oz soothed.

As another contraction overcame her, Riley growled. She honest-to-God growled. "I mean it, Porter. I can't do this againnnnnn!"

The last word was more of a wail than an actual word.

To be honest, Oz hated this. Not her having his baby—*that* he freaking loved. But he hated seeing her in pain. Millions of babies were born every year, but seeing Riley struggle to bring their child into the world was torture.

He couldn't deny that he loved kids though. He loved everything about them. The chaos in their house. The sleepless nights. The warm baby snuggles. But he knew having three babies in about as many years was overwhelming for Riley. Not to mention, throwing Logan and Bria into the mix. They were all good kids, but still, four was a lot. Five was going to be even harder.

"Okay, no more kids," he reassured his wife.

"Are you just saying that because I'm in the middle of labor and you know I'll seriously hurt you if you even talk about knocking me up again?" she raged.

Oz knew better than to laugh. "No. We should've waited before having our third so soon."

"Too late now," she groaned.

It was. And Oz couldn't wait to meet to meet his son. Riley had given him Amalia, then Brittney. Now it was Charlie's turn.

The discussion about whether or not to have any more kids was cut short when the doctor arrived and told Riley the "good part" was about to happen.

Three hours later, Riley held their son in her arms. She was sweaty, exhausted, but Oz still thought she was the most beautiful woman he'd ever seen. Even more so because she'd just given him another child.

Oz forgot their chat about future children because he was too busy introducing his other kids to their new brother. Then he was celebrating with his Delta Force team. Then it was time to give Gillian and Trigger last-minute instructions on what to let Amalia watch before she went to bed, how much to feed Brittney for dinner, about what time Logan needed to be at baseball practice the next day, and how Bria's friend's mother would drive her home after dance practice.

His life was hectic, and Oz didn't have a second to relax, but he wouldn't have it any other way. He planned to spend the night in the hospital with Riley and Charlie. The Army forced him to be away more than he liked, so he wasn't going to waste a single night, even though Riley was in the hospital.

It was now dark outside, and he was sitting right next to her bed as they watched TV.

"Porter?"

"Yeah, Ri?"

"I was serious. I can't do this again. Three is enough for this body."

"And I said I agreed," Oz reminded her.

"But that doesn't necessarily mean I don't want more children…"

Oz turned to give her his full attention.

"I love our kids. Our life is insane, but I never thought I could be this happy. I like the chaos, even if it drives me crazy sometimes. I'm not saying now, and probably not even for a few years, but I wouldn't mind looking into fostering, with the option to possibly adopt."

Oz's heart swelled in his chest. Fuck, he loved this woman.

"Say something," she urged, looking concerned.

Standing up, Oz perched on the edge of her bed. He gently lay down on his side and took his wife into his arms as carefully as he could. The last thing he wanted was to cause her any pain. He snuggled her close and sighed. "I'd love that."

Neither said anything else. They had a lot of time to figure things out. Their son's birth day wasn't the time to plan when to bring more people into their already crazy lives, but he was still thrilled at the idea. Nothing was as satisfying to Oz as when his kids turned to him for advice, for help, for protection. It was heady to be needed, to be the one to help guide them, and he couldn't imagine his life without at least one child in it.

"Sometime in the future," Riley stressed, as if she knew what he was thinking.

"All right. I love you, Ri. You've made me happier than I ever thought I could be. And every day my happiness increases exponentially." He knew he was being cheesy, but if he couldn't be cheesy on the day his son was born, when could he?

"Same," Riley said, before yawning huge.

"Get some sleep," he ordered.

"Wake me up if they bring Charlie in," she mumbled.

Oz smiled. Of course he would. It wasn't as if *he* could nurse their child. But instead of teasing her, he simply agreed. "I will."

As his wife fell asleep in his arms, Oz closed his eyes in contentment. If someone would've told him several years ago that he'd have five kids in the near future, he would've laughed his ass off. Now he couldn't imagine his life any other way.

Three Years Later

. . .

"I can't believe you finally let me talk you into marrying me," Doc told Ember. They were in Los Angeles at the Four Seasons honeymoon suite. Their one-year-old little girl, Jemila, was currently being spoiled rotten at her grandparents' house. As much as Doc loved his child, he was definitely ready for some alone time with his wife.

Ember was one of the hardest-working women Doc knew. Her gym back home, The Modern Kid, had over four hundred kids attending now. There were classes from eight o'clock in the morning until nine at night. And while Ember didn't teach all of them, she insisted on spending more than her fair share of time at the gym.

One of her greatest achievements to date was when one of her older kids, a Black boy who'd started with her program three years ago, shortly after she'd opened, qualified for the junior national championships for the modern pentathlon. Ember had been so proud of him, of how much he'd learned and improved.

She'd taken her fame and used it for good, just as she said she would. Her social media was famous now, not for selfies or for hawking products, but for helping to find missing people. The press had attributed her posts to finding fifty-three so far, as of this month. There were so many more men, women, and children who needed finding, but as of now, there were fifty-three people who were no longer missing, which Doc found amazing.

He'd asked Ember to marry him three months ago. Jemila was nine months old and they'd been together for more than three years. Neither of them had been in a hurry to get married. They loved each other, and that had been good enough.

Until one day three months ago. He'd woken up...and just knew it was time. He wasn't content to be Ember's boyfriend any longer. He wanted more.

So he'd asked, she'd said yes, and now here they were in Los

Angeles.

Her parents had organized a low-key and beautiful ceremony on their property. They'd thankfully behaved, not going overboard with the huge reception he and Ember both knew they'd wanted. But they'd splurged on getting them this hotel room for the night.

They'd just made long, slow, sweet love for the first time as man and wife, and were lying snuggled together on the bed when Ember's phone vibrated with a text. Because Jemila was with her parents, she immediately reached for it.

"Is it Jemila?" Doc asked anxiously.

"No. It's from the photographer. She sent me the picture I asked her to send as soon as she could," Ember told him. Then she turned the phone so he could see the screen.

Doc sucked in a breath. The photographer had captured the exact moment Ember had walked into the yard, and he'd seen her for the first time. Of course, the photo was taken from behind him, so his face wasn't in the picture.

It was exactly the picture of their wedding he'd promised she could post on her social media, once upon a time, but even better...because Ember was carrying their child in her arms.

His wife looked absolutely beautiful. She'd lost a little of her muscle tone over the years, and having a baby had filled her hips out a bit more, but to Doc, she was even more beautiful than she'd been when they'd first met.

Doc rested his head on her shoulder and wrapped his arm around her belly as they lay together in the luxurious bed. "Are you going to post it?" he asked.

She pulled her head back to catch his gaze. "You think I should?"

"Absolutely. Your followers will love this."

"But it's not who I am now. I don't post selfies anymore."

"This isn't a selfie. It's a picture of a mature, beautiful woman about to marry the man she loves. Jemila's face is turned away from the camera, so our rule of never posting pictures of our kids still applies."

Ember nodded, and she immediately began clicking on the screen of her phone. It didn't take long. She once again turned the screen to face him, so Doc could read what she wrote.

She'd posted the picture with only one word. *Bliss*.

Doc reached for the phone and practically threw it on the table next to the bed, then he rolled on top of Ember and smiled as she giggled.

"Something wrong?" she sassed.

"No. Something's right. I love you."

"I love you too," she said immediately.

Doc knew the real world would intrude soon enough, so for now, while he had his wife to himself, he was going to enjoy every blissful minute.

Four Years Later

"It's beautiful," Lefty's mom breathed.

Lefty was in Paris with Kinley and his parents. They'd loved his wife on sight, which he knew they would, and the feeling was definitely mutual. This was their second trip to the City of Lights, and his mom was just as excited this time as she'd been the first.

They'd been standing in front of the Eiffel Tower for the last five minutes. Both his mom and Kinley were simply staring at the structure. They hadn't said much, were just taking it in.

Lefty's dad nudged him. "How long do you think they're gonna stand there?" he asked.

"I'm guessing at least another five, ten minutes."

"That's what I thought." His dad leaned over and plucked Lefty and Kinley's son out of his stroller. "I'm gonna go on a walk with this guy. I'll be back."

Lefty wasn't surprised. His dad doted on Dominic. And his son loved his grandpa. Lefty would have to be careful not to let the boy get too spoiled.

Jerking in surprise when he felt an arm wrap around his waist, Lefty looked down at Kinley. She'd stepped away from his mom, who was still studying the tower.

"Hey," Lefty said softly.

"Dominic's gonna be so grumpy this evening," she said, not sounding too upset about it.

"But he'll be tired. Which means he'll go to sleep without any issues," Lefty said.

"True." Kinley smiled up at him. "Which means we'll have more time to ourselves."

He smiled back. "Yeah. We will." His mind was already racing with all the things he wanted to do to his wife when he got her in bed later.

Kinley smirked as if she knew what he was thinking, and she probably did. She most likely had ideas of her own. They were well matched in just about every aspect of their lives. They simply fit.

"Remember when we were here that first time?" she asked quietly.

"Yes." It was where he'd started to fall in love with her.

"I was so rude," she said with a wrinkle of her brow.

"What? No, you weren't," Lefty said.

"I sat here for like twenty minutes and didn't say one word to you. I just stared up at the tower. And you let me."

"You intrigued me. I loved how you embraced being here for

the first time. The joy in your heart was easy to see, and I was honored to experience that with you," Lefty said.

"I know our path wasn't easy, but I feel so blessed to be here today." Kinley looked up at him. "I have you. Your parents have been so amazing; I feel as if I've known them forever. And of course we have Dominic. I honestly never, ever could've dreamed I'd be as happy as I am today."

Their life definitely hadn't been easy sailing. She'd struggled with postpartum depression after having Dominic...and there were even times when Lefty thought he'd come home from work to find the depression had gotten the better of her. But she'd fought hard to overcome it, and with therapy and the right medication, she'd finally managed to do so.

"I love you, Kins."

"I love you too," she told him with a contented sigh.

They stood there for several minutes, in the middle of the chaos of tourists and locals alike. Finally, his mom turned away from the tower and said, "Time for lunch! Where's your father?"

Lefty chuckled. "There's no telling, Mom."

"Darn that man. He took Dom on another adventure, didn't he?"

"Yup."

Lefty didn't worry about his son's safety when he was with his grandpa. Kaden Haskins was even more protective of the toddler than his parents were.

"I'm gonna go find him. Stay here," his mom ordered.

Kinley giggled as his mom stomped away.

"They're a pain in the ass," Lefty muttered.

"They're awesome," Kinley countered. Her hands snuck under the waistband of his pants and Lefty felt her fingers brush against the top of his ass.

"Watch it, woman," he warned.

"This is the City of Love, you know," she whispered with a grin.

It was hard for Lefty to believe his wife had been a virgin when he'd met her. She was adventurous and almost insatiable now. And he freaking loved it. Leaning down, Lefty took her lips in a long, slow kiss, trying to tell her without words how much he appreciated, loved, and admired her.

When he pulled back, he was proud of the glazed look in her eyes. *He'd* done that. He felt a little dazed himself.

"That was mean," Kinley said after a moment.

"No more mean than feeling me up in public," he retorted.

"You know, I never thought I'd be able to come back here. Not after everything that happened. But now I think this is my second-favorite place in the world," she said softly.

"What's your favorite?" Lefty asked.

"Wherever you are."

Lefty closed his eyes and sighed in contentment.

"Mommy, poop!"

At that, Lefty's eyes sprang open, and he looked down to see Dominic running toward him with his unsteady, wobbly gait.

"So much for romance," Kinley quipped.

"You're my favorite place too," Lefty told her. Then he kissed her hard and fast before leaning down to snatch up their son as he ran up to them.

Life wasn't boring, that was for sure. And Lefty didn't mind in the least.

Five Years Later

. . .

Brain watched with pride as his son went through the obstacle course on the Army base. At almost six years old, he was a handful. He'd come a long way from the premature baby he once was. He was outgoing and energetic, keeping both him and Aspen on their toes from morning until night.

Spending time running through the obstacle course was one of his son's favorite things to do, and since he'd gotten an award from his teacher for being the "helper of the week," Brain thought he'd reward him.

Knowing that his wife had something special planned, he also arranged with Annie Fletcher to meet them there. The young woman had just graduated from high school and would be heading off to college in a month or so. She'd joined the ROTC program and was planning on following in her dad's footsteps by joining the Army after college.

Annie had gotten to know Chance fairly well during the last few years, and they'd bonded over their love for the obstacle course.

Aspen had talked to Brain about what she wanted to do, and he'd been all for it.

At the moment, Annie was helping Chance go hand over hand through the rings, and they were both laughing.

"She's gonna be amazing," Aspen said, her gaze fixed on Annie. "I just know it."

"She is," Brain agreed. "Fletch told me she has her eyes on the Green Berets."

"I have no doubt she'll make it," Aspen said.

"Did you see me?" Chance yelled as he ran toward them. "I did it! I wented through the rings!"

"I saw," Brain told his son.

Annie followed behind Chance with a smile on her face.

"I've got something for you," Aspen blurted.

"For me?" Annie asked, obviously surprised.

"Yes. I wanted you to have this." Aspen held something out, and Annie lifted her hand to accept it. She looked down at the pin his wife had placed in her hand, frowning in confusion.

"It's my Ranger pin," Aspen explained. "It's not quite as cool as a SEAL trident, but for me, it meant the world when I finally got to wear it. I was one of the first female combat medics attached to a Ranger unit. Most people thought I wouldn't be able to hack it. Some even *wanted* me to fail. But I didn't. I know you're heading off to college soon, so I wanted you to have this. To look at it when things get tough. When people tell you that you can't do something. When they look down on you simply because you're a woman. Look at this, and know that you *can* do it. That you're strong and smart enough."

Annie's eyes filled with tears. "I can't take this! It means something to you."

"It would mean more to me if you had it. If it inspires you to be better. To follow in my footsteps," Aspen said simply.

Annie nodded as her fingers curled around the pin. "Thank you."

Aspen smiled.

"Can I see?" Chance asked, tugging on Annie's shirt.

She laughed and kneeled down to show the little boy what his mom had given her. Then he quickly lost interest in the old pin and begged Annie to help him on the obstacle course some more.

"Just a bit longer," Brain told his son. "Then we need to get going to your language lessons."

"Okay!" Chance said happily. He didn't have quite the same aptitude as his dad for learning foreign languages, but he was close. He spent thirty minutes every other day with various instructors, learning the basics of several different languages.

Brain and Aspen had discussed it, and as long as their son was having fun and enjoying the lessons, they'd keep them up.

Brain kissed Aspen's temple after Annie and Chance walked away. "You're amazing," he told her.

Aspen shrugged. "It's not going to be easy for her. I know that firsthand. But I truly believe she can succeed. She'll need to be tough and remember that people are on her side. Because when you're being yelled at, told that you'll never make it because you're female, you need all the encouragement you can get."

"She's gonna make it," Brain said with confidence. "From everything I've heard about her from Fletch and everyone on his team, once she puts her mind to something, she does it. Including getting engaged to her Frankie, just like she always said she'd do."

"Yup. And damn if she hasn't stayed one hundred percent faithful to him, even all these years later," Aspen added. "You think they'll last? College can really change people. Not to mention the fact that she wants to join the Army. It will test them."

Brain turned her around and cuddled her from behind. He rested his chin on her shoulder as they watched their son and the young woman in question on the obstacle course. "You know what? I think they will. When you meet the person for you, sometimes you just know it deep down inside. I think that's what happened with them."

"And us," she said.

"And us," Brain agreed.

"I think if anyone can do it, Annie can," Aspen said after a moment. "She's mature and has had the best examples of how good relationships work with her parents and everyone on her dad's team. I'm rooting for her and her young man."

"Me too," Brain said.

"I love you," Aspen told him.

"No more than I love you," Brain returned.

Eight Years Later

Trigger was nervous. He and Gillian had been disappointed so many times. He felt like a failure for not being able to give his wife the one thing she wanted most in the world.

When they'd first been married, neither had wanted kids, happy and content to enjoy each other. Four years ago, they'd both agreed that it was time.

But it hadn't happened.

At first, racing home to make love to his wife while she was ovulating had been fun. Exciting. Naughty. But when month after month passed, and she still hadn't gotten pregnant, they'd started to get worried.

Now it was four long years later, and Trigger was worried it was *too* late. He knew there were other ways they could have children...adoption, fostering, even surrogacy, if it came down to it...but Gillian desperately wanted to have biological children.

They'd both been tested, and the doctors had said it was unlikely Gillian would conceive naturally. That's when the trips to the fertility clinics had started. And every time an insemination procedure failed, Trigger watched his wife's world collapse a little bit more.

They'd both agreed this would be their last attempt. Trigger couldn't keep watching his wife go through the hopefulness of being artificially inseminated, then the agonizing disappointment when the embryos weren't viable.

Today, they'd find out if the latest, and final, procedure had worked. If any of the implanted eggs had taken.

"Breathe, Di," Trigger said.

Gillian was holding his hand so tightly, her fingers were white around his own.

She inhaled sharply and nodded. They were in a small waiting room at the fertility clinic. There were cheerful flowers painted on the walls and photos of smiling babies and children in frames. The last time they'd been told the procedure had failed, Trigger felt like those pictures were a painful slap in the face.

"If I'm not pregnant, it's okay," Gillian said softly, looking up at him. "I'm okay with it just being us for the rest of our lives. I love you, and I know I've been blessed. I have amazing friends, and an even better husband."

Fuck, Trigger loved her so much. He ached to give her the baby she'd wanted for so many years. "I love you too," he said softly. He couldn't say anything else. He was too nervous. Too worked up. Too scared of the disappointment he had a feeling was coming. Gillian would put on a brave face, pretending she wasn't absolutely devastated. The one thing Trigger hated most in the world was seeing his wife hurting.

The door pushed open and their doctor walked in. Trigger examined her face, trying to see some clue as to what the pregnancy test had shown, but her expression was completely neutral.

"How are you both today?"

"We're okay," Gillian said. "How're you?"

"I'm good. Thanks."

Trigger clenched his teeth. He just needed this to be done. Needed to know one way or another.

"I won't keep you in suspense," the doctor said. "I know

this has been a long, hard road for you both. There's never any guarantees with artificial insemination, and the body's a strange and wonderful thing. As you know, we implanted five eggs, as we have every time with the hopes that one would become viable."

Trigger held his breath and felt Gillian squeeze his fingers even harder. He felt as if he were in a long tunnel, watching the doctor from the far end. Her voice seemed to echo around the room and he braced himself to console his wife one last time.

"I double, then triple-checked. As of right now, it looks like two of the eggs are viable. Congratulations—you're pregnant with twins."

Trigger's breath came out with a long, painful whoosh. He stared at the doctor in disbelief.

"What?" Gillian asked, obviously as gobsmacked as he was.

The doctor had a huge smile on her face. "I said, you're pregnant. It worked! You've got not only one child, but two growing inside you."

"Oh my God..." Gillian whispered.

Trigger's eyes filled with tears. They'd done it.

"I have to warn you though, you are extremely high risk. You need to take it easy. I'm not comfortable saying both the babies will make it until a few more months pass...but for now, the embryos seem to be right on track."

Trigger nodded. He'd make sure Gillian took it easy. She wasn't going to be lifting so much as a finger for the next several months.

He turned to his wife and saw the same look of awe and excitement on her face that he knew was on his own.

She reached up and wiped the tears off his cheeks. "We did it," she said softly.

Carefully, Trigger took Gillian in his arms and buried his face in the side of her neck. "We did it," he breathed.

He vaguely heard the door shut quietly behind the doctor, but didn't move from where he was sitting. Trigger knew he'd have a million questions later, and the shock of having not one, but two babies would hit him, but for now, he needed to hold his wife close.

It had been a long, hard road to get here, as the doctor said. But Trigger couldn't be happier. He pulled back and put his hands on either side of Gillian's beautiful face.

"You'll always be my Wonder Woman," he told her.

She shook her head, smiling at him. "And you'll always be my Steve Trevor."

"Love you, Di," he told her.

"Love you too."

Twenty Years Later

"I can't believe we're here!" Riley said excitedly.

"And that we're in a private box!" Devyn agreed.

"Or that Shin-Soo Choo is sitting *right over there*," Aspen stage whispered.

Oz listened as his wife and her friends chattered happily. As for himself, he couldn't take his eyes off the field in front of him. His heart felt as if it was going to burst out of his chest.

Logan had done it.

He'd worked his ass off in high school and had gotten a scholarship to a division-one university. There, a scout had noticed him, and he'd played in the minor leagues for a few years before being drafted by the majors.

Now, here they were. At the Olympics.

Logan had been invited to play for the United States Team, and he'd invited everyone to come watch him play. The Olympic Games were being held in Dallas, and they'd all made the journey to see their favorite baseball player's dreams come true.

Gillian, Trigger, and their son and daughter were there. At nearly twelve, the twins were as different as night and day. Joe was athletic and thrilled to be at the Olympics. While Josie was more interested in people watching and checking out what everyone was wearing.

Kinley and Lefty had come, as had their son, Dominic.

Aspen, Brain, and Chance were there, although Chance was currently sitting with Shin-Soo and his family, chatting away in Korean. While Brain's son didn't know quite as many languages as his father, he'd come close.

Devyn and Lucky sat to his left. They hadn't had any children, by choice, and were perfectly happy spoiling everyone else's.

Ember, Doc, and Jemila sat directly behind Oz. Jemila's eyes were huge as she took in the crowds. She was about to enter her senior year. She was absolutely beautiful, and though everyone kept encouraging Ember to let her daughter model, she'd refused. Jemila wasn't interested in anything like that, anyway. She was her mother's daughter for sure, and had been kicking ass in the modern pentathlon for years. Oz wouldn't be surprised if they were all sitting in the stands at a future Olympics, watching her compete.

Sierra and Grover rounded out the group. They'd never had children, but had given at least two dozen foster children a temporary home. Mostly teenagers, who needed a safe place to stay while their home lives were figured out. They'd all eventually moved on, but almost all of them kept in touch with the couple who'd given them unconditional love during confusing and unsteady times in their lives.

They'd also filled their property with abused and neglected animals. Grover had expanded his barn, adding other buildings, and the couple now housed over four dozen horses, cows, donkeys, goats...even a few pigs. Oz had never seen two people so in tune with animals as his friends. They'd definitely had the favorite house for everyone's kids over the years. And why not? They basically had their own petting zoo to visit whenever they wanted.

Oz turned his attention to his own family. Amalia and Brittney almost looked like twins. They were only a year apart, and as close as best friends and sisters could be. They were currently entertaining the two foster children who were living with them at the moment.

Over the years, Oz and Riley had taken in more than forty-six kids themselves, occasionally two, three...even four at a time. Some had only stayed a month or so, others much longer. They hadn't ended up adopting any of their fosters, which was all right. Oz was extremely proud every time a child was able to return to family members who loved them.

But never quite so much as the pride he felt for the young man his son, Charlie, had turned out to be. He was tall and handsome, smart and kind, and he looked quite mature at the moment, discussing something with Grover.

Bria was a mother herself now. She'd met and married a military man, which hadn't made Oz overly happy at first, simply because he knew how hard the life was. But she and her husband seemed blissfully happy, and they'd made him a grandfather last year.

Noise from the crowd made Oz turn. The players were

running onto the field, and seeing Logan wearing red, white, and blue made Oz's eyes tear up.

He'd done it. After all he'd been through. After the hard start he'd gotten in his life, he'd accomplished his greatest dreams.

It didn't matter if the US won or lost this game. Logan had made it.

An arm snaked around his waist, and Oz knew immediately it was his wife. She was so tiny compared to him, and he'd recognize her touch anywhere. He didn't take his gaze off Logan though. He didn't want to miss a second.

Riley rested her head on his arm and said, "He did it."

Oz wasn't surprised she was on the same wavelength. "Yeah."

"It was nice of Shin-Soo to come with his family," Riley continued. "I know it means a lot to Logan that he's here. Remember the first time he met him? God, I thought Logan was going to pass out. And now they're friends. It's kind of crazy."

It was. It really was. Ember had facilitated that first meeting, and a lifelong friendship between the veteran and an up-and-coming player had been formed. It was as improbable as Oz becoming a father to a ten-year-old boy twenty years ago. But here they were.

Three hours later, Oz was just as awed as he'd been when the game first started. The US lost, but Logan had caught an incredible fly ball, getting his team to within one point of winning. There would be more games, and time would tell if Logan and his team would earn a medal, but for now, Oz was as proud as he could possibly be.

Their entire group waited outside the gates for Logan to come say hello before he went back to the athlete village with his teammates, and everyone made the drive back to their respective homes. Oz waited patiently when Logan finally emerged to greet everyone.

When it was finally his turn, he found himself utterly speechless. He remembered when Logan was just a scared kid. When he got upset anytime his throws went wide. How happy he'd been when he'd caught his first fly ball in a game. Logan was a grown man now, with a serious girlfriend who Oz had a feeling would become his daughter-in-law sooner rather than later. But Logan would always be his little boy.

He grabbed Logan in a bear hug and held on tightly, trying to come up with the words to tell this man how proud he was of him.

But he didn't need to say anything, Logan knew. He pulled back and held his hand out to his uncle. In it was a baseball.

"It's that last one I caught," Logan said. "I thought you might want it."

Oz chuckled. He had over a dozen baseballs displayed back home. His first homerun ball. The ball he caught at his high school championship game that had won the title for his team. One from his first college game, and a half dozen others from important games throughout Logan's life. And now he had this one, the last ball Logan had caught in his first Olympic game. "Thanks," Oz choked out.

"You were amazing," Riley said, pushing her way between them and hugging Logan fiercely. He towered over her, but neither seemed to notice their height difference.

"Not bad for a pain-in-the-ass brother," Bria said, shoving her way in as well.

Oz wrapped his arms around all three of them. He heard everyone talking in the background, but this moment was precious for the foursome. "Your mom would've been so proud," Oz said softly.

Logan and Bria both nodded.

"The best day of my life was when the two of you became mine," Oz said. "I admit that I wasn't prepared to be a dad, but once I settled in, I couldn't imagine anything better."

"You mean after you begged Riley for some junk food to feed me that first morning," Logan joked.

"Yup. I would've been lost without her," Oz agreed readily.

He wanted to stay there with his kids forever, soaking in the moment, but someone yelled Logan's name. He apologized and said he had to get going. It was too soon before Oz was watching him jog toward his teammates. Bria hugged him and said she needed to get her baby home, since it was late. Slowly, everyone began to drift away to the parking lot, but Oz still stood where he was, watching where Logan had disappeared.

"It's hard to believe how far we've come, isn't it?" Trigger asked as he came up next to him.

"Like, how in the hell did we all get so damn lucky?" Lefty asked.

"I know how *I* got lucky," Lucky said with a chuckle. "It's all in the name."

"Whatever," Doc said with a roll of his eyes.

"Today was amazing," Grover added.

"I think Shin-Soo told my son that if he wanted a job at the multimillion-dollar company his son-in-law runs back in South Korea, it was his," Brain said. "Now I have to worry about the kid heading halfway across the world, where I won't get to see him as often."

Everyone laughed. Oz turned his attention from where Logan had disappeared to the men at his side. Out of the corner of his eye, he saw all their families waiting a short distance away.

It had been a while since they'd retired from the Army, but he was just as close to these men as he'd been twenty years ago, maybe more so. They'd gone through hell and back together, and this was their reward.

"At risk of sounding cheesy, I love you guys," Oz said.

Not one of his friends made fun of him.

"Same," Trigger agreed.

"Don't know what I'd do without you all," Doc agreed.

"I can't imagine not having any of you in my life," Lucky said.

"Best friends are the best," Brain said with a grin.

"Love you too," Lefty echoed.

"We're all sappy old men tonight. But who cares? You're all the best friends I've ever had," Grover said.

Then a car backfired in the lot behind them, and the moment was gone. All seven moved as one, heading for their women and children, wanting to keep them safe from whatever evil might be lurking in the dark, even if it was only a car badly in need of maintenance.

Life was full of twists and turns, but Oz knew his friends all felt the same way he did...they wouldn't change anything that had happened to them. Nothing they'd seen or done, if it meant ending up right here, right now, with their women and families at their sides.

* * *

I hope you enjoyed the Delta Team Two series...and in case you're wondering about the guys at The Refuge...YES! They're all getting stories!
Book one, Deserving Alaska, is available for preorder now!

And if you haven't checked out my other series, based on former military guys who form their own search and rescue team, you should get on that!

Book 1 is *Searching for Lilly*

And...I KNOW you've all been waiting on sweet Annie Fletcher's story! You can find out all about if she made it to be a Green Beret and if she's still with Frankie in *Rescuing Annie*

**

Want to talk to other Susan Stoker fans? Join my reader group, Susan Stoker's Stalkers, on Facebook!

Also, sign up for my newsletter to keep up with all the new releases and Stoker info!
https://www.stokeraces.com/contact-1.html

Finding Elodie
Finding Lexie
Finding Kenna
Finding Monica (May 2022)
Finding Carly (Oct 2022)
Finding Ashlyn (May 2023)
Finding Jodelle (TBA)

Silverstone Series

Trusting Skylar
Trusting Taylor
Trusting Molly
Trusting Cassidy

SEAL of Protection Series

Protecting Caroline
Protecting Alabama
Protecting Fiona
Marrying Caroline (novella)
Protecting Summer
Protecting Cheyenne
Protecting Jessyka
Protecting Julie (novella)
Protecting Melody
Protecting the Future
Protecting Kiera (novella)
Protecting Alabama's Kids (novella)
Protecting Dakota

SEAL of Protection: Legacy Series

Securing Caite
Securing Brenae (novella)

Securing Sidney
Securing Piper
Securing Zoey
Securing Avery
Securing Kalee
Securing Jane

Delta Force Heroes Series

Rescuing Rayne
Rescuing Aimee (novella)
Rescuing Emily
Rescuing Harley
Marrying Emily (novella)
Rescuing Kassie
Rescuing Bryn
Rescuing Casey
Rescuing Sadie (novella)
Rescuing Wendy
Rescuing Mary
Rescuing Macie (novella)
Rescuing Annie (Feb 2022)

Badge of Honor: Texas Heroes Series

Justice for Mackenzie
Justice for Mickie
Justice for Corrie
Justice for Laine (novella)
Shelter for Elizabeth
Justice for Boone
Shelter for Adeline
Shelter for Sophie
Justice for Erin

Justice for Milena
Shelter for Blythe
Justice for Hope
Shelter for Quinn
Shelter for Koren
Shelter for Penelope

Ace Security Series
Claiming Grace
Claiming Alexis
Claiming Bailey
Claiming Felicity
Claiming Sarah

Mountain Mercenaries Series
Defending Allye
Defending Chloe
Defending Morgan
Defending Harlow
Defending Everly
Defending Zara
Defending Raven

Stand Alone
Falling for the Delta
The Guardian Mist
Nature's Rift
A Princess for Cale
A Moment in Time- A Collection of Short Stories
Another Moment in Time- A Collection of Short Stories
Lambert's Lady

Special Operations Fan Fiction
http://www.AcesPress.com

Beyond Reality Series
Outback Hearts
Flaming Hearts
Frozen Hearts

Writing as Annie George:
Stepbrother Virgin (erotic novella)

ABOUT THE AUTHOR

New York Times, *USA Today* and *Wall Street Journal* Bestselling Author Susan Stoker has a heart as big as the state of Tennessee where she lives, but this all American girl has also spent the last fourteen years living in Missouri, California, Colorado, Indiana, and Texas. She's married to a retired Army man who now gets to follow *her* around the country.

She debuted her first series in 2014 and quickly followed that up with the SEAL of Protection Series, which solidified her love of writing and creating stories readers can get lost in.

If you enjoyed this book, or any book, please consider leaving a review. It's appreciated by authors more than you'll know.

www.stokeraces.com
www.AcesPress.com
susan@stokeraces.com

facebook.com/authorsusanstoker
twitter.com/Susan_Stoker
instagram.com/authorsusanstoker
goodreads.com/SusanStoker
bookbub.com/authors/susan-stoker
amazon.com/author/susanstoker